Memories of Empire

django wexler

Silver Imprint
Medallion Press, Inc.
Florida, USA

Dedication:

For my parents,
who convinced me that I wasn't half bad at this after all.

Published 2005 by Medallion Press, Inc.
225 Seabreeze Ave.
Palm Beach, FL 33480

The MEDALLION PRESS LOGO
is a registered tradmark of Medallion Press, Inc.

Printed in the United States of America

Library of Congress Cataloging-in-Publication Data

Wexler, Django.
  Memories of empire / Django Wexler.
    p. cm.
  ISBN 1-932815-14-7
  1. Women slaves--Fiction. 2. Fugitive slaves--Fiction.
  3. Mercenary troops--Fiction. 4. Soldiers--Fiction. I. Title.
  PS3623.E94M46 2005
  813'.6--dc22
                              2005016312

ACKNOWLEDGEMENTS:

Many people to thank:

—*Konstantin Koptev, aka Zombie, who struggled alone through the primitive early drafts.*

—*Caine Gordan, Elizabeth Hoeim, and James Pearson; the Pittsburgh writing group who read the first full version.*

—*Hillary Masters and Jane Bernstien, my writing teachers.*

—*Mike Eisenberg, who taught me to put a sentence together.*

—*Dr. Charles Berlin, without whom I couldn't have done it.*

—*The rest of my family, too numerous to list.*

chapter 1

> "The fundamental flaw in their culture is a certain stubbornness, a continued resistance to the world as it is. The clearest example is their religion, worshipping ghosts six thousand years dead, but this trait runs throughout their entire culture. It makes them fearsome in times of strength but pathetic in times of weakness, and it leaves them unable or unwilling to adapt to changing conditions . . ."
>
> –Kabiru Shun, *The Fall of the Sixth Dynasty*

THERE'S ALWAYS ONE perfect moment, when the mind has just awoken and consciousness has yet to fully engage—still half-wrapped in dream, eyes open but uncomprehending, until the weight of the world crashes down with all its harsh reality. That moment, Veil had decided, was something to be savored. It slipped away all too quickly. The very act of thinking about it kicked her mind into action, and what had been mere patterns of light and shadow resolved into familiar objects. She managed one clean breath, held it for one perfect moment.

Then memory returned, and Veil settled in for a nice long scream.

ONE MAN. IT didn't seem possible.

The scream was very uncharacteristic of Veil. She was not,

1

as a rule, a person who screamed or cried or threw tantrums. Growing up in Kalil's massive household had taught her a number of important lessons about life, and not the least of these was that screaming and crying rarely accomplished anything.

But, in this case, she felt she deserved a good scream. It helped to burn off tension, that was the main thing, And, once she was done, she was able to look at the situation with a great deal more equanimity. Under other circumstances she might have been worried about her reputation, but since there wasn't another human being for at least fifty miles in any direction that was also not a concern.

The sun was up, having just cleared the eastern horizon, and was beginning to make itself felt. The day promised to be a scorcher—the sky was blue from edge to edge, not even a wisp of cloud to blunt the heat. Veil could feel the sand, gritty and cold against her back, but already starting to drink in the sun's rays. In a few hours it would be too hot to touch.

Mahmata lay on top of her, and blood from the wound in the fat woman's belly had crusted over Veil's legs. Once she was done screaming, Veil set about freeing herself. This took some time, since Mahmata was quite fat and Veil might have described herself, charitably, as 'wiry.' Eventually, though, she managed to wriggle out from underneath the corpse and survey what was left of the camp.

Most of Bali's men were sprawled on a blood-soaked stretch of sand halfway to the bluff. Low as it was, it was the only decent shade for miles; it was no surprise they'd run into someone. That was where they'd confronted the stranger, and it didn't look like any of them had gotten more than two steps. Veil wandered over to inspect them, in a stunned state of idle curiosity. Dead bodies didn't bother her—the spirits were gone, after all, settling into the Aether or snapped up as food for something bigger and meaner.

So what was left to be afraid of? They were all dead—seven men. Vosh, who'd boasted so around the campfire, hadn't even gotten his sword out of its scabbard. Vosh had voted to pass Veil around at night, as a kind of bonus for the guards. Thankfully Bali had overruled him—apparently her virginity was worth more than a sellsword could offer—but Veil gave Vosh's corpse a kick anyway and felt a little better.

The other slaves had died, too, tied together and unable to even run. Veil hadn't known the pair of dark-skinned aborigines very well, since they spoke no Imperial and only a few broken words of Khaev, but fair-haired Silel had come from a clan to the west of Kalil's. Veil had gotten to know her in a month of traveling—a pretty, empty-headed thing. It was no wonder her father had gotten rid of her; still, she hadn't deserved to be slashed open like a Mourning fowl, spilling purple and black on the sands. Veil looked at her a moment, and shook her head. In clan lands the corpse would already be covered with flies, or torn apart by coyotes, but nothing lived in the high desert. Not even insects.

Bali, himself, had gotten the farthest. She assumed he'd started to run as soon as his sellswords started falling like trees in a sandstorm, but he'd made the mistake of stopping at his pack to dig out his purses. She found him there, slumped over his gold, run through from behind. Blood had coated the open purse and dulled the gleam of the coins.

She thought about kicking Bali, too, but he was so pathetic in death that adding further insult to his corpse seemed pointless. Instead she bent down to look in the purse. It was filled to bursting, a not-inconsiderable load for a grown man and a hopeless encumbrance for a girl of fifteen. She reached in, delicately, and extracted two fat golden eyes. That had been the slave-price Bali paid her father; more than the usual one-six he paid for children, she remembered, because there was a shortage of virgin girls in Corsa and the brothels were paying double.

Veil tucked the coins into the pocket of her ragged shorts and sat down heavily on the already-warming sands, trying to decide whether or not she wanted to die.

Even that was a bit egotistical, she had to admit.

It's not as though I have much of a choice. A hundred miles from home, in the middle of the trackless high desert, with no food and no water other than what she might salvage from the wreckage of the camp. The right thing to do, the logical thing, would be to lie down in the sun, enjoy the warmth, and slowly wither to a mummified corpse. Either that or, if she was feeling brave, borrow a dagger from one of the guards and end it herself. *That would be the logical choice. No food, no water, no help, no chance.*

On the other hand, why not? Veil's life had ended two months ago, when Kalil lost a war against Siorn and came up short on the reparations. *And yet, I'm still here. Might as well make the most of it. What's the worst that happens:, I die in the desert?*

She permitted herself a tight, sarcastic grin and went about stripping the bodies. She acquired a white cloth robe, suitable for desert wear, from Mahmata; it was a bit used and had a bloody hole through the middle, but Veil felt she wasn't in a position to pick and choose. From Silel, after a brief internal struggle, she took shoes —real bound-leather shoes, better by far for loose sand than the sandals Veil was wearing. The two biggest water skins - which Bali had been carrying - she hoisted over one shoulder. The little canteens that everyone had carried she drained, drinking until she squelched at the edges. There was no food—presumably the stranger had taken it. Veil shrugged. *If I live long enough that food becomes an issue, I'll have gotten farther than I expected.*

She hesitated over the last item. It seemed pointless, really—there wasn't a human for miles and miles , except for maybe the stranger, and there were no animals in the high desert. Nevertheless, she finally unstrapped Vosh's short sword and slung it awkwardly over her other shoulder. It was only a piece of pointed steel, but it made her feel better.

That left one last choice to make. *Which direction to go?*

Two options presented themselves. She could backtrack, heading west toward the Red Hills and home. That did not sound promising—the hills themselves were rife with bandits and rebels, and soldiers hunting both. Not to mention it was at least two weeks' walk through the high desert that way. *And if I turned up again at Kalil's door, what would he do? Probably chastise me for being disobedient and sell me to the next caravan that passed by, counting himself lucky to get paid twice for the same girl.* Veil's memories of her father were understandably colored by recent events, but, even in the past, Kalil had not been the kindliest of men. Not that he'd been particularly cruel, either—he didn't have time, with seven wives and uncounted children to manage, and there had been nannies and tutors to dispense the punishments. But she remembered him as distant, and cold.

Still, she hesitated. There was someone at home who would welcome her. *Kyre.* He was her truebrother, sharing both a father and a mother, born almost two years to the day before her. He'd cried, a little, when Kalil announced that she was to be sold. Afterwards, as she'd sat on her bunk in stunned silence, he'd kissed her lightly on the cheek and told her not to worry. *Kyre would be happy to see me.*

The other choice was south. The trail was clear enough, for the moment, a line of footprints running straight as an arrow across the sand. The first wind would obliterate them, but the baking air had barely stirred. The stranger had gone that way.

Bali had been heading vaguely south, she knew. There were oases, and little towns where you could buy water. She'd searched his body for a map, but either the slaver had navigated by memory or the stranger had taken it; probably the former, since Bali was—had been—only barely literate. Go south far enough, and the desert ran out. The city of Corsa was out there, somewhere. Every vile, nasty story Veil had ever heard had been set in Corsa; apparently the place was populated entirely by slavers and pirates, and operated beyond the reach of Khaev law.

It was ultimately curiosity that helped her to make up her mind. *One man against seven.* Her memories of the fight were confused, a blur of blood and flashing steel, but she remembered the stranger. All in black, and he'd moved like a phantom. *He won't last, in the heat. He'll have to rest. I can catch up with him, and he has the food.* He'd killed everyone, even the women and slaves. *He didn't kill me.* In all likelihood, he hadn't even noticed her—Mahmata had fallen on top of her, and Veil had fainted. *But, still . . .*

The sun had climbed higher, and the sand was getting hot. Veil struggled to her feet, water skins clonking heavily against her breast, and started south. *One step at a time, one foot after the other.*

JUST AFTER MIDDAY, when the sun was at its hottest, she finally caught sight of him.

The air felt like it had been cooked, so dry she could feel her skin cracking every time she moved. It was like the inside of the bakery, back home, when she was standing next to the oven and feeling the waves of heat it threw off; except here the oven was the whole world, and she couldn't duck outside the hut for a quick break. Everything Veil wore—her new boots, her flimsy shirt—was soaked in sweat.

Her burden felt heavy, so heavy. Taking the sword had been a mistake. Just carrying the water was hard enough; the sword flapped against her back at every step, as though chastising her for her errors. She couldn't summon the energy to reach back and get rid of the damn thing, either. It would have meant putting everything down to rearrange the straps, and if she stopped walking, Veil was certain she wouldn't start again.

The dunes went on forever. At the crest of each one, she felt as though she could see to the end of the world—the desert receded eternally to the blue-hazed horizon. Only on her right, in the east, was anything else visible: the dim shapes of the Cloudripper range rode like ghosts on the edge of vision.

By chance, she crested a dune at the same moment he did. A tiny black ant, ten or twenty dunes ahead, crawling across the boiling sands. Veil stopped and shouted herself hoarse, trying to get his attention, but if the ant shifted in its progress she couldn't see it. She spent the next hour damning him in every way she could think of, coming up with creative torments the spirits of the Aether could subject his soul to before devouring it utterly. She saw him again a couple of hours later, a bit closer than she remembered—this time, when she shouted, the distant speck definitely paused for a moment to look back at her. Then he continued on his way, unconcerned. Veil rasped her tongue over cracked lips, took a swallow of precious water, and started down the dune.

IT SHOULD HAVE been getting cooler, by rights, but it seemed to only get hotter. Her burden got heavier with every step, the straps dug into her shoulders until she was sure they'd drawn blood. And the desert only went on and on. She saw nothing more of the stranger, just dune after dune after dune forever. Climbing each new one was a fresh agony, and descending was a losing fight not to stumble and fall.

At some point she began to hallucinate. Veil was not given to visions; when her siblings appeared and started to run alongside her, she knew they couldn't be real. That helped, a little. They were jeering at her, laughing at her imminent failure, mocking her weakness.

Von, one of the eldest, walked backwards in front of her and grinned like an idiot.

"Come on, Veil. One more lousy step. You can't take one more lousy step? Look at you!"

"Look at you," sneered Jayli. She was a pretty, buxom girl, only a year older than Veil but prone to lording herself over all the younger children and sucking up to the elders. "I could do better than that. My grandmother could do better than that."

Seth, also a year older but built like a tree-trunk, had a biting tone in his thick, slow voice. "Poor, stupid Veil. Stupid, stupid little girl. You deserve to be a slave. Nobody needs you."

Seth. Veil gritted her teeth. Seth had been the worst of her siblings. He was the third son of Kalil's first wife, which gave him a good deal of status, and his size and strength made him unchallenged among the other boys. Most of her childhood bruises had come from him.

Seth. Won't leave me alone. Even now. She couldn't laugh—the best she managed was a dry rasp of a chuckle. *Damn him. Damn all of them.*

"Not worth keeping. Not worth killing. Not worth dragging to the brothel." Seth gestured at her, laughing his dull-witted guffaw. "Who'd want to fuck that? It'd be like screwing a board."

Veil started up the next dune. Each step was agony, but she was determined not to stop, not to give him the satisfaction.

Give who the satisfaction? I'm hallucinating! The slope seemed to go on and on. Her heart pounded as though it were about to burst. *What the hell am I doing this for?* Another step. *I'm not showing him anything. He's not even here. There's no one here.*

Veil crested the dune and saw the stranger, no closer than before. His shadow was drawn large by the setting sun, a malevolent shape flickering across the sand. The desert had taken on the red tint of the sky, as though it were slowly soaking in blood. Veil looked over her shoulder, half-expecting to see Bali's caravan right behind her. Instead there was nothing, only desert until the end of the world.

She wasn't conscious of falling. Just the sudden feel of sand on her knees, a gentle scrape, and then the world disappeared. The sand, giving its heat up into the cool of the evening, felt pleasantly warm against the side of her face. The sword stopped its ceaseless torment. There was silence, cool and complete.

I'm dying. She felt her breath rasp in her throat. *I knew it was going to happen, and it has. Nothing unexpected. Nothing illogical.*

I'm dying. Her eyes squeezed shut, trying to prevent tears from leaking out. Precious moisture dripped onto the sand and vanished instantly. She thought about praying; the gods were dead, though, six thousand years dead, and even had they been alive she saw no reason why they would concern themselves with a little girl in the desert, dying alone. And she didn't know how to pray to the Khaev demons, didn't have any of the incense or fancy jewelry the monks and maidens used.

Nevertheless, Veil prayed.

Please. She squeezed her eyes tighter. *I don't want to end. Let there be something—even if I wake up in the Aether with a thousand demons flaying the flesh from my bones, let there be something. This can't be it.*

Please.

VEIL AWOKE WITH those words running through her head. Her body felt as though every inch of skin was being ripped by flaming knives. For a wild moment she thought her prediction had come true, that she would open her eyes to find Zazei, the Thousand-Hooked Horror, working her over in preparation for devouring her soul.

There was still no sound but the silent hiss of the desert, though, and gradually the pain resolved into distinct sensations. Her throat burned, and her skin, even under the robe, was cracked and broken. Blisters had formed and burst around her ankles, and a line of bruises ran down her back where the sword had been.

Had been. The sword was gone. Veil tried to roll over, too suddenly, and managed a little flopping motion with one arm. What was intended to be a shriek came out as a weak rasp.

"Awake?"

The voice was quiet, with a trace of Khaev slur. It sounded nothing like the voices of her siblings, who spoke Imperial stained by the languages of old. *Another hallucination?*

"Well? Are you awake?"

Veil made the most noise she could, which was another dull rasp. The voice grunted, satisfied.

"You are. I wonder, though, if you're going to live."

I am, I am! Tears started to leak from Veil's eyes, and she blinked them away furiously.

"No sense in wasting water on you, you see, if you're not going to live."

Water. Just the thought made her gasp. She heard the voice sigh.

"I must have been an idiot." The heavy glonk of a water skin. "Or a madman. That makes sense. Who else wanders the desert, dressed all in black? Open your mouth." This last was directed at her, and Veil did as she was told. A moment later, a thin stream of pure, cold crystal descended. It was better than anything she'd ever tasted, even though her throat burned at the touch of it, and when the stream tapered off she almost cried again. Veil swallowed heavily and tried to work up a voice.

"More." It came out as a croak.

"Oh?" said the voice, sounding surprised. "It speaks. Answer a question then. Are you going to live?"

"Y—Yes," Veil managed. "Water."

There was a pause.

"About the best I could have hoped for, I suppose." There was another glonk and the stream of crystal returned. Veil gulped greedily. She could *feel* darkness creeping up on her, like a silent assassin, and she drank as much she could before her consciousness dissolved into flowing shards.

VEIL AWOKE AGAIN, and found herself curled up under the white robe. It was cold—once the sand had given up the heat of the day, the temperature plummeted. The ragged hand-me-down shirt and shorts she wore weren't enough to do much against the chill, and she pulled the robe tighter, like a cloak.

The burning in her throat had subsided, though she was still thirsty, and all her limbs still felt like lead weights, numb and frozen. Aside from that, Veil felt almost human again. She wriggled her fingers to make sure they still worked, then tried to sit up and open her eyes. That went mostly as planned—she almost fell over again, though, and had to steady herself with one hand.

It wasn't dark, not really—a half-moon burned overhead, and the sky was full of stars. Her eyes took a moment to adjust—she was sitting amidst a cluster of rocks, sticking from the top of a dune like lonely sentries. Across from her . . .

Veil's breath caught with a hiss. The stranger sat across from her, sitting cross-legged with his back to a rock and watching with half-hooded eyes.

He was not, by any stretch of the imagination, a handsome man. His face was angular and somehow cruel, with eyes set deep in their sockets and a cruel gash of a mouth. His skin was Khaev-pale, and he had the straight dark hair that most of the invaders shared, cut raggedly short. His clothing was black from head to toe—black leather, mostly, though his shirt was black cloth with a hint of chain beneath. Across his knees was a sword which provided the only hint of color, its hilt and scabbard carved from the same piece of reddish wood. It looked old, even in the half-light; the resin that coated it had darkened until it, too, was almost black.

Veil wasn't quite sure how long she spent staring at him. He made no move until she finally blinked and shook her head, wondering how in the Aether she was supposed to start a conversation.

The man in black solved the problem for her, holding up a half-full skin. "More water?"

"Please." Veil took the skin gratefully and swallowed, savoring the taste. She passed it back nearly empty, but the stranger took it without comment.

"You'll want some food, too."

Veil nodded, suddenly aware of how hungry she was. The stranger rummaged in the pack next to him and tossed her a loaf of the flat, hard trail-bread that had been Bali's staple. Two days ago, she'd been so sick of the stuff she'd seriously considered eating her own sandals; now she tore into the bread without a second thought, quickly reducing it to crumbs which she licked from her fingers. The man in black watched with a thin smile that didn't touch his eyes.

Once the bread was gone, Veil looked back at him. Again, she had trouble thinking of anything to say.

"So where have you come from? The chances of the two of us meeting in the desert are very small." He gestured to the emptiness around them. "You must be following me, then."

Veil nodded again.

"But from where?" He leaned a bit closer, as though to examine her. "Ah. The caravan from last night?"

"Y—yes."

"I did not think I left anyone alive."

"I—fainted." Veil scolded herself for being too hesitant. "Underneath someone."

He snorted. "Fainted. I see. So you wake up, find your family slaughtered, your food stolen. Why would you follow the murderer across the desert?"

"I—"

"Revenge?" His eyes glittered. "You must hate me."

"No!" Shouting was a mistake; it brought on a coughing fit that took a couple of minutes to fight off. The stranger waited until she continued, weakly. "No. They weren't my family. Slavers. Bali was a slaver."

"Ah." He shifted his position against the rock. "But still—I killed them all. What makes you think I won't kill you?"

"Nothing."

"I could have left you to die."

"Yes."

"So . . ."

"Where else am I supposed to go?"

There was a long silence. Eventually the stranger shook his head.

"What?"

"I believe you. It's crazy, but why not? Do you have a name, little crazy girl?"

"Veil." She almost added se'Kalil, her family name, but stopped herself. *He sold me.*

"Just Veil?"

"Just Veil."

The stranger nodded. There was another pause before Veil returned the question.

"What about you?"

Something flickered across the man's face, some emotion she couldn't quite place. "Corvus."

"Just Corvus?"

His thin smile returned. "Go back to sleep."

Veil could feel exhaustion waiting for her. This time sleep came like a friend, to soothe the aches from her limbs and the pain from her chest.

SHE DREAMED OF Ebon Death, the demon who walked the land in the guise of a man and came in the night to take bad children away. He towered over her, nothing but a billowing black cloak outlined against the stars, but she wasn't afraid.

He's come to take me away. She giggled in the dream. *My friend.*

IT WAS DAWN when she woke up, stretching her arms and rubbing a crust of sand from her eyes. The ache in her legs still throbbed, deep and painful, but her muscles had apparently decided they would submit to a little bit more abuse before giving out entirely. Veil struggled to her feet, gathering the white robe around her.

Corvus was rooting through his pack. On the ground in front of him was a growing pile of food—more flatbread, some dried meat, even a few of the limes that Bali had saved for special occasions. Meager as it was, Veil found her mouth watering at the sight. Next to the pile were four heavy water skins. Once the pack was nearly empty, the stranger closed it and swung it over his shoulder.

"What are you doing?"

"Leaving."

"Wait a minute."

Corvus was already turning away, starting out across the sand. Veil hurried after him.

"Wait!"

"I left the food and water I had." He spoke without turning. "Take it."

"What about you?"

"I'll survive."

"But . . ." Veil stopped, looking back at the pile of supplies and then at the stranger's retreating back. "I can't carry all of that."

"So take what you can. It's nothing to me."

He'd reached the edge of the dune and started to shuffle down. Veil ran to catch him, throwing up a spray of sand.

"Would you wait?"

She tripped, right on the edge, and slid down the slope on her stomach. Corvus was waiting at the bottom; Veil got up, spitting sand.

"What do you want from me?" Corvus fixed her with a nasty glare. "I saved your life yesterday. I returned the supplies I stole from you."

"There's nowhere to *go*. I can't carry that much water."

"So?"

"So I'll just die!"

"That's not my problem."

"But—"

"Stay, go, live, die. Whatever you wish." He shrugged. "I have a desert to cross."

"Corvus!"

She stumbled toward him, reaching for his shoulder. The man in black reacted so fast she didn't even see him move; a moment later she was standing carefully upright with the chilled steel of his blade pressed against her throat.

"Look, girl." His face had become a death's head. "You're lucky that you found me on a good day. Let's leave it at that."

"Fine." Veil swallowed. Even that slight motion pressed her skin against the razor's edge. "Do it."

"What?"

"You're leaving me to die in the desert. I'm not stupid, I can see that. So do it."

"You're serious?"

"Better than starving." Veil closed her eyes. Her heart thudded wildly. "Do it!"

There was a long, long moment. She wondered what it would feel like, hot blood spraying from her throat across the sand. Veil started to tremble.

"Damn you, *do* it! Before I lose my nerve."

The pause continued. Finally, the pressure at her throat vanished. Veil cracked one eye, hardly daring to hope.

Corvus was trudging up the slope of the dune, back toward the food. She hurried after him, catching a bit of his muttering.

" . . . a madman, for certain. Saving little girls in the high desert. El's blood."

"So . . ."

He whirled. "Not a word."

Veil started.

"I don't want to hear a word out of you. Bad enough that I have to carry your food and water; I will not listen to your prattle. Understood?"

She nodded, lips pressed closed. Corvus bent, and started refilling his pack.

THAT PROMISE LASTED perhaps three hours.

Not having to carry everything made walking across the

dunes tolerable, barely. For the first hour Veil trudged in silence, periodically rubbing her throat as though to excise the memory of Corvus' blade. It stung, a little, although she eventually decided that was merely her imagination.

Corvus, sword hanging at his side now and pack heavy with food and water, seemed not to even notice the weight. He walked lightly, barely leaving a trail beside Veil's big, messy footprints, and, watching him, she was reminded of some sort of feline on the prowl. There was the same feeling of barely contained motion, as though, at any moment, he might explode into violence. The black drank in the sun, and he must have been baking, but Corvus gave no sign of discomfort.

They stopped around noon, and he gave her a drink and another chunk of trail-bread. Veil chewed gratefully while sitting on the hot sand, robe pulled up over her head to keep the sun off. Corvus was cross-legged, staring into the distance. Once she was finished, she broke the silence for the first time that day.

"Corvus?"

Veil flinched preemptively, in anticipation of a rebuke. Corvus turned his stare on her. "What?"

"Where are we going?"

"Isail. An oasis. We should get there tomorrow."

"Oh." Veil stuffed the rest of the bread into her mouth and Corvus climbed to his feet. She followed, wearily.

That was it for conversation until the afternoon. Perversely, Veil found herself feeling better. Her legs ached abominably, and the blisters where her boots were tight around her ankles prickled at each step. But for all that, a kind of euphoria descended. It was not having death in her immediate future that did it—the prospect of getting out of the desert and reaching civilization, previously laughable, suddenly seemed within reach. She spent the day constructing elaborate fantasies of what the rest of her life would be like freed from her obligations to Kalil; for Veil this was more of an intellectual than an emotional exercise, and a futile one at that. The farthest she'd ever been from Kalil's town was twenty miles south, to visit Hizan, to whom Kalil was related via a chain of uncles and cousins too complex to express in traditional terms. There had been talk of marrying Veil to one of Hizan's sons in order to add security to some trade deal, and so she had been carted down like a horse to have her teeth checked. The deal had fallen through at an early stage, and she'd never met her intended.

In any case, by the time the sun was once again sinking below the sand Veil couldn't help but say *something*. Corvus seemed content to trudge forward, like a beast of burden. Veil followed a path that wove behind him, falling back on the up-slopes of the dunes and hurrying ahead on the downhill.

She was hurrying to catch up with him when she broke the silence. "Corvus."

He didn't answer, even with a grunt, so she took that as license to continue.

"Look, I understand your situation. I wouldn't be happy, either—walking across the desert" —*Gods only know why*— "and burdened with some girl who can't pull her own weight."

"And who won't shut up."

She carefully ignored that comment. "I just want you to know that I'm sorry. You know. For being a burden."

"That helps a lot."

She ignored that, too. "So here, let me make a deal with you. I'll be as helpful as I can, and then as soon as we get some-place halfway civilized I'll get out of your way. I don't think I'm being too selfish here—I wasn't really looking forward to dying in the desert, but now that you've saved me the least I can do is leave you alone once I get the chance. So," she caught her breath, "how does that sound?"

The swordsman merely grunted in response. Veil shook her head and followed him down the slope of another dune; their shadows grew longer and longer against the sand, stretching to the east.

THEY STOPPED FOR the night in the shelter of another boulder, nearly buried on one side under the sand that had drifted up around it. Veil stretched out awkwardly on her stolen robe, wadding one end up as a pillow. Corvus merely sat, leaning against the boulder. He didn't sleep, or even close his eyes. Instead, he stared, his gaze settling on her and not moving. She could feel the weight of it, even facing the other way. It had a curiously penetrating quality; his eyes, sunk deep in their sockets, glittered in the starlight. Veil turned over again and looked back at him.

"What's wrong?"

The question seemed to rouse the swordsman from his reverie. "You really want to know?"

"Sure."

"I'm bored."

"Aren't you going to sleep?"

"If I went to sleep, what would happen when the next band of slavers found us?"

Veil looked at the desert, empty for as far as the eye could see, and didn't comment. "But . . ."

"You're suddenly very concerned with my welfare." Corvus smiled, but there was no humor in it. "I'm bored. Want to come entertain me?"

Veil blinked. "I . . ."

"You did promise to be as helpful as you could." His eyes were haunted. "Want to come over here, and be my bedwarmer?"

She sat silent for a moment. *He did save my life.*

"Is that—I mean—is that what you want?"

Corvus stared a moment longer, then snorted. "Go to sleep."

Veil curled up under the robe, shivering a little from the cold, and tried not to feel the eyes on her back. Eventually she managed to sleep; in her dreams, steel flashed and blood fountained beneath Corvus' humorless grin while Ebon Death cackled madly.

chapter 2

> "And Gideon wept, and said: What is the use of pray-
> ing now?
> "Fear not, said Illyard. The gods' design reaches far
> beyond these cratered walls. They knew all that was,
> and all that will ever be, and all is proceeding accord-
> ing to their design."
> —*Godsdoom*, from the Book of Gideon.

IN HER DREAM, as it had been in reality, Kei was bundled out of
Yamika in nothing but a nightshirt. She had been all of nine
years old at the time, but in the dream it was as vivid as though
it had happened yesterday. Her skin pebbled into goose bumps
at every breeze—the late autumn wind cut like a knife through
the thin cloth she was wearing.

Shuzan's hand was warm, though. His boots clicked on the
cobblestones of the dock path, a little too quickly for her to keep
up comfortably. She had to jog to match his adult-sized strides.

By day, the ancestral fortress of the Kagerins was a dark and
gloomy place—the outer walls were high enough that the buildings inside were kept in near-perpetual shadow. Kei was used
to crawling through its passages, wandering the stone alcoves for
hours without ever seeing the sun. By night, though, it was terrifying. The dock road ran along the outside of the main walls,
which blotted out half the sky; Shuzan had chosen a moonless

night for her escape, and all that showed in the other half was a faint scattering of stars.

"Almost there, Shia," said Shuzan. He gave her hand an encouraging squeeze. "Are you scared?"

That's right, she thought. *I wasn't Kei then.*

Little Kei shook her head mutely. They rounded the corner together and came to the docks, a long set of wooden piers jutting out into the river. The guard who usually patrolled the area was absent; later, Kei would understand that Shuzan had bribed the quartermaster in charge of duty schedules. In the dream, though, she thought nothing of it. Shuzan hurried her toward his boat, a simple two-person skiff that could be easily managed by one. It was perfect weather—the water was glassy smooth, and the boats barely bobbed at their ties.

Click, click. Shuzan's boots on the cobbles, the gentle lap of the river, and . . .

"Don't be a fool, boy."

Shuzan spun around, his hand falling to his sword. Kei darted behind him as the sudden flare of a lantern revealed an armed man, leaning against the wall. He raised the lamp, and Kei recognized Lin Murai, the castle's master-at-arms. He was responsible for the guards, and the training of new recruits and Kagerin princes alike; Kei had watched her brother practice against the old man often enough, looking down from her balcony on the courtyard where they fenced back and forth.

"Murai." Shuzan sounded, at least momentarily, taken aback. "What are you doing here?"

"Stopping you from making a nasty mistake." Murai stepped forward. "That's little Shia with you, isn't it?"

"Stay where you are." Shuzan lowered himself into a fighting stance, an instant from drawing.

"Are you going to fight me, Shuzan?" Murai shook his head.

"Not if I don't have to. Turn around, old man, and walk away."

"You'll be found anyway."

"I'll take my chances."

"It's not worth it, boy! You're risking everything—"

"I won't let them kill her."

"Kill her? No one's talking about killing her."

Kei, her hands around Shuzan's waist, felt her brother tense. He practically spat the next word. "Liar."

"Get away from the boat, Shuzan." Murai drew his sword, a line of glittering steel in the starlight, and set the lantern down beside him. "We can still keep this quiet."

Shuzan gently detached Kei's hands and pushed her away. "I'll be only a moment, Shia," he said, softly.

Kei backed away and squeezed her eyes shut. She heard the faint hiss of steel, then a short pause broken by the faint clicking of boots on the cobbles. Then, too fast to follow, there was the scream of blade on blade, and the sound of shattering glass, as though someone had kicked the lantern. After that there was a moment of silence, and a splash as something heavy hit the water.

"Come on," said Shuzan. "We don't have much time."

That was the end of the dream, as it always was. Kei found herself in her own bed, half-asleep and half-awake, with the peculiar clarity that comes with that state. Then she sighed, rolled over, and went on to dream of more pleasant things.

THE CORRIDORS OF Kaiune Palace stretched, maze-like, from one end of the castle wall to the other. Bisected by the river Tsel, the palace was full of little bridges, unexpected gardens, and hidden alcoves. On most days, Kei thought it was gorgeous; when she was actually trying to get somewhere in a hurry, though, it was easy to curse the Third Dynasty predilection for form above function.

She was trying to remember whether it was the third or fourth left that led to the Lady Tashida's suite when she heard Kit, well behind her but coming up fast.

"Keikeikeikeikeikei*kei*—"

Kei sidestepped adroitly, letting Kit flash past her and stumble to a halt just short of a doubtlessly priceless tapestry depicting Fourth Dynasty troops beating hell out of some outlanders. Kit almost lost her balance, poised on one toe—more for the look of the thing than because she needed to, Kei thought—and then teetered back to her feet, spinning to face her commander with a mock salute.

"Reporting for duty, Wing Leader!"

Kei sighed. Like all draekeres, Kit was short and compact—a bit shorter than Kei's five feet, without a spare ounce on her frame. With Kit, though, it was as if all the energy of a more normal person had been compressed into her smaller body. Her hair was cut close to her skull, her blue eyes gleamed with intelligence, and she looked completely out of place in her red-and-black dress uniform. Kei could feel her practically vibrating at the indignity of being forced to stand still.

"Kit, would you please calm yourself?"

"Calm? I'm perfectly calm."

"Calm people don't sprint down halls."

"I had to catch you before we got there. Have you heard?"

"Heard what?" Kei suppressed a groan. Palace gossip was never good news.

"Shuzan's Blade got back last night and delivered some sort of serious news to the High Commander. Mai says it's got them all stirred up. Rumor has it Shuzan's going right back out and Shiori, too."

Kei's eyes flickered automatically, looking for servants. The corridor was thankfully deserted. "Please don't call Lady Tashida by her first name."

"Don't you get it? We're probably going out with her!" Kit bounced in place.

"I had guessed that, Kit. I don't think the Lady Tashida calls in a lowly Wing Leader and her sidekick for a friendly chat."

"But this means it's important!"

"Yes, fine. Now calm down before you get us both killed."

Kit took a deep breath, closed her eyes, then bounced again. "So what are you waiting for?"

"Nothing." Kei shook her head and continued toward the suite with Kit in tow.

"How come I'm the sidekick, anyhow?"

"Because I'm older than you."

"Hah."

"SHOUTA." TASHIDA SHIORI's voice had a gentle, friendly sound that Kei knew from experience meant trouble. It was not a voice that suffered being contained; in this case, for example, it was clearly audible outside the closed door to her chambers. The door was an Imperial monstrosity, a heavy monolith of old oak banded with steel and carved with fantastic figures. Kei could dimly remember, if she tried hard enough, finding such things unusual. That had been during the Pacification, when she'd first arrived in the Empire.

Kit, on the other hand, had been born during the Pacification and had her draekere training at the Imperial fortress at Steelgod. *She would probably think of a proper door as odd.*

Shouta—a menial of some sort, Kei assumed—had been around Lady Tashida long enough to recognize a brewing storm when he heard one. She could *hear* him cowering, through the closed door, but he maintained his decorum. "Yes, my lady?"

"I have been told by Mistress Moriseki that the Lord Kagerin returned to the castle last night."

"Yes, my lady?"

"Did I not leave instructions that I was to be informed the very moment Shuzan returned?"

"Y—My lady, Lord Kagerin's Blade returned in all secrecy. They met with the High Commander under cover of darkness— no one was told . . ."

"Did I leave such instructions?"

"Yes, my lady."

"Then why did I have to be informed of his return by the Mistress of Draekeres?"

"I . . . it was my miserable failure, my lady."

"The fact that Lord Kagerin is sneaking about the castle is no excuse for not knowing his whereabouts. Is that under-stood?"

"Yes, my lady. Absolutely."

"I will contemplate your punishment."

"Yes, my lady." Kei could picture Shouta's sigh of relief. While Lady Tashida's wrath was often terrible, her moods were short-lived and she was quickly distracted. The menial had most likely escaped, and he hurried to capitalize on his good fortune. "My lady, the two draekeres you requested are waiting."

"Excellent."

The door opened, revealing Shouta, bald-headed and sweat-ing. He bowed low, and Kei nodded in return. "Lady Tashida will see you now."

Kei shot a quick glance back at Kit, to make sure the girl was following, and stepped into Lady Tashida's audience chamber. It was lushly appointed—screens in the corners and a wild vari-ety of potted plants made an effort to soften the harsh, angular

Imperial architecture. Shiori sat at a gilt table, legs crossed delicately, smiling like a shark.

The Lady Tashida, though not tall, topped either of the diminutive draekeres by at least a couple of inches. This effect was enhanced by her dress, which was dull gray snakeskin dappled with red and green. It was slashed shockingly low at the bodice, revealing the sides of her small, round breasts. Under normal circumstances that might have caused a scandal; she was a Tashida, though, and, moreover, niece to the High Commander of the Occupation. As such, she was not subject to the same rules of decorum as lesser mortals.

The snakeskin faded into worked metal scales at the shoulders, giving Lady Tashida the illusion of battle armor and making her seem much larger than she really was. Kei felt a bit dwarfed—she bowed low, to compensate, and was gratified to find Kit doing the same. The noble yawned and nodded ever-so-slightly in return.

"Wing Leader Keimani."

"Lady Tashida. We are most honored."

"Of course." Lady Tashida's smile glittered lazily. "I'm not sure if you've met Serenity Shikidai."

Startled, Kei looked up. There was indeed another man in the room, standing close to one of the screens and blending in so well he was almost unnoticeable. Shikidai was bald and clean-shaven, dressed only in loose black robes cinched at the waist. He bowed as his name was mentioned.

"Serenity."

"Wing Leader." Shikidai's speech had the crispness of Khaevar, with none of the lilt of the plains.

"This is Wing Kitsu." Kei gestured to Kit, who bowed again and murmured something about being honored.

With propriety settled, Lady Tashida got down to business.

"Wing Leader. You've flown for my Blade in the past?"

"I have had the honor to fly close support for your Blade, my lady."

"And I have been more than pleased with your performance."

Kei bowed again. "I do not deserve such—"

"Spare me. You have proven to be one of the most able Wing Leaders, and I have convinced Moriseki to lend me the two of you for the duration of the present campaign."

Kei felt something crawl at the back of her neck. *I don't like this one bit.* "Present campaign, my lady?"

"Yes." She yawned again. "Terribly secret, of course, but we ride tonight."

Tonight? Kei felt her eyes go wide and clamped down hard. "I was not aware, my lady."

"Of course not. But you will find that everything has been arranged. Serenity Shikidai will be accompanying us."

Kei nodded uncertainly. She could feel Kit at her shoulder, vibrating with pent-up questions and realized she needed to end the audience before the girl exploded.

"We leave, Wing Leader, under cover of darkness. I expect you and your Wing to be packed and ready by sundown, and to meet us south of the city."

"Of course, my lady. May I confirm this with the Mistress of Draekeres?"

"You don't trust me, Wing Leader?" Tashida's eyes, a dark and malevolent purple, sparkled dangerously. There was a long pause until she finally laughed. "Of course. Confirm the orders, but discuss this with no one else."

"Yes, my lady."

"I cannot overstate that last command. *No one.* Not your friends, not your lover. No one but the Mistress of Draekeres."

What the hell is going on? "Understood, my lady."

"Good." Tashida glanced from Kei to Kit and was apparently satisfied by whatever she saw. "You may go."

KEI WAITED UNTIL they had left the vicinity of Lady Tashida's suite to sigh with relief. *You can never tell when the servants might be watching.*

"Tonight." Kit was talking to herself, as though she couldn't believe her luck. "We leave tonight."

"Calm yourself."

"I'm not allowed to be excited? This is the first really exciting mission I've ever been on. And it sounded like Lady Tashida asked for us personally."

"That's what worries me." *Serves me right for doing a good job, I guess.* "That and the fact that this whole thing is so secret."

"That just means it's important!"

"But who are we hiding it from?"

"Everyone knows the Imperials have this place filled with spies. She just doesn't want anyone talking."

"Can't you be a little bit worried?"

"Why would I be worried?"

"Don't you remember Green Fork?"

Kit blinked. "No. What's Green Fork?"

"Oh." It was easy for Kei to forget, sometimes, how young the girl was. *One year out of Steelgod, a couple of scouting missions under her belt, and she thinks she's invincible.* "About six years ago, Lady Tashida took her Blade across the river to chase down some rebel by the name of Konair. She chased him around the riverlands for a while, but could never quite catch up with him. The river lords, even when they're not outright rebellious, aren't exactly helpful. Tashida requested draekere support. Moriseki sent her three wings, and she managed to chase Konair south, right up against the forest. Konair ducked into the woods at a place called Green Fork, a known entrance. Lady Tashida decided to follow him."

"Oh." Kit's eyebrows went up. "That's . . ."

"Insane?"

"I was going to say 'unwise.'"

"Whatever. In any case, as soon as the report got back here, Lord Tashida sent a couple of Blades and one of his cousins to go and fetch her. If you believe the stories, they fought practically every step of the way until they found what was left of her Blade holed up a couple of miles deep in the Doomwood. They managed to pull her out again, losing half their own men in the process."

"How romantic." Kit was beaming. "It's like a fairy tale."

"The *point*, Kit, is that Lady Tashida led almost a thousand men into the Doomwood in a fit of pique, and practically none of them came back. Does that not make you just a little bit nervous?"

Kit paused a moment, as though in self-examination. "No. Not really."

Kei rolled her eyes. "Great. Fine. Just don't expect me to come charging to your rescue."

"Aw. You don't want to be my prince on a white charger?"

"Why would I be riding a *horse*?" said Kei, which made Kit dissolved into giggles. "We should get ready. Are you going to see Sami?"

Kit blushed. "N . . . No."

"No?"

"She's not speaking to me at the moment."

"Ah." Strictly speaking, her subordinate's affairs were none of her concern. Kei felt like she couldn't just let it lie, though. "Are you . . ."

"We'll have to see." Kit's smile returned, bright and unbreakable. "When we get back from wherever we're going."

"Right." Kei resolved to worm the story out of her. *She'll feel better for talking to someone.* And Kit was never the most close-mouthed of people. "Let me throw some things together. I'll meet you at the stables in an hour?"

"I'll be there."

THE STABLES WERE high in the north tower, which had been known under Imperial rule as the Spire of Memory. It was the tallest in the castle, rising a hundred feet above the outer walls, and had originally been empty most of the way up. The Imperials had used it for lookouts and warning bells; since the arrival of the draekeres, however, it had found much more useful employment.

Kei found Kit on the wooden floor that had been installed about halfway to the top. The center was a smooth bowl, heavily supported from below, where food could be dumped. It was big enough that Kei could have lain down it, comfortably, and the bottom was a perpetual sludge-pit of rotting meat and flies. Every day, menials filled it with scraps and carrion, which the draeks loved. Around the edges of the feeding pit and hanging from the walls were the various tools of the draekere's trade, such as saddles, prods, fixbows, and bombs.

Up above, holes had been drilled in the stone, and mammoth wooden posts, often the trunks of whole trees, had been levered into place. It was from these the draeks hung, upside-down. It was only a few hours after their noon feeding, and most of the creatures had gorged themselves and were busy sleeping it off. Only a few of the nearest rumbled a half-hearted greeting as Kei pulled herself up through the trapdoor and let it slam closed behind her. She sniffed to gauge the smell, which wasn't bad.

On, a good day, when the breeze was flowing through the huge hole in the side of the tower, it was tolerable. When the air got stagnant, spending time with the draeks was not pleasant.

Kit was there already, of course, picking out her equipment. Kei gave her a moment longer and stared up into the vaults of the tower. There were twenty-six draeks in residence, plus the pair that were out on patrol. They ranged in color from dirty brown to off-green, scaled from head to tail except at the shoulder, where they folded huge, leathery wings. Sleeping, they seemed tiny. They were twelve feet long, most of that tail, wings wrapped around their bodies. Periodically, though, one of the draeks would shift and stretch in its slumber. And when those wings unfolded, they just went on and *on*, out to twenty feet or more.

"Hello, Kei," said Kit, without turning around.

"That's the last time I try to sneak up on you."

"I just listen to them." She hooked a finger toward the ceiling. Kit had changed from her dress uniform to a much plainer and more useful riding uniform. It was almost entirely leather, designed to protect one's skin from the draek's rougher scales, and colored a drab gray so as not to show up against the skyline. Kei wore her own, and had the sack containing the majority of her personal belongings slung over one shoulder.

"About ready?" Kei glanced at the sun, angling in through the massive holes near the top of the tower. "We should go and meet Lady Tashida soon."

"Did you go and confirm the mission with Moriseki?"

Kei shrugged. "The Lady wouldn't lie to us. If she gave us permission to confirm our orders, it's pretty safe to assume they're confirmable."

Kit chuckled. "Nice logic."

"I plan to focus my energy on staying alive."

"You're still worrying?"

"Always." Kei sighed and made her way to her subordinate's side. She ran a practiced eye over the line of saddles. "Still, nothing to be done about it."

"Nope!" Kit gave her another bright smile. "Nothing at all."

"You're still happy about this."

"Going to hang me for it?"

"Just be careful." Kei sighed again. "It'd be nice if we knew what we were getting into. Then at least I could bring the right gear."

"True. Are you taking a fixbow?"

Kei nodded. "It's light and better than nothing."

"Good idea." Kit picked out an unstrung fixbow, which looked like a long wooden staff with a complicated metal hook at either end, and added it to a pile of stuff that was already growing worrisomely large. A draek couldn't carry more than around a hundred and fifty pounds, so for draekeres the choice was often between a little extra armor or more ammunition. For her part, Kei preferred the extra arrows, since pounding about at close range was too risky. Kit was, by nature, a member of the sound-the-charge school of thought; given that Kei was in command, though, she eventually gave up the wooden armor in favor of more quivers.

"If I get torn open by some demon, I'm going to blame you."

Kei chuckled. "The idea is to not let them get close enough. Besides, I dearly hope that won't be a problem."

"You really think Lady Tashida would go into the Doomwood again?"

"I'm just trying to be prepared for the worst."

Kit shrugged. "That always seemed like kind of a stupid outlook to me."

"Just wait until the worst happens to you. It always does,

eventually."

For all her uneasiness, Kei had to admit it was good to be in the saddle again. Things had been so quiet recently that she'd gone out only once in the last fortnight, and that had been just a quick patrol around the castle. Now she revisited all the familiar sensations, hanging from her saddle straps as the big green climbed the wall of the tower, the little moment of wild panic as it launched itself into the night. The draek fell for nearly a second, trading height for speed, and the castle walls rushed upwards terrifyingly fast. The lizard snapped its wings out, catching the air with a whump, and Kei's breakneck dive turned into a gentle glide. They cleared the wall with height to spare; Kei gave the reins a tug, and the draek beat its wings once and drifted into a lazy spiral.

Moments later, Kit's blue plummeted past, accompanied by her trademark dopplering shriek. She pulled out of the dive too close to the wall—*probably on purpose*, Kei thought sourly—and made a tight turn, practically pivoting the lizard on one wingtip. Kei straightened out her own path and headed south. Kit quickly fell in beside her.

They passed over the castle wall and Crossroads glittered darkly below with a thousand fires, reminding Kei of a sparkling, smoky hell. The banners on the wall snapped with the wind of their passage. There were ighty-six of them, Kei knew without counting, one for each Blade in the Empire. It was a not-so-subtle reminder to the Imperials below to behave. Kei smiled and pulled up higher.

As usual, the city went on beyond any reasonable expectations. The sheer size of it always amazed her; almost half a million dark-skinned barbarians, huddled together on both sides of the Tsel. No walls, no defenses. When Tashida Kuron had laid siege to the palace, Crossroads had burned nearly to the ground. That had been barely forty years ago, and now it was back, more haphazard and ramshackle than ever.

Further south, away from the Tsel, the city lights began to peter out. There were still a few fires, here and there, campfires for caravans, no doubt, or other travelers. Kei dipped lower until she spotted a point of green light.

"There's the flare!" She had to shout to be heard over the slipstream, but Kit nodded. Kei pulled on the reins and put the draek into a dive, leveling out at tree-top height and pulling up short. The draek flared its wings, dumping air, and settled down gently onto its claws. It grumbled a little complaint—the lizard's claws were made for hanging, not for walking on the ground—but, it was well-trained and lowered its neck so Kei could get off. Kit's draek settled in behind her, the rush from its wings sending leaves skittering across the ground. Kei waited for her to get down and waved her over. The signal fire was just ahead. Beside it was a set of campfires.

Not a lot of campfires, Kei noted, and as they drew closer she realized there were perhaps twenty people clustered around them. It was a long way from Lady Tashida's full Blade, even after its decimation at Green Fork. Most of those she saw huddled around the two outer fires were Imperials. They had the dour, suspicious look of sellswords. All— were armed, and most wore some ragtag ends of armor. Kei hurried past them to the last fire, looked around, and wished she hadn't.

Lady Tashida was there, of course, in real battle-armor this time. If a bit ornate for Kei's tastes—there were gilded snake-heads on either shoulder and an elaborate abstract design across the breastplate—it looked perfectly functional. She wore a short blade on either hip, their bone-white hilts a matched pair, and sat comfortably beside the fire as though tramping through the wilderness was a perfectly normal thing for the daughter of a noble family to do.

Across the fire from her sat the monk, Shikidai, in the same costume in which she'd last seen him. He greeted her once again with a nod; the firelight gleamed off his bald head as though it had been oiled. His staff, a thin, flexible piece of wood that probably served as a weapon, lay across his knees.

It was the third person that caught her attention. Directly across the fire from Kei sat a figure swathed in black cloth from head to toe. There were no slits, not even for the eyes, but it managed to look up as the two women approached. The unseen glare of the thing made Kei break out in goose bumps immediately. She shivered and seriously considered making a run for her draek.

Kit, as always, was undeterred. Seeing that Kei wasn't about to make the first move, she stepped brightly in front of her Wing Leader and bowed low.

"My Lady. Serenity. We're honored to join you."

"Of course." Lady Tashida inclined her head. "Sit down, both of you."

Awkwardly, Kei sat. She couldn't take her eyes off the thing.

"If we use titles the entire trip, things are going to get very dull around here," said Lady Tashida, airily. "You may call me Shiori, Wing Kitsu."

"As you wish." Kit flashed Kei a triumphant glance. "My friends call me Kit."

"Kit." Lady Tashida snapped the syllable off. "Welcome. Feel free to address Serenity Shikidai as Gota, and . . ." She trailed off, looking at the thing in black. It spoke, finally, in a sibilant rasp.

"Jyo-raku." Kei caught a whiff of its smell—like damp, wet stone—and the fire flickered.

"Jyo-raku," mouthed Kit, uncertainly. She lost her place for a moment, then gestured to Kei. "You know my Wing Leader.

Everyone calls her Kei."

"Kei, who is unaccountably silent." Tashida smiled. "So, now we are all friends here."

The monk, silent until this point, grunted in agreement. Kei blinked and nodded frantically.

"My apologies, Lady Tashida . . ."

"Shiori."

Kei stumbled over the name. "S . . . Shiori. It's been a busy day, getting ready to leave on such short notice."

"Of course. I'm sorry to have put you through such a trial, but time is of the essence."

"If I may ask a question . . ."

"Ask," snapped Lady Tashida impatiently. "I told you, we have no time for formality."

"Where are we going?" She blurted the sentence out, horribly aware of its impropriety. *In for a penny, in for an eye.* "And why all the secrecy?"

The noblewoman's expression froze, and she spent a long moment staring before giving Kei an uneasy smile. "Of course. I'm not surprised you're curious."

Kei waited stoically, aware that it was too late to backtrack. Lady Tashida cleared her throat.

"I won't bother swearing you to secrecy again—that this must be kept quiet should be obvious. Lord Kagerin returned last night with bad news. One of the exiled river lords, a man named Justin Valos, has been waging a quiet war against our interests for some time. He has enjoyed some success, and his reputation has spread. They call him 'Valos the Wolf.'"

"This Lord Valos has recently returned from the Diem highlands, somehow evading our forces at the Anvil, and since then he has been tearing up and down the riverlands. He's broken elements from at least three local Blades, and with the river lords harboring him, we've been unable to back him into a corner. Shuzan led the latest force sent to engage this man. He enjoyed some small victories, but Valos got away from him in a way that seemed, frankly, supernatural."

Lady Tashida glanced over at the monk, who'd been listening to the story with his eyes closed. He opened them now and spoke in a deep, commanding voice. "One of my order happened to be with Lord Kagerin at the time. It was his opinion that Lord Valos has enlisted the aid of a sorcerer, a powerful one."

Kei nodded. That put an entirely different complexion on things. Two-bit rebellions were common; one trait that all Imperials seemed to share was a stubborn refusal to recognize when they were beaten. Usually the local Blades wrote a bloody end to them, and that was that. But a powerful sorcerer on the loose was an entirely different matter.

"Shuzan is leading his Blade south again, as we speak," continued Lady Tashida, "in an attempt to catch Lord Valos by surprise. In the meantime," her nasty smile spread, "we have a different task."

"Find this sorcerer and eliminate him," rumbled Gota.

Oh. Kei sat for a moment digesting that. It was worse than she'd feared, worse than she'd really imagined. She asked the first question that came to mind. "How?"

"I've brought enough local guards to protect us from bandits, and the two of you to scout. Once we find the man, Gota will deal with him."

Gota inclined his head toward the figure in black. "Indeed."

Jyo-raku hissed, the low, mournful sound of a fire sputtering out. Kei was, once again, almost overcome by the sudden urge to run for her life.

"So you see the importance of secrecy," Lady Tashida went on. "We must catch this sorcerer unawares."

"Of course," Kei murmured.

Tashida shrugged. "You're worried."

"Excited, my lady."

"Good. You should get some sleep. We have long days ahead of us."

"Of course." She bowed, again. "Come on, Wing, let's set up our tent."

"I'm not . . ." Kit caught Kei's glare and bobbed her head obediently. "Tent. Right."

"*I* THINK IT'S exciting," said Kit. She was lying on one side under the newly erected tent, a simple, easy-to-build cloth and wood affair that was light enough to carry draek-back. There was barely enough room inside for two, wrapped in cloth against the chill of oncoming autumn. Kei hadn't even bothered to change out of her uniform.

"Did you *see* that thing?"

"Jyo-raku?"

"That's a demon, Kit."

"I should hope so." Kit shrugged. "Gota's a monk, and probably a good one. If we're going up against a sorcerer we'll need a demon on our side."

"You weren't talking like that back there."

Kit blushed a little, and cleared her throat. "I admit he's a little . . . intimidating. But he's on our side, Kei."

"For now," said Kei sourly.

"You're worried about Gota?"

"I'm more worried about what happens when this sorcerer sends his demon after us, and we happen to be between the two of them. Even if Jyo-raku's bound to obey the monk, he can look for loopholes."

"You really worry too much," said Kit. "All we have to do is find the guy. Then we pull out and leave it to him."

"I really hope it works out that way."

Kit smiled. "Relax. This is exciting! And think of what'll happen when we get back. Personally assisting Shiori on an important mission . . ." The girl stared dreamily into the distance. Kei half-suspected that Kit had a crush on Lady Tashida, which couldn't lead anywhere good.

"Try to stay focused, Kit."

Kit flopped onto her back, staring at the canvas ceiling. "Right. Focused."

Kei reached up, and pulled the string that let the tent flap fall closed. She lay on her back, arms crossed behind her head, and tried to sleep.

Sorcerers and demons. She worked hard to suppress a little shiver of fear. *Maybe Kit is right. There's nothing to worry about— they wouldn't send someone as important as Lady Tashida out here if it was really dangerous.* That was a comforting thought, until she remembered Green Fork. *If it gets dangerous, she won't pull back.* Ironically, it was a trait the noble shared with Kit. *It's me that has to pull her ass out of the fire if things go badly.*

The embarrassing thing was, she was well aware of what her first thought had been. *Ebon Death, come for my soul.* Kei snorted, softly. *As if actual demons weren't bad enough, I've got to conjure up children's stories.*

Kit was already asleep, by the sound of her breathing. She'd rolled back up onto her side, one arm groping blindly against the wall of the tent as if looking for something. *Sami, probably.* Kei envied Kit her casual relationships. *How long has it been for me?*

Outside, the dying campfires popped and spat. One of the sellswords swore, and guttural chuckles filled the night. Kei closed her eyes and listened to them banter in Imperial, which she only half-understood. Eventually, she fell asleep.

chapter 3

> "Everyone was so worried—like the Khaevs were
> going to march an army across the High Desert or
> through the Cloudrippers. I used to laugh at them;
> got thrown out of many a bar, let me tell you.
>
> "'The Khaevs are coming! The Khaevs are coming!'
> If anyone had stopped to think for a few seconds, they
> would have known it was bullshit. Forget the moun-
> tains and the deserts and the thousand miles between
> here and Khaevar. Fact is, they need the slave trade
> and they know it. Without us they'd have to get their
> precious hands dirty.
>
> "*That*'s why no Blade ever showed up at the gates.
> Whether the Imperials or the Khaevs are in charge
> doesn't matter. They can't do without the rats."
>
> > –Captain Vin Morrenson as recorded by
> > Leo Fairtooth, *Memoirs of a Pirate King*.

VEIL WOKE UP and was surprised to find herself freezing.
Her teeth chattered, despite instructions to the contrary, and her breath steamed instantly in air so cold it leeched
the warmth from her skin. She found her toes numbing rapidly,
and quickly curled into a ball. It was at this point that she noticed she was naked.

Oh. Veil breathed a chattering sigh of relief. *This is a dream.*

That didn't make it hurt any less, though. She brushed her eyes and looked around. A flat landscape of what felt like ice extended underfoot in every direction, until it merged with a sky that was nearly the same pale blue-gray. There was something in the distance, huge spires or spikes that cast weird, translucent shadows.

"Hmm," said a voice, so whispery and soft that Veil wouldn't have been aware of it but for the utter silence that prevailed. "So this is Veil."

She turned, with some effort, to look for the speaker. Veil's limbs were going numb, too, and the feeling of cold was starting to fade, replaced by a light-headed nothingness. She managed to scrape herself around, though, and found herself facing a woman made of ice.

It was like looking at a statue, the most perfect statue ever made. Every detail of the woman's features was visible. The ice was pure and perfect, too, as clear as glass. She could actually see through the woman's body. Her face was soft, but colorless, and her blank eyes were unblinking. Her hair, which was long and waving, was a single sheet of shimmering aquamarine crystals. She was naked, too, with small, flat breasts and a lean figure.

"W . . ." Veil couldn't force the words out. The woman tipped her head to one side, as though studying her subject. Her body moved without the slightest creak or groan of ice, sliding supplely from one position to another. When her hair shifted against her back, Veil could hear the tinkle of crystals.

"Not exactly who I would have chosen," the woman said after a while. "But everyone has talents. And after having her dropped quite literally into my lap, I can't very well say no."

Veil was not happy being discussed like a piece of livestock, but she couldn't say anything. Even her shivering had stopped— she lay frozen in place, watching the woman ponder. Finally, the statue shrugged, with another crystalline tinkle.

"Very well. She needs some work, but she'll do." She leaned closer, and smiled, revealing a mouth full of icicle teeth, sharp as needles. "Off you go."

VEIL AWOKE WITH a start, and sat bolt upright. She felt the grittiness of sand underneath her, and was relieved to find that she was still fully clothed and that the sun was just peeking over the edge of the horizon. The high desert, as usual, stretched in all directions—the phantom chill still clung to her limbs, though, so it was almost a welcome sight.

Corvus, still in his blacks, was sitting cross-legged a few feet away. His eyes were open. He hadn't slept since he'd picked her off the dune. *He must eat and drink while I'm asleep.* An odd thing to hide. *He carries the food and water anyway, so it's not like he needs to sneak any extra rations.*

"You're up?"

She nodded and yawned. He tossed her a full water skin, which she barely caught, and rose smoothly to his feet.

"That's the last one, so be sparing. We should get to Isail today."

Veil took a shallow drink and slung the skin over her shoulder. "What are you going to do when you get there?"

"Find a caravan headed to Corsa and join it. I'm sick of walking."

He didn't ask what she was planning to do, and she didn't mention it. Frankly, Veil wasn't sure she considered Isail civilization. From what she'd heard of the desert oases, they were little more than a spring and a little fort, where travelers could buy food and water at grossly inflated prices. *Speaking of which . . .*

"Do you have any money?"

Corvus was already trudging away across the sands. "No."

Veil fingered the two eyes in her pocket, and wondered how much water they'd buy in the high desert. *Not a lot. Slaves are cheap, and water is hard to come by.* "I've got a little. We can buy some more water."

"Thanks for the charity, but no."

"But—"

"Save your concern." Corvus looked back long enough to glare, then returned to trudging south. The sun had started to warm the sand, and for the moment it felt delicious on Veil's back.

MOST OF THE day passed before they reached the oasis. Corvus spoke only in monosyllables. They stopped just after high noon so Veil could have something to eat, but, other than that, it was straight-arrow progress across the dunes.

It occurred to Veil only after they'd crested the last dune and caught sight of the little fortress that, had Corvus been wrong about distance and direction, they both would have died horribly. It wasn't as unsettling a thought as she might have imagined. *It honestly never occurred to me.* She looked at Corvus in his black leather and silk and he seemed depressed and slightly scary but, above all, *competent*. The idea that he might die, lost in the desert, seemed somehow too ridiculous to entertain.

Isail was a welcome sight, in any case. It was nestled halfway up a giant rock formation which poked toward the sky as though the landscape were making an obscene gesture at the horizon. Halfway up, some long-forgotten spire had cracked off and left a relatively flat spot. It was here that water trickled from the rock, and that the desert merchants had thrown up walls of rough-cut stone. There was nothing else to build with. Wood would dry and crack in the heat, and shipping it overland would be prohibitively expensive. The whole place was smaller than Kalil's mansion, but far more defensible. Crude as they were, the walls overlooked a fifty-foot staircase carved into naked rock, with no protection from anything the defenders might choose to drop. And it would cost such a fortune in water to besiege the place that she doubted anyone would ever try.

A couple of caravans were camped around the base of the rocks in a haphazard jumble of tents and cloth thrown up from the sides of carts. A fenced enclosure had been thoughtfully provided by whoever ran the place, and at least a dozen mules were stabled there, mostly sleeping.

Veil's stomach lurched at the sight of the carts. Each one had wooden slats reaching high on all sides, forming a cage in which slaves could be safely left for the night. Two of the four were empty, while the other two were covered in white-clad forms, sleeping as best they could on the rough wooden flatbed. Veil glanced at Corvus and found him smiling.

"Excellent."

"What?"

"Full carts mean they're headed to the city. We'll tag along with them."

"But . . ." Veil bit her lip and stayed silent. None of the slaves so much as stirred as they approached, but there were a pair of sellswords in ragged red-and-blue coats sitting on a barrel, and one of them stood to greet the strangers. One man was chewing *rhigar*. H e looked the pair over for a while, then spat a thick red glob on the ground.

"Yeah?"

"I need to purchase water." Corvus inclined his head toward the fortress. "I'd also like to travel south to the city with your caravan."

"Oh, you would?" He elbowed his partner in the ribs. "Zon, you hear that? He wants to come along. I'm sure the master would love that, some desert loony hanging around, eating our food and drinking our water." He took a *rhigar* cube out of his pouch, took a long, loving bite, and started to chew.

"I can work."

"Doing what?"

Corvus put one hand on the hilt of his sword, but said nothing. The guard scowled.

"Happens we've already got all the guards we need."

"I challenge you, then. When we're done, the guard will have been improved."

The guard spit another heavy red glob an inch from Corvus' boot. Veil flinched, but the black-clad swordsman didn't move.

"First of all," said the guard. "There's no fighting within sight of the fortress, or none of us gets water. They like to keep the peace. And, second of all, the master knows me and trusts me. Even if you were better, which is not likely," he said as he elbowed his companion again, who guffawed, "what makes you think he'd hire some stranger?"

"Very well."

Here it comes. Veil almost closed her eyes, but was afflicted by an odd desire to see the blood fly. Corvus did not seem like the type who would take an insult like that kindly.

"I can pay."

What?

"Oh?" The guard smiled. "That's a different matter."

"Do you want to fetch your master?"

"Master trusts me to handle the finances. He doesn't like to be bothered."

"As you wish." Corvus shrugged. "I will pay two eyes."

"You'll drink more water than that."

"I can also offer your master a half-interest in my slave, who I plan to sell when I reach the city."

Veil barely had time for a confused squeak before his hand

landed heavily on her shoulder and squeezed, hard enough to be painful. She swallowed hard.

"Half-interest?" The guard looked at Veil with the air of a man examining a piece of livestock, muttering to himself. "Not bad, not bad. She'll fetch at least six at market." He looked up again, smiling. "That's acceptable."

"Excellent."

"I'll get her into the cage. Then I'm sure my master would like to speak with you."

"I should have a word with her first."

"A word?"

"She trusts me." He shrugged. "It'll be less trouble this way."

The guard shook his head but made no comment. Corvus retreated a few steps, and Veil followed anxiously.

"What in the Aether do you think you're doing?"

"Doing things the easy way."

"The *easy* way? They're going to put me in a cage!"

"Trust me." He said it gravely, and Veil suppressed a hysterical giggle. *How can I possibly trust him?*

"But . . ."

"Unless you'd like to fight your way into that fortress, I suggest you play along."

Veil's lip twisted. *I don't have much choice.* Corvus could sell her by force if he wanted to. *Still . . .*

"How long are you going to keep me in there?"

"A night, no more."

"I . . ." She caught the satisfaction in his gaze. "Six Lords, Corvus. If I get raped tonight I'm going to *kill* you."

"Nothing will happen to you. Trust me."

"This is by far the stupidest thing . . ."

Corvus was already turning back to the guard. "She is convinced."

47

"Odd way to talk to a slave."

"She's not properly broken in yet." The guard nodded. "Another thing."

"Yes?"

"She must remain undamaged in order to fetch a good price."

The guard nodded again, more slowly. "Not properly broken in, eh?"

Corvus raised a dry eyebrow, and the man shrugged. "She's your property. Too bad, though, I was going to ask if I could rent her for a night."

Mentally, Veil decapitated the man and left his head to drain on a pike. She kept up her blank smile.

"Too bad."

"Zon, take her to the girls' cage." The other guard, a huge bear of a man with hands wide enough to wrap around Veil's neck with room to spare, unfolded himself from his seat. "And be careful with her."

"Right," Zon grunted. He took her arm, surprisingly gently, and led her toward one of the carts. Veil looked back at Corvus, who was still talking to the other guard.

Trust him. Much to her surprise, she did. *He just sold me into slavery, and I didn't make a peep.* Though, she reflected, it's not as though there was a lot she could have done. *Kicked him, bit him, something.*

If nothing had happened by tomorrow afternoon, Veil resolved, she was going to make her own escape.

THE CAGE WAS not as bad as she'd expected. One of the two carts was dedicated to girls. There were four in there already, ranging from a pair of sisters her age to a snuffling child of seven. They were asleep when Zon opened the door to the cage and stayed asleep while Veil struggled over to a corner and wedged herself in.

The smell was atrocious, so bad that after the first few minutes her nose practically shut down. The worst part, she decided, was the tickling on her arms and legs as the various vermin who had traveled a hundred miles with this caravan jumped at the chance for some new food. Veil took deep breaths and tried to ignore them. Aside from that, it was almost peaceful, with the occasional sigh of the wind, the raspy breathing of the other girls, and the intermittent laughter of the guards as they drank and played cards.

Veil wouldn't have laid odds on being able to sleep in a cage, but she managed it. Once again, she found herself on a freezing plain. This time she remained standing, wrapping her arms over her naked chest and shivering.

"Am I . . ." She inhaled too much of the frigid air while trying to shout, and ended up coughing, which pretty much ruined the effect. Veil finished the statement as a wheeze. "Am I going to end up here *every* time I fall asleep? Because as dreams go, this one is pretty awful."

"Only when I need you," said the soft, crystalline voice. Veil whirled, not a smart move while standing on ice, and ended up flopping to the ground. The ice-woman chuckled. The sound was like the ringing of tiny glass bells.

"Well, whatever you want, get it over with." Veil hugged herself tighter. "It's cold in here."

"My apologies. I will be brief."

Despite herself, Veil found her curiosity piqued. *Given that none of this is real, figuring it out is kind of a waste of time. Unless this is a demon.* That thought had occurred to her before. Demons often tempted their victims through dreams before dragging them off into the Aether for torment and consumption. *She hasn't exactly tempted me, though.*

"Who are you?"

The ice-woman smiled, just a little. "That's a complicated question. For the sake of convenience, call me Sybian."

"W . . . W . . . what do you want with me?" The stutter was from cold, not cowardice. Secure in the knowledge that she was dreaming, Veil was unafraid.

"I'm using you as a pawn."

"Oh." *At least she's honest.*

Sybian shrugged, her hair tinkling. "There's not much you can do, so I suggest you relax and enjoy things. Assuming everything works out, you won't come out of it badly at all."

The cold was intense. Veil could barely move her lips to frame the next question.

"What if things . . ."

"Don't work out?" Sybian's grin widened. "You'll probably end up dead. That's the way things go. I'll take care of you, either way."

"I . . ." Veil's jaw clamped shut and refused to open again. She shivered violently. Sybian tilted her head and looked at her with a trace of pity.

"You have to learn to let go, Veil. This is a *dream*, after all. What do you need to be warm for?"

Veil couldn't answer. Sybian leaned closer.

"You let him lock you in a cage, and now you're trusting him to get you out again. Really, you're going to have to do a bit better than that."

VEIL PRIED HER eyes open. They felt dry and crusted, as though she'd been sleeping for weeks. The floor of the cage jostled in a regular rhythm that suggested they were on the move; a quick glance outside revealed the dunes sliding slowly past. Men walked on either side of the cart, easily keeping pace with the lazy mules. Nearest on the left side was Corvus, who nodded to her as she sat up.

Veil nodded back, absent-mindedly scratching at her arms. Various small creatures that had colonized her during the night cracked under her fingernails, and some of the bites itched furiously.

"Well?" asked Corvus. "How did you sleep?"

"Fine," she answered dryly. "And you?"

He chuckled. "Hospitality compelled Master Morzeban to offer me some wine. Pride made him try to drink me under the table."

"I take it that didn't work?"

Corvus shrugged. "He's sleeping it off."

Veil nodded, as though this conversation were being held under normal circumstances. "Good, good. Can I ask you a question?"

"If you must."

"How about getting me *out of this fucking cage?*"

"You're impatient."

"If you had to bear the company in here, you'd be impatient, too."

"Other girls keep you up late?" He glanced at the other slaves, who were still asleep.

"They're not the ones I was referring to." Veil scratched her arms again. "Now—"

"You know," Corvus mused, "I could just leave you in there. Slaves bring a good price in Corsa . . ."

"Corvus!" He smiled, and she glared at him. "You wouldn't."

"I would." He shrugged again. "But I owe Furoc for talking to me like that yesterday. So you're off the hook, this time."

Veil let out a long breath. "If you're going to do something, do it."

Part of her impatience, she had to admit, was curiosity. It had always been her curse. Corvus seemed too confident. *He has to have some kind of a plan.* There were a dozen guards with the caravan in total, mostly clustered around the men's wagon, with a few of the sharper ones acting as advance guard and another couple loitering behind. A man on a horse, who Veil assumed was Master Morzeban, rode between the two wagons at a walking pace and cradled his head as though every step brought him pain. *Serves him right.*

"Furoc!" Corvus called out. The guard who'd greeted them yesterday dropped back from his position by the lead wagon until he was walking alongside Corvus. He smiled, revealing blackened teeth and a couple of gaping holes.

"Corvus! You are amazing, my friend. I have never seen anyone out-drink the master."

"Indeed." Corvus smiled thinly, and Veil could see he prickled at 'my friend.' "Furoc . . ."

"What do you need?" Furoc leaned closer. "More wine? The hair of the dog, they say . . ."

"I have reconsidered our bargain. Free my slave, and provide me with enough water to reach the city."

Furoc blinked. "Corvus . . ."

"You can keep the two eyes."

"Corvus, you must be joking." Furoc shook his head. "You'll drink at least four eyes worth of water. The master would never consent . . ."

"So don't ask him." Corvus' hand dropped to the hilt of his sword. "I'm asking you politely."

Furoc's smile faded. "I'm not sure I like your tone, my friend."

"I'm not your friend, and I've never liked yours."

A couple of the other guards had noticed the altercation and were drifting over. Emboldened by this support, Furoc drew his own short-sword, an ugly piece of notched metal.

"I advise you to drop that."

"Oh?" The guard no longer sounded friendly. "I think we will just keep your slave." His eyes flickered to Corvus' side. "And your sword. We'll leave the rest of you to the desert."

"Drop it." Corvus sounded bored. "Last chance."

Dear dead gods, thought Veil. *He's just going to fight them all.*

"Last chance, he says." Furoc half-turned, laughing. "He tells *me* last . . ."

That was as far as he got. Blood sprayed from a gash in the guard's neck, coating the sand with red. Veil, who'd been watching closely, had barely seen Corvus move. The other guards didn't have a chance; they were still looking at Furoc, whose body had begun to wobble. Corvus stepped forward and ran one of them through, contemptuously, then whipped his sword out and plunged it into the bowels of the other as he fumbled for his sword. The guard groaned and slid off the blade, hitting the ground just as Furoc's body finally decided it was dead and toppled over.

Corvus straightened up. Blood ran down the length of his blade, pooling at the tip and dripping to clot the sand. Veil blinked.

"Anybody else feeling brave?" He allowed himself a tiny smile as his eyes found Morzeban, the caravan master. The merchant's jowly face contracted, and he pointed frantically.

"What are you waiting for? Kill him!"

There were six guards at the front of the caravan, and three at the rear. They had Corvus nine-to-one, and they knew it. Veil could read their faces as they edged closer. The black-clad swordsman was *fast*, viper-fast, and whoever went for him first was probably not going to survive. *Let someone else do it*, they thought. *Why should I be the first one?*

Veil almost laughed. *They're all going to die.*

Corvus waited until the guards had come closer, almost within striking distance. He was watching their faces, too, and he moved just before they were committed.

He charged the left-most of the group of six. The guard threw up his sword, desperately, trying to parry a stroke that never arrived. Corvus landed heavily on one foot, throwing up a spray of sand, and brought his blade around in a low arc that removed the adjacent guard's leg at the knee. The man fell screaming as his companions backpedaled.

Corvus charged the next pair in the moment that bought him. Steel shrieked against steel as the first parried and the second attacked, but Corvus ducked the stroke and lopped the man's hand off at the wrist. His companion thrust desperately, but his target was no longer there: Corvus had moved on to the final pair.

Those two had enough warning to try to defend themselves, for all the good it did them. The black swordsman feinted them out of position, opened the belly of the one on the right, then stepped past him as he fell and brought his blade almost casually across the other's throat. Blood fountained again onto the thirsty sand as Corvus stepped away and raised his sword, still smiling.

"Nine on one." He glanced at the sand, where two of the guards were still writhing. "Now five on one. Anybody else?"

The guards looked at each other, then back at Morzeban. The merchant was sweating profusely.

"A bonus! I'll give you a bonus if you kill him!"

Zon, the big leg breaker, shook his head slowly. "I don't know if we can take him, boss."

"As long as you're in my employ, you'll do as I say!" the

merchant shrieked. "Now kill him!"

Corvus shrugged. "Let me make it easy for you."

He moved again, pushing off with another spray of sand. The guards started, splitting up to stay out of his way; Corvus ignored them and bore down on the merchant. Morzeban barely had time to yank his horse's reins before Corvus was on top of him, grabbing the edge of his saddle and swinging himself up. He turned the momentum into a kick that sent the merchant sprawling off his mount and rolling across the sand. Corvus followed him down, sword-first, and landed with a crunch. Morzeban gurgled and kicked a few moments longer, then lay still. None of the guards had moved.

"That make it easy enough?"

Zon was the first to throw down his sword. "Easy enough."

"Let her out."

Veil got to her feet, a little shakily, as Zon opened the door at the back of the cage. She slipped past the huge guard carefully and wobbled a little bit when she finally got back on solid ground. The other slaves cowered in their corners, unwilling or unable to move.

Corvus didn't take his eyes off the guards. "Veil, get the supplies from the back of the wagon."

"Right." She hunted through the packs until she found a wrapped bundle of dried fruit and meat and a pair of lashed-together water skins, and hefted them onto her shoulders. The weight staggered her, but she managed to make her way over to Corvus before letting them slip to the ground.

"Take the wagons back to Isail. I'll keep the horse. Any objections?"

One by one, the guards shook their heads. Zon slammed the door of the cage, and they began the laborious process of turning the mules around. Corvus took the horse by the reins and tugged; it followed him placidly, apparently undisturbed by the smell of blood. He handed the reins to Veil.

"Hold this."

"Right." Veil couldn't stop staring at him. *Twelve on one. He didn't even blink.*

Kalil's master of arms was a short, wiry northerner named Yenn. Veil had watched him give lessons to the older boys, her older brothers. Yenn had been quick, no doubt about it, but, compared to Corvus, he looked like an arthritic old man. *It's unearthly.*

Corvus finished strapping the food and water to the back of the horse and gave it a pat on the rump. It started walking south, slowly and Veil hurried to keep up with it. Corvus gave the retreating caravan one last glance. He produced a square of black cloth from some pocket and wiped his sword, deliberately. Then he turned away to follow Veil.

They had walked for a good half hour before Veil could force herself to broach the subject. "You . . . I mean . . . that was incredible!"

Corvus shrugged wearily. "Fools. A pack of fools."

"But twelve against one! You're like a hero from the stories. Like when Ebon Death killed the four Khaevs, or when Dominarius fought the entire Perkat clan, one after another, or when . . ."

"Right."

"I'm just . . .impressed, that's all."

"Thank you. That means so very much to me."

Veil kicked some sand from her path, but remained silent for a few moments longer.

"The other slaves . . ."

"What about them?"

"You could have let them go."

"Go where? This is the high desert. Nothing but slavers and dust for a hundred miles in any direction."

"Right." Veil nodded, slowly. "I guess it's better this way."

"In any case, I couldn't be bothered."

"You let *me* out."

He rolled his eyes. "Don't make me regret that decision."

"Right." Veil sighed. "Right."

LORD JUSTIN VALOS rode alone toward the blasted hilltop and the tower house that crowned it. He was dressed to avoid notice, wearing a brown cloak, with simple leathers underneath and an unremarkable sword at his belt. Just another man-at-arms, running a message for one of the ever-talkative river lords. He wore no tabard on his shoulder, but that was not uncommon during the occupation; a lord could fall out of favor with the Khaevs for no reason at all. No one displayed colors if it could be avoided.

His horse might have marked him as unusual. A high-spirited stallion, young and full of fire, it was not the tired old workhorse that a man-at-arms should have been riding. But his horse also looked as though it hadn't been cleaned in a week. Its dappled hair was well-coated with mud, and only an experienced eye would look past that to the magnificent beast beneath.

All in all, Justin felt, he had done a fair job of concealing his station. Not that any of it was necessary, if everything was as it seemed. *But then again, when have things gone according to plan?*

During the autumn, thunderstorms washed up on the shores of the riverlands like great black jellyfish. They floated in off the sea and drifted west across the plains, losing strength until they dissolved of their own accord or smashed themselves to bits against the mountains. Justin could see one in the distance. The riverlands were flat, or nearly so, and the tower house commanded the highest hill for miles. The shadow of the dark clouds moved slowly, but unstoppably, swallowing farms, fences, towns, and anything else in its path.

Justin shivered, then shook his head to clear his mind of such foolish thoughts. *I am in a dark mood today.* He was never particularly happy, going to see the Prophet, but the events of the last week had thrown him into a black, angry depression.

As always, the tower house looked abandoned from the outside. A two-story stone building supported a much taller wooden tower, which had fallen into disrepair since the river lord who had built the place had abandoned it. The stables, which were big enough for thirty horses, were empty as well. Justin tied his stallion to a support beam, since the hitching posts had long since fallen over or been uprooted. From there he went in the stable entrance and threaded his way through a series of crumbling kitchens and empty servants' quarters until he arrived at the main hall.

He found the Prophet sitting at the bottom of the great stone staircase that led up to the tower. A fallen ceiling blocked it at the top, but the bottom made a convenient bench. The old man was occupied with his dogs, the only living things in the building besides himself. They were huge, black-furred creatures, imported from the Diem highlands as puppies. They loved the old man and tolerated his guests, but Justin would have given long odds to any intruder.

The dogs noticed him first, taking time out from licking the Prophet's fingers to treat Justin to a stare and a brief growl, just in case he was thinking of trying anything. Justin spread his hands, and that seemed to placate them; they withdrew to their master's side and curled up, panting. The Prophet looked up and nodded at him.

"Lord Valos. It's good to see you again." His voice was solemn, with an odd touch of authority. Justin would have guessed the Prophet's age at perhaps sixty. His skin had toughened to the consistency of old leather and the hair that remained on the sides of his head was pure white. But his eyes, the blue of old ice, had lost none of their intelligence. They fixed Justin with a gaze that was both penetrating and somehow cold.

"You as well." There was always the ticklish issue of what to *call* the man; addressing him as 'Prophet' was a bit too reverential for Justin's taste, but he had no other names that anyone had ever heard of. "You're doing well here? For food and so on?"

"I have sufficient, thank you." He scratched one of the dogs behind its ear, and it rubbed against his leg. "You're troubled, my Lord."

"You don't exactly have to be a sorcerer to see that." Justin's mouth twisted. "Adrian's gone."

"Gone where?"

"Nobody knows! He's just gone. Took his personal guard and cut out, sometime after Mourning."

"Sorcerers are notoriously fickle."

"I know that!" Justin shouted. He took a deep breath. The Prophet's placid expression remained unchanged. "I know. This just comes at a particularly bad time. Tashida Shiori has left Crossroads, and the rumor is she's hunting me."

"With her Blade?"

"No. Just she and some special agents, which makes matters worse. Shiori's no tactician, not like that damned Lord Kagerin, and we could easily stay one step ahead of her Blade. But if it's just she, and maybe some draekeres and maidens . . ." He paced back and forth. "And my gods-damned sorcerer has decided to go on vacation without telling anyone!"

"Perhaps Adrian will return soon."

"Perhaps. I'd rather not stake my life on perhaps." He eyed the Prophet doubtfully. "I take it you don't know anything?"

"On that subject, no."

That the old man had some supernatural source of information, Justin didn't doubt. His warnings had been right more times than Justin could remember. His title as the "'rophet" was somewhat facetious. H e didn't see the future, just the present, but he did so in an extremely precise, if maddeningly inconsistent, way. Still, his advice had helped Justin in more than one major battle, most recently against Kagerin Shuzan's vaunted elite cavalry.

Adrian, though, was one subject on which the Prophet would never give a forecast. The sorcerer hated the old man with a passion born of madness, and was constantly railing against his advice. Justin often wondered if he'd shielded himself somehow from the Prophet's awareness. *Who knows how sorcerers do what they do?*

"And on other subjects?" Things that the Prophet thought were important were usually worth paying attention to, even if they seemed a little far-fetched. Justin had learned this from experience.

"The girl." The old man hooded his eyes and sat back, looking pleased with himself.

"Your strategic genius? Max Senar come again, and just in time to help us fight the Khaevs?" Justin couldn't keep the doubt out of his voice, but the old man just kept smiling.

"The same." He caught Justin's expression. "You laugh, but you've done everything required of you."

"Zhin and Isobel were headed back to Corsa anyway. We need all the help we can get, and if there are any mercenary bands of note that will work for us—" Justin's trailed off, sourly. Most mercenaries could tell which way the wind was blowing, and it had been blowing firmly behind the Khaevs for more than ten years. The groups that would sign up to fight for the Empire were few and far between. *Ungrateful scum.* Most of the mercenary companies were led by ex-Imperial veterans, farmed out in the peaceful pre-Conquest years, and many of their recruits came from the conscripts who'd deserted in droves when the Khaevs broke the Imperial Army at Tsankuun.

"They will not be bringing any mercenaries back with them." The old man shrugged. "But they have the girl and her companion, and that is all that matters."

"And is this girl going to conjure up another ten thousand men with her brilliance?"

"She will win the battles that need to be won," said the Prophet placidly. "You should have more faith, Lord Valos."

"Faith in what? Gods that have been dead six thousand years?"

"Their plan guides us still. They have considered all things, even the Khaevs. Even you."

Justin snorted. "Where were the gods at Tsankuun? Or on the beaches at Sunnyshore, when they might have made a difference?"

"Some things are inevitable."

This was old territory, and Justin choked off his anger with a snarl. He wasn't mad at the Prophet, not really. The old man's outmoded faith in the gods was an eccentricity, nothing more. The rage that burned in Valos was directed at the Khaevs, at the cowards who'd fled rather than fought, and, most of all, at the corrupt lords who'd bled the Empire dry. *So dry that a passel of backwoods barbarians set it aflame.* As always, Mika's face rose in his mind, blurred by time—bright, shining blue eyes and a radiant, clever smile. *You should have listened to me, Mika.* His throat clenched. *You all should have listened.*

"Have I disturbed you, my lord?"

"No." Justin waved a hand. "Old ghosts."

"When you reach my age," said the Prophet dryly, "you may speak of old ghosts."

"I have taken enough of your time." Justin nodded, respectfully. "I will take my leave."

"I am an old man, Lord Valos, and I have time to waste. But go. You have an army to train and a war to run. Take advantage of this respite. Even now Tashida Ikon prepares for his offensive against Tellen, and I doubt very much he intends to launch his invasion with you in his rear."

That made Justin smile, grimly. He had no doubt what the outcome of that offensive would be. The stories of the Empire's first and only attempt to conquer the cursed island were still told after a thousand years.

"Until next time, Prophet."

"Until next time, Lord Valos." The Prophet smiled, and his blue eyes glittered like ice in the sun. "Until next time."

chapter 4

> "The Empire stood for six thousand years with these horrors on their doorstep. The greatest power in the world, and they ignored it. They were *content* with the status quo. Dynasty after dynasty was *content* to cede some part of their 'empire' to the monsters, to put up with the disappearances and ignore the growing threat. These creatures have been allowed to build their power unmolested for six thousand years!
>
> "I will not permit this one moment longer! I am *not* content! And we have the power to end this, now and forever!"
>
> —Kagerin Semike's last speech to his Blade before their final expedition to Godsdoom

THE MAN WITH no name sat alone in the clearing.

He'd had a name, before. He even remembered it. *Ilam Adrian*. A name, a family, a purpose. None of it mattered now. Nothing remained but a strange satisfaction that came from killing Khaevs. Everything else came through Vaalkir.

The spirit was in the clearing, too. It sniffed the air, distastefully. Every movement kindled fire at its joints, little spurts of flame that ran across its armored body in waves. The armor shone silver wherever the ash had flaked off. It covered the spirit from head to toe, completed by a solid visor without even an eye slit. As it paced, steam flashed from ground dampened by recent rain, so that Vaalkir's every step was accompanied by a baleful hiss.

"They are still following." The spirit's voice was the harsh crackle of flame.

"I don't understand," said the man with no name. "Why don't you simply destroy them?"

"The humans are nothing. Less than nothing. The one who accompanies them is another matter entirely."

"But . . ."

"It has taken a long time to convince him to show himself. Now that I have a chance to destroy him, I must be certain."

"But you could defeat him?"

"Of course." Fire bloomed all over the spirit's armored form, for a moment encasing it in an aura of heat that frizzled the man's eyebrows. "But he must be forced to commit himself. There can be no retreat this time."

"In that case, things are proceeding well!" The man smiled. "They follow where we will."

"The humans may balk, and he will not proceed without his cover. They must be convinced."

"Won't he be suspicious?"

"He is suspicious by nature. Also arrogant. My hand will be obvious in what follows."

"I don't—"

"You are not required to understand. Just obey."

"Yes."

JYO-RAKU STRAIGHTENED. HE looked uncomfortable in direct sunlight, shifting his weight as though he was considering making a run for it. Each time, though, he glanced back at the impassive Gota and returned to the task at hand.

The rest of their little band was gathered on the road. The sellswords hung about in twos and threes, talking and laughing with the air of those who are employed on a pointless task, but are getting paid anyway. Lady Tashida, the monk, and the two draekeres were paying the shrouded figure close attention, though, as he scraped the earth between his fingers and considered.

"He has turned northwest," Jyo-raku hissed.

Gota blinked heavy-lidded eyes. "Are you certain?"

"Of course I'm certain."

Lady Tashida spoke in a conciliatory tone. "We've seen no sign of them. And the last report from our scouts has the main body of Valos' force still headed southwest, toward the mountains. So . . ."

"The sorcerer's minions hide his trail from your eyes. I would expect nothing less. But I can feel his demons. They are there, to the northwest."

"But there's nowhere to *go* that way," Kit objected. "It's just some little farm towns and then the mountains."

It still irked Kei that her subordinate felt far freer to speak up at these meetings then she did. Part of it was innate deference to Lady Tashida, and part of it some lingering fear of Jyo-raku, despite the control that Gota clearly exerted. And part of it, Kei had to admit, was just natural. Kit was talkative and happy to share her opinion. Kei was more inclined to simply obey. *I've spent twelve years not drawing attention to myself. It can be a hard habit to break.*

Lady Tashida smiled. "Maybe they're trying to hide from us. They do know we're following?"

"They do," nodded Jyo-raku. "I have concealed my own presence, however."

"So he could be running scared."

"No." The demon shook his head. "In that case they would

continue south, and take refuge in the Doomwood. They are going somewhere in the mountains."

The noble shrugged. "At this rate, we should catch them long before they get there."

"Yes." Jyo-raku seemed distracted, as though lost in thought. Kei wondered briefly what the world looked like to the demon. "We can reach the next town by nightfall. After that we enter the hills. If they continue at their current speed . . ." He trailed off, staring into the distance.

"Jyo-raku!" snapped Gota. The demon's head whipped around, and he bowed low.

"My apologies. We should continue."

"Yes." Lady Tashida clapped her hands. "We're moving out! Northwest."

There was more laughter among the sellswords, who clearly considered this a wild goose chase, but they shouldered their packs and weapons and began preparations for departure. Lady Tashida nodded to Kit.

"We'll meet you two at this town unless something happens."

"Understood," said Kei, attempting to retain at least some of her authority. The noblewoman favored her with a bland smile, then turned away.

"You still don't like her," said Kit, as the two draekeres made their way down the road.

"It's not that I don't *like* her. This whole mission just seems a little . . ."

"I know, I know." Kit sighed. "I don't like her either."

"You certainly don't show it!"

"You know I'm not fond of the Tashidas, or any of the nobility for that matter. But we have to work with Shiori, and that's that."

"You have to admit it's weird."

"Of course it's weird! Stuff like this doesn't happen every day. *You* have to admit that Jyo-raku's been well-behaved."

"So far," Kei muttered.

"And Lady Tashida has been very careful to try and be nice to us vermin." Kit grinned. "I think you just need to relax."

"Maybe."

The girl stretched her arms behind her back. "Absolutely! And tonight we get to stay in a real town."

That, Kei had to admit, sounded good. After two weeks of sleeping on the road by night and flying all day, the aches had started to build up. A night in an actual bed, even a too-soft Imperial-style bed, would definitely be welcome.

The draeks rumbled a welcome as their riders rounded a hill. Kit's blue was still lying on its side. They had eaten two days before, a whole deer each, and they were still showing the bloat around their stomachs. Draeks were amazingly hardy, given their fragility, and Kei had known them to go for more than a week on one meal. It never ceased to amaze her that the things could get into the air after eating; her own mount looked liked its weight had nearly doubled. As she got closer, it clambered lazily to its feet and shook out its wings, blowing a twisting whirlwind of leaves into the air.

Kit laughed. "I think it's anxious to get going."

"Are you kidding?" Kei patted the green on the side as she pulled the saddle straps tight again; it let out an angry snort. "I think if we weren't around it'd be perfectly content to just lie here until it got hungry. Yours, too."

She mounted, using the rope that hung from the pommel of the saddle to help herself up, and started tightening her straps. She tested each line, carefully. The straps were connected by spring-loaded hooks to rings on the saddle, which was in turn

<u>bolted into the lizard's shoulder blades.</u> Riding a draek bare-backed was possible; it had been done, though not often. But without a saddle there was nothing to even hold on to if the thing decided to bank too sharply or, gods forbid, flip over. A saddle also provided a good mounting point for a fixbow.

Kit was mounted and anxious to be off by the time Kei was ready. The blue shared her mood, pawing at the ground and leaving deep gashes in the grassy soil. Kei rolled her eyes and gestured. "Go ahead."

Kit snapped the reins and the draek was off, moving with an ungainly, waddling gait that reminded her of a giant chicken. For all their grace in the air, a grounded draek was somehow pathetic. They landed on flat ground only reluctantly in their natural state. These two were trained mounts, of course, and would land wherever they were told.

In a surprisingly short distance the lizard had gotten up to speed. It snapped its wings out and its legs up in one smooth motion, dropped disconcertingly until its belly almost brushed the ground, then flapped and shot upward. Kei kicked her own mount onward, clinging tightly to the forward straps as it bounced along the ground and went through the same routine. A few moments later, the two draekeres were gliding peacefully through the morning sky, the riverlands unfolding beneath them like a living map.

Just to the north was the Fuyuun, one of the innumerable tributaries that fed the mighty Tsel as it curved to the sea. The river ran roughly northeast-southwest. Further upstream, in the mountains, it worked itself into a froth. Here the Fuyuun was peaceful and nearly flat, curving back and forth through green country that was lightly forested and heavily farmed.

To the west, the Shieldwall rose imperious and impenetrable, blued by distance. Kei looked for the Anvil but couldn't find it. The legendary Imperial fortress was supposedly buried in the side of the mountain itself with only two massive towers showing above ground. It had been built during the Third Dynasty, when the Empire still knew a thing or two about building. The Palace at Crossroads dated from the same era, and she had to admit it was impressive in scale, if not in content. The Anvil had never been taken by storm; the draekeres that had proved so effective against the open castles of the river lords had been worthless against a buried fortress.

Kei remembered her history lessons—Tashida had been forced to starve the defenders out, and the siege had lasted more than two years, with the better part of another year going by before every last warren was cleared of defenders. *You have to give that to the Imperials. They're persistent.*

To the south . . . Kei tried not to look to the south. The patches of forest got larger and darker, and the farmsteads smaller and more isolated, until in the distance the dark patches merged into the black mass of the Doomwood. For now the trail led northwest, and Kei was grateful. She was still unsettled. Something in Lady Tashida's pursuit seemed too dogged to be real. She would follow this sorcerer through the gates of Hell, Kei was sure of it. *The question is why.*

"I can see the town!" Kit shouted, her voice nearly lost in the slipstream. Kei shaded her eyes with one hand and waved. A castle on a hill and a collection of wood and stone buildings nestled under its walls. She pulled the draek into a lazy turn, crossing over the path the others would take far below; flying was faster than riding a horse, much less walking, so she and Kit were supposed to scout far to each side of the road to look for hidden dangers.

Why are we here? That was another question that had been bugging her. *Tashida said she wanted us to scout, to look for this sorcerer and his men. But Jyo-raku seems to be doing a excellent job of following them, and he says whoever this guy is, he's good enough to hide himself from the likes of us. So why bother bringing a couple of draekeres along on a high-secrecy mission like this? Unless Moriseki knew about this from the beginning, bringing her in on it had to be a big risk.*

Another question without an answer. Kei shook her head and concentrated on the ground. From above, the country seemed practically empty. Here and there, ant-sized peasants worked the fields, cutting and drying the beginning of the harvest. Some of the fields had already been stripped bare, but most of them were still covered in green plants or golden wheat. The wagons of Lady Tashida's caravan crawled along like beetles, and a few riders were visible on the road. Messengers, perhaps, or merchants traveling light.

However boring the terrain, it was nice to fly. Kei closed her eyes for a moment, enjoying the solitude, the rush of the air and the gentle creak of the draek's wings. *I'm sore in places I'd never admit, and this mission is crazy, but,* damn, *it feels good to fly again.* Up ahead, Kit's blue playfully rose a few hundred feet and then dove nearly to the treetops. Technically, Kei should have been offering a reprimand, but at that moment she felt too content to bother. *There's another six hours of daylight before we have to land. That's six hours before I have to try to figure this thing out again.* Kei intended to enjoy those six hours while they lasted.

IN HER DREAM, Kei was back at Steelgod.

The young draekeres were not allowed inside the fortress itself at that point. It had fallen only three years before, and Pacification was in full swing, so no one had had time to repair the damage. One entire wing was gone: Walls and towers were crushed into fine powder by the abomination the Imperial sorcerers had summoned with their last, desperate magic. What was left of the place still sprawled over an immense amount of ground. The outlying towers had their feet in the valley, three hundred feet below, and were solid stone for at least the first hundred. The only doors were at the top, , connected to the keep itself by as-yet-to-be-replaced rope bridges.

Beyond that were the famous silver walls, scorched black near the breach on the east side, but no less impressive on the others. Just after noon, when the sun caught them, one couldn't even look at the fortress without being blinded. And behind that was the looming bulk of the main keep, butting up against the stone face of the mountain. The east side of that, too, was breached, and, in the stories they told at night, the soldiers swore that the castle rock had glowed cherry red and flowed like melted butter. Kei had been close, once or twice, daring her superior's wrath in order to get a better look; some of the stone did indeed have a rounded, molten look to it, so she assumed the stories were true.

More than a hundred monks and Maidens had lost their lives to bring down the god of fire and light the Imperials had unleashed. In most cases there were no remains, so the High Commander had built a memorial garden under the east approach, a nice stretch of grass and trees with a pond in the middle, scattered about with grave markers. It was well known that the place was haunted. Many of the girls, giggling nervously, claimed to have heard the gentle songs of the lost Maidens' spirits or caught a glimpse of a stray demon.

That was why nobody visited the garden at night. And *that* was why Kei came here, after dark, once even the sergeants were asleep in their barracks. There were guards, of course, but they were more concerned about keeping people out of the section of town the draekeres had claimed than keeping the girls in. Anyway, stealth was a big part of the curriculum at Sora. The draekeres had trained against each other, and against the monks. Getting by a couple of lazy swordsmen was hardly a challenge.

It was the dark of the moon, and the garden was lit only by the endless march of stars. Kei padded across it by memory, avoiding the square grave markers that loomed suddenly from the dark. The pond rippled faintly in the light, and something went 'plop' as she approached.

She heard him coming a mile away, of course. Kino was light on his feet for a swordsman, but in the utter silence of the garden his footsteps were as loud as if he'd been wearing steel-toed boots. Kei sat down on the grass, feeling the chill of the pre-dawn dew, and willed herself into stillness. As he got closer, she even held her breath. Kino walked within a foot of her without noticing; once he was past, she glided silently to her feet and came up behind him. The swordsman pulled up short as she pressed her finger into the small of his back.

"You're dead," Kei whispered.

Kino put up his hands and turned around, slowly. He was wearing a big, goofy smile, As usual.

"I'm always dead."

"That," said Kei, "is because you're bad at this." She stepped closer, poking her finger into his stomach and looked up at him. Kino was at least a foot taller than the diminutive draekere.

"I am, am I?" Kino shook his head. Without a change in his wicked smile, one of his hands shot out, finding her breast under the loose black shirt and giving it a playful squeeze. Kei squeaked, and the swordsman took the opportunity to grab her poking hand by the wrist and twist it behind her back, pushing her toward the ground. Kei had to go down, or else dislocate her shoulder. Pretty soon she was lying on her back, with her arm trapped underneath her. Kino was kneeling next to her. Once he let go, she leaned up impulsively and kissed him.

"That," she said when he finally let go, "was not fair."

"Not fair?" He put on a shocked expression. "You never know when some guy's going to make a grab for you."

"Not fair because I don't want to kick *you* anyplace sensitive."

"That would probably ruin our evening, I must admit." He lay down next to her, on his side, propping his head up with his elbow on the ground. "Well, in that case, I thank you for restraining yourself."

Kei blinked. Kino's features were almost invisible in the darkness, but his eyes reflected the stars. She smiled. "Accepted."

"So." The swordsman traced patterns on her stomach with one finger, raising goose bumps. "What brings you out here so late at night, young lady?"

"Hunting for ghosts."

"I see." He moved his hand higher, pulling her shirt up with it, and she shivered. "And have you found any?"

Kei leaned over and kissed him again, throwing one arm over his shoulder. "You seem solid enough."

"So tonight's a failure, then," he murmured.

"Absolutely." She kissed him again. "A total failure."

He shifted over, putting his knee between hers and sliding it slowly up her thigh. Kei shivered deliciously and wrapped her arms around him.

KEI WOKE UP in the small hours of the morning, sheets tangled around her, feeling hot, flushed, and decidedly uncomfortable.

Why tonight? I haven't had that dream for a long time. She hadn't even thought about Kino in ages.

Part of the answer to that was obvious. A quick glance across the room revealed that Kit's bed was still empty, still neatly made.

Kei sighed, and rolled to the floor. *Just because she's found someone's bed to share shouldn't make* me *feel bad.* Bad memories, maybe. Kino had been killed during the Pacification, just a few months after that night, marched off to certain death. She'd cried for a week or so, but in the meantime she'd done her duty. *We were at war. Things were different.* That brought a little smile. *That's the problem. We've gone soft.*

Maybe it's just been too long, she mused, as she unlocked the double doors that led out onto the balcony. The night air rushed in, cool and invigorating. Kei wore only a simple sleeping shift, which flapped around her legs in the breeze. She took a couple of steps out and leaned on the rail, looking down at the town of Ravensor. There were remarkably few lights. Kei was used to the bustle of Crossroads, where business never seemed to stop, or to the well-lit hallways of the Palace. A few lonely sentry fires burned on the turrets of Ravensor castle, and here and there a window was lit by a candle, but that was all.

They'd arrived, as Lady Tashida had predicted, in late evening. Lord Ravensor had not come to meet them personally, which seemed like an insult to Kei, but Lady Tashida surprisingly chose to ignore it. Instead she thanked the delegation he'd sent to escort them to the town's only inn, and nodded politely when asked to be outside the gates by morning.

Ungrateful scum. Castle Ravensor bore none of the scars of war. Most of the river lords had resisted the Khaev invasion fiercely, and ruined castles were ranged up and down the Tsel and its tributaries. Some, like Lord Ravensor's father, had surrendered with the defeat of the Imperial legions at Tsankuun. The High Commander had left their lands and titles intact, provided they swore fealty to their new masters.

The inn, Kei had to admit, was luxurious. It was in the Imperial style, of course, big rooms with stone floors and layer after layer of rugs to blunt the chill. The beds, as she'd anticipated, had been heavenly. After ten years in the Empire, Kei had managed to get used to sleeping a few feet off the ground; she still woke, occasionally, with the feeling that she was going to roll out of bed and fall on her face. Each room had its own balcony overlooking the town's main street. And the food had been good, for Imperial cuisine. *Another thing I've learned to tolerate.*

Kei put her chin in her hands, leaning on the railing. *So what's wrong with me?*

She stared out into the night, looking without really seeing. People moving on the street below were vague shadows in the moonlit darkness, and it didn't really register that a whole group of them had paused directly below her balcony until she caught the gleam of moonlight on barbed steel.

Even then, it took a moment to sink in. Luckily for Kei, her legs decided what to do on their own, a split second before her mind really caught up with current events. A triple *hiss-thunk* was nearly simultaneous with the bloom of pain in one shoulder, but she was already throwing herself to one side. She landed awkwardly, clapping one hand to the stinging wound, and it came away slick and bloody.

Kei finally felt awake, sort of. *What the hell is going on?*

The railing was mostly thin, decorative wood that stood no chance against a crossbow bolt. Keeping her head down, Kei rolled back toward the doorway and made it just in time. Another volley from the men outside sent splinters flying as the bolts punched through and embedded themselves in the wall above the balcony.

Now, while they're reloading. Kei risked getting to her feet, realizing a moment too late that if there were two groups of archers, she was giving the second batch a perfect target. Her luck held, and she scampered back into her room and dragged the heavy balcony door shut. The door that led to the corridor was still closed and locked. Kei looked frantically around the room for a weapon.

Find a weapon. Step one. They'd done this drill in training, a million years ago. *Find a weapon, find your partner, then get out. The attacker has chosen his ground—get off it, make him work.* She bit off a curse. Most of her luggage was still tied to her draek, asleep in a clearing a mile or so from town. *This place was supposed to be guarded!*

Leaning in one corner was a long wooden pole with a hook at the end, for opening the topmost of the windows. Since nothing else was handy, she grabbed it. It was too heavy to be much good in a fight, but would do for one swing. *Weapon.* Next she checked her shoulder, automatically. The bolt had ripped a ragged trail across her skin, but it wasn't deep enough to be more than irritating. *Good. Now.* Kei stood next to the door, holding her makeshift club, and stopped for a moment to listen.

Still lucky. She'd picked just the right moment. The lock clicked as someone outside turned the key. Kei raised the pole and waited.

The door opened, slowly, and the lights outside threw long shadows through the doorway across the floor. Someone eased into the room, bare steel in one hand. That was good enough for Kei; she brought the pole down on his head as hard as she could.

At Sora—Steelgod, now—the draekeres were trained in many different forms of combat. Kei could fight with a sword, a knife, a bow, or with no weapons at all in a pinch. All of these forms possessed a certain grace, but there was definitely something to be said for just bringing a heavy object down on the opponent's skull. The intruder dropped like a stone, sprawling in the doorway and spoiling his friends' entrance.

There were two more behind the first, both with short swords drawn. One, a narrow-faced man with a ponytail she vaguely remembered lounging around the common room downstairs, had stumbled over the recumbent body of his companion and half-fallen into the room; the other was backing off into the corridor.

Kei wasted no time; another lesson that had been drilled into her at Sora. *When you've got them off balance, don't let them up.* Before the one who came through the doorway could recover, she planted her knee neatly under his chin, which sent him toppling back out again, blood spraying from his mouth. The third had to step even farther back, which bought her another moment to make sure the one she'd hit with the pole was still down, and to scoop up his sword.

There was a shrill scream from further down the corridor. Kei quashed her first thought—*Kit!*—almost instantly; it was hard to imagine Kit screaming, anyway. The second intruder didn't seem inclined to get up, and the third was circling warily away from the doorway. *Keeping me contained, until he can get help.* Guessing he was the cautious type, she attacked, flicking the ugly short sword toward his face in a series of feints. As she suspected, he gave ground; she let him back up until he was against the wall, connected hard with one of his parries to throw him off balance, and kicked his legs out from under him. The man fell with a clatter, and by reflex she brought her blade backhand across his throat. Blood splattered, soaking instantly through the thin fabric of her nightgown. Kei ignored it. She grabbed a dagger from the dead man's belt, for her off-hand, and hurried down the corridor toward Lady Tashida's room.

Weapons. Partners. Then out. Number one was accomplished. *But where the hell is Kit?* Another thought struck her. *Could she have been outside? They had crossbowmen out there, probably waiting for us to make a run for it. Maybe they picked her off on her way out.*

She put that thought firmly from her mind, as well. The top

floor of the inn was arranged as a single corridor running along three sides of a square, with staircases at either end. Kei's room was near one of the corners, Lady Tashida's on the opposite side. As she headed across she caught sight of another pair of men, undoubtedly left behind as rear guards. At their feet lay a pair of bodies. Kei recognized a couple of Lady Tashida's sellswords.

The two guards weren't expecting trouble to come from Kei's direction so fast. They'd heard the fight, of course, but apparently weren't prepared for a half-naked woman charging them with steel in either hand. Kei threw the dagger as she closed—a terrible shot, but enough to scare the guard on the left, who put up his sword and took a step back. The other leaned toward her and cut across; Kei checked the blow on her sword, wincing a little at the ring of steel on steel, and twisted inside his reach. An elbow to the gut and a kick to the back of the knee sent him sprawling, and she got her sword around just in time to engage the other one. Steel scraped on steel. The fight was brief, though, since Kei was faster and the guard's greater reach was wasted in the corridor. He gurgled and died, clutching his stomach, and Kei bent briefly to retrieve her dagger and make sure the other guard stayed down with a quick kick to the back of the head.

She paused before rounding the corner. If there were any more of them, standing at the doorway to Lady Tashida's room, they'd have heard the scuffle. That meant they'd be ready by now. Kei spent a moment gathering another pair of daggers before proceeding.

She'd been right. There were more attackers around the corner, and they were ready for her. Another pair were blocking the corridor with drawn swords, while two more framed the doorway Kei guessed was Lady Tashida's. A young woman she didn't recognize, dressed only in a flimsy nightshirt, was backed against one wall and nearly weeping in terror.

Kei matched gazes with the pair that were waiting for her, holding her sword at the ready while she considered her options. *These guys aren't great, but without surprise, and two against one, I could be in trouble. But where else is there to go?* Out, maybe, back toward the other staircase and out of the building. But that meant leaving Lady Tashida, whose life she was supposed to be protecting, to the mercy of these thugs. *Not to mention Kit.* Kei shifted her grip on the sword and took a deep breath. *Here goes nothing.*

She'd no sooner made the decision than a body came hurtling out of the door and landed against the opposite wall with a tremendous crash. The pair waiting by the doorway reacted at once as people came charging through after it. Kei recognized the bulky figure of Gota, who grabbed the thug's wrist to stop his swing and ran him headfirst into the wall. The other thug thrust toward his back; unable to get entirely out of the way, the burly monk spun to the side, taking a grazing blow along the ribs, and hammered the guard to the ground with one massive fist.

The pair of guards facing Kei had turned at the commotion. This belatedly struck them as somewhat unwise, but Kei had already taken advantage of the situation. She threw a dagger—a good throw, this time—and sank it into one thug's back, right between his shoulders. She was charging before he'd hit the ground, and crossed the distance before the other man had returned his attention to her; Kei parried his half-hearted strike and ran him through.

There was a sudden silence. Kei's ears rang with impacts of steel on steel. Gota, still dressed in his brown monk's robe, nodded respectfully.

"Wing Leader."

Kei nodded back, feeling idiotically formal. "Serenity.

What the hell is going on?"

"We're under attack."

"I can see that. Where are Lady Tashida and Kit?"

Gota hooked a finger over his shoulder, silently. Kei ducked past him, into the room, and found Lady Tashida rummaging in the wardrobe while Kit calmly stripped three more dead men of their steel. Kit wasn't wearing a stitch; Kei hastily averted her eyes. The girl looked up with a fierce smile.

"Good to see you, Wing Leader." She nodded toward the rear, where one of the thin walls between rooms had been smashed through. "They were waiting outside my door, and I figured there was strength in numbers. Serenity Shikidai was kind enough to make me an entrance."

"Get some clothes on. We're getting the hell out of here." She caught Kit's eye. "What were you doing over there, anyway?"

"Mary invited me up after dinner . . ."

Kei held up a hand. "Never mind."

"This place was supposed to be guarded," complained Lady Tashida, struggling into a leather vest. "What am I paying these people for, anyway?"

"At least two of them won't be needing any more pay." Kei shook her head. "I doubt they'd take on a dozen armed men if they didn't have to, though. Easier just to make them a better offer." Her lip curled, disgustedly. The Empire was rife with sellswords. Sometimes it seemed like every young man, and some women besides, who knew which end of a sword to hold wanted to make his living by it.

"Any idea who these people are?" asked Kit. She'd pulled on her underwear and thrown a light robe over it. Relieved to have everyone decent again, Kei shook her head.

"I didn't get to ask any of them. I know there are more outside, though."

"There are probably more downstairs," said Kit. "Just to make sure we don't get out that way."

"Is there any other way out? Windows, or the balconies?"

"Not unless you want to drop thirty feet. Plus, you said they're waiting for that."

"So we're going through them." Kei took a deep breath. "Okay." With Kit at her side, she felt surprisingly at ease. "Are you planning to use all those swords?"

"I was saving one for you." Kit chose one of the short swords and tested the balance. "Shiori?"

Lady Tashida shook her head with a faint air of disgust, to no one's surprise. Kei sighed and looked around. "Where's Jyo-raku?"

"He will accompany us." Gota stuck his head in the door. "My lady, Wing Leader. I suggest we move on. I think those waiting for us downstairs are getting restless."

Kit whistled when she saw the number of thugs lying unconscious or dead in the hallway.

"Leave any for the rest of us, Wing Leader?"

Kei blushed, just a little. "Serenity Shikidai helped."

Gota had moved up to the staircase, peering down it for a moment before pulling back. "It turns a corner halfway down," he reported.

"Ten to one they're waiting at the bottom with crossbows," said Kei.

Kit snorted. "Why not just come in and get us?"

"Because they've probably guessed by now how well that worked." She gestured at the bloody corridor. "These are just sellswords—they're no more eager to die than anybody else."

"Ahem." Lady Tashida cleared her throat, reminding everyone of her presence. "Regardless of their motives, we need to leave. The question of how to take bloody vengeance on Lord

Ravensor and his thugs comes later."

Lord Ravensor? For some reason, the thought hadn't occurred to Kei. *I guess this could be his work. It feels wrong, though.*

"Wing Leader?" Lady Tashida looked at her seriously.

"Me?"

"This sort of situation falls under your authority."

"Yeah," said Kit, grinning. "What should we do, Wing Leader?"

Send the damn demon, was the first thing that came to mind. Gota didn't seem inclined to, though. *So we need something else.* Her brows creased for a moment, and then she chuckled.

Imperial architecture may finally come in handy for something.

"Kit, can you break one of these doors off its hinges?"

"Probably." Kit paused for a moment, then got it. "Ah. Right." She laid down the sword and pulled out a knife she'd acquired from one of the thugs, and set to work. Kei turn to Gota.

"Serenity, I'm going to need you to carry that thing." *Because you're the only one who can,* Kei thought sourly. "Will your wound bother you?"

Gota looked down at the cut as though noticing it for the first time and shrugged. "No."

"Lady Tashida?"

"Yes?" the noble said, looking innocent.

"We'll be going down the steps after Serenity Shikidai. We need to kill everyone in the room before they get a chance to reload."

"I'll do my best to stay out of the way," she said dryly.

"Got it," Kit announced. The heavy oak door sagged outward into the corridor until Gota caught it with one hand. He hefted it, experimentally, and managed to get it in front of him by putting one hand on either side. Muscles stood out like cords of rope on the monk's forearms.

"Heavier than I thought," Gota grunted. He edged around Kit and made it to the top of the staircase. "Ready."

Kei looked at Kit, who nodded. The girl had a dagger in her throwing hand and a sword in the other. She looked, if anything, excited by the prospect of charging into an ambush. *She's crazy.* Kei hefted her own dagger.

"Go."

The monk lifted the door again and started down the stairs. Given the weight of the door, it was more of a stumbling half-fall than a run, but he managed to turn the corner with a respectable amount of speed. Kei and Kit followed him closely, with Lady Tashida another step behind them. The door blocked any view of the common room, but there was shouting, followed quickly by a couple of loud *whap-thuds*.

Gota understood what to do after that. He kicked the door savagely, sending it flying the rest of the way down the stairs, and charged. Apparently, not all the crossbowmen had been as surprised as Kei had hoped. There was another *whap*, but the bolt flew over the monk's shoulder and buried itself in the ceiling. Then Gota was leaping over the door, with the two draekeres right behind him.

Kei dove to the left as soon as she cleared the stairwell, and saw Kit go the other way. She gave the room a quick once-over as she did so. Four men with crossbows, no other clientele—they must have been cleared out—*wait,* four *men*—

Kei ducked as the last crossbowman, a fuzz-cheeked boy of no more than eighteen standing on a table near the entrance, pulled his trigger and sent a bolt into the wall right where her head had been. She came up throwing; the boy clutched his gut and took a step to the side, tipping the table and sending him crashing to the floor. Another crossbowman screamed as Kit's dagger scored in his shoulder, and one of the others was backing away hastily as Gota came toward him like a runaway bull. The last was trying to reload, and Kei charged him. He'd almost gotten the bolt slotted when she ran him through the throat.

She turned, looking for another target, and caught a glimpse of something orange and yellow in the doorway. *What the hell . . .*

Whatever it was, it moved so fast it was a blur. Gota had reached the last crossbowman and bludgeoned him to the ground with one punch; he saw the thing just in time and dove to one side as it passed. It seemed to jump from place to place, barely touching the ground; where it did, it left scorches.

The creature came to rest on another table, across from the entrance; Kei finally got a good look at it. It seemed vaguely canine, or more accurately vulpine—four legs, a couple of feet high, with three bushy tails that swayed constantly back and forth. Discerning more than that was difficult because its entire body was wreathed in living flame, crackling yellow and orange and occasionally blue. Or maybe there was nothing *to* it but fire. It was hard to be sure. The wooden table it was standing on burst into flames almost instantly, so the creature was quickly surrounded by a roaring inferno. Kei stared.

A demon. A gods-be-damned demon.

The creature waited a moment, as though sizing up its prey. Lady Tashida had ducked behind a table near the stairway, Gota dove under some benches, Kei was trapped in the open at the center of the room, and Kit was...

Kit was creeping behind another table, slowly getting closer to the thing.

She's crazy. Dear gods. Kei felt the demon's attention on her, and she could feel the heat as the flames spread. *Here goes . . .*

The demon jumped. Kei dodged, whipping her sword around. It scored on the creature's midsection, and it yowled a complaint in a voice filled with shrieking, crackling fire. The cheap steel in Kei's hand went cherry-red almost instantly She dropped the sword with a clatter, clutching at her palm as she backed away. The thing followed, trailing smoke from where she'd cut it, little flames springing up even on the hardwood floor around its feet. Kei caught another glimpse of Kit, closing in on the demon from behind, and tried to mouth a command.

"Don't—"

Too late. Kit charged, driving her sword nearly to the hilt in the creature's rump. Like Kei, her blade became too hot to hold; Kit let go as the demon whirled and struck with one paw. The blow carried a strength far beyond the thing's size. Kit actually flew backwards before crashing to a halt amidst the ruins of a table. Kei didn't have time to scream before the demon turned back toward her.

"Jyo-raku!" Gota's voice rang out over the crackles of the fire.

The flickering shadows thrown by the flame moved, flowing like water until they merged. Jyo-raku's black form came out of nowhere, jumping upward as though he'd come through a hole in the floor and bringing one hand down edge-first on the demon's neck. There was an awful hiss, like a bucket of water thrown on a bonfire, and the demon's head came off entirely. Smoke gushed from its neck as its body wobbled and collapsed, flames rapidly guttering out.

Kei didn't bother watching it die. She was already headed across the room, toward where Kit had fallen. The girl was sprawled in the wreckage of a table—she'd hit hard enough to split wood. Kei knelt next to her, anxiously. There wasn't any serious bleeding, but patches of her robe and the skin beneath were scorched black.

"Kit? Are you okay?"

Kit didn't answer. Kei leaned closer, anxiously, to check if she was breathing.

django wexler

"Kit? Come on . . ."

Her last word became a squawk as Kit put one hand around the back on her head, dragged her down, and kissed her firmly. Kei tasted the girl's tongue, briefly—*honey and smoke*—before she dragged herself away; Kit let her hand fall to her sides, chuckling weakly.

"Sorry, sorry." She laughed. "You should have seen the look on your face. Priceless."

"Are you okay?"

"Fine." She sat up and groaned, slapping a hand on the burn on her side. "Ow. Maybe not fine. I'll live."

"I suggest we get out of here," said Gota. "This building is on fire."

Kei helped Kit to her feet with one hand and noticed the monk was right. The flames were spreading quickly from where the demon had died, and most of the furniture was already ablaze. Jyo-raku had vanished again. Lady Tashida and the monk were waiting by the front door, Gota wearing his usual non-expression while the noble had one eyebrow raised, archly.

There was a moment's pause.

"The building?" suggested Gota.

THE SELLSWORD LEADER was a thin-faced northerner named Dathem, a mountain man who styled himself a lord but was instantly betrayed by his accent and manner as nothing more than a common thief. He was fuming now, and no wonder; a sellsword captain's worth is measured only by the number of men whose loyalty he commands, and most of Dathem's were dead.

Karl watched him with an idle curiosity, keeping his expression studiously bored. The little clearing was packed full on both sides; a dozen of Dathem's men backed him up, while Karl had the rest of Lord Adrian's guard behind him. If it came to swords, he was pretty confident that his hand-picked half-dozen could dispatch a gang of weaselly mercenaries. *But it won't. This Dathem is a coward.*

Everyone seemed to have arrived. Dathem looked impatient, so Karl gave him another couple of moments before he yawned and spoke.

"I'm curious, my lord"—he gave the self-styled mercenary's title a sarcastic spin—"why you bothered to show up here."

"Karl . . ."

"Sir Karl, please."

Dathem's face twisted. "You promised me another three hundred eyes."

"You promised me four heads, which you failed to deliver."

"But—"

Karl leaned forward. "I'm not pleased. Lord Adrian is not pleased. Our time and gold have been wasted, and yet here you stand, demanding more. It seems to me, *my lord*, that you are in a very precarious position."

"I need compensation. It's not my fault—you told me that demon of yours could handle things!"

"I said two draekeres, one high-born lady, and one monk. You sent how many men—twenty?"

"Twenty-two. But . . ."

"But what?"

Dathem looked down. "Three women and a monk. We didn't think—"

"Obviously not."

"I need compensation." The sellsword captain looked up, suddenly. "For my lost men."

"Your lost men are your own concern. Get out of my sight."

Dathem's hand dropped to his sword, and the dozen scruffy men behind him perked up. The northerner was sweating inside his ridiculous furs. Karl just smiled. Finally Dathem looked away with a scowl.

"Curse you and your fucking Lord Adrian." He turned on his heel and strode out of the clearing. "Let's go."

Karl gave this Dathem about a week to live, before one of his men decided they'd be better off with a new captain. That was the way of things, with sellswords.

Once they were safely gone, Erin hopped down from her perch on a fallen log. There was a chorus of sighs and groans from the rest of the men as they stretched, stiff from the staring match. Sarth, the big Diem, cracked his knuckles with a sound like a forest giant crashing to earth. Aff carefully unstrung his bow and folded the string neatly into an oilskin pouch, while pig-faced Morg wandered off in the direction of camp, muttering something about a drink. Only Melody remained sitting, perched on a branch ten feet off the ground and leaning against the trunk of an old oak. She played idly with her hair, flipping one of her long red braids back and forth, over and over.

Erin stretched her arms over her head, cracking both shoulders in rapid succession. She wasn't wearing her usual armor, just a light shirt patterned in red and gold with a jacket over it to ward off the slight mountain chill. Sunlight glinted from the links of chain at her belt, and the hilts of the little recurved daggers that sat on either hip. Her hair was pale-blonde and short, and her eyes the usual pale blue of the river-folk.

"I'm surprised, Sir Karl." She smiled, revealing a gap where one of her molars had once been. "I didn't think you could lie with a straight face."

Karl frowned. "Who was lying?"

"Misleading, anyway."

"I was completely straight with the man."

"Of course. And of course you expected him to return with

Lady Tashida's head?"

Karl chuckled. "His own fault. He should have planned more carefully."

"But our objective is accomplished nonetheless, isn't it?" She leaned toward him, probing. "They'll keep following us now."

"A sane party would break off pursuit. If they know that we know they're following, they should also know that we could set traps, ambushes."

"Not while they can keep watch from above."

"True. But that advantage is about to be negated."

She raised an eyebrow. "Really?"

"So Lord Adrian has promised."

"Good." Erin's grin widened. "I was starting to worry that this job would get boring."

Melody hopped down from the tree, absorbing the fall with a crouch. Blades clattered, all over her body, and the tight-fitting leather armor she wore creaked almost audibly. She gave the pair a bright, green-eyed smile, and followed Morg toward the camp.

Karl eyed her as she left. Erin raised an eyebrow.

"Still worried about her? Or just admiring her other salient characteristics?"

He shrugged. "I still think she's crazy."

"All Tellenna are crazy. You should count yourself lucky she's on our side. Anyway, I like her better than Morg."

"Granted." Karl chuckled.

"So what's next?"

"We wait for Lord Adrian's word."

"And then?"

"Into the mountains."

"Rest the gods. Are you serious?" When he nodded, she groaned. "I signed up to fight Khaevs, not be a damn rock climber."

"Lord Adrian knows a trail, so we won't have to do any serious climbing."

"Or so he says. What about the natives?"

"The Valdiem are shy. We shouldn't have any trouble."

"Great. Just great. And he really thinks the Khaevs are going to follow?"

"Yes."

"It just seems awfully pointless to me. We should just go down there and kill them."

"I'm not privy to Lord Adrian's plans." Karl stood from the boulder, and Erin took a step back. "But I suspect he has something besides death in mind for them."

"Great," said Erin again. "I love a good mystery."

chapter 5

> "The Khaevs believe that, when you die, your soul is judged according to how it has performed relative to your duties in life. So if you were a king, you get judged on the scale of kings; if you were a beggar, you get judged on the scale of beggars. Then, depending on how you measure up, you either get sent back for another shot, admitted to some kind of paradise, or sent below to burn forever.
>
> "This says a lot about Khaevs.
>
> "Imperials know, on the other hand, that the gods died six thousand years ago and the afterlife went with them. So after you die, unless you're very lucky, your soul just drifts into the Aether and becomes food for creatures too horrible to describe.
>
> "This says a lot about Imperials, when you think about it."
>
> —Lord Zhorin the Historian, *The Pacification*

ISOBEL WAS NOT, by most lights, an attractive young woman. For one thing, there was no flesh on her. Her limbs looked like sticks wrapped in cord, her hips were slender, and she had only the barest suggestion of breasts, even in a tight shirt. Her fingers were long and thin, and half-covered with calluses. And her face looked as though someone had boiled the meat from her bones: The orbits of her eyes protruded, while her eyes themselves, a deep purple-blue in color, were sunk well back in her head. Her hair was a brown so dark it was almost black, and looked as though it had been hacked off at a convenient length on the point of a dagger, which, in fact, it had been.

Nevertheless, when she walked into a dockside tavern unaccompanied, she was invariably approached within minutes. Zhin attributed it to the boundless hopefulness of human nature and the persuasive powers of alcohol. Most of the time, a glare and a growled word were enough to get rid of the drunken dockworkers, who often made gestures of protection against evil spirits while retreating. Every once in a while, though, some genius didn't take the hint. It was usually when he had friends to impress and felt like he'd been insulted.

This was one of those times. Isobel sat alone at a wide, circular table and a pack of bravos had pulled chairs up to the other side and started banging their mugs for a drink. Isobel gave their leader a glare, which he ignored. He was a big guy, with a black mustache and tattoos covering both his bare shoulders. His friends bore similar markings. *Probably some kind of gang colors.* Zhin sighed and ordered another glass of T'bach stiff; it got there just before the fighting started.

The big guy opened the conversation.

"So, what're you doing here all alone?"

It was not, Zhin thought, particularly effective as an opening gambit. *Then again, there are only so many ways one can say, "I'm drunk. Will you have sex with me?"*

Isobel, seeing that her glare had failed to deliver the message, looked the guy in the eye and didn't smile. He didn't flinch, protected by the invincible armor of intoxication.

"Fuck off," she said. "I'm busy."

The big guy took this as a joke and burst out laughing. After a strained moment, so did his friends. Once he was done, he reached into his belt pouch and tossed a silver crescent across the table. It bounced in front of Isobel, spun for a moment, and settled down.

"That enough?" The big guy smirked.

"I said I was busy."

He flicked another silver deftly, so that it landed on the first with a chink. "And I'm saying you're not."

"I also said to fuck off. If you need to rent a woman, there are a dozen waiting for you just down the street."

His expression flickered, dimly aware that she was making fun of him. "What did you say?"

"I told you where you could find a whore." Isobel stretched, languidly. "My guess would be that you're too drunk to take advantage of one, though. And you'd probably have to pay her a lot just to stop laughing."

"You little slut," he roared.

"That's not really of much consequence. I told you, my business isn't with you. It's with him."

Isobel pointed out one of the followers, the quietest of the bunch. He wasn't as heavily muscled as the leader, but there was something dangerous about him. H e wore the same weather-beaten half-shirt and trousers as the rest of them, and bore them same tattoos, but he projected an air of quiet menace totally unlike the blustering drunk.

"Boss . . ." said the quiet one. The big guy waved angrily.

"Shut the fuck up. If you have business with one of my guys, you have business with me. Understand?"

"I feel sorry for your men, then. They must not get a lot of action."

"Funny." He put one heavy hand on the table. "Very funny. Ron, Cord, take her." The boss leaned across the table. "We're going for a little walk."

"And by 'walk' you mean 'rape and painful torture'?" Isobel's expression didn't flicker. "No thanks."

"You don't get to choose!"

I love this part, thought Zhin. Ron and Cord got up from their chairs, a little unsteadily, and made their way around the table, one on each side. Cord was grim-faced, but Ron leered.

"Come on, girl. We ain't gonna hurt ya. Just a bit of—"

Zhin barely saw Isobel draw, and he was watching for it. Her arms moved, and there was a flicker of steel in the air, and then Cord crashed forward onto the table and Ron's head wobbled a little bit and fell off. Isobel ignored both of them, pushed her chair back calmly, and got to her feet. She had a long knife in either hand.

The boss still didn't quite understand what was going on, looking from one body to the other. His half-shirt was spattered with Cord's blood. But the quiet guy behind him had figured it out, and he got to his feet.

"Jhal the Knife." Isobel nodded to him, respectfully.

Jhal had produced his namesake weapons from somewhere, holding them backhanded; a street-fighter's grip. He eyed Isobel doubtfully. "Do I get to know your name?"

"Isobel," said Isobel.

"Fucking *kill* her!" said the boss, who was just now catching up to things. "Jhal!"

Jhal nodded again, slowly, and slid back into a fighting stance. Isobel held her blades casually, and waited. There was a moment of frozen time; then Jhal rushed forward, and the pair became a blur of steel too fast to follow. It lasted only a second before Isobel stepped aside and let the bravo slump to the floor.

The boss was sweating now, fumbling for his sword. Isobel turned away without a glance.

"Zhin. Let's go."

Zhin got to his feet and shrugged his jacket on, falling into step beside her. The hostess of the tavern had vanished, of course, at the first sign of trouble. Isobel flipped an eye onto the counter anyway and stepped out the door, with Zhin behind her.

They were immediately assaulted by the smell of the docks. Under the salt water spray there was the stench of rotting fish, sewage, and blood. Isobel turned right as soon as they reached the street and headed directly for their own inn, leaving Zhin looking frantically to see if they were followed. Once he was satisfied, he caught up with his partner.

"No good?" he asked.

Isobel snorted with contempt. "When I find what I'm looking for, you'll know."

"How?"

"I'll be the one who falls over afterwards."

"That's a cheery thought. Good thing no one can beat you."

"If I thought that was true, I'd kill myself."

"That would be a tragedy. Then there'd be no one to laugh at my various witty remarks."

She snorted again, but said nothing.

"Lord Valos doesn't exactly approve of these little side jaunts, you know."

"I don't care what Lord Valos thinks."

"He *does* pay the bills around here."

"And he's tolerant. He certainly tolerates *your* little hobby."

"My little hobby is more useful." *And I'm under orders, though I can't mention that.*

"So you say. It has yet to produce any results."

"I'm just looking for the right person."

"And will you know him when you see him?"

"Of course."

"There's a hole in your purse that says you're a liar." It might have been a joke, but Isobel didn't smile.

"You'll see."

"Indeed." Anybody else might have worn a self-satisfied smirk. Sometimes Zhin wondered whether his partner had killed herself already, and not bothered to inform anyone of it.

VEIL FELT HERSELF tearing up at the sight of a cloud, which she concluded was a definite sign she'd been in the desert too long. It hovered on the southern horizon like a distant, silver promise, and it was some time before she convinced herself that it wasn't a mirage.

They were walking by night, now. Veil had gotten in that habit after traveling with Bali's caravan, but Corvus didn't seem to mind the heat and for a while she'd been hesitant to bring it up. He didn't seem to care when they traveled, though. Every day, at dawn, she'd look around for changes in the landscape. It was happening, slowly. More rocks stuck up through the dunes, and the ground underfoot began to look less like sand and more like soil. After a while she began to see plants, struggling to gain a foothold. Before too long there were trees here and there, and patches of grass.

When they finally reached the edge of the desert, it was more sharply defined than she'd been expecting. A wall of rough-cut stone, five or six feet high, with sand drifted against it on the desert side. Veil climbed the little dune and looked over the wall. Beyond, the land was green from edge to edge, hundreds of little bushes in neat rows. In the middle distances, a young man was on his knees, working around the base of one of the plants; before Veil could duck back, he caught sight of her and started over at an unhurried walk.

"Corvus."

The black-clad swordsman was waiting impatiently at the base of the dune. "What?"

"Someone's coming."

"Oh?" That perked him up. Corvus' hand dropped to the hilt of his sword.

"I think it's just a farmer. Maybe we can find out where in the Aether we are."

"Go ahead." Corvus shrugged. "Shout if you want me to kill him."

"You've killed everyone I've met in the last two months. I think you need a break."

"Hello!" shouted the young man. Veil returned her attention to him. His coloration looked alien—his hair was blond, and he was paler than the Red Hills people, though not quite as pale as a Khaev and without their distinctive eyes.

Veil waved, hesitantly. She wasn't really sure what to say. He didn't look hostile; he certainly wasn't armed, except with a spade.

"Hello." She settled on that. It was non-committal.

"You lost, young lady?"

"Absolutely," said Veil.

"Do you belong to somebody around here?"

Slaves. They think . . . Veil thought furiously. "No. I mean, my master's back here, with our horse. We're headed for the city, but I think we got lost on the way out of the desert."

He laughed. "You're lucky you made it out at all!"

"Yeah." Veil chuckled weakly.

"You're not too far off, anyway. Go that way." He pointed along the wall, to the east. "Just a couple of miles, and you'll find the main road." He had a funny accent, to her ears, with long A's and rolled R's.

"Great. And how far from there?"

"Couple of days ride."

She nodded. "Thanks!"

"No trouble." He turned back to his task as Veil scrambled back down the dune and rejoined Corvus and the horse.

"Well?"

She pointed. "That way. There's a road."

Corvus pulled on the animal's reins, and it sullenly turned eastward. Veil took up her usual place at his side.

"They thought I was a slave," she said after a while.

"Not surprised."

"They must have slaves working these farms." She looked at the wall, which continued as far as the eye could see. It changed composition periodically, as though it had been constructed in sections. "There's no guards, though. Why don't they just run away?"

"Where is there to go?" Corvus gestured to the north. "Why bother guarding the desert side?"

"That's true." Veil shook her head. "Still..."

"There." Corvus pointed. "The road."

His other hand went to his sword. A long caravan, at least six wagons, was rumbling past.

"Relax," said Veil. "We're just walking to the city, not fighting anybody."

"It never hurts to be careful."

WALKING PAST THE wall was like entering a different world.

There were still walls on both sides of the road, of the same rough, uncut stones. They'd passed the lumbering wagons of the caravan and found themselves nearly alone. On either side, though, people worked the fields, alone or in pairs. Every once in a while they could see the distant, hunched shape of a house, and they passed gates in the wall, locked but usually unguarded.

At even longer intervals, they were passed by other travelers, mostly riders coming from the south. None of these even gave them a second glance, though Corvus tensed every time he spotted one.

They spent the night by the side of the road, leaning on the wall. Veil found it disconcerting to sleep on rough ground, instead of sand, and the smell of living, growing things was vaguely nauseating. Corvus, as usual, never closed his eyes.

By noon the next day, the sky was full of clouds, and the towers of Corsa began to peek over the horizon. They crested a rise, a few miles outside the city; after that the land fell away, and the road twisted and turned down the slope until it merged with the city streets. Corvus seemed unaffected by the view, but Veil stopped and stared.

Corsa. In the Red Hills it was more legend than place. It was where slaves went, after they were sold, and occasionally young men, off to make their fortune, would announce they were headed to the city. The traders would go on about it for hours, if asked—how high the towers were, how wide the docks, how cheap the whores—and the Khaevs refused to acknowledge that it existed. Everyone agreed that getting there was hard, at least by land.

All this had failed to prepare Veil for the sheer size of the place. If pressed, she'd have admitted she was expecting something like Kalil's town, only bigger—one mansion/fortress, at the top of a hill, surrounded by a ring of perhaps a hundred dwellings. Maybe double that size, to account for the traders' stories.

Instead the city sprawled for miles. Four massive towers commanded the harbor, flat-topped and rooted in the water. Even at this distance she could make out men working on their roofs, an infestation o crawling black flyspecks. The city grew outwards from the harbor in a confused, organic jumble. Here and there little neighborhoods showed some stamp of order, like little islands in the sea of chaos. There were hundreds of buildings, thousands, tens of thousands. And the docks. The sea was barely visible as a distant silver line, but the masts of ships crowded around the piers looked like a leafless forest, swaying gently in the breeze. Further out she could see a couple of ships under sail, headed out to sea on the tide.

The wind was blowing inland, so she could smell the city, too. Salt water, with an undercurrent of rancid filth. Veil caught a little too much of the scent and gagged.

Corvus seemed unimpressed.

"Have you been here before?"

He shrugged. "I know how these places work."

"So what now?"

"How much money do we have?"

Veil looked into her pouch. She'd assigned herself the task of keeping track of their funds after she'd thoughtfully swiped Morzeban's pouch, since Corvus didn't seem to care one way or the other. Gold clinked as she opened it, along with smaller silver crescents.

"About fifteen eyes, I guess."

"Is that a lot?"

Correction, thought Veil. Corvus didn't even seem to understand the concept of money.

"Not really."

"How long will it keep us?"

"I have no idea! I've never been here before."

The swordsman snorted. "Fine. You'll be in charge of making sure we don't starve. That way you can make yourself useful for a change."

"And what are you going to be doing?"

"Mostly making sure we don't get killed. Anything else is

my own damn business."

"Okay." Despite the snide tone of his comments, Veil felt pleased. "So where to?"

"Brothel." Corvus smiled.

"You're not serious."

"Of course I'm serious. I just walked across the high desert, mostly alone. Where else would I go?"

"You can't . . .I mean . . .we can't afford it!"

"I say we can. Unless you're volunteering?" He raised an eyebrow, then laughed. "Nah. Too skinny for my tastes."

"I can't believe this."

"Lighten up." His smile turned crafty. "Maybe we'll buy you a good time, too, it might help you relax."

With that he started down the track that led to the city, switchbacking down the hill. Veil hurried after him, dragging the tired horse.

"You really do need to relax, girl. We made it."

"I just think . . ."

"You think too much."

Veil sighed.

THERE WERE NO brothels in the Red Hills. There were certainly women willing to sell their affections for money, a practice which was tolerated by lords like Kalil with a wink and a nod. Not that such things were ever spoken of to children, but the brighter ones, like Veil, figured it out from scraps of overheard conversations. There were certain houses you went to if you were in search of a good time. The older boys, when they got up the nerve, would save up their allowances and sneak out of the mansion to see if the rumors were true.

But a real *city*, like Corsa, was something she'd only read about in books. When brothels were mentioned at all—usually as a place for the hero to rescue the virtuous young maiden from—they seemed to be seedy, hidden places concealed from the local authorities. So despite Corvus' intentions, she wasn't at all sure how to go about finding one.

As it turned out, though, one needed only to follow the giant red signs, and there were a good many establishments to choose from. Whatever authorities ruled in the pirate city certainly did not seem to mind brothels. Veil stuck close to Corvus as they made their way from the outskirts to one of the major streets, slightly in awe of the crowds. She'd never seen so many people in one place, not even at a fair, and she'd certainly never seen so many different *kinds* of people. Fair-haired easterners made up the definite majority, but there were a good number of her own people, too, along with a scattering of others. She caught sight of a couple of dark-haired, white-skinned Khaevs, sneering at the narrow beehive of streets and rickety buildings and staying well apart from the crowds. Further down, there was an enclave of dark-skinned youths she guessed were Diem, sitting outside a café and already starting on the afternoon's drinking. There were more, too, that she couldn't even recognize—a young man with skin as pale as a Khaev, but dressed in flowery reds and blues that no Khaev would ever wear, and a pair of giggling young women in dark red leather, slim as knives and bristling with weapons.

Corvus moved through the crowd like a solid ghost. The way he walked revealed a measure of his self-assurance, and people unconsciously gave him a wide berth. Veil stayed well inside the clear space that developed around the swordsman and kept one hand on her purse, remembering some of the less savory parts of the stories of Corsa. But as far as she could tell, no pickpockets even considered approaching her.

Following the red signs, Corvus made his way to a street that seemed to be composed entirely of brothels and pleasure houses. The buildings themselves were mostly rickety and wooden, each supporting a sign that jutted out into the street as far as it could manage and was luridly painted to advertise the services available within. The crowd here was almost entirely men, laughing and pointing in groups of three or four and eventually ducking through a particular doorway or past a beaded curtain. Most of the brothels had bouncers standing outside—large, well-armed fellows whose primary function seemed to be glaring at passers-by. The customers ignored them.

For a moment, Veil felt a touch of claustrophobia. The crowds pressed in around them so closely she couldn't move in any direction without touching someone, and even Corvus' grim expression didn't keep them back. She shook her head dizzily and tugged on his shoulder.

"Are you sure about this?"

He rolled his eyes. "Come on."

The swordsman dragged her by the hand toward one of the doorways, selected apparently at random. The name of the place was spelled out on the sign, both in Imperial and in Khaev glyphs she couldn't read, as "Fara's". The door swung open at a touch and closed gently behind them, cutting off the noise from the street.

It was like stepping into a jewelry box, Veil thought. The downstairs was a common room, almost like an inn, except the walls were draped with velvet in many colors and there were fewer tables and more couches. A great many young women were hanging around, of course, mostly wearing sheer silks that were hardly better than nothing at all. They, too, seemed to come from all races, though there were more copper-skinned Red Hills people and aborigines than anything else. An older woman, who seemed to be the only one fully clothed, made her way over to Corvus with an ingratiating smile, which flickered just slightly as Veil entered behind him.

"Welcome, sir." She had the hard accent of an easterner. "What might you and your daughter require?"

Veil bristled. *First of all, I look nothing like him, and secondly, what kind of person would bring his daughter to a place like . . .*

"A room? Or perhaps you are here to sell her?"

"Actually—" began Corvus, but stopped when Veil fixed him with a furious glare. He shrugged to cover his hesitation. "We need rooms and entertainment for the evening."

"For both of you?"

"*Separate* rooms," Veil put in. Corvus raised an eyebrow but said nothing. The woman shrugged.

"As you wish, of course. Take your pick.". She waved her hand around the room. "I will get your keys."

The woman bustled off into a back room, and most of the girls smiled at Corvus. A couple of them smiled at Veil, too, which made her decidedly uncomfortable. She stayed close behind the swordsman as he made a quick circuit of the room, looking over the merchandise. Veil pretended to be interested, too, and waited until she had a chance to whisper in his ear.

"Just to check. You aren't planning to kill everyone here, are you?"

"Don't be silly."

"I figured it might be best to be prepared."

Corvus pulled up sharply in front of a couch facing a window. One of the girls on it sat up eagerly. She was an easterner, perhaps a year older than Veil, with blonde hair past her shoulders and a wide, freckled smile. The other remained half-slumped over against one of the armrests. She had the pale skin and dark hair of a Khaev, and when she finally turned her eyes confirmed it. Corvus looked at her blankly, then rattled something off in the liquid Khaev tongue. The girl spat back something that sounded nasty, but Corvus just smiled. Hurrying footsteps behind them announced the return of the proprietress.

"I'm sorry," she said. "That girl is a recent acquisition. She has not learned the proper courtesies yet."

"No trouble." The girl glared daggers, but Corvus didn't look at her again. He pointed to her companion on the couch. "I'll take her."

"Very good. Allydra, room twelve." The woman held out a key, which the girl took. She bounced buoyantly off the couch and grabbed Corvus by one hand, dragging him toward the stairs.

"Corvus!" said Veil, almost involuntarily.

"I'll see you in the morning." He winked back at her, and she watched him go up with something akin to panic.

Stop it, Veil. This isn't like you. Corvus had been her constant companion for nearly two weeks, to be sure, but she'd been relying on herself for much longer than that. There was something visceral in her reaction, though. Her bile rose as he disappeared around the corner, and she felt almost ill. *What the hell is wrong with me?*

"Miss?"

Veil looked up, wildly, to find the proprietress staring at her with some concern. "What?"

"Would you care to make a selection?"

Veil suppressed her initial 'Of course not!' and looked around the room. *I might as well talk to someone. Find something out about this city. Corvus isn't going to be doing much information-gathering.* Her lip twisted. She pointed to a girl with the Red Hills coloring, around her age. "Her."

The woman's head bobbed. "Of course, miss. Seelie, room thirteen."

The girl nodded obediently and took the key from her

mistress' hand, beckoning Veil up the stairs. Veil followed uncertainly. The second floor was a pair of corridors with numbered doors all along them, and Veil followed Seelie to the one labeled Thirteen. From behind a number of the doors she could hear sounds—moans, grunts, and the occasional loud thumping. Seelie unlocked the door and gestured Veil in; she entered a little uncertainly.

It was a tiny room, barely big enough for a bed and an end table with a couple of drawers. The window was closed and tightly shuttered, so the room was very dark. Seelie squeezed past Veil, letting the door close behind her, and struck a match to light a couple of candles. They filled the tiny place with flickering shadows. There was nowhere to sit but on the bed, so Veil sat down, hearing the 'groink' of abused springs. Seelie stood by the door, waiting.

"Um." Veil cleared her throat, nervously. She was suddenly aware that she didn't know if the girl even spoke Imperial. By her coloring, she could be Red Hills or aborigine. She was also aware that Seelie was wearing only two thin wisps of silk, which seemed even more inadequate in the closeness of the bedroom than they had in the common room downstairs. "Hi. I'm Veil."

"Seelie."

Veil was relieved when she spoke in a familiar accent. "I didn't really mean . . . I mean . . . I just . . ."

"Nervous?" Seelie tilted her head to one side. "Is this your first time?"

"No!" Veil blushed. "I mean, well, yes. But it's not . . . I don't want to . . ."

Seelie smiled and went to the end table. From one of the drawers she produced two thin glasses and a heavy bottle. She half-filled each of the flutes with a translucent green liquid, picked one up by the stem between two fingers, and offered it to Veil. Veil accepted the glass uncertainly; it smelled sharp, like sour apples but with a heavy bite to it. Not wishing to seem impolite, she took a sip. The taste was marvelous, fizzing and dissolving on her tongue.

The other girl laughed at her hesitation. "You need to relax, Veil."

"That's what Corvus keeps telling me," she muttered. "I'm sorry. This is just a little uncomfortable for me."

"Why?"

"For one thing, you're the first person I've really talked to in months. Besides him."

"You've just arrived in the city?"

Veil nodded. "From the high desert."

Seelie took a long sip from her own glass and chuckled again. "That's a long walk."

"I know."

"Move over." Seelie gestured, and Veil scooted sideways to give the other girl a chance to sit down.

"I told you, I don't want to . . ."

"Relax. I get it." She smiled. "Besides, it's nice to have someone to talk to for a change."

"Right." Veil took a longer sip of the drink, whatever it was.

"So who's Corvus, anyway? He's not really your father."

Veil shook her head.

"Is he your master, then?"

"No! I mean . . . I'm not . . ." Veil stopped abruptly, staring at Seelie. The other girl laughed again.

"You ease up, you know. So you're not a slave. So who is he?"

"Just . . . a friend, I guess?" It sounded odd. "Someone I met in the desert. He saved my life." *After he almost killed me.*

Seelie nodded. "So he brought you here?"

"Yeah. This was the first place he wanted to go when we got to the city." Veil rolled her eyes, but Seelie shrugged.

"It's only natural, I guess. Being in the desert, all alone for so long . . ."

"He could have at least pretended it wasn't the only thing on his mind."

Seelie grabbed the bottle from the end table and filled Veil's glass, which she'd barely noticed was empty. Veil took another sip, savoring the fizzy texture.

"Men." The girl snorted. "What are you going to do?"

"Right." Veil recalled her original objective. "So how long have you lived here?"

"All my life, practically. Supposedly I was brought across the desert with my mother when I was two years old, but I don't remember."

"And you're a . . ." Veil hesitated again.

"A slave? I've heard the word before, you know." Seelie smiled, and shrugged. "Yeah. But I'm pretty lucky."

"Lucky?"

"There are places I could have ended up that are a lot worse than this. A T'bach army, for instance, or one of the cheap whorehouses on the docks."

"But still! You have to . . ." Veil's face colored again. "You know."

"Fuck people?" finished Seelie, indelicately. Veil smiled nervously.

"Yeah."

"It has its moments." She refilled her own glass, and Veil's, which had once again mysteriously emptied itself. The green liquid was starting to slosh rather low in the bottle.

"Really?"

"This is a pretty nice place." She waved a hand at the furnishings. "So the people we get have some . . .some class, I guess. And Fara will probably let me go once I get too old."

Veil nodded, a little unsteadily.

"What about you? What are you doing in the city?"

"I don't . . .I don't really know." Veil was having trouble finishing a sentence without giggling a little. "In the desert I thought I was going to die. Knew I was going to die. Something like that. I'm just glad to be . . .to be out of it, you know?"

Seelie shivered. "It sounds awful."

"A little bit." Veil took the bottle from the other girl's hand and upended the last of it into her cup. "A little bit awful."

They sat in silence for a moment, finishing the last of the drinks. Veil finally spoke, in a low tone.

"They were going to sell me, you know. To a place like this."

"If you end up in a place like this you're lucky." Seelie hiccupped, and giggled. "What happened?"

"Corvus."

"He bought you and set you free?"

"No." Veil leaned closer to Seelie and felt herself giggle, too. "He killed . . . everybody. Including me, almost. Almost almost."

"That sounds terrifying." Seelie put her glass on the end table with exaggerated care.

"I was scared. I was so fucking scared." Veil laughed, and her own glass slipped through her fingers and fell a few inches to the floor, rolling under the bed.

"But you're still following him?"

"Where else do I have to go?"

Seelie nodded, sympathetically. Veil wobbled, her shoulder brushing against the other girl's. She shook her head, suddenly dizzy.

"I think . . ." She concentrated on enunciating. "I think I need to lie down."

"Feel free."

Veil stretched herself out on the bed. Seelie shifted so she was sitting beside her. After a moment, Veil felt the girl lay down beside her.

"Seelie . . ."

"Relax."

"But you don't . . ."

"I told you to relax."

Veil closed her eyes.

GAMEH LANI STARED pensively into the turgid water of the harbor at Corsa. Farther out, as her ship had wended its careful way through the razor-edged deathtrap known as the Tears of Heaven, the water had been crystal blue and as transparent as well-blown glass. Coral reefs had surrounded the tiny islands on all sides, giving them an oddly defended look, as though they were ringed by fortifications; row after row of spiky white fingers, draped in the blues and greens of seaweed. The reefs were alive with fish, many of them brightly-colored varieties that Lani had never seen before she'd come here. The tuna and steel fish that could be found in the waters around Khaevar seemed pale and lifeless by comparison.

The boy was a local, Corsan born and bred. He kept his eyes lowered, deferentially, and spoke in the manner of someone who knows exactly where his loyalties lay. He was one of innumerable boys and girls who, by some tangled chain of agents, were on Lani's payroll. This was most likely his first time laying eyes on his mistress. Rumor had it that she never left her private ship, which cruised around the bay over and over, day and night, with supplies and passengers brought to it by small boat. Lani had fostered this image, though she did in fact leave her floating headquarters from time to time. It made it all the more surprising when she showed up where no one had expected her to be.

She'd considered trying to remain completely hidden, when she first arrived. But while one more Khaev in this city of thieves and murderers would certainly have gone unnoticed, someone spreading around the amount of gold she needed to spend—Council gold—would have been like blood in shark-infested waters. So she'd moved carefully, and cultivated a reputation for danger and secrecy. It had paid off, so far. No one had been willing to tangle with the shadowy Khaev woman whose fingers seemed to be in every pot. It helped that she didn't have to interfere with the local 'businessmen' to generate an income. The Tashidas, Kagerins, and the other great families of Khaevar were more than willing to trade gold for information.

"A stranger coming in from the north is hardly unusual."

"Yes, m'lady."

Lani found that form of address irritating, since she wasn't nobility and didn't deserve it, but 'mistress' carried unfortunate connotations in Imperial, so it couldn't be helped. "So why the urgency?"

"He matched the description m'lady circulated, on her watch list." He rummaged in his pocket and produced a much-folded piece of paper. "Here, m'lady. Number three. A tall, thin Khaev, dressed all in black, carrying a fine Khaev sword and approaching alone from the north."

"I see." Lani looked at the paper distastefully. That particular description was more than four years old. It had been one of the first things the Council had instructed her to look for. They hadn't bothered to explain why, but Lani had formed her own conclusions. In theory, no outsider was supposed to know what was locked in the secret histories of the Two Hundred, but the evidence was there if you knew where to look.

The boy stood, waiting for her command. Lani hooded her eyes and tried to look bored.

"Very good. I want you to follow him, keep track of his movements. Send regular reports. I want to know who he talks to, in particular, and where he plans to go." She picked up a small bag from one of the end tables near her armchair and tossed it at the boy. When he caught it, they both could hear the heavy clink of gold. "That should cover your expenses."

"Yes, m'lady." The boy bowed, awkwardly to Lani's eyes, and backed toward the exit. "Thank you, m'lady."

After he'd left, she returned to her desk, opposite the big windows at the stern of the ship, and pulled the cord that rang the little silver bell. Daggerwind appeared a moment later. Her chief of staff topped his mistress by at least a foot, was thin as a blade and gave a gangly impression that belied his impressively organized mind. He was one of the few people with whom Lani felt comfortable sharing her secrets.

Almost all of my secrets. She smiled. "I need you to put together an ambush team."

The Imperial nodded. "Very good, mistress. How many men?"

"Ten should be sufficient."

"Did you have anyone in particular in mind?"

"No one we can't afford to lose."

He only hesitated a moment. "Ah. I know just the men."

"I'll give you a target for them in a day or so. Make sure it's someone who doesn't mind working in broad daylight."

"Understood, mistress. Will there be anything else?"

"No."

"As you wish."

He bowed his way out, leaving Lani to her thoughts. She turned back to the picture windows and stared at the bay, her eyes not really seeing it.

Ebon Death. A real person, if the secret histories could be believed. *They have to be jumping at shadows. He'd be two hundred years old by now.*

In any case, ten men ought to put an end to the question. If the stranger was not who the Council thought he was—at least, who she suspected the Council thought he was—he'd be dead, and that would be the end of it. *If he is . . .*

She steepled her hands. *Then things are likely to get very interesting indeed.*

GHOSTLY HOWLS ECHOED through the dark Corsan night. The air was sluggish, and heavy with the scent of salt and sewage. All over the city, people shivered and shut their windows; a chill wind ripped from alley to alley, from street to street, leaving little patterns of frost on glass that melted almost instantly in the autumn heat. Puddles froze, cracked, and melted again in a space of minutes.

A young slaveboy, sent into the night by his master to empty a slop bucket in an alley, found it already occupied. First, by a young woman who walked unsteadily and used the wall to support herself, and second by a pair of huge dogs. The canines in question had shoulders higher than the boy's head and seemed to be made almost entirely of ice. Spikes jutted from their shoulders, and the street's light refracted through their translucent bodies and threw crazed patterns on the alley walls.

The young woman looked up at the dogs, injured but unafraid. She had skin the color of polished gold, and hair that hung heavy and limp and glittered like silver. Her eyes glowed in the darkness.

The dogs growled, a creaking, groaning sound. The boy would have run, then, but his feet were rooted to the spot. A moment later, another voice issued from the dog's throat, words forming themselves from the creaks and cracks of rotten ice.

"I warned you not to interfere."

The woman smiled, a little shakily. "I've never been much for warnings."

"This is my chance, Saya. My shot. I will not tolerate your meddling in my affairs."

"I couldn't care less about your chances, only your choice of implements."

"That is also my own affair."

"Mine, too."

"I seem to recall you divesting your interest in the matter."

"You're a fool." The woman stuck out her chin defiantly.

"Under the circumstances, it would not do to insult me." The dog growled, and stepped forward a pace. The boy watched, silent; he could feel the cold radiating off the thing, leeching the heat from his skin. Ice started to form on his hands and feet. "I'll tear you limb from limb."

"You'll have to catch me."

The dog growled again. "Not a problem."

Saya jumped straight up, as though she were weightless, and landed on an adjoining roof after a backward somersault. The dogs followed a bit more heavily, and the roof creaked and complained under their weight. The cold wind blew on.

The boy saw none of this, however. Ice had long ago closed over his eyes, leaving him motionless in a block of crystal. Even a late autumn night was warm near the sea, though, and the ice melted quickly. When they went looking for him in the morning, all that was left was a puddle.

chapter 6

> "The Khaevs and their bloody Two Hundred. Bah!
> I could take the lot o' them with one hand tied behind
> me back."
>
> –Uther Rockfist, Imperial General.
> Slain during the next day's fighting in personal combat
> with Furiena Sumero, Ninety-Seventh of Two Hundred.

NEXT!" SCREAMED WAIN. His voice reminded Kit of a vulture's guttural squawk.

Although her eyes were closed, she could feel the heat of the sun on her face. On the left side, a heavy liquid drop curved past her eye and started down her cheek. Kit flicked out her tongue to catch it, tasting sweat and blood. The air was calm and still, but overhead, outside of the protective walls of Steelgod, the wind screamed and shrieked like a legion of demons. The soft murmur of her classmates was barely audible. Kit could tell, by its tenor, that no one was standing up.

She smiled. *I did it. Fourth in the history of the draekeres. I* . . .

There was a shuffling as someone got to her feet. Kit winced.

"Kimira Zaneh. Fifth year. I request the honor." The voice sounded determined, a little scared, but above all *young. Fifth year?* Kit felt her lip curl into a smile. *On the other hand, I can barely stand up.*

Wain cleared his throat. "Kimira, I . . ."

She cut him off. "It is permitted, is it not? She must face all challengers."

"Yes, but traditionally challengers only come from the seventh-year . . ."

"Come on." Kit opened her eyes and spread her arms, ignoring the pain from the bruises that covered her chest and back. She smiled broadly. "One fifth-year more or less won't make a difference."

A roar arose from the circled draekeres as Kimira made her way down from the benches hastily thrown up for the audience. The girl threaded her way through the crowd of fifth- and sixth-years who had come to watch, and stepped carefully over the seated circle of seventh-years that defined the edge of the arena. Kit lowered her arms and watched her opponent.

Kimira was a slender girl, with oddly luminous purple eyes. At fifteen—a fifth-year—there was hardly any shape to her at all. Kit estimated she had at least six inches and thirty pounds on the younger girl. *And I'm stiff and tired and I can hardly see.* She stretched her arms, wincing at the pops in her shoulders, and pulled the sweat-soaked training uniform away from her skin to let some of the heat out.

Wain gestured for silence, and the audience quieted down. Kimira bowed respectfully, and Kit returned the gesture. Her peers, ranged in a circle twenty feet across, were to a woman leaning forward intently. The teacher turned to the fifth-year.

"You understand the rules?"

"There are no rules."

"Very good. Leave the circle and you lose. Are you ready?"

Kimira nodded and dropped into the standard draekere fighting stance, hands up and apart, weight back and low. Kit waited a moment before lowering herself into her own position.

She's good. Kit watched the play of muscles in the girl's legs, shifting almost unconsciously in response to her own movements. *Probably going to be quick, not a lot of power. Learned to fight here at Steelgod, so I know what she can do. But she knows that I know, so . . . what?*

Kimira seemed content to let her opponent make the first move. *If it goes to endurance, I lose. She's fresh. Have to drop her quickly.*

Kit planted a foot and closed the gap between them, feinting to the left. It was a standard opening gambit against an unarmed opponent, feigning a weakness on the right, and the proper follow-up was to grab an opponent's counter-attack and throw them to the dirt. Kimira saw it, ignored the feint, and bulled forward.

Perfect. Kit planted her left foot and brought her right around. The kick would have taken Kimira in the side of the head, but the girl twisted and took it in the shoulder instead. It was still enough to drive her to the ground; she turned it into a roll and popped back to her feet a little way away. Kit resumed her stance, a little wearily, and saw new calculation in her opponent's eyes. She was barely aware of the cheering of the other draekeres—for or against her she couldn't say—as a distant background roar.

One, however, was not cheering. Tashida Sumi sat in the front row, arms crossed, glaring defiantly at Kit through a black eye. She had been, predictably, the first to challenge Kit today. *She's never liked me. Ever since . . .*

Kit shook her head and returned to the present. *Drifting. That's dangerous.* Kimira had shifted into another stance, her eyes never leaving Kit's, and the distance between them drifted closed. Kit barely had time to think of a response before the younger girl erupted in a series of lightning-fast blows. Kit threw up her arms to block, wincing again at the crunch of bone meeting bone, and looked for an opportunity to throw. It didn't come. Kimira was too fast, and Kit was exhausted. She fell back, letting her opponent press her toward the edge of the ring in a widening spiral.

I'm going to lose. Kit felt her blocks getting closer and closer to missing, and she still couldn't find an opportunity to counter. *She's too fast—no fifth-year has any right to be that fast! If I could just* think *straight I could take her . . .* Pain clouded her thoughts as one of the girl's punches scored on her side. Kit danced away, clutching her ribs with one hand and breathing painfully. *Maybe I should just give up before I get hurt.* She smiled, though it came out as more of a grimace. *Hah.*

And then the answer was behind her, smirking visibly at Kit's discomfiture. Kimira closed the distance again, but now Kit had stopped giving ground, right at the edge of the circle. She blocked two punches, waited for the fifth-year to try a kick, and ducked. Kimira's blow whistled over her shoulder, catching Tashida right in the forehead. The seventh-year toppled backward with a screech, and Kimira bent toward her, one hand extended.

"Gods! I'm sorry! Are you . . ."

That was as much as she got out before Kit brought her elbow down, right between Kimira's shoulderblades. The fifth-year went instantly limp, collapsing on top of Tashida and twitching spastically. Kit got back to her feet, with some effort, and looked over at Wain.

The teacher cleared his throat and spoke into dead silence. "Kitsu wins."

"But—" The shout came from somewhere in the audience, but Wain cut her off.

"But nothing. Kimira took her eyes off a dangerous opponent. Let this be a lesson to the rest of you. Now." He looked over the assembled students. "May I assume there are no others?"

Kit wobbled a little. *Please let there be no others.*

There was a long moment, but no one got to their feet. Wain nodded. "Let it be recorded, then, that in fourteen hundred and eighty four, Kitsu Meru, seventh-year, defeated all challengers. She is the fourth in the history of our school to do so."

Kit smiled. The roar of the crowd rose around her, but she couldn't hear it; she was unconscious before she hit the floor.

IN HER SEVEN years at Steelgod, Kit had come to know the infirmary pretty well. it was run by some of the gentler Maidens, those whose spirits focused exclusively toward the light side of the spectrum, plus a number of learned peasants trained in the coarser arts of medicine. Kit had been in and out so frequently that the head Maiden, a jocular middle-aged woman named Sera, knew her by sight and joked that she kept a bed reserved. For all her frequent bruisings, though, she'd only forced them to call up spirits for her twice—once in her second year, when a fall from one of the towers had broken her skull and almost certainly would have killed her, and once in her fifth year, when a particularly bad back injury had left her unable to move her legs.

Sorcerous healing was difficult and sometimes dangerous, so the Maidens mostly relied on the same devices as everyone else. Kit had had her share of casts and poultices, and so when she woke this time she was relieved to find nothing more wrapped around her limbs than a damp cloth. Her body ached, but it was a deep, sweet ache in her muscles that left her feeling clean. Kit let out a sigh and lifted her head, to check if any of the Maidens were present.

They weren't. The long stone room was empty except for the cot immediately next to Kit's, where Kimira sat. She had a bandage wound around her head, but whatever wounds she'd sustained apparently weren't too bad, since she was sitting up and reading by candlelight. Kit peered at the slim volume and recognized the library's much-abused copy of Kagerin Morida's *Subdual*, covering the climactic battles of the Conquest. An odd choice of reading for a fifth-year, to say the least.

Kit tried sitting up and found her muscles protested only gently. The cot creaked—it was leather straps and a cloth cover over a wooden frame—but Kimira apparently didn't notice. Kit cleared her throat.

"Um . . . hi."

The fifth-year shut the book with a snap, and Kit cringed. *She hates me. It's understandable. I did humiliate her in front of the whole school. Irrational, maybe, since she was the one who challenged me, but still. What in the hell do I say now? I'm so bad at this sort of thing . . .*

"Hi!" said Kimira brightly, setting the book aside and turning. Her smile and the light catching her oddly purple eyes made her face look much friendlier than it had a moment before. Kit blinked, and the fifth-year looked at her curiously. "What's the matter?"

"Nothing." Kit felt herself color. "I just thought you were going to be mad at me."

"Why would I be mad at you?"

"For knocking you unconscious earlier." *Idiot. That's the first thing you bring up?*

Kimira shrugged. "Fair fight. I shouldn't have stopped to look after Tashida—I figured that out a moment too late, and I thought, 'Zaneh, you're in for it this time . . .'"

Kit chuckled. "I hate that moment of dawning realization."

"Absolutely." She paused. "Can I ask you a question?"

"Sure."

"Did you do that on purpose?"

"Y . . . yeah." Kit blushed again and scratched the back of

her head.

"'Cause that Tashida girl is *really* pissed off at you."

"What else is new?" said Kit automatically. To her great surprise, Kimira laughed. "How'd you find out?"

"She was in here earlier with a bunch of her cronies, whining about the bruise on her temple." Kimira sniffed. "If I whined like that about every little bruise . . ."

"She's a Tashida. I imagine she doesn't get knocked around much."

"You do, though." Kimira leaned forward. "I can tell."

"Y . . . you can?"

"Sure. You're not afraid of getting hit. They teach us not to get hit, 'cause the whole theory is that we'll almost always be fighting someone bigger. But most of the girls end up too scared of it."

"Sometimes you have to take a punch or two to get what you need."

"You're lucky I'm not some two-hundred pound guy, though."

Kit laughed. "If you were some two-hundred pound guy, I wouldn't have fought like that. Besides, no bruiser's that fast." She shook her head. "Where'd you learn to fight like that?"

"From a Tellenna."

Kit stared. "You learned to fight from a *Tellenna*?"

"Yeah. When I was little."

"But they're crazy!"

"Absolutely. Min got herself killed in a tavern brawl when I was nine — that's how I ended up here. She knew how to fight, though."

"A tavern brawl?"

"It was about fifteen to one."

"How many of them got away?"

"Six, and one of those had to crawl."

Kit nodded. "That's a Tellenna, all right. I didn't know they taught anybody."

"They don't, normally." Kit sensed a closed door in that avenue of conversation, and didn't pursue it.

"I don't think we were properly introduced." Kit bowed as best she could from the cot. "I'm Kitsu Meru, seventh year. Everyone calls me Kit."

"Kimira Zaneh, fifth. Go ahead and call me Zaneh."

Kit could see the question burning on the younger girl's face, and nodded sympathetically.

"Go ahead and ask."

"Ask?" Kimira—Zaneh—squeaked. "I mean, I don't want to be impolite . . ."

"Ask. Everyone does eventually."

"Okay." She took a deep breath. "Are you related to . . ." She cast about for a word.

"*That* Kitsu? Kitsu Sendameh? Former Fourth of Two Hundred?"

Zaneh nodded, looking embarrassed.

"Yes. He's my father."

"Oh!" Her eyes opened wide. "Oh. I mean, I'm sorry."

"It's okay. I barely knew him. My grandfather Sumai raised me."

"I imagine being the Fourth is sort of a full-time job."

"Yeah." Kit shrugged. "And since my mom died before he got the chance to marry her, I was always sort of an embarrassment to him. He packed me off to granddad, who sent me to the draekeres as soon as it was obvious I was going to be short and light enough."

"You must be great with a sword, if your granddad showed you anything."

"I guess." Kit's blush threatened to return.

"Really? How good are you?"

Kit looked at the floor. "I don't . . ."

"Go on."

"I don't know. I've never met anyone who could beat me."

"Not even Wain?"

She shook her head mutely, embarrassment coloring her neatly.

"Wow." Zaneh sat back. "And I challenged *you*. Gods."

"It wasn't with swords," said Kit hastily. "You're *good*. If you were my age I doubt I could beat you bare-handed."

"Want to trade?"

"What?"

"Show me what your granddad taught you, and I'll show you what Min taught me."

"I . . ."

"Come on, it can't hurt."

"I'm not sure I'm allowed to train with a fifth-year."

Zaneh raised an eyebrow, exasperated. "Kit, you just defeated all challengers in the Fire Tournament. Right now, you get to train with whoever you want."

It was true. Wain had a quiet word with her after she got out of the infirmary, letting her know that attending the unarmed combat or fencing classes was probably a waste of Kit's time. When Kit asked if she could train with one of the younger students, the teacher seemed delighted that she would bother. After that, although she continued to attend classes in the more exotic weapons like throwing knives and axe-chains, sparring with Zaneh became the best part of Kit's day.

The Tellenna fighting style was totally unlike the soft, throw-based style the draekeres were taught. It was fast and ruthless, just what one expected of the infamous Blood Angels, and relied on precise placement of strikes to make up for raw stopping power. What Zaneh had shown off in the ring wasn't the half of it, either. The Tellenna style included close-in knife fighting, which the Blood Angels were supposed to prefer above all else. What it didn't include was much defense, focusing on taking cuts to non-vital areas of the body in order to get a killing blow in.

In return, Kit showed the younger girl some of what she'd learned from the man who'd taught the Fourth of Two Hundred. Granddad had taken her seriously when she'd said she wanted to learn the sword; he was the kind of man who took everything seriously. And Kit, who'd grown up on stories of her father's prowess and his great standing at court, was a willing student. She never complained, not even when her arms ached from doing stroke after stroke or when her grandfather battered her hard enough to rattle the teeth in her skull.

"I wanted to be the First of Two Hundred," she said to Zaneh, during one of their breaks. They'd been practicing swordplay, up on the battlements of the main keep. Now both girls were slumped against a merlon, back to back, drinking from a jar that was still half-ice. It was getting into autumn, and the wind whipped shrill and cold past the towers and the outer wall, but it felt good after two hours of thrust and parry.

"You did?"

"For a while." Kit shrugged. "When I told Granddad, he just smiled at me."

"I guess a lot of kids want to be First."

"When they're eight years old, sure. I was pretty determined, though. When Granddad told me a woman had never risen above One Hundred Twelfth, I just told him I was going to be the first one to make it."

Zaneh laughed. "You must have been an odd little girl."

"Speak for yourself. How did you end up hanging around with a Tellenna?"

"I didn't know, at the time. I only really found out after she died."

There was a pause. Kit took a sip of water and swallowed uncomfortably.

"You don't have to . . ."

"It's okay." Zaneh took a deep breath. "My mother was a guard on a merchant ship, making the T'bach run, when they were attacked by pirates. Some of the pirates were Blood Angels, which meant it was a fight to the death. They don't take prisoners. Mom and the rest of the guards were winning. Then one of the Blood Angels got kicked, and it looked like she was going over the side. Mom dove to catch her."

Kit nodded. "She saved her life."

"Yeah. After that Min kind of followed her around. You know Blood Angels."

"So what happened?"

"A couple of years after I was born, Mom got killed by Imperial raiders out of Corsa. I don't really remember her. But Min took care of me, best she could. She was getting old for an Angel—thirty, maybe?"

Kit whistled, softly. "She must have been spectacular."

"Apparently." Zaneh shrugged. "So that's it. Not much of a story. After she died I ended up here. All I really knew how to do was fight, a little, and I had the right build for a draekere."

There was another, longer, silence. Kit slipped an arm companionably around her friend's shoulder, and the younger girl leaned against her.

"Five years, this Shadow." Zaneh sighed. "Three years to go."

"I'll be an eighth-year." Kit shook her head. It seemed

unbelievable—sometimes she felt as though she spent her entire life at Steelgod.

"You're lucky. Eighth-years learn to fly."

"I have to say I find the prospect a little nerve-wracking."

"Come on." Zaneh poked her shoulder. "You've never wanted to fly?"

"Wanted to, yes. But it's a long way down."

Kit shifted her grip on Zaneh's shoulder, and felt her friend wince.

"What's wrong?"

"Nothing. Just an old bruise."

"From training?"

"Y . . .yeah."

Kit noticed the slight hesitation, but made no comment.

Training for fifth-years was in the basement of Tower West, on one of the many floors fitted out as practice rooms. The hundred-and-some girls had instruction for a couple of hours from Wain or one of the other teachers, and then they were turned loose for sparring and practice duels. Mostly they broke up into pairs or fours, but a few sought out older students. Kit thought it a little odd that Zaneh had never asked her down here to spar, but the fifth-year seemed a little bit embarrassed about her friendship with the prodigy.

On this particular day, well into autumn and getting on toward Shadow, Kit was on her way to retrieve her friend in preparation for an evening's excursion. First snow was expected soon, and there were a couple of rumors that she wanted to check out before winter made the mountains deadly. Kit descended the long spiral staircase two steps at a time until she reached the right floor, and pushed open the big double doors that led to the training room.

It smelled of wood and sweaty young bodies, and the air was filled with the click-clack of practice swords and the occasional thump and groan. Kit looked around for Zaneh and didn't immediately see her. There was a knot of girls in one corner, though, and she recognized a couple of seventh-years. Kit drifted toward them to see what was going on.

"Get up!" *That* voice she'd recognize anywhere. Only Tashida Sumi could hit that glass-shattering note in everyday conversation. "Come on. I hardly touched you."

Kit felt her bile rise, and she ground her teeth as she got closer. The seventh-years at the back of the crowd noticed her and gave way at once, but she had to push through a bunch of younger girls to get to the center. In the middle was a clear space, and after that...

Zaneh. She was on her knees, breathing hard, a little blood trickling down her forehead. Tashida stood over her, unarmored but leaning on a wooden practice sword. A couple of her friends stood behind her, girls whose primary skill seemed to be sucking up to the grand-niece of the High Commander. They were armed, too.

Tashida was too occupied in what she was doing to notice the newcomer. She gave Zaneh another little kick, still shrieking.

"What's wrong? You did better than this yesterday, Kimira."

Before she could kick again, Kit interposed herself. Tashida's face clouded with fury until she focused on who the interloper was; then she blanched.

"Kitsu." The seventh-year laughed, nervously. "What brings you here?"

"Looking for a friend." Kit smiled, not at all pleasantly. "What about you?"

"Practicing, of course." Tashida shrugged. "We're supposed to be prepared for all situations, so I thought it best to try a few drills against unarmed opponents. I asked some of the fifth-years to assist me."

"Asked?"

"Of course." She pointed. "See, she's ready for another go!"

Zaneh had pulled herself to her feet, using Kit's arm to steady herself. Blood flowed freely from a scrape on her temple and another ugly cut on one shoulder. Kit half-turned.

"Zaneh . . ."

"It's the rules." Her voice was soft. "Have to assist older students. Required."

"That's right," said Tashida. "It does say something about that in the rules. I'd almost forgotten."

"Get out of here." Kit kept her face calm with an effort.

Tashida surveyed her unarmed classmate and raised an eyebrow. "I'm not done with my drills. Unless you're volunteering—"

Kit held out her right hand, without looking, and felt gratified when one of the watching fifth-years slapped a sword hilt into it. Her fingers curled around the wood.

"Get out."

Tashida swallowed nervously. "I'm going to tell Wain about—"

"Out."

She bobbed uncertainly and ran, in none too dignified a fashion, with her cronies trailing behind her. Kit let the practice sword clatter to the floor, and looked around to find every girl in the room staring at her. She slipped her arm around Zaneh, feeling the gazes like a weight on her back until the heavy doors slammed behind her.

"How long has this been going on?"

Zaneh stared at the floor. "Since the tournament, more or less."

"Why didn't you tell one of the instructors?"

"Tashida's right, technically. I'm supposed to assist her . . ."

"Not like this! Wain would see that it's abuse. Tashida wouldn't get away with it."

"What's he going to do? Whip the High Commander's own blood?"

Kit paused. That was true. Because of her birth, Tashida basically had the run of Steelgod. None of the instructors stood up to her, except on the smallest of matters.

"Zaneh," said Kit. "Why didn't you tell *me*?"

"I didn't . . .I didn't want to . . ."

Kit looked at her gently. "Why?"

"I should be able to deal with someone like Tashida." Zaneh swallowed, eyes tearing. "I should be able to do it. I shouldn't have to . . ."

She buried her head in her friend's shoulder and cried, silently. Kit held her, a little awkwardly, and mentally committed murder.

FOR ALL HER training, all her sword work, Kit had never swung a weapon at someone in anger. She'd never even really wanted to kill someone before. When she was nine, she'd sworn revenge on Zenda Fumai, who'd defeated her father to become Fourth of Two Hundred. The white-hot rage had only lasted for a few weeks, though. Zenda had defeated him in a fair duel, after all, and there had been nothing personal in it. It was hard to hate someone over something like that, and she'd barely known her father.

Now Kit had someone to hate. Rage coiled white-hot within her, ripping her apart from the inside out.

The quarters for the seventh-years were on the top of Tower East. By this age, the girls had rooms of their own, tiny djava° we×ler

little closets off the whistling cold corridors that the Imperial architects seemed so fond of. But they still had to share a toilet with an entire hall, which people like Tashida undoubtedly found a terrible indignity. There was no way around it, though. Steelgod had been built as a fortress, not a pleasure palace.

Kit waited in silence, sitting in a nook behind an extinguished brazier. It was after lights-out, and technically she was confined to her own wing, but none of the instructors took that prohibition seriously anymore. The moon was high, throwing little bars of light across the flagstones through the arrow slits. Kit sat on the floor, and waited.

It was only a few hours before she was rewarded. The door to the room she knew was Tashida's opened, and the girl emerged, letting the thin wooden portal close quietly and tiptoeing across the cold stones. She wore only a sheer white sleeping shift, which was swishing about her legs as she moved.

Kit sprang so suddenly Tashida didn't have time to let out more than a strangled yelp. The two girls went down in a tangle of limbs, with Tashida's furious struggles coming to an abrupt halt as she felt the cold touch of steel at her throat. Kit could feel the other girl shivering underneath her.

"Quiet." She kept her own voice low. "And listen, because I'm only going to say this once."

Tashida didn't even nod. Kit continued.

"I know you don't like me. That's fine. If you want me, name your weapon, and I'll take you on. Live steel if that's what it takes." She pressed the dagger into the terrified girl's neck, just enough to break the skin. "Like I said, that's fine. But if you *touch* Zaneh again, if you so much as lay a finger on her, you're dead. I don't give a shit who your great-uncle is, understand? Unless he gave you iron skin." She pulled the dagger back a little. "Nod if you understand."

Tashida nodded.

"Now, you've got two choices. You can go to the teachers, and say that I threatened you. I'll deny it. Then I'll challenge you to a duel. Or you can stay quiet. I really don't care."

Tashida nodded again, hastily. Kit pulled the dagger away and climbed off her, quietly. Tashida remained on the ground, staring at the floor as Kit faded back into the darkness and padded away.

"WINTER IS COMING," said Zaneh with a sigh. She shaded her eyes with one hand and looked around at the spectacular view. Steelgod was built into the eastern flank of the Cloudripper mountains, and from the points where the battlements met the mountainside there were a half-dozen paths and stairways carved into the rock, so that the particularly intrepid could hike toward the peaks.

The day was a little cool, but not quite cold, and the sun was alone in a brilliant blue sky. Kit wore thick pants and a halter top, with a heavier shirt tied around her waist; climbing up to their present altitude she had worked up quite a sweat. From up here, well above the tops of the fortress towers, she could see for *miles*. The riverlands stretched to the south and east like a blue-and-green carpet, farmland and little forests and the occasional glint of water as far as the eye could see. Behind her were the tallest peaks of the Cloudrippers. The highest was Mount Koltos, forever wreathed in clouds, where Imperial legend said the gods had once had their court.

It was well past Shadow, and nearing the end of autumn. First snow could be any day, and the quartermasters were already laying in supplies for the winter, stocking the fortress' stores with firewood, food, and water. Now that Khaev engineers had rebuilt the eastern wall, no army in the riverlands could hope to lay siege to Steelgod; the High Commander, though, believed in being prepared.

Zaneh stared off to the southeast, toward the Tsel and Crossroads. The city was invisible in the distance, of course, but Kit still felt a little chill thinking about it. *One more year. Then I'll go there. I'll* fly *there.* The thought was simultaneously thrilling and terrifying.

"So!" Zaneh turned on her heel with a cheerful smile. "Where are we going?"

"Uh . . ." Kit looked around, lost in thought for a moment. She'd forgotten she was the one leading this little expedition. Finally she pointed. "Just over that ridge, if I recall correctly."

"Then what?"

"We settle in and wait, and see if the rumors are true."

"And if they are?"

"Then we'll know. Plus you owe me twenty eyes." Kit shouldered her pack again and smiled. "Still up for it?"

Zaneh rolled her eyes. "Please. I could hike you into the ground."

"You may get that chance. Come on."

After the last bit, which had been a mad scramble up a more-or-less sheer rock wall, hiking up a gentle ridge was a relief. There was even a trail, of sorts, a little goat-track that cut a narrow path through the stunted trees that thrived at this height. All the pines had branches and needles only on the west side, green arms stretching out like little flags. The eastern wind was so strong at mid-winter that driven ice had stripped the other side of the trees bare.

"Here we go." Kit scrambled up the last boulder and glanced over the side. "Don't look down too fast."

Zaneh peered down and stifled a gasp, grabbing Kit's arm so tightly she cut off the blood flow. Kit chuckled.

"I warned you."

The other side of the ridge was a sheer drop, falling into a tiny valley at least a few hundred feet down. The other side of the valley was shockingly close, a massive rock overhang that made it more of a crevasse extending almost a mile in either direction.

The vertigo was almost unbearable. Kit forced herself to stare down until the world started to wobble and flow at the edges, then threw herself back onto the boulder, giggling. Zaneh fell down beside her, dropping her pack and hugging her friend's arm.

"What is it?"

"The map called it Venom's Cut." Kit shook her head, a little bit in awe. "Some old Imperial explorer found it. It's so deep the sun never touches the bottom, and it's thick with ice and snow, even at Fire."

"And there's a snow spirit here?"

"So the journal says. He claimed it appeared to him in the evening."

"I've always wanted to see a snow spirit."

"It seems a logical place for one." Kit shivered a bit. Once she stopped moving, the chill of the afternoon closed in on her bare arms. "I'm going to break out the blankets. Let go of my arm."

"Nope!" Zaneh pouted. "You'll have to do it one-handed."

That took some effort, but Kit finally managed to extract the pair of wool blankets they'd snuck out of the dormitory. The pair wrapped themselves up, leaning together for warmth, and sat in companionable silence as the sun slowly sank toward the western horizon.

Kit found herself drifting. It wasn't too windy, thankfully, but the cold air brought a bloom to her cheeks. Under the blankets she was toasty warm, though, with Zaneh snug against her shoulder. The combination made her feel sleepy and safe. In the

django wexler

distance, the sun touched the clouds around Mount Koltos, and the entire western horizon came alive with colored fire.

"Kit?"

It took Kit a moment to realize that she'd closed her eyes. "Yeah?"

"What am I going to do next year?"

Kit swallowed, past a lump in her throat. "What do you mean?"

"This time next year you'll be gone. Off to Crossroads, right?"

"Probably. Most new draekeres spend a year around Crossroads."

"So what am I going to do?"

Kit shook her head. "Work. Train."

"For two years?"

"I guess."

Zaneh gripped her arm tighter. "I don't want to."

"Zaneh . . ."

"I'll miss you."

"So miss me."

Zaneh looked up, on the verge of tears. Kit ran one hand across her cheek and tried to keep her face disciplined. "But . . ."

"Two years isn't forever. You'll miss me, and you'll get over it."

"No." Zaneh shook her head.

"Trust me. You . . ."

The kiss was light, and fast, like the brush of a butterfly in the bitter cold. Zaneh leaned back almost as soon as she'd done it, her ears burning. Kit sat for a moment, not really able to speak.

"You'll survive."

"I . . ."

"Trust me."

Kit leaned over and kissed her more thoroughly. Neither

134

spoke again. The sun slipped behind the mountains and, eventually, Kit fell asleep. No snow spirit was in evidence, but it didn't seem to matter.

TASHIDA WAS WAITING for them, shortly after dawn.

Kit had just disentangled herself from the still-sleeping Zaneh and managed to slip out of the blanket, savoring the chill on her arms. The scrape of boots on rock behind her was instantly out of place. She hadn't heard another man-made noise since they'd left the fortress the previous day.

Tashida was wearing a long black coat, silk, with her family crest embroidered along the borders. Totally impractical wear for mountain-climbing, of course, and it was a bit dirt-stained now. It took Kit a moment to notice that she was also wearing steel, the short straight blade of the draekere. A pair of her friends followed behind, also armed.

Kit forced herself to relax. *This is just more of her bullshit.*

"Kitsu, Kimira." Tashida nodded slightly. "Nice spot you've chosen."

"What the hell are you doing here, Tashida?"

"Just admiring the view."

Kit's eyes narrowed. "Admire all you want, then. We were just leaving."

Zaneh was awake by this point, looking from Kit to Tashida with something like panic in her eyes. Kit spared her a glance that was intended to be reassuring.

"I'm afraid not." Tashida's little self-important smile was incredibly irksome.

"You're not serious." Kit forced a laugh, looking from one girl to another.

"You didn't leave me much choice!" Tashida's voice rose to a screech. "You held a fucking *knife* on me. Me!"

"I should have slit your throat."

"Then the teachers would have had you hanged." Her smile returned. "This way is much better. Mountain-climbing is pretty hazardous. You're not even supposed to be up here, did you know that?"

Oh. Kit swallowed hard. "So that's how it is."

"That's how it is."

Kit nodded, mouth dry, but maintained her composure. This seemed to irritate Tashida.

"Aren't you going to say anything?"

Kit shrugged.

"I just told you I'm going to kill you!"

"So get on with it." She felt her heart pounding madly in her chest, and it was all she could do to maintain her demeanor. *But it's making her angry. That's good. Right?*

Zaneh got to her feet. "Kit?"

"Stay behind me, okay?"

"The hell with that." She smiled shakily. "I'll handle the other two and leave you to rip Tashida's head off."

Kit couldn't help but smile. "I love you, you know that?"

"Right."

Tashida's lip trembled, on the verge of pouting, and she put her hand on her sword. "Kill them!"

The three girls drew in unison, a long scrape of steel on steel. Kit raised her hands, but they felt pitifully inadequate. Real blades, with real edges. She tasted bile at the back of her throat, and forced herself to concentrate. *Look at them.*

Tashida was ready to kill, no doubt about that. *What about the other two? They're just her cronies.*

The moment broke, and Tashida charged with a screech, swinging in vicious horizontal arcs. Kit dodged one way, and Zaneh went the other. Kit closed in on one of Tashida's followers, a horse-faced seventh-year, and just charged. It was an idiotic move. All the girl had to do was extend her sword and her opponent would neatly spit herself. She moved to do so, but at the last minute she hesitated. *Not quite ready to kill me? Too bad.*

The moment of hesitation was all Kit needed. She ducked under the half-extended blade, grabbed the girl's wrist in one hand, and smashed the weight of her body against the other's mid-section. The air went out of the girl with an 'oof', and Kit dropped to one knee and flipped her neatly. She landed on rocky ground with a nasty-sounding crunch, but Kit was more concerned with the sword. It had slipped from the girl's fingers and gone slithering down the slope, out of reach.

She looked up, frustrated. Zaneh was baiting her opponent, ducking aside from her half-hearted pokes in an attempt to force her out of position. She was giving ground as she did so. Kit snatched a dagger from the belt of the unmoving girl at her feet and turned to face Tashida, who was closing on her like a runaway bull.

Tashida used the short sword correctly this time, pulling up short and thrusting at Kit, who barely managed to step aside. When she tried to close, Tashida backed up and tried again, using her greater reach to good effect. All Kit had was a little belt-knife, useless except up close. All she could do was back away and try to dodge.

Unless . . .

Tashida thrust again, and this time Kit brought the knife up to parry. She barely pushed the larger blade aside—it nicked the side of her hip, drawing blood—but it got her close enough to Tashida. Kit brought her other hand down in a carefully judged blow, and Tashida's sword skittered to the ground. She followed with a kick at head height, but the other girl had enough sense to duck and it whistled over her head. Tashida backed off and drew her own knife, rubbing her forearm. Her eyes were wild with rage.

Kit spared a moment to look over at Zaneh, just as she took another step back and tempted her opponent into an ill-advised thrust. The seventh-year was out of position long enough for Zaneh to grab her by the wrist and drag her forward, pivoting on her heel . . .

Kit saw what was about to happen, and sprang forward, not wasting breath with a shout. Time seemed to slow. Zaneh twisted into her throw, and Kit could *hear* the crunch as the edge of the ridgeline gave way under her outstretched foot. She was sprinting up the ridge, but not fast enough, nowhere near fast enough—Zaneh's expression changed from triumph to terror in a heartbeat.

The shock of Tashida's dagger burying itself in her stomach barely registered. Kit kept running, helplessly. She had time to catch one last look at Zaneh—screaming—before she toppled backward, letting go of her opponent as she fell. Then she vanished into Venom's Cut.

Time returned to normal, and Kit pounded up the ridgeline in what seemed like an instant. The dagger twisted in her gut, but she was blind with rage—the girl whom Zaneh had been fighting barely had time to turn before Kit hammered her to the ground with a fist to the side of the head. She scooped up the girl's sword as she fell and whirled to face Tashida, whose face had turned a very pale shade. She turned and ran for it, stumbling down the rocky slope.

Kit followed only a few steps before sagging against the rock, clutching the hilt of the knife. Her sword fell from suddenly nerveless fingers, and her hands were slick with blood.

Zaneh . . .

She closed her eyes, and the last image she saw before consciousness fled was the bottom of Venom's Cut, a hundred feet of ice and snow and one tiny, broken body.

KIT OPENED HER eyes and found herself in semi-darkness.

It was warm, and quiet, and close. Only a few inches separated Kit's sleeping roll from Kei's, and she could hear the older woman's quiet breathing.

"Kit?" murmured Kei. "Are you awake?"

"Yeah."

"Something wrong?"

"Not really." Kit lay still, and shivered. "Just bad dreams."

"So how was she?"

"What?"

Kei brought her draek closer, until she could make herself understood over the whistle of the slipstream. "How was she?"

"Who?"

"The girl at the inn!" Kei raised an eyebrow. "You know what I mean. Or were you just trying to get close to Shiori?"

Kit giggled. "Maybe a little of both."

"I thought you hated her."

"I can't hate her and want to fuck her?"

"Generally those are considered opposites."

"Let's just say it pleases my sense of irony, then."

"You have a strange sense of irony."

Kit smiled wickedly, but said nothing. Kei shrugged and shook her head.

"I'd like to go on record as saying that this is insane."

"What is?" The huge lizards glided more than flew, only occasionally flapping their wings to make up for a deficiency in the updrafts. They'd entered the hills, precursors to the impenetrable Shieldwall range, and the signs of human civilization had begun to thin out. The land had gone from cultivated farms to rocky hills and scree broken by patches of forest wherever the streams ran. The rocks basked in the sun as though they knew that full autumn would soon be upon them, and heat would be a thing of the past. This far inland, the seasons were fierce and the weather could change overnight.

"Going on with this mission."

"We didn't need the sellswords for anything more than cover, anyway. Now that we're past the river lord's territory—"

"Forget the sellswords, Kit! I'm more worried about a sorcerer that obviously knows we're after him."

"What do you expect? He is a sorcerer."

"Doesn't that bother you? We could be walking into death-traps from here till we finally catch up with him."

"Shiori thinks that Jyo-raku can handle him."

"Jyo-raku certainly took his time about it at the inn. You nearly got killed!"

Kit stared at the distant mountains, which were getting closer all the time, and shrugged.

chapter 7

"Swordsmen are like cats. They have to know who's number one."

–Khest 'The Doomhammer' Morel

ZHIN SHUDDERED, GRUNTED, and lay still, breathing deeply.

"Done?" Isobel's voice from beneath him was a little muffled. Zhin rested his head on her shoulder, feeling beads of sweat trickling down from his hairline and dropping silently onto the mattress. He took a moment to breathe, and Isobel continued. "I'm just a little bit uncomfortable here."

"Sorry." He rolled off her, onto the other side of the mattress, and she promptly rolled off and dropped cat-like to the floor.

"Not your fault." Isobel brushed the hair from her eyes, and wandered over to the mirror and basin at the far end of the room. She was unselfconsciously naked. Clothes or not, she moved as though he didn't exist. He took a moment to admire her figure, such as it was. "It's too hot."

"That it is." Zhin let his head fall back to the mattress, enjoying the slightly cooler air on his skin. Isobel paused for a moment, then dipped her face into the basin of lukewarm water. She emerged dripping, hair slicked to her head, and proceeded to scrub herself down with a relatively clean rag.

"So when are we leaving?"

"Day after tomorrow." Zhin sighed. "Empty-handed, as usual."

"Lord Valos isn't gong to be happy."

"Lord Valos knows the problems. It's not *worth* recruiting from Corsa unless we find someone really good."

"I sometimes wonder if it's worth recruiting from Corsa at all." Isobel began pulling on her clothes—first pants, then belt and sword. She added a shirt as an afterthought. "It's not particularly logical. It takes a lot of gold to get us here, and more to bring anyone back with us."

"Lord Valos is of the opinion that the riverlands have been scoured clean of the best strategic thinkers."

"I realize that." Isobel looked at her reflection in the mirror and nodded, satisfied. "I'm just saying it's an expensive experiment."

"Lord Valos can apparently afford it." Zhin sat up. "And you shouldn't be complaining, anyhow. It gives you a chance to indulge your little hobby."

"I'm not complaining." She checked her sword in its scabbard and headed for the door. "Just observing."

"Going out already?"

"It's too hot to lie around all day. I've got a few more leads to check on before we leave town."

"Great. Try not to kill anyone important."

She shrugged and opened the door. "Try not to lose any more money than you have to."

"Right. And be careful."

Isobel snorted and let the door slam behind her. Zhin waited another moment, then flopped back to the mattress, feeling exhausted.

By rights I should ride out to one of those cold springs and spend the day in a nice cool longhouse with a couple of pretty young things feeding me grapes. That did not seem to be in the cards, however. Lord Valos would most certainly not approve, and Isobel would raise her eyebrows in no uncertain fashion. *'This is essential to our mission too, Zhin?'* *That's exactly what she'd say. Damn it.*

He rolled out of bed and went to the basin to wash some of the sweat from his body. Sex with Isobel was amusing enough, but hardly satisfying in the long term. *It's like making love to a board.* Sometimes he found himself checking that she was still breathing. Her position, as far as he could tell, was that if he wanted to make use of her body while she wasn't using it for something else that was his business. *Still, it'd be nice to hear a little moan now and then.*

He pulled on his own outfit, a loose-fitting summer weave, and retrieved his coin-pouch from its hiding place under the mattress. Thus attired, Zhin looked at himself in the mirror and spent a moment adjusting the cut of his shirt, then favored the glass with a brilliant smile. *Perfect.* He glanced at the sun, angling in through the eastern window. *Still a while till midday. So, something to drink, someone to drink it with, then off to the dominion tables.* A jaunty tune found its way to his lips as he shut the door behind him and turned the key in the lock.

FROM HIGH ON a rooftop across the way, Saya watched the pair leave. First the thin little girl and then the soldier. She glanced around at the surrounding rooftops and found them reassuringly empty. *Too hot for little ice bugs today, anyway.*

If they're here, I've still got time. Vaalkir's not one to leave anything up to chance, and that girl is definitely his shot. She wondered, briefly, if Sybian knew about her. *Probably. The bitch knows everything. Though if she thinks she can wrap Vaalkir around her finger like some fire-sprite, she's got some surprises in store.*

In any case, I've still got time. She looked up, across the city, and her eyes narrowed. *So on to problem number two.*

VEIL AWOKE TO find the sheets tangled and stained with sweat, her shirt on the floor, and no sign of Seelie. The previous night was a bit of a blur, but the empty bottle of green stuff stood on the bedside table. The sun had woken her, peeking in through the open window. It was hot, which she was used to from the desert, but also *wet* and muggy. Veil rolled out of bed with a groan. She felt sticky and generally disgusting, and pulling her shirt on was something of an ordeal.

Once that was done, she ventured out into the corridor. The brothel had the relaxed, sleepy feel of a building during its off hours. A couple of the girls were cleaning the rooms, carrying armfuls of sheets down the stairs and replacing them with fresh linens. Veil edged past them and headed down to the common room, where she was greeted by the matron from the night before.

"Miss Veil," the woman crooned. "So nice to see you. I trust you had a pleasant evening?"

What I can remember of it, anyway. "Very pleasant." She bobbed her head respectfully. "Have you seen . . ."

"Sir Corvus? He left earlier this morning."

Left? Veil felt her heart skip a beat. The matron continued, oblivious.

"He gave me the name of an inn—I have it somewhere—where you're to meet him tonight. Said he had business to take care of and didn't want to wake you. I don't blame him. You slept like the dead, poor dear."

Veil breathed out. "Great." That didn't seem adequate. "Thank you."

They stood for a moment. The matron cleared her throat, quietly.

"Sir Corvus also mentioned that you'd be settling the bill."

"Right." She put one hand in her money pouch. "How much?"

"Three eyes."

Three eyes! In the hills you could *buy* someone for that much. *Three eyes for one night. Lost Gods!* Veil dug into her purse and came up with three fat golden coins, which the matron accepted gracefully. In return she received a scrap of paper, on which someone had scrawled 'Red Stripe' in a delicate hand. She showed it to the matron.

"Do you know where this is?"

"Of course, dear. Follow Center to Stable Square, and turn left. There's a banner with a red stripe on the outside, you can't miss it."

"Thank you again."

"Thank *you*. I hope you'll favor us with your custom again. Seelie seemed most pleased."

Veil colored a little, but managed another respectful nod. "I—I look forward to it."

A few moments later she was out on the street, which was a bit less crowded this early in the morning but still thronged with people passing through. Veil took a moment outside Fara's to check her purse. She counted twelve golden eyes. *We're going to need more money.* Corvus had said that side of things was up to her and hadn't bothered even taking any money for himself. *He'll probably just kill anybody who looks at him crosswise*, she thought sourly. Veil jingled the coins and looked down the street, weighing her options.

We're going to need more money whatever we do. So he can't begrudge me a few coins for myself. He was the one who wanted to stay the night at a brothel, anyway. That line of logic was only vaguely satisfying, but the hammering heat lent it some weight. The city was muggy and thick with the stench of tens of thousands of sweating people, and the air made her feel like she was breathing soup.

Veil found the general direction she needed to travel in by

asking one of the heavy-set bouncer types who guarded the out-side of the brothels, and walked until she started to see shops with fabric in the windows. The north side of town, being the wealthier districts, had a couple of streets that were absolutely thick with shops of all kinds. She poked her head into the first place she saw and found it filled with a variety of stunning gowns, all with jaw-dropping price tags. The next place sold evening wear for men, but was staffed by a friendly young fellow who was happy to direct her to a more reasonably-priced establishment across the street. Half an hour later, Veil emerged with one less eye in her pocket and some new clothes over one arm.

Another brief search produced a bathhouse, nearly deserted at this hour. Kalil's mansion had its own private baths, and Veil was used to cleaning herself in a crowd of siblings. Here in the city, apparently, people had to pay money for that privilege. The old woman who ran the place sniffed at being offered a gold eye, but eventually produced eleven half-moon shaped sil-ver crescents as change and let Veil in. She was the only one on the women's side of the bath, and having the huge tub entirely to herself seemed an unspeakable luxury. The water was only luke-warm, but it felt like heaven in the heat. After getting out and changing into her new outfit—sensible short pants and a shirt that left the arms bare, a style she'd seen other young women wearing in the city—Veil felt almost civilized again. The desert already seemed like a fading dream, or perhaps a nightmare of sand and sun and stone. *And blood.*

After soaking, Veil wandered. Corsa was the site of half the tales she'd heard in her childhood. Even if it lacked slavering de-mons on every corner and Ebon Death stalking the streets, there was more than enough to make up for it. There were open-air markets, filled with goods of every imaginable kind. Long rows of stalls sold food and drink, at which another silver crescent bought her water and strips of pork, fried and glazed in honey. A few entertainers plied their trade, too, even so early in the day, playing guitar or pipes for donations. Veil drifted through it all like someone who had just stepped into a storybook.

She turned another corner onto a major north-south avenue and found it lined on both sides with tables, most of which were occupied by people playing games. A fair number were playing at cards, something she'd seen the visiting merchants do back home but had never quite figured out. Quite a few were playing games she'd never seen. An odd one involving triangular stones printed with differently colored dots seemed fairly popular. Almost everyone was playing for money, and there seemed to be as many spectators as gamers. Veil kept walking, glancing from table to table until she found something she recognized.

Capture! There was a whole section devoted to it, stretching quite some length down the street. The stones were red and green instead of black and white, but a few minutes of observation confirmed it was the same game they played in the Red Hills. *Now* that *I can play.*

It took her a moment to find an open board. A young man, thin as a whip and wearing a terminally bored expression, was playing against an old coot. Actually he was playing against three old coots—the other player had two friends who pointed at the board and prodded him, but the young man didn't seem to mind. He clicked his stones onto the board with one hand, staring into the distance, and the old men moaned every time he made a move. Finally they gave up, muttering and drifting into the crowd, and the young man swept the stones from the board and started separating them into colors. He didn't look up as Veil took the seat opposite him.

"One eye for the first game, then double or nothing," he rattled off, with the air of someone who has said the words so many times they'd lost all meaning.

Veil blanched a little bit. *One eye on each game?* "C . . .can we make it a crescent a game instead?"

He looked at her, finally, and gave her a perfunctory smile. "Don't waste my time, little girl. Kid's tables are down that way."

Veil was fumbling in her pouch before she was even really aware of it, slamming a gold eye down on the table. "One eye per game, then."

He blinked, and his expression softened a little. "Look. You don't want to waste your money."

"Are we playing or not?" 'Little girl' had rankled, she had to admit. It had also been some time since Veil had gotten to do something she was genuinely good at, and being patronized had always irritated her.

The young man gave her a hard look, then shrugged. He pushed the pot of green stones across the cross-hatched board. "You're green."

Veil took the stones and thought for a moment. "Do I go first or second?"

He rolled his eyes. "Look—"

"Where I come from it's white and black, okay?"

"Green goes first."

"Fine." She slammed a piece down in the upper-right corner, a good deal harder than was probably necessary. He gave her an odd look and made his own play.

Veil's anger faded a little as the pieces clicked into place. *I love this game.* She always had. Kyre had taught her to play, on a lazy winter afternoon when there was nothing else to do. She'd taken to the game at once. The shape of the pieces and the sound of clay clicking on wood brought back good memories; sitting in front of a fire, watching the patterns take shape.

Five minutes later, the young man was staring at the board

and gritting his teeth. Veil gave him an innocent little smile.

"I—" he began, but she cut him off.

"Are we done?"

He shook his head.

"All your stones are dead."

"But . . ."

Veil waited while he worked it out. Finally he swept the stones from the board, angrily. "Double or nothing."

"If you want . . ."

"I was going easy on you." He gave a thin smile as he sorted his stones from hers.

Veil shrugged, and opened again. This time the young man played viciously, rather than lazily, but to the same result. She cut his overextended attacks to shreds and filled the lid to her pot with red stones. It took ten minutes for him to admit defeat, staring glumly at a board covered with interlocking green shapes.

"Two eyes." She fixed him with a glare. "Unless you'd like to go again?"

For a moment she thought he would, or else run off without paying. The street was crowded, though, and a few curious eyes were turned in their direction. Veil had the feeling that gamblers who ran out on a debt wouldn't find the environment friendly in the future. Finally, with bad grace, he dug two tarnished coins from his waistband and tossed them across the table. Veil scooped them up and tucked them into her purse.

"Get out of here."

She gave him another teasing smile, which he didn't return, and started to wander down the rows again. Veil looked over the capture tables, at pair after pair of concentrating players, and grinned like a shark.

THE CLOSER ONE got to the docks, the rougher the city became. The alley Corvus had finally tracked down was only a block from the water, so the buildings were of crude, tough stone, blackened by years of smoke and stained with all manner of unmentionable substances. The day's work had already started, which meant the doors to the brothels and taverns were closed and barred and the street was deserted. After sundown, the place would probably come alive with dockworkers, pirates, and criminals.

It hardly seems promising. Corvus strode quickly down the alley, feeling uncomfortably obvious. *If that little punk was lying to me—* It seemed unlikely, considering where Corvus' sword had been at the time, but a back alley like this one hardly seemed like it would be the abode of a wealthy tradesman.

"Number fourteen," he muttered aloud, glancing at the closed doors. Fourteen was heavy oak, locked and barred like the rest. He spat another dire threat against the immortal soul of the man who'd sent him here and knocked on the door, feeling foolish. He waited a moment or two, then knocked louder.

"What?" The voice from inside was faint, but there. Corvus leaned close to the wood. "What do you want?"

"I'm looking for Alled."

"Never heard of him." It sounded like an old man, tired and whining.

"I've got something for him to appraise."

"I told you, I never heard of him."

Now we see if my hunch was right. "Tell him Corvus is here."

There was silence from the other side of the door. Corvus sighed. *So much for that idea. I was hoping I was someone important.*

The door swung open.

"F . . .forgive me." The old man was stooped by too many years of sitting hunched over a desk, and only a fringe of white hair remained at the edges of his spotted head. He bowed low.

"I am Alled. You can't be too careful here, that's what I always says, can't be too careful."

Corvus gave him a look, and he paled visibly.

"C . . . come in, come in! The place is a mess, I'm sorry, I keep meaning to tidy it up but you know how things get. Would you like something to drink?"

"No." Corvus looked around the room. It was big, but absolutely cluttered with knick-knacks and oddments. At least a dozen swords hung from the walls, with another pile on the central table. Books were everywhere, mostly open or sporting a collection of bookmarks torn from old notepaper. The whole place smelled of stale food and paper, with a heavy hint of oil. Alled bustled amid the clutter, shifting a few piles of books from place to place with no effect whatsoever on the overall mess.

"Sorry, sorry. I had a bottle of something somewhere, I know I did. Shut the door, would you?"

Corvus kicked the door closed behind him, his boot leaving a mark in the varnish. He waited impatiently while Alled cleared a space on his table by the simple expedient of sweeping a half-dozen books and a plate of sandwiches onto the floor.

"Okay, okay." The old man sat down in his chair. "Now. What's this about Corvus?"

Corvus slid his sheathed blade from his belt and held it in front of him. Alled leaned closer, peering nearsightedly.

"Well-made, certainly. Resined cherry wood, of course, in the old Khaev style. Hilt and sheath from the same piece, very nice. An old blade, or an imitation?"

"That's what I came to ask you." Corvus pulled the first foot of blade out and let Alled puzzle over the characters burned into the steel. The old man blinked, and stared. "What does it say?"

"It says Corvus." He traced a finger along the blade,

wonderingly. Corvus gritted his teeth and tried to control his impatience.

"I know. I mean after that."

"After that, after that." Alled nodded. "Old Khaev characters. Pre-Conquest, pre-Tashida. Not in use anymore."

"Can you read them or not?"

"Don't need to. I know what it says."

"And?" Corvus felt his patience wearing thin, but Alled was clearly enjoying dragging this out.

"'First of Two Hundred.' And the date—1267, by the Khaev calendar I assume. More than two hundred years ago."

"What does that mean?"

"Assuming it's genuine, it means you're holding an artifact. The actual sword used by the First of Two Hundred." Alled tilted his head, surprised by Corvus' blank expression. "The best swordsman in the world?"

"This is his sword?"

"It would appear so. Unless someone has managed a very clever forgery." Alled looked up from the blade again, a calculating glint entering his foggy eyes. "Where did you acquire it?"

I have no idea. "None of your business."

"Of course, of course." He shrugged. "I assume from your presence here that you're interested in selling it? I could probably arrange a buyer, but that would take time. On the other hand, I can take it myself. Hate to tie myself down in a single artifact that way, but no way around it if you're in a hurry. Shall we say fifty eyes?"

Corvus snorted. *Even I can tell that's a scam.*

"Fifty, fifty, of course not." Alled was sweating. "But I'm assuming a substantial amount of risk here, you understand. It could be fake, and then I don't know what I'd do. A hundred. I'll give you a hundred."

"It's not for sale."

"Not for sale?" The old man shook his head violently. "But—"

"I need to find out where it came from. Who's the First of Two Hundred?"

"No one!"

"What do you mean?"

"He's dead. Mysterious circumstances. The Two Hundred won't say. Nobody's been promoted. There isn't a First. Hasn't been for years."

"Mysterious?"

The old man shook his head again. "Enough. You've gotten enough information for free."

Corvus took a step closer, and Alled yelped. "Mysterious?" the swordsman repeated.

"Mysterious! Nobody knows."

"Somebody knows."

"A Khaev, then! One of the Two Hundred."

"Right." *Then that's who I have to see.* Corvus tucked the sword back into his belt and turned on his heel. Alled sagged behind him.

"Wait! You can't just—"

"What?"

"Where did you find that? You have to tell me!"

"Why? So you can go there and dig up the artifacts?"

"No! I mean—"

"Goodbye, Alled. You've been most helpful." Corvus pulled the door open and let it slam behind him. The old man waited until he was sure the swordsman was gone, then sank back into his seat with a sigh.

"Corvus, Corvus. Most unusual. Unusual indeed." He thought for a moment, scribbled quickly on a piece of notepaper,

django wexler

then pulled on a thin cord that caused a bell to ring somewhere in an adjoining room. "Boy!"

A boy of eleven or twelve entered, wearing leathers and an insolent expression. Alled regarded him solemnly.

"I need a message taken to Daggerwind's man at the Silver. As soon as possible, you understand?"

"Yeah." The boy accepted the folded note with a shrug. Alled tossed him a pair of crescents, which he snatched out of the air and pocketed. "I'll get it to him."

"Tell him the matter is urgent." Alled turned back to his books. "Most urgent."

CORSA WAS NEVER really silent, but the normal background noises were drowned out by the sound of a large number of people being very quiet at once. The old man's hand hovered over the board, red stone gripped between three fingers. He set it down at the junction of two lines with a click that seemed to ring up and down the street.

Veil stared at the board, motionless, and murmurs started to grow toward the back of the audience.

"He's got her this time . . ."

"No way out. That south group can't make eyes, and there's no way for her to join."

"Six to one on the girl. You're on."

"It's a shame to take your money."

Veil smiled to herself and plucked a green stone from the pot, and the murmuring suddenly doubled.

"She's going to fall for it . . ."

"Not a chance. You didn't see her play Maki."

"Morris has been playing capture fifty years, he won't lose to someone like this . . ."

Click. Veil put the little stone down and sat back from the

board. The old man nodded, quietly, and folded his hands.

"Your game, my dear."

Veil squeezed her eyes, dry from the effort of concentration, and nodded. *Whew.* "Thanks a lot."

"Thank you." He shook his head and smiled. "It's an honor to play against you."

She blushed. "It's nothing."

"Did you study?"

Not really. But saying that would embarrass him. *It's just easy.* "I . . . practiced. With my older brother."

"He must be a master."

He never beat me. "He was."

The old man pushed his chair back and got up with a groan, one hand on the head of his gnarled walking stick. Behind him was a young fellow in dockyard leathers who claimed to be the old guy's manager. He was staring at the board, distraught.

"Morris!" The young man shouted after him. "You can't just . . ."

"The game's over." Morris shrugged, tiredly. "Pay the girl."

"Fuck if I will." The youth turned to Veil. "You got lucky. Get lost, kid."

This prompted angry mutterings from the crowd. Veil got up from her chair and held up her hands. "It's okay . . ."

"You heard her!" he shouted. "She said it's okay."

"I don't want any trouble. So just pay up."

"Right. What?" He looked down at her, snarling. "You little . . ."

"Pay her." Another man stepped to the front of the crowd. He was short and heavily built, in the thin white shirt male Corsans seemed to favor in the heat. He was also armed, and had the gnarled look of a soldier.

"Who in the Aether are you?"

"Her manager."

Veil flashed a glance back at him, but he didn't bat an eye. The young man hesitated.

"It's fifty eyes, man!"

"If you couldn't make good on the bet, it was unwise of you to make it. Now."

The crowd muttered again. Trapped, the manager dug in his coin purse and counted stacks of gold eyes onto the table. He glared at Veil.

"You're finished. You'll never play here again."

"I wouldn't worry about it." The newcomer put his hand on her shoulder, and Veil made an effort not to flinch. She stayed quiet for the sake of the charade. "She won't be wasting her time here anymore."

With a last snarl, the young man followed his charge. Veil swept the stacks of coins into her purse, which was starting to feel comfortably fat. She swept her ""manager" 's hand off her shoulder and headed away, into the crowd. When she looked back, he was following, so she ducked off the street into an alley and waited for him. He rounded the corner a few moments later, shaking his head.

"Not even a thank you?" The man shook his head. "Kids these days."

"Who *are* you?" She put one hand on her purse. "If you think you're getting a cut of this . . ."

"Relax. I already cleaned up betting on you at six to one."

Veil snorted. "Whoever took that bet hadn't been paying attention."

"Their loss." He bowed, deep enough to show respect. "I'm Zhin, by the way."

"Veil." She bowed back, cautiously. "Thanks, I guess."

"No trouble." He waved a hand. "I hate people who welch

on gambling debts, because it's usually me they owe money to."

"Right." She shook her head. "Well—"

"I have a proposition for you."

"Not interested."

"Not that kind of proposition." Zhin raised an eyebrow. "How much money did you make today?"

Seventy-six eyes, counting the last game. Veil shrugged and said, "Enough."

"Do you want to make more?"

"I suppose." It hadn't really occurred to her. *We've got enough for a few weeks, now.*

"Have you ever heard of a game called dominion?"

"No."

"Picture capture, but on a bigger board and with four players. I think you'd be good at it."

Four players? "That sounds . . . odd."

"The purists hate it, because it's not as simple as capture and the king making is fierce, but the dominion games draw big crowds. That's where the real money is."

"Why do you think I could play?"

"Because you're good at capture, and I don't think you've studied very hard."

That was true enough. "What exactly are you offering?"

"Let me take you to a dominion parlor. I'll cover your buy-in, and you can pay me back if you win. If you lose, it comes out of my pocket."

She didn't quite understand that, but got the gist. Veil tried to keep her voice cool and professional. "That sounds very generous. What do you get out of it?"

"Side bets. Nobody will expect a girl like you to even get past the first round. I should be able to get good odds."

"You have a lot of faith in me."

He hooked a finger over his shoulder. "Morris has played capture every day for almost his entire life. Mostly against weak players, granted, but you beat him without breaking a sweat."

Veil gave it a moment's thought. *Something still seems off. Zhin was too eager. But if he wanted to rob me, he could just try it now. Maybe he's taking me somewhere so a bunch of his friends can jump me?* That didn't make any sense, either. No need for a complicated story. He could have had a gang of thugs waiting in the alley.

What the hell. I have nothing to do until tonight, anyway. An inner voice pointed out that she didn't really have anything to do after tonight, either. Veil ignored it and nodded, slowly.

"Fine."

"Excellent!" Zhin smiled lazily. "This should prove to be quite profitable, Miss Veil. For both of us."

THERE WAS ANOTHER knock at the door. Alled waited until after it had been repeated once before getting up, grumbling, and making his way over to the peephole. A quick glance revealed a young woman—a good-looking young woman—with silvery hair and a wide smile. Alled opened the door.

"What do you want?"

"Alled Mirka?"

"That's me." He peered at her. "Do I know you?"

"I doubt it. You saw a sword earlier today."

"I see swords every day."

"Not a sword like this."

"Ah." He cleared his throat. "You understand . . ."

"You want to sell me the information."

"I . . ."

"Have you sold it to anyone else?"

"Young lady, that's not something I'd like to discuss."

"You have." Saya sighed. "Damn it, Corvus."

"Corvus?"

"Alled," said Saya, as white fire began to glow around her hands, "it's nothing personal."

THE SHADIER THE business, Daggerwind had found, the better it was to resolve it in a public place. Late nights in smoky taverns only encouraged treachery. It was easy to think highly of your cunning at midnight in a back room and much harder in a busy café at noon. Less cunning meant less mess, and less mess meant fewer bodies to clean up; as far as Daggerwind was concerned, this was a good thing.

The leader of the White Tigers looked like someone who didn't care where his business was transacted, and didn't care who knew he was transacting it. His jacket, dyed pure white and embroidered with an elaborate tiger-motif, proclaimed his allegiance for all the world to see. A couple of his compatriots sat beside him, clearly unused to eating in such relative luxury. Daggerwind sipped his tea and watched them fidget in the complicated wicker chairs with a secret smile.

"Are there any questions?"

"Yeah," said the White Tiger. Daggerwind hadn't bothered to remember his name. "What's the catch?"

"Catch?" Daggerwind did his best to look innocent, which was not actually a very good effort. "Why does there have to be a catch?"

"A hundred eyes to kill one guy? Why do you need the White Tigers?"

Daggerwind shrugged. "The 'guy' in question is quite dangerous. We want to be sure he goes down without . . . unnecessary complications."

"How dangerous?" The White Tiger glared. "A sorcerer?"

"No. Just a swordsman of some skill. I don't expect you to

have any trouble."

Caution warred with greed behind the man's eyes. On the one hand, the job smelled funny. Daggerwind didn't blame him for being suspicious. On the other hand, a hundred eyes was a hundred eyes. What finally tipped the balance were the implications for his reputation should he decline. Admitting that Daggerwind had frightened him by offering too much money was apparently out of the question.

"Fine." The gang leader snatched the purse that was sitting in the center of the table with bad grace. "The guy'll be meat by tonight."

"Excellent." Daggerwind tossed a crescent to the table, to cover his tea, and got to his feet. "I'll meet you here tomorrow, gentlemen, to deliver the balance of your fee. Until then." He bowed politely and made his exit.

On the street outside, a nondescript pedestrian who'd been leafing through the offerings of a book store put down the volume he'd been investigating and fell into step with the tall Imperial. Daggerwind barely glanced at him.

"Everything go okay?"

"Fine." Daggerwind kept his voice low. "Follow those men and alert me when they're about to make their move. This is a fight I'd like to observe."

"As you wish."

VEIL ATE A late lunch with Zhin at a corner restaurant that purported to serve Tellenna cuisine, which apparently meant adding dried pepper to everything until it was practically inedible. Zhin paid from a double roll of coins that hung from his belt, and chattered almost non-stop about the food, the city, or the passersby. It might have been irritating, but Veil felt a little bit relieved. The thought of having to make small talk was somewhat intimidating, since she didn't have the slightest idea what to talk to a Corsan about. She did notice, though, that Zhin scrupulously avoided asking her about her origins, and similarly made no mention of his. She thought about calling him on that, but in the end decided to respect his discretion.

After lunch, the Corsan guided her toward the southern half of the city, closer to the docks. The buildings got lower and meaner as they descended toward the sea, and the nice brick-and-stone houses and shops began to give way to wooden buildings, with windows that could be covered by flaps of canvas instead of glass. Zhin seemed to know where he was going. He led the way straight to an imposing stone structure that stood out like a tower in a sea of wooden shanties. The Corsan rapped the door with his knuckle, twice, and it opened a fraction on groaning hinges to reveal a pair of suspicious eyes.

"What?"

"First round started yet?"

"Not yet." The eyes narrowed. "But you're not getting in without cash." The unseen watchmen caught sight of Veil. "Unless you've turned to pimping?"

Why does everyone assume I'm a whore? Veil was feeling exasperated, but managed to keep her mouth shut. Zhin laughed, curtly, and jingled the rolls of coins at his belt.

"I've got the buy-in and plenty besides. Are you open or not?"

"Yeah. Hold on." There was the sound of a chain being drawn back. "We have to keep out the deadbeats, you know."

"Since I'm a deadbeat more often than not, I won't take it personally."

The doorkeeper turned out to be a round little man, sweating profusely in the heat. He stepped aside. The entrance was barely big enough for one, so Veil and Zhin had to squeeze past. Another set of doors behind him opened out into a wider space,

django wexler

through which Veil could hear the buzz of conversation.

"You've only got a few minutes. Find Calio. He should be on the main floor somewhere. There were a couple of house spots last time I checked."

"Great." Zhin motioned. "Come on, Veil. Stay close."

She would have done so anyway. The great room beyond the doors was bustling with people—not nearly as crowded as the street had been, but made all the more claustrophobic by the low ceilings. The crowd was made up of all kinds—dockside types in leathers and uptown pimps in brilliant silk, with a healthy smattering of armed guards. Most of these wore black, which Veil took to mean they belonged to the owner of the establishment, but here and there some particularly important personage was followed by a knot of sellswords. Waitresses circulated, wearing sheer silk that must have at least provided some relief from the heat. And, at one end of the room, two uniformed bartenders served liquor from a huge variety of bottles.

What drew Veil's attention were the tables, sixteen of them arranged in a four-by-four grid. They were large, square, and covered with cross-hatchings, many more than a capture board—thirty lines wide at the least. The center of the table was apparently not part of the board, and contained four pots she assumed held the gaming stones. None of the games had started yet.

Veil tapped Zhin's shoulder, which was easy because of his relatively short stature. He bent down to listen.

"Are you sure this is a good idea?"

"Of course." He raised an eyebrow. "Nervous?"

"Damn right. I don't know how to play this game."

"It's just like capture."

"With four people!"

"You'll get the hang of it. And even if you don't, it's my

money, right?"

"I guess . . ."

Something still didn't ring true. There was insincerity behind Zhin's smile. Veil thought about it as she followed him
toward a tall man she took to be Calio; he was blue-eyed, but his
face betrayed a hint of Khaev blood. A couple of guards stayed
a step behind him at all times, and everyone else in the parlor
seemed to know to get out of his way. Zhin ducked past a wait-
ress and planted himself right in the manager's path.

"Calio!"

"Zhin." Somehow Calio looked less than pleased. Veil
cringed inwardly, but Zhin ignored the other man's tone.

"Looks like the place is doing great!"

"Business is tolerable, yes." Calio bared his teeth in what could
have been interpreted as a smile. "What can I do for you?"

"I've got a player for you."

"Sign-up ended an hour ago."

"I heard you've still got a couple of house seats, though."
Zhin raised an eyebrow. "Those are no good for profits."

"Mmm." Calio focused on Veil, who looked him in the
eye with as much boldness as she could muster. "This is your
player?"

"Ah . . .yes. Veil, meet Calio. Calio, this is Veil."

"Charmed." He bowed ever-so-slightly and turned back to
Zhin. "I trust you have the buy-in?"

"Right here." Zhin undid the string on his belt roll and
pulled out a stack of coins. "A hundred eyes, right?"

"Indeed." Calio accepted the coins gravely. "You need to
hurry and get to your table—number four. We're about ready
to begin."

"Great." Zhin bowed politely. "It's great seeing you again,
Calio."

The manager's lip twisted upward. "Likewise." Then he swept off, guards clinging to his heels like faithful dogs. Zhin took Veil by the shoulder again and directed her toward one of the tables.

"You're in."

"I gathered." *A hundred eyes just to play?* "What exactly is the prize here?"

"Let's see . . . one hundred per, minus five percent parlor fee . . ." His lips moved silently. "A little more than six thousand eyes."

"Six *thousand?*"

"Six thousand and eighty, to be exact. Sixty-four players, one hundred each—"

"Stop." She held up her hand. "I don't want to hear it."

"You'll do fine."

She rolled her eyes. *But, as he keeps reminding me, it is his money.*

Three of the chairs around the table were occupied. Veil headed to the fourth one and sat down, evidently to the amusement of many of the onlookers. Little chuckles and muttering spread through the crowd, which she ignored. Zhin patted her shoulder.

"I'm off."

"Off where?"

"To find some suckers, of course." He smiled broadly. "I have to make money off this somehow, don't I?"

"Right." Veil rubbed her forehead. "Right."

ZHIN SLIPPED INTO the crowd, shooting a last glance at the little girl.

I don't believe it. He had to work to keep his expression calm. *I don't fucking believe it. The old bastard was right.*

Maybe, he amended. *There's no knowing if she's everything he predicted.*

If she is, though, I have to find Isobel, and ask if she has any more flip remarks about my hobbies.

He ducked through a gang of T'bach in their ridiculous colors and put his back to a pillar, having chosen a position where he could both keep an eye on Veil and watch most of the room.

If she wins, we may have a hard time getting out of here. His practiced eye found Calio's guards ranged along the walls, which was a little bit comforting. *That's not going to help much if this turns into a riot.* He wished, absently, that his partner were here. What Isobel lacked in personality she made up for in ability to carve people into bloody chunks.

"First round!" The announcer's voice was barely audible above the clamor. "Begin!"

Sixty-four players reached for the pots in the center of the table, almost simultaneously, and pulled off the lids. Sixteen green stones clicked onto the board. Zhin found his smile growing. *Here goes nothing.*

CORVUS STOPPED IN the middle of the street, hand dropping to the hilt of his sword.

"You might as well come out now."

He was walking along the docks, and the street was crowded with workers. Attention gradually started to focus on the swordsman in black. M ost people turned to look, but kept a respectful distance. A few came closer, pushing past the edge of the crowd. Though wearing dock leathers, they were all armed, and they spread out into a rough circle.

"Do I know you guys?"

"Nope," said one of them. He was a thin, lanky type, who sported a hammer almost as big as he was. "We're the White Tigers, if you care."

"Whatever." Corvus rolled his eyes. "What do you want?"

"It's nothing personal, you understand."

The crowd started to chatter.

"What'd he say?"

"It's a hit . . ."

"The White Tigers . . ."

"Gods," said Corvus, turning in a slow circle. "People are so stupid sometimes."

"This guy thinks he's a hotshot." The thin man looked around at his companions, who chuckled happily. "What're you going to do now, hotshot? Going to . . ."

He didn't get any further because Corvus cut off his head, drawing and striking in a single smooth motion. The pair of White Tigers who'd been standing behind him managed to get their hands on their weapons before they dropped with a spray of blood; the rest of the gang closed in, too angry for the moment to think logically about what had just happened. There was a frozen instant of slashing, gleaming steel and the scream of metal on metal.

Then Corvus was stepping away from the press of suddenly toppling bodies, already reaching into his pouch for a black cloth to clean his sword. The crowd looked on in a kind of shocked awe, not sure whether to applaud or run for their lives. The circle of clear pavement around the swordsman in black moved with him, since no one wanted to get too close; he finished wiping his sword and resheathed it with a silky metallic sound.

"Interesting." Daggerwind, looking on from a second-story balcony, rubbed his chin thoughtfully with one hand. "Very interesting."

Business was already resuming on the docks. A mere gang fight wasn't important enough to get in the way of commerce for very long. Daggerwind watched Corvus step out of the circle of bodies and continue on his way. He half-turned, heading back into the building, then returned to his post as someone else came up behind the swordsman.

THE MAN IN black let out a heartfelt sigh, thrust his hands in his pockets, and stopped walking. He didn't bother turning around.

"Another one of these White Tigers?"

Isobel shook her head. "No."

She was trying to control her excitement, but her breath was already coming faster. The man sighed again.

"And you want to fight, too?"

"Yes."

"Doesn't anybody *pay attention* around here!" He whirled, angrily. "Gods. Just some little boy."

"I'm a girl, and my name is Isobel," she said, calmly. "Might I have the honor of knowing yours?"

"Why not? Everyone else apparently does." He shook his head. "Corvus. My name is Corvus."

"Corvus." Isobel nodded, and drew a long knife with either hand. The swordsman looked at her disdainfully.

"Look, kid. I don't know who's paying you to do this, but it's not worth it."

"No one is paying me."

"Then why? Just a death wish?"

Isobel nodded solemnly. "Something like that."

"Great. Why does every suicidal girl pick me to latch on to?"

"Time to draw your sword, Corvus."

"Right." He rolled his eyes and drew. "I knew I was forgetting somethi . . ."

Isobel went for him, slashing at neck height with one dagger. Corvus checked the blow and sidestepped the follow-up. He lashed out with a knee that she avoided with a lithe twist, bringing the daggers around again. This time he had to duck and weave, and she caught his right arm with a tip, slicing cloth and drawing a bright line on the black leather underneath. Corvus backpedaled hurriedly and raised his sword, eyes narrowed.

"So that's how it is." He nodded at her. "Fine."

Isobel licked her lips. Her heart was pounding hard enough that she could feel it in her wrists, and her skin had broken out in gooseflesh all over. She shifted her grip on the knives and waited.

Corvus attacked, and this time she could tell it wasn't a joke. Blades flickered back and forth faster than the eye could follow, brief zings of scraping metal blending together into a kind of fugue. In close, fighting with two hands gave her an advantage, but Corvus used the longer reach of his blade to keep her at bay quite effectively. Isobel found herself forced to give ground, and finally to dodge aside entirely. Corvus' blade scraped the ground, raising sparks, and she dove toward him in a last-ditch effort to regain her balance. It didn't work. He ducked under the knife and twisted to plant his shoulder in her stomach, sending her rolling across the pavement and gasping for air.

She blinked to focus as he walked over and put the blade at her throat.

"Are we done here?" He wasn't even breathing hard.

"No." She smiled, shakily. "Walk away and I'll plant a knife in your back."

"Unbelievable." He shook his head.

"You'll have to kill me." She looked up at him, holding her breath.

"Don't tell me what I have to do."

"But . . ."

Pain jabbed her shoulder as Corvus kicked her, hard. Isobel rolled over, off the edge of the waterfront and into the none-too-clean waters of the bay. The chill of the ocean was such a shock it was a moment before she thought to kick her way to the surface; by the time she hauled herself out, dripping, Corvus was hidden by the crowds. Isobel let out a long breath and found her knives, right where she had dropped them.

THREE HOURS LATER, Veil felt like she was getting the hang of dominion.

The problem was that it was easy to capture territory with someone else helping you, but hard to ensure your safety. A betrayal could always turn the game around. The first round had begun with an apparent alliance between red and blue, who glanced at each other knowingly before the game started. Veil guessed they were prior acquaintances. She ended up allying with green almost out of necessity, and that lasted until almost the end of the game. Once her territory and green's covered more than half the board, with the other two solidly wedged against the side, the old woman playing green turned around and started attacking her erstwhile ally.

Veil had been expecting this, since a quick glance showed that she was ahead of green in territory and would thus win the match. The fighting in what had been their backfield was still savage, degenerating into a complicated double capture race that Veil pulled out by two moves. Green looked over the board glumly and found no escape for a group that had grown over half her territory. She tossed a handful of green stones onto the board with a clatter and a muffled curse and pushed her way away from the table.

Sweat dripped from Veil's forehead as she leaned back in the chair, listening to the tumult going on around her. Their game had apparently taken shorter than usual, but the other fifteen first round games were winding down, too. The crowd that had chuckled earlier was now chattering animatedly, and one or two even came up to Veil to offer their congratulations, which she acknowledged with a nod and a wave.

Zhin reappeared, with a glass of something cold which she grabbed at and downed in one gulp. He smiled and jingled a pouch at his belt.

"Cleaning up?" She let out one wonderfully cool breath before the heat of the day started to reassert itself.

"Absolutely." Zhin looked very pleased with himself. "Apparently word doesn't travel fast enough. Nobody had heard of your exploits this morning."

"Great."

"Second round is going to be tough, though. I looked at some of the winners."

"Great."

"Are you having fun?"

Veil nodded, limply. "Yeah."

That was the odd thing. It *was* fun. This was not a concept Veil had a lot of familiarity with. In Kalil's household, everyone worked, down to the very youngest; she'd had a list of chores and tasks every day that often kept her up until after sunset. Only occasional holidays broke the monotony. At some households, less pious than Kalil's, Mourning was a weekly break, but Veil spent her Mournings all in white, regretting the loss of the gods.

All of that seemed practically a lifetime ago, separated from the here and now by the desert and two months working each day for survival. The idea that now, less than a week later, she was entertaining herself simply for the sake of entertaining herself seemed ludicrous.

Something will come along and ruin it soon enough. She smiled grimly. *If nothing else, I have to meet Corvus tonight.*

"Great." Zhin patted her on the shoulder. "Now they know

that you're not a total novice, but I should be able to get even better odds on the second round. It's the cream of the crop."

"I might lose."

"I have faith in you."

That came out odd. A bit too sincere. Zhin must have realized it, because he faded back into the crowd a moment later, replaced by the two young men who'd played red and blue. They had outfits with matching colors—a little blue-and-white design on the edges of their sleeves—and nearly identical haircuts. She nodded to them, uncertainly, and managed to flinch only a little when the one on the left brought his hand down heavily on the board.

"Who the hell are you, anyway?"

"Veil." She sketched an approximation of a bow. "Nice to meet you."

"What do you think you're doing?" said the other. He leaned forward, in an attempt to look menacing; Veil actually found him a bit pathetic. Calio's guards were everywhere, and she didn't think they'd allow a fistfight between rounds.

"Winning?" she said with an innocent smile.

"This should have been our game. Teammates don't get paired in the first round very often, and you've ruined it for us." The leftmost banged his hand on the table again. "We're not happy."

"I plan to win, so it doesn't matter when I beat you, does it?"

"Win?" The rightmost chuckled. "You're not going to win."

"Not if you know what's good for you," said the other.

"That," answered Veil, "has never been one of my strong points. Now, if you'll excuse me . . ."

Calio was in the center of the room, shouting something about the second round. Veil slipped past the two angry players and worked her way through the crowd, grinning gleefully.

That was fun, too. She spared a kind thought for Zhin. *Whatever he's up to, this is working out rather well.*

"Didn't I tell you to stop causing trouble?"

Saya grinned, her teeth a brilliant contrast against the gold of her lips. "I like causing trouble."

"There's nothing you can do, you know." Sybian, as usual, sounded smug. Saya walked quickly along the waterfront, with the ice spirit's voice echoing in her ear. "He *wants* to find out, and he'll chew up anything you throw in his way."

"Probably."

"Oh? Do I detect a hint of pride for your little monster?"

"Just realism."

"Why don't you just give up?"

"It's a long way from here to Godsdoom, Sybian."

"When you fall from the top of Mount Koltos, it's a long way to the ground, but you're bound to get there eventually." The smirk came through the ice spirit's voice; Saya didn't even need to see her face. "There's nothing you can do. You turned him loose on the world, and now there's nothing you or I or anybody can do to stop him."

"You seem awfully sure of yourself. What if he takes a dislike to you?"

"By the time he realizes what I've done, I'll be a god."

"Or he will."

"Not that one. He's mortal through and through." Sybian lowered her voice to a suggestive whisper. "People like that wouldn't have any fun being a god."

ISOBEL, STILL SLIGHTLY damp, was working her way through the alleys of dockside.

She'd traced Corvus' movements by the simple expedient of threatening people until they told her where he'd been. It was a technique she'd used in the past, and one she felt a certain fondness for. Today, though, her heart hadn't been in it. Every time she described him she couldn't help but remember the fight, the sheer joy in grating steel on steel. And then, finally, feeling the prick of his sword at her throat and the sweet agony of realization.

He's better than me.

She rubbed her throat, almost unconsciously, as she walked, trying to recall the sensation.

He's better *than me.*

Isobel had lost count of the number of sword fights she'd been in. *A lot, certainly.* And every time, if the opponent had walked away it was only because she'd let him. *Not this time.*

Who is he? To think that I just happened to be watching him fight. If I had turned back one block earlier . . . The thought made her knees wobble. To have found what she'd been looking for for so long, just by chance. It had to be the jape of some long-dead god. *Corvus.*

She shook her head and returned to the present, peering at the numbered doors along the alleyway. It was not a nice section of town, and, under other circumstances, it was quite possible that she might have been set upon, robbed, raped, or even murdered. But bad news like Isobel got around quickly in a culture as interconnected as the Corsan underworld, and she was left strictly alone as she poked through streets.

Fourteen. Here we are. She raised her hand to knock on the door, and stopped when she noticed it was slightly open. *Hmm.*

Isobel was not the kind of person who sidled quietly into a situation like that. Her hands dropped to her belt, and she gave the door a gentle kick.

"Hello?"

She didn't really expect any response, and didn't receive any. The alley door opened onto a room filled with books, loose paper, and swords. It was a total mess, but a somehow organized mess. Books lay open to marked pages, carefully balanced on stacks of other volumes, and the swords were hung neatly on wall racks. It didn't look like the place had been deliberately trashed.

A man, who she had to assume was Alled, lay in the center of it all. Isobel's lip twisted, curiously.

So where's his head?

Alled's head was nowhere in evidence, and no blood had spewed onto the floor. Still keeping a wary eye on the rest of the room, Isobel knelt and poked at his neck, which was sealed by a heavy black ash, as though it had been burned.

Sorcery, then. Some demon did this. But why?

The answer seemed obvious. *Alled talked to Corvus, told him something Corvus didn't want anyone else to know, and Corvus killed him.* But that didn't quite fit. Though their interaction had been admittedly brief, Corvus didn't strike her as the type to randomly murder harmless old men. *After all, he didn't kill* me. She rubbed her throat and put a stop to that line of thinking.

So where does that leave us? Corvus came here. We know that for certain. Alled told him something. Corvus left, and then someone else *killed Alled. Either a sorcerer or someone who could afford to hire one.* Or a demon acting on its own, but Isobel preferred not to consider that possibility. *If Corvus has attracted* that *kind of attention—*

She headed back for the door, still thinking. At the threshold she paused, then turned back and helped herself to a couple of the nicer blades hanging from the walls. *Alled certainly doesn't need them anymore.*

So Alled was some kind of an expert on swords. Old swords, from what she could see. Pre-Conquest, even Fourth or Fifth Dynasty. *Corvus went to see him about a sword. Makes sense. Is he looking for one? Does he have one that he needed looked at?*

If someone else killed Alled, they must be looking for this sword, too.

Maybe they've asked someone else. Time to ask around.

Isobel smiled, and turned her steps toward the taverns.

THE SECOND ROUND was a pushover. She drew green this time, and got to watch, amused, as red and black got into a furious fight on the left hand side that let her and blue split most of the rest of the board between them. Blue, played by an old man with a shock of white hair that made him look like a dandelion puff, was skilled but a little too cautious, willing to cede territory to establish a sure defensive line rather than fight it out. Veil got her line stabilized against him in short order, then occupied herself fighting off a futile last-ditch attack from black. It left him overextended. Veil let him leap through a hole in her own line and drove her own wedge behind him, cutting his territory in half. Red, eager to salvage something from the game, jumped on him from behind. In a few more rounds black had been almost completely wiped out, and three-quarters of the table was behind Veil's green stones.

Zhin checked in again as the game was winding down, with another cold drink and a meat sandwich, both of which Veil accepted gratefully. She noticed that he looked a little bit worried, and said so, between mouthfuls.

"Betting not going well?"

"What? No, that's going fine. No problems."

"Then what's wrong?"

"Nothing, really. My partner usually checks in around now, and I haven't seen her."

Partner? "You think something happened to her?"

"More likely she happened to someone."

Veil chuckled. "Sounds like my kind of person."

Zhin rolled his eyes. "So how was the second round?"

"No problem." She gestured at the board, which was still

standing. "See?"

"Great. The last table's going to be you, Nazareen the T'bach, some kid from up north, and Velyn."

"That means nothing to me."

"Nazareen's in it for the money, a professional gambler. If he's come this far, chances are he's working out an agreement with one of the others to split the pot. Velyn's the head of a rather nasty gang, owns a couple more gambling joints of his own. I don't know the kid. Probably just got lucky."

"Great." A gambler and a gang leader. Veil didn't like the sound of it. "Any chance these guys are going to try to spit me and take the cash once the game's over?"

"Quite possibly. They won't do it in here, though."

"What about when I leave?"

"Let me worry about that." Zhin flashed his crooked smile. "In fact, I was just about to go take care of it."

Veil raised an eyebrow, but said nothing.

LANI WAS FACING the windows, which were, in turn, facing out to sea, when Daggerwind opened the door to her chamber. She nodded without turning around. He was the only one, besides herself, who could open that door and remain in one piece.

"Well? What news?"

"The man in question has indeed recently arrived from the north, in the company of a Red Hills slave. He answers to the name of Corvus."

Lani controlled her tone of voice rigidly, determined not to show any emotion. "And the ambush?"

"As you apparently suspected, mistress. Corvus cut down nearly a dozen men in a few heartbeats. I've never seen anything like it."

"Who did you use?"

"The White Tigers."

She permitted herself a smile at that. "Thus neatly fulfilling our obligation to Gorman. Very clever, Daggerwind."

"You are too kind, mistress."

She could tell, just by his tone of voice, that he was anxious to ask about Corvus. Lani wasn't sure how much information she was ready to divulge and, in any case, needed to think about the next step.

"Mistress . . ."

"Yes?"

"There is more."

"Go on."

"Corvus visited a scholar named Alled, who had achieved some notoriety as an expert on Fourth and Fifth Dynasty era swords, both Khaev and Imperial. He also had a reputation for being willing to purchase interesting finds, no questions asked."

"Did Corvus buy or sell?"

"Neither, apparently. Our man says he brought a sword in with him and consulted Alled as to its provenance. I also received a message from Alled himself, stating that he had acquired some very interesting and potentially profitable information and was willing to part with it for the right price."

"Purchase it," snapped Lani. "Now."

"I anticipated your decision in this matter," said Daggerwind smoothly, "and acted to obtain the information. Unfortunately, someone else acted faster. Alled was dead when we arrived."

"Dead." Lani turned around to face him, finally. "Dead how?"

"Sorcery. His head had been burned off."

"Corvus?"

"No. Our man definitely saw Alled alive after Corvus departed. He may have had a sorcerer or a demon as an ally, however."

"A sword." Lani sat down, then leaned back in her chair, musing. "A sword . . ."

"Mistress?"

"What?"

"If we're going to act, we need to act quickly. Corvus has proved most adept at avoiding pursuit. I've already had to replace two tails who let themselves be spotted, and I'm not sure how long we can keep him under observation without him realizing it."

"That makes the decision easy enough." *The Council told me to watch for him, but didn't tell me what to* do *if he showed up.* "I want him killed. Seriously, this time."

"As you wish, mistress, but news of the slaughter at the docks has spread. It may be difficult to find someone willing to take him on."

"Only a lunatic would fight him," Lani agreed. "I want the Judge."

"The Judge?" Daggerwind's calm exterior cracked, just for an instant. "Mistress—is that *entirely* wise?"

"I don't see how it endangers us. Find the Judge and turn him loose on Corvus, then stay out of the way."

"I . . ." Daggerwind caught his mistress' expression, and resumed his calm mask. "As you wish, mistress."

"Keep me informed of how things progress."

"Of course."

"Anything else?"

"A minor point only, mistress. After the fight with the White Tigers, a young girl challenged Corvus, apparently for personal reasons."

"Did she die?"

"No. He knocked her into the bay."

"What happened to her?"

"I'm afraid I didn't keep track. All my tails were busy trying to keep Corvus in sight . . ."

Lani waved. "It's probably not important. If she turns up
again, let me know."

"As you wish, mistress." Daggerwind bowed his way out of
the room, and Lani swiveled her chair to face the window. The
ship had turned, so her view now looked out along the coast-
line, where chalk-white cliffs alternated with dark outcroppings
of forest.

Corvus. There were, officially, only one hundred and ninety-
nine people in the world who knew that name. *The Two Hundred.*
Although I'd be surprised if Tashida Karikin didn't know. His nephew is
Forty-Fifth, after all.

Ebon Death. The First of Two Hundred.

She shook her head. *It's not possible. He'd be long dead by now.*
Perhaps the name has been passed on. Or maybe someone is playing a
dangerous game.

Either way, I'll settle him. She set her jaw. *The Council need not*
be informed.

Unless something goes wrong, of course.

MARKET DAY IN Crossroads—a synonym for chaos in the raw.
There were always street vendors, particularly in the two main
market squares on either side of Triplespan bridge, but on market day they overflowed their designated district and took over
the entire city. It was like a fair and a holiday rolled into one.
There was no question of any work being done except for buying
and selling, haggling and stealing.

"Only the thieves and the guards work on market day," Lord
Justin Valos muttered under his breath, "and only the thieves
are glad of it." It was an old proverb, but no less true for it.

Market day did have the singular advantage that the

Khaevs would have something else to worry about. Most of the guards would be busy chasing pickpockets, and the rest would be so blinded by the swirling crowds that the number one criminal on the High Commander's bounty list could walk the streets with impunity.

Criminal. They don't even dignify us with the title of rebels. Just criminals, causing mischief against the rightful order. Market day tended to put Justin into a black mood, though truth be told he was often in a black mood these days. *But still. Look at these people.*

He was wandering through Southside, at some distance from the river, so the crowds were composed mostly of commoners in brightly dyed leather or homespun fabric. A little further north were the estates of the merchants and lesser nobility, and then across the Tsel were the real palaces, converging on the Imperial seat atop Sentinel Hill. If Justin had cared to look up, he could have seen the Kaiune Palace, its polished marble walls winking in the afternoon sunshine.

Marble is brittle. You can break it with a hammer. I told them to rebuild the walls with granite. He smiled grimly. *Not that they put up much of a fight.* Once the Imperial Army had been beaten and the city mostly burned, the supposedly elite division of Imperial Guards had yielded Palace and Empress and vanished like smoke. *Well-trained. Ha! Well-trained at taking bribes, perhaps, and polishing their armor for parades.* An anonymous arm jostled him out of his reverie, and he pushed back. The man moved on without apology.

Justin shook his head. Sometimes he wanted to scream.

This isn't your city anymore! The commoners milled back and forth, looking for bargains, while a harassed-looking squad of Khaev guardsmen tried to keep order. Their pikes, heads peacefully shrouded in white, stuck up like a copse of dead trees amongst the milling Imperials. Justin saw Khaevs in the crowd, haggling and buying as much as anyone else. A young woman smiled as she handed over a beautiful wrought-iron necklace to a Khaev nobleman; on the other side, a young Khaev servant girl berated an old man for charging too much for his rice.

How can people forget so quickly? All those smiling faces. Dark hair and light, side by side. *The Khaevs burned this city to the ground! How can they be so content?*

"Hands up," said a voice behind him, "and no sudden moves."

Justin held still, and spoke without turning. "You're taking a big risk, you know. If Isobel were here, she would have spitted you."

"Isobel's in Corsa. Every lowlife and mercenary east of the Shieldwall with pretensions to swordsmanship is breathing a sigh of relief."

"I don't think she's that famous."

"Bad news like her gets around." The man cleared his throat. "Turn around, damn it. I'm not going to spend all day talking to your back."

Justin turned. Lord Ethan Fallar; Justin still thought of him as 'Lord,' though the lands the Fallar family had once possessed had been annexed by the High Commander. He was tall and heavily built, with a speed that belied his bulk, and unlike many he had not lain idle in the years since the Empire had been crushed. Ethan sold his swords to the highest bidder, so successfully that, even after the loss of his familial estates, he'd amassed a small fortune.

It hadn't been without cost, though. A bandit's arrow had taken his left eye, which he covered with a strip of red cloth tied around his head at an angle. The right twinkled, blue and merry, but Justin noticed that touches of gray were beginning to show in Ethan's once-dark hair and beard.

django wexler

His fighter's body and reputation concealed a sharp mind, with a penchant for nasty tricks. For the past six years he'd been the head of Justin's spy rings in Crossroads, sending regular reports on the movements of Khaev nobility and their Blades. Keeping track of people like Kagerin Shuzan at all times was one of the things that had kept Justin and his men alive.

Three years since I've seen him. Justin felt like embracing the man, but that would only have drawn attention to them. He settled for shaking his hand warmly. Even that was getting rarer. Nowadays, shopkeepers bowed like the Khaevs. The sight of their bobbing heads made Justin ill.

"You're looking well," said Justin, and meant it. Despite evidence that old age was approaching, Ethan still looked hard and tough. The big man waved a hand dismissively.

"I look old, you mean."

"You're only, what, eight years older than me?"

"Ten."

Justin raised an eyebrow. "Tell me the rumors aren't true."

"You heard that?" Ethan grinned, embarrassed.

"The great Ethan Fallar, whose cutlasses were the terror of every pirate and brigand from Crossroads to T'Bach, has sold out and settled down." Justin shook his head. "I never thought I'd live to see the day."

"Neither did I." Ethan looked wistful for a moment, then shook his head. "Come on. Let's go somewhere we can talk."

Justin followed his friends through the twisting streets of the city. Crossroads had been grown rather than planned; combined with the detritus of millennia of building, it made for a very complicated road system. Some avenues were wide enough for a cart and a team of four, while others couldn't fit two men side by side. Ethan appeared to know where he was going, though, and finally stopped in front of a low stone building with

182

a heavy oak door. He fumbled in his pocket for the key and stepped aside to let Justin in.

Once they were inside, Justin whistled. The exterior was unassuming, but the place was huge by Crossroads standards, with floors of polished hardwood and furniture that would have done credit to a noble mansion. A marble sideboard boasted a dozen bottles of fancifully-colored spirits, and a central hearth and chimney was flanked by two huge sofas overburdened with animal skins.

"I see," said Justin, "that being a sellsword has its rewards."

"Only if you're good at it." Ethan closed the door behind him. "You can speak freely here. I had this place built myself, so there are no rat holes for a spy to scurry in."

"I wonder if I might ask for a glass of the T'Bach Gold, first?"

"Of course." Ethan busied himself at the sideboard. "I'll join you."

Once the glass was pressed into his hand—thin glass, Justin noted, of an elegant Khaev design—the pair collapsed onto one of the overstuffed couches. Justin swirled his drink thoughtfully.

"So what's the story on your retirement?"

"I thought you'd heard already."

"I'd rather hear it from the horse's mouth, so to speak."

"I'm retired." Ethan raised his hands. "That's all there is to it."

"Just like that?"

"Just like that, he says. It took me twenty years."

"You used to say that going blade to blade with human scum was the only thing you lived for."

Ethan scratched his beard. "I suppose I did, at that. Things change, Justin."

"I never thought you'd change." Justin slugged the drink back and put the glass down on the table.

"Truth be told, I found myself sitting in taverns more often than not. There's no work anymore, unless you're willing to sign up to fight for the Khaevs."

Justin frowned. "There are always caravans that need guarding, or ships."

"Only if you go far afield, through the Highlands to Corsa. I'm telling you, there isn't a bandit gang worthy of the name east of the Shieldwall."

"There used to be."

"Used to be." Ethan shrugged. "Used to be the local lords would shelter 'em, as long as they preyed on the Khaevs. When his lordship Tashida Ikon found out about that, he put a stop to it in a hurry. Went over to the Siltoi castle with his Blade, ordered old Lord Siltoi to open his gates. When he did, Ikon had everyone in the castle hung."

"I heard," said Justin grimly. News like that *did* travel fast.

"After that, the high lords weren't so eager to let the bandits hide in their woods. Since then, work's been scarce for my kind. So one day I thought, 'Ethan, you're not getting any younger. Time to sit back and spend the money you've been killing for all these years.'" He spread his hands. "And here I am."

"Well enough, I suppose." Justin shifted on the couch. "So what's the news from the Palace?"

"N . . .not much." Ethan swallowed. "Justin . . ."

"What?" He could tell, by his friend's face, that it was something bad. "Did one of your spies get captured?" That could be disastrous, depending on how much the man knew, though Ethan was usually careful about that sort of thing.

"No, nothing like that." He let out a deep breath. "I'm retiring. All the way retiring. That means the spy business, too."

"Oh," said Justin carefully. He groped for words. "I see."

"I've been cultivating a young man for almost a year now. Dvaeric. I'll give you his address, he knows you're coming. He has everything, all the codes, the drop points . . ."

Justin waved a hand. "I understand."

"I'm sorry, Justin," Ethan mumbled into his beard. "I just couldn't . . . live like this, anymore. You'll be all right, won't you?"

"Of course." Justin blew out a long breath. "We did survive before you signed up. I imagine we'll manage."

"Good, good." Ethan looked like a man who'd expected a scolding. "You know how I feel about the Khaevs, but I'm getting on in years. Time to let the next generation take up the work, and all that."

There was a sound from the door, the click of the lock. Justin jumped to his feet, hand already on his sword. Ethan held up a hand.

"I'm home!" A young woman's voice, followed by the young woman herself. "I came back early, sorry . . ." She stopped, eyes narrowing. "I didn't know you had guests."

Justin looked her over, carefully. She was sixteen or seventeen, short but slender, with steel-gray eyes and long, dark hair. There was no mistaking Ethan's features in hers. The set of her jaw and the orbits of her eyes made her a close image of him. But there was also no mistaking the other side of her ancestry; she had the almond eyes and pale skin of a Khaev.

"Ami," said Ethan uncertainly, "this is . . ."

"I was just leaving." Justin removed his hand from his sword and pushed past the girl, with Ethan trailing behind him. He managed to make it out the door before rounding on his friend, who shut the oak behind them.

"Who is she?" Justin's voice was icy.

"My daughter," Ethan mumbled. "Ami."

"I didn't know you had a daughter."

"Neither did I, until a few years ago. You remember Ballin Woods?"

"Of course," Justin snapped. It had been the site of one of their greatest triumphs, nearly an entire Blade belonging to an incautious young noble wiped out in a series of ambushes. That had been back during the Pacification. *Before everything went to hell.*

"Well, you know. You do things, when your blood's up. Things you regret later. And there was this woman—girl, really—and she'd taken a poke at me with a spear, so I figured she was fair game. I left her afterwards. Didn't think she'd live." He sighed. "It was one of those things you can't stop thinking about. So when she turned up on my doorstep . . ."

"With your daughter."

"She was fourteen!" Ethan was close to tears. "Her mother was sick, very sick. What was I supposed to do? It's not like I could deny it. You've seen how much she looks like me."

"So she just moved in with you?"

Ethan nodded miserably. "Her mother died a month later. It's been the two of us ever since."

"I understand." That explained a lot, Justin realized, including this whole 'retirement' business. "Look, I still have some friends in the country. We'll take her out there, and then you can . . ."

"You don't understand." Ethan shook his head violently, and paused. "I'm out, Justin. I don't want this for her."

"But . . ."

"Here." Ethan pressed a scrap of paper into his hand. "Go see Dvaeric."

Justin said nothing.

"Goodbye, Justin." Ethan turned around, wrenched the

door open, and jerked it shut behind him. Justin, still a bit dazed, drifted back onto the busy streets. A merchant's wagon rumbled past, followed by a squadron of Khaev cavalry with gray-and-gold banners. He felt the world rolling onward as well.

chapter 8

"The Imperial attitude toward sorcery is fundamentally flawed. They revile all spirits as 'demons', and cast out those who work with them. They deny themselves the tools necessary to deal with the army of monsters that sits on their very doorstep!
"I fear we will never understand them."
    —Gena Souko, First Maiden during the Conquest

THE SORCERER WITHOUT a name waited patiently, leaning on the twisted trunk of a dead razor leaf tree. His men were safely out of sight, in a clearing slightly further along, and Vaalkir stood motionless on the track in front of him. Little fires blazed sporadically across the steel giant's armored form, but aside from that he was absolutely still.

The sorcerer shifted, uncomfortably, as he felt energies move in response to his master's call. Fire, of course—that had been his specialty, before—fire with a healthy touch of shadow. He felt the response from somewhere in the Aether, like the stirring of something ancient and forgotten. The spirits snapped into being as Vaalkir called their names with a voice like the roar of a bonfire.

"Ba'lel. Kir'vah. Ghae'mar. Tor'quai. Fen'zir. Ya'blik. Dryldamar."

Fire energy surged, stronger than the sorcerer could have

ever hoped to control. Vaalkir's power was beyond mortal reach, nearly beyond comprehension. By the time he was finished, sparks were rising from his body, drifting lazily into the night air, and the ground at his feet was scorched and blackened. The spirits were ranged in a rough half-circle before him, great leathern wings covering their bodies like cloaks. They were the color of ash, gray and charred, and specks of brilliant red sparkled beneath their skin. Vaalkir faced the one in the center, who stood to meet the armored spirit. Under the wings the newcomer was only vaguely humanoid. It had a pair of arms that ended in wicked claws and short, ungainly legs tipped with talons. Its face was frozen in a permanent grimace, like something locked in stone, and the only sound it seemed to be able to make was a low hiss.

"Dryldamar. You will obey my commands."

The spirit tilted its head, considering. Vaalkir did not seem pleased.

"You will obey my commands or I will scatter you to the four winds!"

Finally, insolently, the thing nodded. Fire encased Vaalkir for a moment, but he did not press the issue.

"Go to the southwest, find the women on their flying beasts, and kill them. Then come back here. Nothing else. Understand?"

Dryldamar hissed and nodded.

"Go."

As one, the seven spirits vanished, falling apart into drifting ashes which wafted away on the breeze. Vaalkir stared after them a moment, satisfied, and then turned back to his sorcerer.

"Tell your men to be ready. The Khaevs will be on foot when they enter the pass."

"Are you sure, my lord, that they won't turn back?"

"Jyo-raku has come too far to turn back now. He should be able to feel the Blade from here, just as I can. The prize will be too tempting to resist."

"As you say." So far, the shadow spirit had done just as his master had expected. "My men will be ready."

TASHIDA IKON WAS not, technically, *lord* of the territory still informally known as the Empire. Instead he was High Commander of a pacification mission, which gave him supreme authority in practice but set certain limits on the way he could conduct his business. An opulent throne room, for example, with all the fancy trappings and servants, would have been considered appropriate by most Khaevs to a lord of Tashida's stature. But because of his military position, his chamber had more of the air of a briefing room. A central table was covered with maps of the territory under his command, and one wall was a giant chart listing available forces and commanders with little notes pinned to it indicating current dispositions. One door led to the High Commander's private apartments—previously those of the Emperor's Chief Adept—and another to the Palace proper. A third massive doorway led to what had once been a private ballroom, now stuffed with worktables and lanterns, where a small army of scribes took care of the tedious business of running the occupation.

It helped that High Commander Tashida had the right bearing. He'd entered the military at a young age and risen rapidly, both due to his high birth and natural ability. He'd commanded a Blade at nineteen, a great honor, and had been one of the subcommanders when an uncle of his, Tashida Kuron, had led the Conquest. Young Ikon had distinguished himself since then, and was eventually rewarded by being given command of the pacification mission.

He was a man who had never in his life done a millimeter less than his duty. This, as far as Kagerin Shuzan was concerned, made him somewhat less than fun to be around. It would have been unwise to say so, however, not least of all because, in addition to commanding all the military power of the Khaev occupation, Tashida Ikon was Forty-Fifth of Two Hundred and the second greatest swordsman in the Empire. The only one ranked above him was Gefura Suron, Thirty-Seventh of Two Hundred, and since the Gefuras were subjects of the Tashidas, Gefura Suron had found employment as the High Commander's permanent bodyguard.

"I'm not sure I see the problem," Tashida said. He was sitting at one of the subsidiary tables with Kagerin Shuzan, commander of the most-honored Blade in the Conquest and Fifty-Fourth of Two Hundred, along with his bodyguard Gefura and Moriseki Hikari, mistress of draekeres. The latter was a hard, compact woman with tightly cropped silver hair. She was well into her fifties but had lost none of her edge. It was unusual to see her even mildly discomfited, as she was today.

"The problem, my lord," said Shuzan patiently, "is that Shiori has gone haring off into the middle of nowhere again."

"The problem," snapped Moriseki, "is that she's taken two of my best women with her."

Tashida cleared his throat. "Firstly, Shuzan, my niece is well within her rights to take her Blade anywhere she wishes."

"But she didn't! Her Blade is still in the Palace."

"She is *certainly* within her rights, as a Khaev citizen, to go where she chooses in our territory. Since her Blade is not active at the moment, I have no concern with how she spends her time."

"What about my draeks?" said Moriseki, sharply. "We're critically undermanned as it is, with the exercises for the Tellen campaign and courier duties on top of normal support."

"That is a bit more puzzling." Tashida leaned forward, crossing his hands under his chin. "Are you saying that the draekeres in question left without permission? That would indicate a quite shocking breakdown in discipline."

"No." She shook her head firmly. "No, Lady Tashida confirmed the mission with me. They simply should have been back by now."

And that's oddity number one. Moriseki was notoriously tight-fisted with Blade commanders, who were always clamoring for more of her precious aerial scouts. For her to have sent two of them on some fool's errand was beyond belief. *There's more here than she's saying.* Shuzan tried to catch the woman's eye and failed. *I'll have to talk with her afterward.*

"My lord, I don't expect to be gone from the Palace longer than a week."

"You and your entire Blade?"

"In my experience," said Shuzan dryly, "Shiori needs an entire Blade to get her out of trouble."

"Impossible." Tashida shook his head. "Your men are slated to move out in less than a week, to head south for marine training. Your Blade is going to be one of the core invasion forces."

Shuzan sighed. "I know that as well as you do! But I can't just leave her out there." *Not exactly a lie, is it?*

"You will remember your duty, Kagerin Shuzan." Tashida stood from the table, adjusting his sword. He, Gefura, and Shuzan were all armed: Only members of the Two Hundred were allowed to carry weapons in the Palace. "And you, Moriseki, will simply have to be patient. Precious as draekeres are, we can't change the entire invasion schedule to go chasing after two of them."

With that he turned and strode back toward his own chambers. Gefura gave the pair a last looking over, sneering behind his bushy mustache, before following his master.

I hate him. Not Tashida. It was hard to hate a man who was simply doing his duty. But Gefura. *Arrogant son-of-a-bitch.* Conceit came easily to the Two Hundred, but Gefura acted as though because the gods had gifted him with quick wrists and a swordsman's mind he was entitled to everything else in life. *I've seen the man fight, though, and he must be accorded proper respect.*

Moriseki was already leaving; Shuzan hurried to catch up with her. She was obviously not interested in talking to him, but couldn't outpace his longer stride without breaking into an out-and-out sprint.

"Lady Moriseki—"

"I'm not a lady and you damn well know it." Like most draekeres, and unlike most Blade commanders, Moriseki came from an unknown, honorless family. It was a source of occasional tension between the aerial scouts and their commanders. Shuzan rolled his eyes.

"Mistress Moriseki, then. I wondered if I might have a word."

"You're having one right now."

"It's a bit difficult while you're walking so fast."

She stopped, so abruptly he stumbled a few steps further before recovering. "Is that better?"

"Much."

"So what do you want, *Lord* Kagerin?"

"I want to know what the hell is going on."

"I don't know what you're—"

Shuzan slammed a hand against the wall in front of her, forcing her to a halt. At better than six feet, he towered over the diminutive draekere, but she looked up at him unintimidated.

"Don't lie to me, Moriseki. Shiori couldn't have gotten those draekeres out of the palace without your approval, and it follows that you're in on whatever crazy idea she's gotten it into her head to follow. Lord Tashida made it very clear that you're not going to be getting any support from High Command, so if you want to get your people back I suggest you tell me the truth."

Shuzan bared his teeth in a snarl, and the draekere leader hesitated, uncertain.

"Even if there were something to tell, what are you planning to do about it? Lord Tashida gave you your assignment."

The snarl turned into a sneer. "The Kagerin family does not simply roll over when a Tashida gives an order."

"There'd be an investigation."

"Father will support me. He's sick of the Tashidas lording themselves over the rest of the Council."

The woman shook her head. "You'd really take your whole Blade and go looking for her? Against Lord Tashida's orders? Why?"

Shuzan smiled in what he hoped was a mysterious fashion. "I have my reasons."

Moriseki reached a decision. "Come with me, then. There's someone you should meet."

"THAT HAS TO be them." Kit swung her draek in lazy circles, pointing at a tiny glow on the distant mountainside.

Kei peered at it, uncertain. "There could be other people around."

"In these parts?" Kit snorted, inaudibly in the draft, and waved. "The last village was six days ago! Nobody goes into the Shieldwall this far north."

That was true, she had to admit. What trade there was through the Shieldwall, mostly caravans making the long passage to Corsa, went through the Anvil and Crimson Pass. Travelers up here would be few and far between.

"Still, we can't just assume it's them. They've been careful so far. We haven't spotted them once, even though Jyo-raku says we're gaining. Why would they slip so badly now?" The speck was tiny at this distance, but that was deceptive; Kei figured it had to be a bonfire or something similarly sized to be visible at all.

"Maybe they found what they were looking for."

"I'm not sure if that's good or bad."

"Me neither."

Kei took a deep breath, coughed, and blinked suddenly, surprised to find her eyes watering. *What the hell?* The air was filling with ash, fine ash, as though someone had pulverized spent charcoal and let it drift in the wind. It was already thick enough that Kit had become a vague outline, off to her left. Kei coughed again and hauled on the draek's reins, trying to climb out of it.

Sorcery! It has to be . . .

There were darker shapes in the murk, fading into existence as though assembling themselves out of the grit. Before she rose out of the cloud they were solid, and four pairs of wings snapped open. Kei barely had a moment to register her disbelief—nothing natural could fly like that, they'd risen straight up without flapping their wings—before they were on top of her.

In that frozen moment, the four things swarmed over her draek. Two of them went for its hindquarters, and two for its head. The lizard reared up, spilling air, and tried to bite its attackers; one of them aimed high, the other low, wicked claws spread wide.

At this point Kei's training kicked in. Air-to-air combat was not a major component of the courses at Sora, but every draekere spent hours in the sky testing herself and her mount against others in mock duels and races. Kei kicked back, her boots knocking on scaly skin, and the well-trained animal obediently went into a dive, kicking its back legs out and slashing through the cloud of smoke in mere instants. This left the two above hissing their rage, and one of the pair behind her tumbled in the draek's wake and snapped its wings open to regain control.

The last creature, though, had lashed out wildly and managed to get one clawed hand on the draek's hindquarters. Its claws dug through scaly skin with ease, ripping three parallel tracks until they finally caught, leaving the thing flapping by one arm like a flag. The draek screeched in pain, and Kei hauled back and left on the reins, banking sharply and pulling up to avoid the rapidly approaching hillside. The demon flailed but kept its grip, swinging its other arm wildly until it managed to get a hold near the base of the draek's tail and start pulling itself forward.

Shit, shit, shit*!* The hillside shot past, a multicolored blur. Kei pulled up harder and brought the draek away from the ground, killing most of the speed she'd gotten from the dive. A moment later, three gray blurs flashed past as the rest of the demons dove for her like stooping hawks, leveling out just above the treetops and rising straight up in total defiance of gravity.

Kei gave herself a couple of seconds to deal with the one behind her before the others finished her off. It had pulled itself forward another foot, nearly within reach of her back, and dug its claws in along the draek's spine. Kei wrapped the reins and pulled her sword from its sheath on her saddle; the demon raised one arm to defend and hissed, contemptuously.

She didn't know if it was capable of stopping a sword with just its claws, and didn't intend to find out. A sideways jerk of the knee made the draek fold one wing and level out upside down, which left the creature momentarily hanging by its arm. Kei, strapped securely to her saddle, fought desperately against the rush of blood to her head and brought her sword around, taking the demon's limb off at its elbow. It broke loose instantly, hissing like mad but lost in the slipstream, and the arm it had left behind flashed into ashes. Another prod of the knees rolled the draek back over, just in time to pull into a climb and avoid the trees.

Kit! Kei looked around for her partner, keeping half an eye on the three demons that followed her, horribly quickly. She spotted the other draek some distance away, flapping hard for altitude with three more of the demons flitting around it. Kei turned that way and looked up.

Here they come. The demons were smart. They split up, one ahead and one behind while another dove for her, claws extended. Kei murmured a silent apology to her beast as she jerked the reins back again and it reared and roared, right in the path of one of the demons. The creature rolled, slicing the draek across the jaw, but the lizard's head snapped out viper-quick and tore off a chunk of the demon's wing, which vaporized to ash in the draek's mouth. Out of control, the demon twirled toward the rocky slope. Kei didn't spare it another thought as she hurriedly pulled the fixbow from her pack and snapped its oiled sections into place.

A twitch of her thumb on the control connected the bow to the ropes around the saddle, and the draek roared at the un-expected effort the next time it flapped its wings. She pulled a bowstring from her saddlebag and looped it around the now-cocked weapon—*too slow, I could do it in less than a second at Sora*—and slotted a heavy bolt into the groove. The whole assembly swiveled on its mount; it made controlling the draek rather difficult, but using the lizard's muscles to cock the bow gave it amazing range and power.

Carefully, Kei wheeled back toward Kit, who was apparently making a run for it, darting to and fro between the treetops. The demons followed her, a bit farther back and higher up, look-ing for an opportunity to dive. They made near-perfect targets, gliding in a straight line. Kei set parallel course, lined one up, and fired.

The sound of the fixbow was shockingly loud, as usual, and the draek swung sideways to compensate for the recoil. The shot went true, tearing through one of the demon's wings and lodging in its midsection, and it drifted quickly toward the ground and impacted a treetop in a spectacular spray of ash. The other two screamed and rose quickly, heading for Kei, but they had apparently forgotten their own quarry. Kit pulled her draek around, rose to a perfect apogee, then dove after her erstwhile pursuers, reins in one hand and sword in the other.

"Kit!" Kei tried to line up another shot on the incoming demons, but had to swerve hastily aside to dodge another dive from her own pursuers. Kit was coming up fast between the pair, who hadn't noticed her. With a quick wing-beat, she was between them, chopping one wing from the one on the left. Ash puffed, and the demon fell. The one on the right, though, rolled onto its back and slid under the draek, coming out the other side with red claws and a triumphant hiss. Thick blood sprayed from the lizard's neck, and it thrashed and started to sink toward the trees.

Kei threw her own mount into a dive before she'd even realized it, ripping the release from the fixbow and letting it pinwheel away toward the ground. Kit's draek was still gliding, sort of, and Kei closed on it from behind. Kit was frantically wrestling with the straps that held her to the saddle as Kei pulled alongside and held out a hand, which Kit grabbed while still fumbling with a catch. For a moment Kei found herself supporting five hundred pounds of woman and draek, and her arm was nearly pulled from its socket. Then Kit found the catch and flew free, gripping Kei's wrist so hard it hurt, and the younger woman's draek spiraled into the trees in a horribly drawn-out crash.

Without breath to spare even for a warning, Kei banked the draek back so Kit fell onto its hindquarters, which were already slick with blood. An order to hang on was unnecessary. Kit was already gripping the back of Kei's saddle as hard as she could. Kei banked again, blindly, desperately, hoping to avoid the demons she knew were coming.

It almost worked. Her last-minute turn threw two of them off, and they streaked past with hisses of rage. The last demon's claws hit the draek right at the shoulder, ripping through skin, flesh, and bone with a truly awful crunch. The draek howled in agony, but the demon held on until the entire wing tore away. The draek tipped over instantly, angling toward the ground and leaving the creature behind.

Kei hauled the reins to the left, aiming for a clear patch of ground, but in its dying agony the draek didn't respond. She found herself watching the growing treetops with a curious sense of equanimity in a single stretched instant.

We might live. Broken bones, maybe. We weren't going very fast. I'd just pulled up, and we weren't very high. If we don't hit a trunk head on, maybe. This is a razorforest, though. If we hit a grove of razorleaves, there won't be anything left but chopped meat.

The timeless moment shattered, the draek plowed into the trees, and Kei lost consciousness with something like relief.

"Two," said Erin, staring at the sky with a satisfied smile. "They both went into the trees."

Karl winced. Plowing into the ground at high speed did not seem like a pleasant way to die. *Then again, are there any?* "As promised."

Morg spat on the ground. "I still say these orders make no fucking sense. Lord fucking Adrian's gone off his . . ."

"Enough." He'd never liked the big Corsan, who he

suspected had been a bandit before he joined up with Valos and Adrian. Morg was quick enough with his notched, ugly great sword, but Karl was beginning to find his mouth something of a trial. "Lord Adrian has yet to lead us astray."

Morg spread his hands. "We should just kill them, is all I'm sayin'."

"You can kill the monk," said Erin, grinning like a cat.

The Corsan snorted, but didn't comment.

"Or perhaps the cold has affected your wits?" she went on. Morg's eyes narrowed, and he turned on one heavy heel and stomped off down the path. Karl looked at the swordswoman quizzically.

"Cold? It's not that cold yet."

"You didn't hear?"

"Hear what?"

"Two nights ago Morg suggested to Melody that they . . . ah . . . share blankets.' Somewhat forcefully, I understand."

Karl rolled his eyes. "I'm surprised she didn't slit his throat."

"Apparently she let him take his clothes off, then marched him into the woods at knife-point and pushed him in a stream." Erin mock-shivered. "Brrr."

He couldn't help laughing. "He should know better."

"I don't think he's the best apple in the barrel."

"How come he never tried it with you?"

"Pre-emptive action. I caught him looking at me one day, while we were cleaning off in the river, and threatened to castrate him if he ever came near me again."

"Under the circumstances, I don't blame you."

"Besides," she said, stretching her arms over her head and yawning. "I prefer the clean cut type."

"Right."

They both tensed at the sound of footsteps on the path, and

relaxed as Aff turned the corner, waving cheerfully. His un-strung bow, taller than he was, was lashed to his back, and his leathers were dyed forest green.

"They're coming up the path," said the youth, once he'd gotten closer. "Sarth is keeping pace with them."

Karl nodded; for all his size, the Diem axeman could be sur-prising stealthy when he wanted to. "Just the two of them?"

"The monk and the lady." Aff raised an eyebrow. "It hardly seems fair."

"Remember our job."

"Kill the monk, threaten the woman until some man in black shows up, then retreat." Aff shrugged. "Doesn't make a lot of sense, but what does these days?"

"As long as you remember. And I want that monk down as fast as possible. He's probably got at least one demon with him, and if he manages to call it in it could be trouble."

"Demons die the same as anything else when you put an arrow in their eye."

"Assuming they even *have* eyes," said Erin. "I've seen de-mons that are nothing but a big gooey mass of tentacles. And when they catch you, they pull your arms and legs . . ."

"Erin," said Karl patiently. If she had been attempting to discomfit the youngster, though, it hadn't worked. Aff just smiled and nodded.

"Good thing I'll be up a tree, then."

"Go and find a spot," said Karl. "And warn Melody and Morg."

"On my way." The archer stepped past Erin and disap-peared around the switchback. Erin was staring down the trail, shaking her head, until Karl put a hand on her shoulder.

"Come on. We should get ready."

"Karl, if I were grabbed by some horrible demon and was

about to be ripped limb from limb, would you come charging in to certain death to save me?"

"Gods no!"

She rolled her eyes. "I thought not."

"I'll admit I've grown fond of your company" —he looked sly, so badly that she laughed— "but certain death is certain death."

"What about nearly-certain death?"

Karl sighed. "Go and find a spot, would you?"

She turned and walked past him. "I just want to know how much I can count on you . . ."

He gave her a prod from behind, and she stumbled off around the bend, laughing. Karl looked down the path one last time, shook his head, and followed her.

SARTH'S SIGNAL WAS a rough-sounding crack, the sound of a limb snapping off a tree. Karl perked up, jammed between the bare trunk of a razorleaf and a boulder, and kept his eyes on the path. Soon enough he could hear the Khaevs coming, two sets of foot-steps, and then they came around the switchback. It occurred to Karl, distantly, that this was the first time he'd actually laid eyes on his pursuers.

The woman was in red-tinted armor, embellished with gold on the shoulder-blades and cunningly crafted to flatter her fig-ure. She wasn't wearing a helmet, and legendary Tashida good looks were obvious in her face. She was a little shorter than he'd expected, and wearing a bone-hilted short sword on either hip. The monk walked one step behind and to the right, in a traditional brown robe; he was massive next to the tiny noble-woman, picking his way up the forest path with a staff in one hand. His head was shaved, and his heavy-lidded eyes scanned the forest constantly.

No man in black. Karl didn't like that. He didn't like anything unexpected. *Lord Adrian did say he was going to show up at
some point, though. Maybe he's scouting in the woods? Or waiting behind
them, for some reason.* That didn't make a lot of sense, but Khaevs
had their own way of doing things. *In any case, it's a bit late to call
things off now.*

He eased his hand onto his sword, but didn't move. Aff had
the opening shot, and the plan was to let the archer pick his time.
Get that monk down. The woman shouldn't be a problem after that.

Something big moved, in the trees on the downslope side of
the trail. The monk half-turned to look, presenting a near-perfect target. Karl smiled tightly.

What happened next wasn't quite clear. He heard the snap-
hiss of the bowstring and saw the monk diving to one side, but
that seemed to have happened in the wrong order. He could
have sworn the man was throwing himself aside *before* the kid
fired. Karl blinked. Either way, the arrow flashed past into
the trees on the other side of the trail, and surprise was blown.
He unwedged himself from the boulder and pounded down the
slope, drawing his sword in one hand.

Aff was ahead of the pair, and Erin had positioned herself upslope as well. Sarth and Melody appeared out of the
brush behind them, and Morg, cursing, kicked his way out of
the brush on the downslope side of the trail, awkwardly drawing his massive sword. For his own part, Karl headed right for
the monk. Outnumbered six to two, normal travelers would
have surrendered, but he didn't expect a Khaev noble to give
up without a fight.

Charging down the hill gave him a lot of momentum, which
he used to his advantage. The monk was already on hands and
knees, and rolled to avoid getting skewered. Karl had expected
that, and swept sideways as soon as he regained his balance, but

the monk had somehow managed to hang on to his heavy oak staff and bring it around in time to check the blow. His eyes narrowed and he shouted something incomprehensible. In Karl's experience, this was bad news.

The noblewoman shrieked as Sarth approached, which left the big warrior somewhat handicapped. He couldn't simply cut her in half, since that would be against orders. Instead he raised his axe, threateningly, and she scrambled away from him.

The monk was back on his feet now, hefting his staff thoughtfully. Karl tried a couple of feints, but the Khaev didn't go for them. At some point, though, his attention shifted. Karl considered running him through but thought better of it at the last moment, ducking low and turning aside. A fist like a small boulder whistled over his head. Karl turned to find a vaguely human-shaped mound of earth had clawed its way free of the track. A pair of the earth-demons were already heading for Erin and Morg, and another had reared up behind Melody.

"Melody!" Karl ducked another swipe as he shouted. The girl heard him just in time, rolling out of the demon's path and simultaneously planting a pair of knives in its stomach. This didn't seem to bother it very much, and the Tellenna backed away hurriedly. Behind her, the noblewoman moved to duck behind the burly monk, and went down with an 'oof' as Sarth caught her in the stomach with the flat of his axe. The Diem stepped past the Khaev to deal with the demon.

Erin poked at one of the demons, ineffectually, and dodged a couple of swipes. The other creature sprouted a pair of arrows, one after the other. When that didn't work Aff jumped down from the tree, landing behind the pair and drawing his sword. Morg took a swing, which the creature blocked with its forearm, and he frantically parried a swipe in return.

In the meantime, Karl found himself in trouble. His short

sword wasn't doing much more than nicking the demon's outer skin. *A good thrust would probably hurt it, but then my sword's stuck in the damn thing.* He backed away and parried, pensively. The creature was slow, at least, and relatively easy to avoid. But a sudden pain at the backs of his knees reminded Karl that he'd forgotten the monk, who drove him to the ground. Karl rolled aside, leaving his sword behind, and the demon followed with a series of blows that shook the ground.

The monk spun around, faster than Karl would have thought possible for a man his size, and advanced on Aff. The archer had just managed to sink his sword to the hilt into a demon's back when the Khaev whipped six feet of oak into the side of his head, knocking him off the path entirely and sending him rolling down the slope. The demon roared—a deep, resounding growl—and Morg's next stroke cut it in half at the waist, both sections losing cohesiveness in mid-air so that a shower of dirt and pebbles rattled to the ground. The big Corsan whooped and advanced on the monk, who dodged his first strike without apparent effort and swept his legs out from under him. Morg hit the ground hard.

Karl rolled, and rolled again, until his out-thrown hand met no resistance—the edge of the trail, and no more room to run. The demon's features were virtually non-existent, but somehow it contrived to look satisfied at finally catching its prey. Before its blow could land, though, Sarth's axe swept its head from its shoulders, and the body collapsed onto Karl as a heap of rocks and dust. Karl nodded his thanks and regained his feet in time to see Erin dueling with the monk, steel clattering against wood, and Melody advancing on the Khaev from behind.

The monk saw her coming, from the corner of his eye, and shouted again.

"Jyo-raku!"

For a moment, time seemed to come to a halt. The whole scene looked as though it had been *stretched*, somehow, as if what Karl could see was paint on a canvas that was slowly being ripped apart. The sunlight faded for an instant and then returned, leaving an extra figure on the trail—a lithe, thin form surrounded by shadows that flowed over his body like heavy black smoke.

The newcomer lashed out with one arm, and his aura of shadows flashed out into a blade thinner than the sharpest razor. Melody flipped backward, , out of harm's way, and Sarth hefted his axe threateningly. Before Karl could call out, the shadow-thing took a step toward the Diem and slashed twice, impossibly fast. Sarth blinked once, then fell apart; neatly sliced into three separate pieces, axe and all. Bloody mist filled the air.

Karl found his voice.

"Out! Get out of here!"

Erin was already leaving, backing away from the monk a few feet before sprinting up the trail. Morg, who'd regained his feet and was fending off the remaining earth-demon, dealt the thing a final slash that reduced it to shards and followed her. Karl ran the other way, leaving his sword behind. Only Melody hesitated. Karl knew something about the oaths she'd taken as a Blood Angel—never leaving a fight while an opponent was still standing was definitely one of them—but those oaths only applied to mortal foes, not demons. She caught up with Karl easily, just around the next bend, and favored him with a wide smile.

Crazy. All Tellena are crazy. Karl panted, trying not to think about Aff or the way Sarth's blood had sprayed. *Fucking crazy.*

KAGERIN SHUZAN SNIFFED the air suspiciously. It had the smell of old, wet stone. A Khaev building would never have been allowed to grow so musty, but the Palace was full of forgotten corridors and hidden sub-basements where the cleaning staff never ventured. To Shuzan, it smelled like a tomb.

"Moriseki . . ."

"I haven't brought you down here to murder you," said the old lady dryly, "if that's what you're thinking. Besides, you're armed and I'm not, and you're Fifty-Fourth of Two Hundred. If anything I should be the one worrying."

Shuzan's mouth hung open a moment, until he closed it with a decisive snap. *That wasn't exactly what I was worried about.* It had obviously been a long time since this corridor had even been swept, much less patrolled. *Who knows who could be lurking down here?* His hand dropped to the hilt of his sword.

When Moriseki noticed, she rolled her eyes. "Please try not to kill anyone, Lord Kagerin. You're quite safe, I assure you."

Shuzan released his sword with an effort. "Of course."

"We're almost there. Around this corner."

There was a shuffle of movement from around the corner as Moriseki's voice carried to whoever was behind it, When they turned a moment later they found a pair of young women greeting them with grim salutes. Both were slight and lithe-looking, in the manner of draekeres, and Shuzan decided the one on the right was actually quite attractive in a too-young sort of way. They stood in front of a windowless wooden door.

"Greetings, mistress," said one of the girls. Both bowed respectfully, first to Moriseki and then to Shuzan. He gave them an absent nod in return.

"Greetings. Has there been any change?"

"None," said the girl on the left. "He eats, sleeps, and waits."

"He has been cared for?"

"In all particulars."

"Good. Admit no one after us."

"Yes, mistress!" they chorused together. Moriseki opened the door with a key from her belt and motioned Shuzan to follow.

He was practically burning with curiosity at this point. *Who is the Mistress of Draekeres keeping down here in the dark?* The palace had its own jail, far from the lords' apartments. *Why not use that? Obviously, because you have a prisoner you don't want anyone else to know about.*

The room beyond the door was lit only by a dim candle in one corner. Shuzan blinked as his eyes adjusted from the torch-light of the corridor. Moriseki waited, too, as though she were used to this. Once she could make out basic shapes, she gestured to what turned out to be a couple of chairs. Shuzan took one, gingerly, and tried to see the rest of the room. There seemed to be a bed, with a single figure on it; a basin and a chamber pot, and not much else. *Still, pretty well appointed for a jail cell.*

"It's Moriseki," said the old woman softly. "I've brought Kagerin Shuzan to see you."

"I know." The voice that came from the darkness was a soft hiss. "Even through a mortal's eyes, I can see well enough in the shadows."

"Who are you?" blurted Shuzan, drawing a reproachful look from the Mistress of Draekeres. The dark shape gave a kind of hissing laugh.

"Somewhat difficult to answer. What this mortal's name once was I have no idea, but at the moment you can address me as Jyo-raku."

"Jyo-raku." Shuzan mouthed the unfamiliar name. "You're a spirit of shadow."

"Very perceptive." The figure turned to Moriseki. "Did you have any trouble bringing him here?"

"None." The woman shook her head. "As you predicted, he seemed interested from the start."

"Of course." It sounded somehow menacing. "Kagerin

Shuzan, the Fifty-Fourth of Two Hundred."

What the hell is going on here? The look in Jyo-raku's eyes was far too smug. *He couldn't possibly know about Shia . . .*

"What do you want with me?"

"I came to Lady Tashida some time ago, Lord Kagerin, in order to enlist her help. A sorcerer named Ilam Adrian, in the employ of the rebel Lord Valos, had located one of the artifacts known as Bound Blades." The figure paused. "I take it from your expression that you're familiar with the legends?"

"I understood that none of the Blades still existed."

"Not quite true, as this Ilam Adrian and his demonic backers apparently discovered. They set out to find the Blade. Having acquired this information through channels of my own, I set myself to stopping them. I asked for Lady Tashida's help."

"Why?"

"Surely you can see that a Blade in Imperial hands would be unfortunate for your occupation."

"I realize that." Shuzan waved a hand impatiently. "I mean why did you come to Shiori?"

"She was a Blade commander, had the ear of the Mistress of Draekeres, and—how shall I put this—seemed like someone who would not object to being contacted by a demon."

"Great." Unfortunately, that assessment was all too accurate. Shiori would jump at the chance to capture a Bound Blade, and the fact that it was a demon doing the asking made things even more exciting. *Empty-headed little idiot.* "And she took two draekeres with her."

"Along with a few mercenaries, a monk, and myself."

"But —"

"This," he gestured to his body, "is only an aspect. At the moment I'm keeping watch over Lady Tashida."

"They're okay, then?" Some of the weight lifted from

Shuzan's chest.

"Yes. Thus far."

"Tell her to come back!"

"I'm afraid the Imperial sorcerer would then obtain the Bound Blade. That cannot be allowed."

"I don't care—" *About the Bound Blade, or about Shiori. Shia...*

"Wait a moment."

The candlelight flickered, throwing shifting shadows all over the room. Shuzan leaned forward. "What?"

"They are under attack."

"*What?* Do something!"

Moriseki cut in. "Attack by whom?"

"I must incarnate," hissed the spirit. "We've come too far to give up now. This aspect will vanish."

"Wait! Where are they?"

"West, at the base of the Shieldwall."

"Where—"

"There is no more time." There was a strange sense of suction, as though something had departed the room, and the shadowed form slumped to the bed. Shuzan rushed to its side. It turned out to be the body of an old man, face twisted in horror, who had apparently been dead for some time. He waited a long moment before rising.

"Moriseki."

The Mistress of Draekeres was muttering to herself. "Something must have gone wrong."

"Moriseki!"

"What?" she snapped.

"I'm going after them."

"Just like that?"

"Are you coming or not?"

"But Lord Tashida—"

"I thought we went over this already. Lord Tashida has not forbidden you to leave, so I will take full responsibility." Shuzan leaned closer. "You helped send them out there. If something has happened, I am not going to be pleased with you."

Moriseki, for the first time, looked a bit intimidated. "Y . . . yes. Of course I'll come. Two of my people are with them."

"Good. We leave at nightfall." Shuzan turned on his heel and stalked out of the chamber.

TASHIDA SHIORI OPENED her eyes, and for a moment there were two copies of Shikidai Gota standing over her. He came back into focus only slowly; she sat up with a groan, feeling a line of pain across her stomach. The armor had helped, but not much.

"My lady," the monk said gravely. "Are you all right?"

"F . . . Fine." Shiori looked around. There was blood everywhere, and pieces of one body, but no sign of the other attackers. "What happened?"

"I called on Jyo-raku."

"Oh."

The demon was standing, arms folded, in the middle of the track. He looked somehow more solid. Earlier, his presence had always been a wavering thing, as though a sudden break in the clouds could sweep him away on a tide of sunlight. Now the shadows around him boiled and snaked, defiant of the light overhead. The chill emanating from him was palpable, even a few feet away.

Lady Tashida remembered herself. "Why didn't you do so earlier? We could have been killed."

"He was reluctant to call on my powers, lady," hissed the spirit, "because doing so is dangerous."

"More dangerous than being chopped limb from limb?"

"Dangerous to me." The spirit inclined its head. "You're

lucky I rescued you at all."

"If it's so dangerous, then why . . ."

Jyo-raku sniffed the air, his expression invisible under a mask of shadow. "I think," he rasped, "that this expedition may be worth my while after all."

KEI STOOD ALONE, in the dark, in another dream.

The same damn dream. Somewhere, her real self grinned cynically. *Too late, this time. I'm already dead.*

She was nine years old, dressed only in a nightshirt.

Footsteps in the dark. She turned, heart pounding. A form emerged from the shadows, familiar but somehow sinister. A face that seemed to float in darkness, disconnected from anything else.

"Kei." The voice was a hiss.

"Sh . . . Shuzan?" *Shuzan wouldn't call me Ke . . .*

No. Another face, cloaked in an aura of shadow that covered it like a boiling mask, its voice a familiar hiss.

"Kei."

Then she found herself standing on rough forest ground. Behind her was an archway, many times the height of a man, the stone engraved with a complex script she didn't recognize. The arch was filled with tiny purple sparks, flowing around and over each other in a complex dance. On the other side of the arch, she knew, lay something horrible. But on her side . . .

. . . the spirit of darkness.

"Heaven's Gate," it hissed.

This isn't right. What is Jyo-raku doing in my dream?

"Kei."

The spirit took her by the arm, and its touch was ice. She felt her flesh numb, freeze, and crack. Then it was pushing her, and she was falling through the archway. The purple light grew, and a barely heard whine ascended to a horrible crescendo. The hissing voice sounded somehow satisfied.

"Kei . . ."

"Kei!"

I'm dead. Leave me alone.

"Kei." The voice sounded familiar, somehow. "Come on. Up."

Something poked her in the ribs, hard. Kei shifted positions and grunted. *It was more comfortable when I was falling.* Now it felt like she was lying on the ground, or more accurately on the twisted root system of some old tree. Her shoulder burned with a dull, hot ache that pulsed with every heartbeat. Darkness threatened again, and behind the darkness she could feel the comforting wind and the fall that never ended.

"Kei!" Something poked her in the ribs again. "You're fine. Time to get up."

Kit . . .

Kei opened her eyes, and found herself staring at the forest canopy dappled by the fading evening light. This high in the mountains, the ubiquitous oaks and maples were mixed with needled pines and razorleaves. The leaves of the trees whipped back and forth, as though trying to escape, and as she watched a dozen of them broke free of their moorings and started the long fall toward her. They only made it halfway before a wind caught them and swept them into the forest.

Kit filled her vision, waving a hand back and forth in front of Kei's eyes. "Hello? You there?" The girl looked mostly unhurt, though her hair was a mess and most of the skin on one side of her face had been scraped and torn away, and was already starting to scab over.

Kei blinked and tried to remember which muscles controlled her voice. She made it, eventually. "Kit?"

"Good! How many fingers am I holding up?"

"One." Kei blinked again. *Fingers? Was that important?* "Kit . . ."

"Take it slow for a minute. I think you hit your head in the crash."

Crash? Memory came flooding back: the demons, the fight, Kit's smaller hand gripping her own so tightly she thought her bones would crack, the horrible spray of blood from the draek's broken wing and the long spiral to the ground. And then, just *before* impact, darkness had surrounded her. Kei gulped a deep breath, as though she'd been punched in the stomach, and blinked tears back from her eyes. *Right, the crash.*

"I think you'll be okay. You don't seem to be bleeding, or even bruising that much, and you didn't break anything major. That shoulder is going to hurt for a while, though." Kit paused, looking at her Wing Leader. "Kei? Keep talking, would you?"

"I'm . . ." She tried to pull herself up with her left arm and it wouldn't support her; her shoulder screamed in agony. She quickly threw out her other arm to hold herself up, breathing hard. "I'm here."

"Good. That's good." Kit sat back. "No hurry."

"What happened?"

"About what you'd expect when you hit the ground that hard."

"And we're still alive?" She laughed through a raw throat. "Who's idea of a joke is that?"

"You did a great job landing." Kit beamed with genuine appreciation. "Dodged a stand of razorleaves and those big rocks."

"I had no control at all." She remembered hauling on the reins, and being utterly ignored by the dying draek. "It was a gods-damned miracle."

"Oh." This didn't seem to faze Kit. "Well, we missed them."

"Are you okay?"

"Fine." Kit patted her chest. "No problems."

Unbelievable. "The draeks?"

This time the younger woman shook her head. "Both dead."

Great. The fact that she'd survived the battle was slowly starting to sink in. Kei felt her daze clearing, just in time to understand the new problems she was facing. "Any idea where the hell we landed?"

"As far as I can tell, we were knocked a bit north in the battle and crashed somewhere on the slope. So the trail Shiori and Gota were following should be somewhere to the south."

"Any idea which way is south?"

Kit pointed. "I could see the sun earlier."

The sun was long gone by now, fallen behind the mountains to the west, and the sky was rapidly darkening. Even in the half-light, though, Kei could tell the eastern sky looked particularly gloomy. Kit followed her gaze and nodded.

"There's a storm coming. Hear the wind?"

"Yeah." Kei tried to move again, and this time got only a twinge from her shoulder as long as she kept it steady.

"Hey! You shouldn't be walking around."

"We need to find shelter." Kei grimaced. "Once the storm breaks, we can try to get back to the trail."

Kit bounded to her feet. "Right. Think you can walk?"

"If not, are you going to carry me?" Kit opened her mouth, and Kei shook her head hurriedly. "That was a joke. I can walk." She got to her feet, painfully. "See?"

"Good."

"Have you looked around at all?"

"Not really. I didn't want to leave you."

"Thanks." Kei glanced about. "Let's head uphill. Maybe we can find a cave or a fallen tree or something. Keep an eye out."

Kit's grin got wider. "Right behind you, Wing Leader."

chapter 9

> "When falling from a mountain, you will find that flapping your arms makes little difference in the long run."
>
> −Diem Proverb

L ATE AFTERNOON HAD worn into early evening by the time the last bet was settled, the last drunk thrown out, and Calio and his men were able to restore enough order to set up the central table for the third game. Veil sat in silence—mandatory, since the players were not allowed to communicate before the game began—and listened to the buzz of the crowd. She found herself to be the talk of the room, at least for the moment.

Her lips curled slightly as she heard the theories that circulated around her. The most common seemed to be that she was someone's slave, raised to play dominion or acquired for that purpose from one of the Red Hills tribes. Some of the spectators thought that Calio was cheating, somehow rigging the games. A few suggested she was a demon in disguise, which made Veil chuckle under her breath.

If I told them the real story, they wouldn't believe me. That made her think of Corvus. *After this, it'll be time to go find him.*

She shivered at a sudden chill wind, totally out of place in the crowded heat of Calio's parlor. It took her a moment to place the feeling. *My dreams.* She closed her eyes, tentatively, and opened them with a gasp when she found the ice-girl staring back from under her eyelids. Veil leaned down and mumbled as quietly as she could.

"Can you hear me?"

"Yes." Sybian's voice was high and distant, the tinkle of falling ice. "You don't have to talk. Just think hard."

"What do you want?"

"Where's Corvus?"

She shook her head, which caused a few of the bystanders to look at her oddly. "I don't know. I'm meeting him tonight."

"Irritating." The spirit radiated disapproval. "Still, it's unlikely Saya would be stupid enough to stand against him directly."

"Who?"

"Saya." She pronounced it with a long vowel, *sei-uh*. "She's the one who's trying to impede our progress."

"Progress toward *what*? I can't be much of a help if you don't tell what you're doing."

That came out oddly, Veil thought. *When did I decide I was helping her?*

"It's not important right now. I just wanted to warn you that I've lost track of her, which probably means she's planning on causing trouble."

"Great. Anything I can do about it?"

"Just be on your guard, and if something happens stay out of the way. I can handle Saya."

That should be comforting, but somehow I don't feel any better.

"Round Three!" shouted Calio, prompting an answering roar from the crowd. "Nazareen the T'bach, Velyn Greenroad, Whitespear House's Hugo, and," he raised his eyes conspiratorially, "'Veil, the mystery girl.'"

Mystery girl? Veil couldn't help but laugh. She got up from her seat and made her way to the table, Calio's enforcers clearing a path through the onlookers. It was the same as before: four pots of stones in a central depression, surrounded by a huge grid. Beyond a small clear space established for the players the spectators were pressed in tightly. The parlor smelled of the sweat of too many bodies in too small a space, mixed liberally with alcohol and various unidentifiable fumes.

One by one, the other players took their chairs. Nazareen the T'bach was a corpulent whale of a man who barely fit into the seat provided for him; leather and wood creaked under the pressure of his weight. He was balding underneath his funny little square hat, but sported a pair of enormous mustaches that made him look as though he'd just swallowed a pair of long-tailed cats. When he waved to the audience, there was a little bit of cheering.

Velyn was thin, with stubble-short hair and ice-blue eyes that missed very little. He wore a jacket with the same blue-and-white sleeve design as the two youths she'd trounced earlier in the afternoon, and he shot her a venomous look as he settled down at the table. His glance at Nazareen was contemptuous, and he didn't bother playing to the crowd. Velyn didn't seem very popular, though there was a great deal of drunken shouting from a corner occupied entirely by white-and-blue cuffed young men.

Hugo, the last, was only a few years older than Veil. He was a handsome young man with dark skin and brown hair drawn back in a ponytail. He could have lived in her mansion in the Red Hills and she would never have commented. His clothing was elaborate, but Veil's eyes were drawn to the collar around his neck. *He must be a slave.* Calio had introduced him as belonging to the Whitespear House, but she hadn't realized he'd meant it literally.

Still, Hugo was the only one of the three to pay her much

attention. He waved, and she waved back, feeling a little bit sheepish. Veil found herself blushing, incongruously, and fought the feeling down. *I've still got a game to win.*

"Choose your colors," came Calio's voice from somewhere in the background. Veil reached into the center for a pot of stones and found Velyn reaching for the same one; their fingers brushed, and he practically snarled. Veil picked another pot and set it down in front of her, pulling the top off to look at the color.

Black again. This apparently had some significance to the onlookers, who gave a kind of collective sigh. Veil wondered if it was a good omen or a bad one. Nazareen drew blue, Velyn red, and Hugo green. That gave Hugo the first turn; he clicked his stone down confidently and sat back in his chair. Veil placed her own piece on the opposite side. Nazareen fumbled his stone between fingers like sausages, but finally managed to get it onto the board, and Velyn slapped his piece down almost without looking at it. He kept his eyes on the other players. Veil found his gaze unnerving, but she could hardly protest, so she looked down at the board instead and ran her fingers over the cool ceramic stones in her pot.

Here we go.

THE YOUNG WOMAN was clearly frightened, and just as clearly trying not to show it.

"C'mon." The man accosting her was typical dock scum, forearms swelled by years of lifting and carrying; the same activity had apparently depleted his wits, not to mention his morals. A couple of his friends lurked behind him, one sporting a braid that fell past his waist and the other a stomach to match his musculature. The latter had long since gone beyond the realm where belts were of any help, and had been forced to secure his pants with a length of cord.

"C'mon," the leader repeated. "You owe, and it's time to pay up."

"I said I don't know what you're talking about!" Her voice squeaked a little. "Would you get lost?"

"Ask your boyfriend over there. It's only a lousy couple of eyes—more than you're worth, I'd say."

"Gregory!" The woman poked the man who'd escorted her to the bar and hissed. "Do something!"

Unfortunately for her, Gregory was in no state to defend her honor. He lay face-down on the bar, muttering slurred accusations between alcohol-scented snores. She poked him again, a little harder, but without any effect. The woman spun as the dockhand put his heavy paw on her shoulder.

"Now, you're comin' with us, you see?" He put his hand on her shoulder, and the woman squeaked. The dockhand grinned, and there was a tremendous guffaw from the fat man.

"I believe," said a new, deep voice, "that the lady does not wish to accompany you."

"Fuck you, you . . ." The three thugs turned, snarling, but at the sight of the newcomer they dropped their angry expressions and stared.

"You were saying?"

The new man was huge, even compared to the dockyard toughs. Not fat, or even over-muscled, he was simply built on a larger scale than normal. His face was hard, with an iron set to his jaw that suggested someone who possessed no sense of humor whatsoever. The man wore gray: gray pants, a gray sleeveless shirt, and a gray cloak that hung limply behind him. His head had been shaved, and the only hint of color on his person was a brilliant red skullcap; his eyes were invisible behind smoked-glass spectacles.

There were three people behind him: a big one, almost as

tall as the leader and much broader of shoulder; a thin one, to the point of appearing consumptive; and a breathtakingly beautiful woman in coarse black robes, her face framed by raven-dark curls. All except the thin man wore bored expressions, as though they'd watched this scene a dozen times before. Tthe thin one couldn't stop giggling, as though he'd also watched the scene before but found it endlessly entertaining.

The leader of the toughs quickly recovered his nerve. "What the fuck do you want?" he shouted, then gaped in surprise as his fat friend elbowed his way to the fore.

"Mercy, y'honor. He didn't mean that. Please, y'honor, we didn't mean no harm."

The big newcomer's expression was unmoved. "Did you, or did you not, intend to accost this young woman?"

"We . . ." The fat man looked at his friends frantically.

"You know the penalty for lying to me," said the newcomer, gravely.

"We did!" he burst out. "Mercy, please, y'honor! Mercy!"

The newcomer tipped his head to one side, considering. "Confession is good for the soul, it is true. But on the other hand, I doubt this is a first offense."

"No! Please, y'honor, we never meant . . ."

"Fuck you!" The big dockhand pushed his way back to the fore. "I'm not scared of you, you freak . . ."

With that he swung a brutal uppercut at the newcomer's chin. The big man—surprisingly swift for someone of his bulk—sidestepped, grabbed the dockhand's arm at the wrist and elbow, and broke it in one clean motion. The tough screamed and fell backwards, and the newcomer raised his hands.

"I've seen enough. Chemura! In the name of the gods, I pronounce judgment!"

"Noooo—"

The fat man's scream ended in a nasty, splattering sound. A whirlwind of flame and blood filled the room. The bar exploded outwards in a thousand shards, and there were screams from the other patrons who hadn't had the sense to leave while they'd had the chance. The whole thing lasted only a few moments, and was punctuated by the thin man's mad giggling.

Once it was over, the place was silent except for the steady drip, drip, drip of blood from the ceiling. There was nothing left of the three toughs except a greasy black stain; the object of their affection lay nearby, torn in half. The big man lowered his hands.

"Good afternoon."

All four turned. Daggerwind entered the bar judiciously, stepping across the corpses of a pair of whores and avoiding a puddle of blood. A drop of the stuff from the ceiling landed on his shoulder, and he brushed it off fastidiously.

"I assume," he said, "that you are the one they call the Judge?"

The big man nodded solemnly. "I am. My followers are Yor, Vincent, and Nala." His expression was unreadable behind his dark glasses; his gray outfit was somehow untouched by bloodstains. "And you are?"

"My name is Daggerwind, and I've come to retain your services."

Vincent giggled, high-pitched and mad. The Judge shook his head gravely.

"My services are not retained. I owe allegiance only to the gods."

"May they rest in peace," rasped Yor.

"Excuse me," said Daggerwind, "I misspoke. More accurate to say we have a convergence of interests."

"Oh?"

"Who is the greatest killer of all time?"

"Elor the Collector," answered the Judge promptly. "In the Fourth Dynasty. When they finally caught up with him, he'd filled an entire basement with his victim's hearts."

"Greater than that."

The Judge's eyes narrowed. "You mean . . ."

"Yes."

Nala looked up at her master. "Who?"

"Ebon Death," said the Judge.

"He's not real," said Yor in low tones. "Never was."

"He's real enough. Or so this man claims." Daggerwind shrugged. "He could be lying about who he is, so I understand if you don't want to bother . . ."

"No," said the Judge. "You've piqued my interest."

"I thought I might have."

"So where is he?"

Daggerwind smiled.

ISOBEL SMILED, SATISFIED, as the group she was looking for rounded the corner of the alley, headed for the end which had only a single door. They didn't notice her. She'd taken pains to find a shadow deep enough to blend with her blacks, but in any case they looked preoccupied. There were four of them—a big one, clearly the leader, plus two other men and a cloaked figure.

Isobel forced herself to concentrate on remaining still and fading into the darkness. Part of her itched to draw and charge, without thought to the consequences. Zhin's opinions to the contrary, though, she *had* learned to suppress that aspect of her personality when necessary.

It's just not necessary that often. Isobel grinned savagely and edged toward the corner. The alley was two turns off a main street, and this late in the evening there weren't any passersby, so all she had to worry about was anyone left behind by her quarry.

If these are even the right people. The bouncer at the Goldspin had assured her that his description was accurate. Given that he was obviously aware of her reputation, it was unlikely that he'd been lying, but there was always the chance he was mistaken. *Though it's a pretty recognizable bunch. How many six foot six men in red skullcaps are wandering around?*

So what do I know? She'd started out trying to find Corvus, but it had quickly become obvious that someone else was making the same search. News got around quickly in Corsa's underground, and after visiting a few establishments she'd learned that the big man—who was called "The Judge", for reasons that escaped her—was after the same target. He apparently had a good source of information, and by following his tracks she'd zeroed in on the swordsman pretty quickly, until they'd finally arrived at this middle-of-nowhere alley.

So what do I know? Are these the guys who killed Alled? Given the Judge's reputation, it seems likely. Everyone seems to agree that he's either a sorcerer himself or has one on his side. But why are they looking for Corvus? Tavern rumor also seemed to agree that the Judge was a raving madman. Everyone stayed out of his way as much as possible, since it was never clear what side he'd come down on. Several of her sources had described him as some kind of religious fanatic. *So why is he after Corvus?*

For that matter, why am I after Corvus? The question set her stomach to fluttering, a feeling with which Isobel was decidedly unfamiliar. *He's the one I've been looking for. The only one who's ever beaten me.* But the fight hadn't gone quite as planned. *He was supposed to kill me, and he didn't. So now what do I do?* Tracking the man down seemed the only reasonable option, but she wasn't sure what she'd do when she found him.

Worry about that later. Here goes nothing.

"Lord," whispered Yor, "is this entirely wise?"

"I thought you were the one saying there was no such thing as Ebon Death," said Vincent. He giggled. "Changed your tune in the dark of the night, have you?"

"Forget Ebon Death." Yor waved a hand. "They could have two dozen men in there."

"Two dozen or two hundred," said Nala, "the gods will protect the faithful."

"Nala is correct," rumbled the Judge. "I will go in, alone, and confront whatever terrors they see fit to send against me. You three remain here and keep the entrance secure."

"Yes, my lord," they chorused.

The Judge opened the door and stepped inside, unafraid, letting it swing closed behind him.

SHE POKED HER head around the corner and there they were, three of them, anyway. The thin man, the bruiser, and the cowled figure. *The leader must have gone inside. Now what?*

She weighed her options. They were too far away for a sneak attack, and it would be difficult to kill them all without announcing her presence to anyone inside. *So maybe it's time for a little subtlety. If I can get just a bit closer, I can probably pull it off.* Assuming none of the three was a sorcerer. If that was the case, all bets were off.

Isobel took a deep breath and stepped into the alley, purposely clapping her shoes against the cobbles. All three spun at the noise, and the little one emitted a high-pitched giggle. Isobel bowed politely, while they were still a bit stunned.

The tall man recovered first, his hand dropping to his sword. "Who are you?" His voice was a deep growl.

"Name's Isobel." She took a calm step forward. "I've been

looking for you."

"Looking for *us*?" said the women in the robe.

"Not for *you*, precisely. I'm looking for the same person you are, and this seemed the easiest way to find him." Isobel spread her hands and took another step forward. She knew, from practical experience, that she could draw her blades from any position in a fraction of a second. "I'm looking for a guy named Corvus. Big guy, black clothes, fights like a demon."

The women gave her an odd look. "Who *are* you?"

"It doesn't matter," said the tall man in a whisper. "This isn't your business, girl. If it's revenge you're after, Corvus will be dead soon enough."

Dead? Isobel found the thought horrifying. *He can't be dead. Not before I get to fight him again.* "Where is he?"

"I said that it was none of your concern."

"Though if you'd like to stick around," giggled the thin one, "we'd be happy to play with you."

"If you've touched him, it damn well is my concern." Isobel put her hands to her sides, still smiling. "Where?"

The tall man rolled his eyes. "One of his companions, then. How touching."

There was a hoarse scream from behind the door.

VEIL WATCHED, ABSENTLY, as a bead of sweat rolled down Nazareen's face. It looked as though it was going to drip off and splash onto the board, but got lost at the last moment in the folds of fat under his chin. The piece in his hand spun, over and over, and he flicked it mindlessly with one finger. Velyn, whose turn was next, was practically vibrating with impatience. He kept trying to catch Calio's eye, as though asking the manager to force the fat gambler to make a move.

Eventually, finally, Nazareen set his piece down exactly

where Veil had known he would. She almost felt sorry for him.

It's too sweet, isn't it? He can't resist. She'd left an opening that looked exploitable; on a border as closely fought as the line between black and blue, that was not something that could be passed up. So the gambler almost *had* to go for it. *But that lets me stabilize that whole east-west line, and link it up over* there, *and that saves the group Velyn was attacking.* It was neat, tidy, and absolutely devastating.

It had been apparent from the start of the match that Velyn and Hugo were in it together. The slave boy seemed almost apologetic about it, shaking his head in Veil's general direction as he defended his corner quite competently and pushed a few attacks in her direction. His heart wasn't in it, and she quickly discovered he had an aversion to close fighting, as he gave up on more than one battle he might have won.

Nazareen, on the other hand, loved close work. He fought for every point, leaving the black-blue border a long standstill. If it had just been him, Veil was fairly certain she could have won easily. H e was too defensive, so she'd turned an early advantage into a permanent gain.

Velyn seemed to think he could kill every stone she put down. He played as though the whole board was his territory, ripping savagely at her black groups with twisted trails of red stones. Fending him off while keeping Nazareen at bay was a bit of a trick, and, for the first part of the game, Veil found herself in retreat. But while Velyn was bent on her destruction, he wasn't above taking a shot at his erstwhile ally. Maneuvering Nazareen to leave an opening facing the gang leader led to a red-blue war that gave her some much-needed breathing space, which she used to neatly demolish Hugo's line. The boy seemed taken aback, playing frantic rearguard as Veil's black stones cut him to bits. By the time Velyn and Nazareen had settled their position, she'd taken enough green territory to ensure a healthy lead.

Hugo had started passing some time ago, his few remaining green groups standing out like jewels in a dark sea. After a few more exchanges, Nazareen sat back from the table, wiping his face with a handkerchief and shaking his head. That left Velyn, who kept throwing his stones into her backfield in a vain attempt to invade. Eventually, with Veil's territory covered in dead clumps of red stones, he had no choice but to admit defeat. The gang leader slammed an angry fist on the table, which made more than a few stones jump, and stalked away into the crowd.

"Veil wins!" Calio materialized at her side. His public voice was completely different from the nasty tone he'd used with Zhin; now he was pandering to the crowd. "The mystery girl is victorious! This is the biggest upset we've ever had!"

Here and there in the crowd were smiling faces, *beaming* faces. Despite her earlier victories, the odds against her must have been long. *I bet Zhin made a fortune.* Most of the spectators seemed a bit angry, though, which meant a lot of them must have lost money. Veil carefully occupied herself with clearing her stones from the board until she saw Zhin approaching with Calio and two of his guards.

Zhin was smiling as broadly as ever, but there was just a hint of a crack in his varnished façade.

"Brilliant. You're brilliant, Veil. I've never seen anyone play like that."

"I must agree." In a private conversation, Calio's voice had returned to normal. "We would love to know a little more about you. Where did you learn to play?"

"My brother taught me." Veil shook her head. "I don't really know how to play. I just . . ."

Her cheeks burned, but she was smiling broadly. Calio

nodded, interested, and she was about to launch into a description of her life to date when Zhin interrupted.

"I know you have a lot of questions for her, Calio, but we really need to get going. The atmosphere in here has gotten a little tense."

"Right." Veil looked up at him and got a 'keep quiet' glance in response. Calio turned to Zhin.

"Of course. Where should I have the purse delivered?"

"We'll take it now, if you don't mind."

The purse? Somehow, Veil had almost forgotten the money.

"Now?" Calio seemed perturbed. "But . . ."

"Now."

"I'm just not sure it's safe to walk the streets without an escort."

"I can handle myself."

What about me? Veil's lip twisted, but she kept the thought to herself.

"As you wish." Calio waved to one of his attendants. "I must admit I've underestimated you, Zhin. After last time . . ."

"Let's forget about last time."

"Can we expect the pleasure of your company again?"

"Not for a while," said Zhin. "I'm going out of town."

"I see."

The guard returned with two heavy leather satchels on a cord, which Zhin hung around his neck. They clinked as he moved, the heavy, dull clink of stacked gold coins.

"What about you, Miss Veil?"

"What?" Veil shook her head; she hadn't been paying attention.

"Will we have the pleasure of seeing you again?"

"Maybe . . . I mean, I . . ."

"She'll be going out of town, too," said Zhin, putting a hand protectively on her shoulder.

"Pity." Calio smiled, not very nicely. "Well, be safe, the both of you."

"Of course." Zhin pulled Veil by one shoulder. "Come on."

Calio's guards cleared a path to the exit by dint of some effort. A number of the patrons seemed interested in talking to Veil, and there were a number of shouted offers or threats. She shook her head, silently amazed, and followed Zhin up the stairs and back out onto the street. Night had fallen, and the moon rode through a half-misty sky. Veil stretched and took a deep breath. It seemed an eternity since she'd gone down into the cramped basement parlor.

Zhin was now visibly disturbed, pacing back and forth in front of the stone building as though looking for something. He kept muttering under his breath.

"Come on . . . Come on . . ."

"Zhin?"

"What?"

"What did you mean, when you said I was going out of town?"

"That?" He laughed. "Forget it. Calio's a crook. He's honest enough when you've got him where everyone can see, but if you'd stuck around he'd have strong-armed you into working for him. His goal in life is to find a slave who can beat all comers at dominion, so he can just sit back and pocket the money."

"You think he'd try to rob us?"

"No." Zhin waved a hand dismissively. "News would get around. It'd scare his customers off."

"So what are you worried about?"

"We just walked out of a den of thieves with six thousand eyes, what do you think I'm worried about?"

"I thought you said . . ."

"*Calio* wouldn't try to rob us. Once we're outside his joint, it's fair game. Most of the guys down there have sponsors to keep them safe, but not us. And Velyn did *not* look happy."

"So what are we sitting around here for? I thought you said to let you worry about this."

"I'm worrying about it, aren't I?" He shook his head. "Our escort should have been here by now."

"Escort?"

"My partner. If she doesn't show soon, we could be in trouble."

"You're in trouble," said a chiming voice that only Veil could hear. It startled her so badly she almost jumped, did a frantic double take, then thought hard.

"Trouble?"

"Saya's people are headed your way. Get moving, I'll try to keep you covered. That bozo any good with his sword?"

"I don't know."

Veil could hear Sybian's smirk. "You're about to find out. If push comes to shove, leave the money and run."

Great. She tapped Zhin on the shoulder, and he spun around.

"What?"

"I think we should leave. Now."

"My partner . . ."

"If she doesn't show up, we're just giving them more time to get ready for us."

"If she doesn't show up, I think we're in trouble no matter where we go."

Veil shook her head. "If we can get to the Red Stripe, we'll be fine."

"Why?"

"*My* partner will be able to handle it from there." *Okay, maybe I wouldn't call him a* partner, *but at least he left me a note . . .*

Zhin raised an eyebrow but didn't immediately comment.

Veil tapped her foot impatiently.

"Come on!"

"I don't know why I'm trusting you on this," he sighed. "Let's go."

"Are you any good with that sword?"

"Why?"

"Just thought I'd ask."

BEYOND THE DOOR was a cavernous space, dark except for a line of windows near the ceiling; these let in a tiny sliver of light, red with the sunset. The Judge let the door close behind him and waited a few moments for his eyes to adjust to the darkness.

"I know you're here," he said, to pass the time. "You might as well come out."

Corvus' voice echoed through the room. "You've been following me."

"I have." There wasn't much point in denying it. The Judge crossed his arms.

"Why? Are you working for those White Tigers, or whatever they were called?"

"I have come to offer salvation, Corvus." The Judge smiled, tightly. "You will thank me, in the end."

"Look." There was a sigh in the darkness. "You're going to die in a moment, one way or the other. Why not make things easier for me?"

"The gods protect their own. Particularly from the likes of you." The Judge squinted. He could make out two faint shapes on either side of one of the many pillars that held up the roof. Either one of them could be the swordsman in black. He slipped one hand behind his back and withdrew a pair of knives from their sheaths.

"You're determined to be unhelpful, then." Another sigh.

"We might as well get on with it."

"Indeed."

The Judge moved, whipping a dagger at one of the dark shapes. There was no sound, no shout or scrape of metal on armor. *So it's the other one.* He was already charging, putting all the power of his considerable bulk behind the long-knife in his other hand. The shadow didn't move, and a moment later he drove his blade to the hilt in . . .

. . . a sack of flour? But . . .

Pain flared across his back and he spun away. Corvus stood opposite him, sword in one hand; he held the Judge's dagger between two fingers in the other, as though he'd caught it in mid-flight.

That's not possible. The Judge smiled as he felt the blood trickle down his back. The cut was superficial. Clearly, Corvus meant to prolong their encounter. *So he is everything Daggerwind claimed he is. Ebon Death come again.* He raised his blade. *We'll see about that.*

Corvus, still mostly shrouded in shadow, raised an eyebrow. "If you've got any other tricks, now's the time."

"No tricks, sinner." The Judge spread his arms. "Just the vengeance of the gods."

"Crazy . . ."

"Chemura!"

The Judge's shout was answered by a roar and a flare of fire. Something huge and bright dropped into being between him and Corvus. The fire-spirit looked like a lion, but it was as tall as a stallion at the shoulder. Its mane and tail blazed with flame, and the claws on its forepaws glowed red-hot. Corvus took a step back, clearly not liking the odds, while the Judge chuckled quietly.

"Destroy him."

The great cat pounced, and Corvus vanished under a nimbus of yellow-white fire. The Judge lowered his arms.

"Too bad," he muttered, mostly to himself. "His soul . . ."

There was a shriek, high and horribly inhuman. A moment later the cat came flying backward, trailing smoke from a long cut on its flank, and hit the wall hard enough to crack the wooden timbers. The Judge barely had time to open his mouth before Corvus charged out of the cloud of smoke. He managed to raise his blade to defend himself, but the swordsman was fast, impossibly fast. His first stroke slipped under the Judge's guard and removed his hand at the wrist. Before he could scream, before the pain could even register, Corvus took off his head on the backswing.

SAYA RAISED HER arms, and light exploded all around her, shooting up into the sky in a column of brilliance that lasted only a tiny fraction of a second. Once it cleared, she looked at the shapes that surrounded her and nodded, satisfied. Saya waved a hand.

"Go. Find him and kill him."

THE SCREAM THREW the three temporarily off-guard. Isobel drew her knives with a flourish, but lost a precious second deciding what to do.

Which one's the sorcerer? The woman seemed the most likely, or the little giggly one. The bruiser was probably just that. *Not certain, though. So be ready to beat a quick retreat if something big comes through.*

One of Isobel's maxims was to never do anything halfheartedly. It took her only a second to decide, during which the tall man looked over his shoulder, then back at her. By the time he'd turned around she'd slipped a pair of throwing knives from their sheaths and whipped them at him, aiming for the shoulders.

She was turning toward the woman as soon as the knives had left her hands. The guy was supposed to go down, or at least be unable to fight. Somehow, though, he managed to draw his sword and strike one of the knives in *mid-air*, sending it spinning off down the alley. The move turned him slightly, so the other blade only scored a line along his bicep and clattered to the ground.

Isobel was already moving the other way, which left her in somewhat of an awkward position. She whipped another knife at the robed figure, watched it catch her in the stomach with a satisfying 'thunk', and started to backpedal toward the corner.

"Nala!" The tall man wasted a moment looking at his companion, while the thin one charged with a nasty, rising shriek. His hands disappeared behind his back and reappeared filled with twin blades. Isobel barely had time to draw her own fighting knives and parry his crazed rush.

For all his anger, though, the man wasn't a particularly effective opponent. He swung wildly, and Isobel danced backward after her initial blocks, waiting for an opening. It came relatively quickly, as a slash left him off balance. She spun sideways, away from his attack, and planted one of her blades at the base of his neck. The giggle cut off abruptly, and the thin man went down without another sound.

The bruiser had risen from where his friend lay on the cobbles. She probably wasn't dead, Isobel reflected. It hadn't been a killing shot. But that didn't mean the man would be any friendlier. She yanked her knife from the corpse's neck and reversed her grip as the man took a step away from the end of the alley.

"You will pay," he grated. "No one crosses the Judge—"

The door burst open, and a figure in black ran down the

alley, terrifyingly fast. Isobel barely had time to step out of the way and recognize Corvus before he was gone, skidding around the corner.

Wait a minute . . .

The wall of the building burst outward in a sudden gout of flame, revealing a fire-spirit the size of a bull. It landed heavily where the woman had been lying, and Isobel winced. In the meantime, the rational part of her brain made a direct connection to her legs, and she started running after Corvus. The tall man hesitated a bit too long. The giant cat pounced on him next, and his scream followed Isobel out of the alley.

Zhin was still looking nervously down every alley, one hand on his sword, but Veil was starting to feel like they'd gotten away with it. It wasn't until they were three or four blocks from Calio's that she realized they were being followed; then her heart jumped to the back of her throat all over again.

"Zhin . . ."

"I know," he said grimly. "It has to be Velyn's guys. I don't think anyone else could have gotten so many on such short notice."

"So what now?"

"Stick to the main streets," he said, turning a corner and walking surprisingly quickly considering the fifty or sixty pounds of gold hanging from his shoulders. "They probably won't attack us as long as there are other people . . . around . . ."

He trailed off. The street ahead, one of the north-south avenues, was blocked by seven or eight bulky men standing shoulder to shoulder. All of them wore Velyn's blue-and-white.

Veil turned around, though she already knew what she'd find. Velyn himself, along with another half-dozen men, were sauntering up the street behind them. The two youths she'd beaten in the first round were there, standing close behind their boss.

"Veil!" Velyn gave her a wolf's grin. "Excellent."

She didn't bother to reply to that.

"That was some spectacular playing today." He shook his head. "Best I've ever seen, and I do mean that. But, here's the thing." He took a step closer. "The money you're carrying is mine. Calio promised it to me; sort of payment for services rendered, if you catch my drift. So I think I'll have to take it. I know you worked hard for it, but there'll be other tournaments. At least" —he hooked his hands into his belt— "there will be, if you hand it over nice and quiet."

Veil considered simply handing over the money. Velyn didn't expect her to, that was certain, but his eye had a murderous glint. She strongly suspected that even handing the satchel over 'nice and quiet' would not be the end of this.

Zhin's mouth was tight, as though the thought of parting with six thousand eyes was almost physically painful to him. Against more than a dozen swords, though, he didn't seem to be able to find any other options. He pulled the satchel from his shoulder and hefted it, getting ready to throw it to Velyn. *He could have at least consulted me.* Not that she had any better ideas.

"I'm glad we're not going to have any trouble." Velyn's smile widened. "Over here, nice and—what in the *Aether*—"

Screams from behind her made Veil glance over her shoulder and gape. The line of thugs that had been blocking the road was gone, scythed down like wheat, and a tide of blood was spreading across the cobblestones. In their place stood three . . . well . . . Veil wasn't quite sure *what* they were. They didn't seem to be quite possessed of a physical form; the panicking crowds up the street were quite clearly visible through them. It was as though someone had taken a man in full armor, polished him till he gleamed in the sun, and then taken the man and armor away but left the gleam. They bore swords in either hand, long ribbons of uneven glints and reflections, and the edges of these were now coated in blood that ran along their nearly invisible surface and dripped slowly to the ground.

Veil felt her eyes go wide, and a familiar voice spoke at the back of her mind.

"Light demons. Saya's butcher boys. Run for it."

"But . . ." Veil glanced behind her. Velyn and his men still blocked the street, though they too were staring at the shimmering apparitions.

"I'll handle them. Run! Meet Corvus."

Veil grabbed Zhin's hand and tugged. "Run!"

"My thoughts exactly."

The pair of them sprinted down the street, right toward Velyn's line. The gang leader was momentarily torn between running from the demons that had just diced half of his men and not letting his six thousand eyes get away, and in that moment Veil and Zhin bulled past him. Once they were through, Velyn decided he could have both. He gestured wildly, and his men followed him away from the demons and after Veil.

"Sybian!" hissed Veil, under her breath. The gang was gaining fast; poor Zhin, still holding on to the gold with one hand, was weighed down considerably. "Do something!"

"Take the next right," puffed Zhin. "Then we can head back uptown . . ."

He ducked, warned by a footfall on the cobbles behind him, as one of the thugs slashed at his head. Zhin fumbled for his sword with his off-hand, unwilling or unable to let go of the gold. Veil skidded to a halt, a few feet ahead.

"Sybian!"

The thug drew back for another strike, was momentarily enveloped in a white mist, and froze on the spot. *Literally* froze.

Veil could see icicles hanging from his arms, and his flesh had acquired a bluish tinge. An instant later, something huge and white came thundering out of an alley and slapped him in the chest with one massive paw. The poor thug shattered on the spot, spraying rock-solid chunks of flesh across his fellows.

The thing that emerged was reptilian, a lizard magnified to a hundred times its normal size and equipped with a long run of dorsal spikes that appeared to be made of ice. It interposed itself between Zhin and the thugs, moving deceptively fast. Velyn's gang skidded to a halt, caught between two demons, and before they could decide which was worse the lizard opened its jaws and covered them in freezing white mist. This didn't have quite the effect the high-pressure spurt had had on the unfortunate leader, but it covered the men with a thin layer of ice which stuck them to the spot quite effectively. The demon stalked past them, disemboweling one of the youths who happened to be standing in its way with an absent-minded swipe of its claws.

Zhin shook his head. "What . . ."

"Don't ask!" The three light demons were already advancing on the lizard, swords raised. Veil pointed. "Just run!"

ISOBEL, FOLLOWING CORVUS and being followed in turn by the giant fire-lion Chemura, turned a corner and started to think that she was having a really bad day.

I mean . . . I found Corvus, that's good, right? Maybe all the rest of it is to balance that out.

The street was empty of pedestrians, unless you counted a few along the sides of the road that seemed to have been frozen on the spot. There was a great deal of blood around, and enough pieces to make up seven or eight people. All this was old hat for her, and Isobel was unfazed.

What *did* attract her interest, though, was the ice-dragon in the center of the street that seemed to be having it out with three other demons. The glittering light-spirits circled the lizard warily, trying to get inside its reach; as she watched, they struck as one, leaping forward to plunge two swords each into the beast's hide. The dragon caught one of them with a concentrated spray of mist, bellowing in agony as swords pierced it but managing to swipe a paw and smash the one it had frozen to tiny pieces. Then the other two struck again, and the creature toppled onto its side and rapidly started to melt.

Corvus didn't even break stride, turning down the street and sprinting right past the shimmering demons. Isobel followed him, but the remaining pair seemed to take an interest in her, catching up with huge, floating strides. She ducked the first one's strike, rolled, and came up with her blades out in time to parry the other. It seemed solid enough. She let its swords slide off and over her head, ducked, and planted both long knives in the center of its chest. The light-demon let out a screech and toppled backwards, blocking its companion's way for a moment; Isobel used the time to start running again, since an angry, smoking form had just rounded the corner.

The last light-demon had regained its footing and was just setting off after Isobel when Chemura hit it from behind. The fire-spirit flattened the thing and tore its head off, angrily, with one shake of his powerful jaws. Then he was off again, bounding after Isobel and Corvus.

THE RED STRIPE was easily identified by the giant streak of crimson someone had painted across the second-floor walls. It was in one of the nicer districts, well away from the chaos of the waterfront, and Zhin and Veil were forced to push through increasingly irritated passersby in order to make any headway. By the time they reached the inn itself, Zhin was completely winded.

He collapsed against the front door, breathing hard. Veil put one hand to her side, clutching a cramp, and pushed Zhin out of the way to knock on the door. He let the gold slide to the ground with a heavy 'clunk' and collapsed on top of it.

The door was answered by a tall, bald man with forearms wider than Veil's neck; he had 'bouncer' written all over him. Veil took a moment to catch her breath as he looked at her, balefully. Apparently the Red Stripe was not the kind of establishment you simply walked into.

"Yeah?" said the bouncer eventually. "Whad'ya want?"

"I'm looking . . .for someone." Veil blew out a long breath. "Name's . . . Corvus."

"We ain't got no Corvus."

"Tall guy, wears all black, carries a sword?"

The bouncer snorted. "This is a qua-li-ty establishment, kid. We don't let thugs and pirates in."

"He said he'd be here."

"Sounds to me like you been dumped." The bouncer slammed the door, almost on Veil's nose. She took a step back, eyes watering. *He said he'd be here.*

"Veil . . ."

She turned to Zhin, already getting an angry retort ready for his sarcasm. Instead he was pointing down the street, where the crowds were dispersing with the silent determination of people who wanted nothing to do with anything.

Corvus trotted to a halt. He had a naked blade in one hand, which was for some reason trailing smoke. He didn't seem exhausted, or even winded; on catching sight of Veil he nodded, wiped the blade with a black cloth from his belt, and sheathed it carefully. Veil felt a tiny knot inside her melt; she shook her head.

"You're late."

"Lay off. It's been a long day." He nodded in Zhin's direction. "Who's this guy?"

"Zhin. He's been making himself useful." Veil's earlier barely-admitted terror was quickly evaporating, replaced with a kind of wobbly-legged giddiness. "Zhin, this is Corvus."

"Charmed." Zhin managed to get to his feet and bow politely, which Corvus ignored.

"Why are you waiting outside?"

"The bouncer wouldn't let us in," Veil explained. "We could probably bribe him . . ."

"Don't waste the money. This is just the place the brothel mistress recommended. We can find something more to our tastes . . ."

Veil was about to explain that budget had become the least of their problems when Corvus spun on one heel, suddenly, and his sword hissed from its sheath of its own accord. Another person—a girl, Veil thought, though it was dark and it was hard to be sure—flew out of the shadows, a long knife in each hand. Corvus parried the strikes with his usual fluid grace and riposted with a cut that would have taken off his attacker's head, had she not backflipped out of range. She—it was a girl, Veil saw, with dark hair and severe features—landed cat-like and sure, flipping one blade around to a reverse grip and starting to circle. Corvus raised his sword and shook his head.

"Crazy little death-wish girl . . ."

"Corvus—" Veil was intending to ask him what the hell was going on, but Zhin interrupted him.

"Isobel!"

"Zhin?" The girl noticed him for the first time.

"You know her?" said Corvus and Veil, simultaneously. Zhin nodded, confused.

"Isobel, what in the Aether are you doing?"

"I found him." Her fierce expression became a kind of

dreamy smile. "I found him, Zhin!"

"Oh, by all the dead gods . . .Isobel, this is *not* the time!"

"You found me?" asked Corvus suspiciously. "What do you mean? Why are you looking for me?"

"Could we please put the swords away?" asked Veil. "I'm really getting a bit nervous . . ."

"I have to finish this duel." Isobel raised her knives threateningly. "Corvus . . ."

"If I recall," said Corvus dryly, "you already lost the duel."

"I'm still alive!"

"That's my prerogative. Planning on making me reverse my decision?"

"I . . ." Isobel hesitated.

"Corvus," said Veil.

"What?"

"Look over there, would you?"

The flaming lion which had been charging the length of the street chose that moment to let out an ear-splitting roar that rattled the fancy glass in the inn windows. Isobel spun around, weapons raised, and Corvus took a step forward so they were side-by-side. The spirit pulled up short, facing three gleaming blades, and seemed to be considering or waiting for instructions. With a final glare at Corvus, it turned away and sauntered back down the street, limping slightly and still trailing smoke. Corvus shook his head.

"What was *that*?" asked Veil.

Corvus and Isobel ignored her. As though mounted on turntables, they swiveled to face each other, weapons still drawn. Veil rolled her eyes.

"*Please*, people. The swords?"

"You really don't want to kill me?" Isobel sounded almost pleading.

"Why should I want to kill you?" asked Corvus. "You're the one who jumped me in the street, if anything I should be asking *you* that question."

Isobel sheathed her blades, slowly, as though not sure what else to do. She looked suddenly lost. Corvus flipped his own sword around and carefully slid it home, turning back to Veil and Zhin.

"There's a lot going on here that I don't understand," he said.

"Tell me about it," muttered Veil under her breath.

"But I know where I have to go next."

Go? "Where?"

"The riverlands."

"The *riverlands*? Why?" If Corsa was the city of legends to Veil, now made flesh, then the riverlands were only distant dreams. The idea of a place where it rained almost daily and trees grew so thick you couldn't see the sky seemed ludicrous. Some of the traders who made it as far as the Red Hills claimed to have visited the riverlands, where everyone had blond hair and blue eyes and the Empire had first been born. The Red Hills had been Imperial since the Fourth Dynasty, but they were so far out of the way they never had to give more than a nod and a bag of gold to the Palace at Crossroads. When the Khaevs replaced the Imperials, it was just another set of tax collectors for Veil's people; if anything, less onerous than before.

"My business." His voice was hard, and softened only a little. "You've proved I don't have to take care of you all the time, so I suppose you can come along if you want."

"How are you planning to get there?"

Corvus frowned. "I'm still working on that."

"If I might offer a suggestion?" said Zhin, smoothly.

"What?"

"My partner and I"—he gestured to Isobel—"are headed back to the riverlands ourselves. As you've no doubt heard, the journey is long and rather perilous. Most travelers go by ship, around the Tears of Heaven and T'bach and through the Straights of Tellen, braving pirates and storms the whole way. The only other alternative is to wait for a caravan to form, and travel the Diem highlands in strength."

"I assume from your tone," said Corvus, "that you have another way?"

"As a matter of fact, I do." Zhin looked exceptionally pleased with himself. "My partner and I have been granted safe conduct by the Diem Council. We need not wait for a caravan, and supplies and mounts will be made available. We could make the journey in a matter of weeks instead of months."

"I'm not frightened of the Diem," said Corvus. "We could ride tonight."

"And the Anvil?" Zhin's smiled widened. "The fortress blocks the only usable pass through the Shieldwall mountains, and the Khaevs are quite strict on who they allow through."

"I suppose you have a way around that as well."

"I do."

Corvus' lip twisted. "I don't appear to have much of a choice."

"I'm only trying to be helpful." Zhin spread his arms. "You're free to ignore me."

"Fine."

"Wait, wait." Veil held up her hands. "You're going with them?"

"Apparently."

"What about her?" She gestured to Isobel. "She wants to kill you."

"Isobel will restrain herself." Zhin's voice was firm. "Our lord would be quite cross with her otherwise."

"Yeah," said Isobel faintly.

"But . . ." Veil shook her head. "Why, Zhin? Why all the help?"

"You won't believe it's out of the kindness of my heart?"

"No."

He shrugged. "Very well. I hope to convince Corvus to assist my lord in some small matters when we reach the riverlands. It's also never a bad idea to have a swordsman like him along when crossing the highlands."

"I thought you had safe conduct."

"Of course." He smiled again. "In theory."

"Great." She turned back to Corvus. "And you're going along with this?"

"You don't have to come," said Corvus.

Zhin opened his mouth, as though he were about to say something, but Veil cut him off, angrily. "Of course I'm coming! Where else on earth or Aether do I have to go? I'm just saying . . ." She trailed off. "It's weird. That's all."

"Things have been strange, lately." Corvus' voice was grim. "This does not surprise me."

Zhin clapped his hands. "If we're all agreed, then, let's get ourselves a room in the Red Stripe. I could do with a fire and something to eat."

"Looks expensive," Corvus growled. "We shouldn't . . ."

Veil shook her head. "*That* we don't have to worry about."

chapter 10

"Trading with the Valdiem has always been a bit of a gamble. Sometimes they'll treat you like royalty, and sometimes they'd rather spit you than look at you. The money's good, though, so you just have to trust to luck and the whims of their demon god."

–Kaylie Tholos, Imperial Trader

Y OU'VE HEARD NOTHING?" rumbled Vaalkir.

"No, lord."

The spirit paused, then shrugged with a grinding crunch of metal. "It matters not. Your men have served their purpose. The shadow senses the trap, but he cannot resist. Now he is committed."

"Yes, lord." The sorcerer nodded eagerly. "They're headed straight for the mountain where the Blade sleeps."

"Small wonder. Jyo-raku can sense it." Vaalkir smiled, eyes burning.

This was a surprise to the sorcerer, but he simply nodded. "That is part of the plan, lord?"

"Of course."

"What of the others?"

"Saya has already withdrawn her interests."

"And . . ."

"The ice-bitch seems content to let us alone for now. She

must believe she has an edge, that she can manipulate me."

"She doesn't know about the Blade."

Flames roared across Vaalkir's body and the sorcerer smiled. "No, she doesn't."

There was a moment of silence.

"It is a pity your men have not returned," Vaalkir rumbled finally. "I had one final role for them to play."

"I am sorry, lord."

"There is always a contingency. This has been long in the planning."

"A contingency?"

"Our way has been prepared."

The sorcerer said what he always said when he didn't understand, which was "Yes, lord."

"Come with me."

He followed the spirit obediently, ignoring the ash that puffed from its footfalls.

MELODY CONSIDERED HERSELF a tolerant individual. By the standards of Tellen, she had to be; otherwise merely walking through a *szandling* town would force her to leave a trail of bodies in her wake. She could stand it when some *szandling* crossed her path without apology, or bumped her arm in a crowd, or even threw her a lecherous look while he thought she wasn't watching. She'd even learned to tolerate their speaking out of turn, which would have been cause for summary execution of a *szandling* at home.

But Morg's complaining was seriously threatening her tolerant attitude. He was nominally an ally, and it took a lot for a Tellenna to think badly of someone who'd drawn blood by her side, but the litany had been unending since the botched ambush. *Considering how close he came to losing his head, you'd think he'd be grateful.*

It was all, Melody reminded herself, part of the Old Ones' plan. She wondered idly which Old One she had offended in order to merit this kind of treatment. Melody glided through the forest, her feet barely leaving depressions on the leafy ground, but it was all for show. Morg was clomping along in his big leather boots a dozen feet behind her, announcing their presence to all and sundry with his constant muttering.

"I told him it was a bad fucking plan. Lord Adrian's fried his brain. That's exactly what I told him. Ambushing a gods-damn sorcerer is never a fucking picnic in the woods, and we had to make sure we didn't hurt his fucking noble bitch. *Fuck*." This last was a veritable explosion, a monosyllabic expectoration that startled a pair of grouse from a bush forty feet away. "Now we did what he wanted, and what do we have to show for it? Sarth's dead. No loss there. Big bastard was loony anyway, but Aff was all right. Fucking monk cracked his head open. What a way to go. You wouldn't catch me buying it like that. Fuck no."

At least, Melody thought, he didn't seem to expect her to keep up half of the conversation. Morg was talking more or less to himself.

"What am I even doing this bizarre shit for, anyway? Shoulda' stuck to the city, stuck to what I'm *fucking* good at. Bashing people's heads for money. I mean, shit, it wasn't even that much money. Fucking Lord Valos. He gives one speech and I come over all teary-eyed. Fuck that. When I get out of these gods-damned woods I'm going to tell Valos where he can stick his fucking revolution, and then I'm going to find a *fucking* whore-house with a nice big bed and . . . *fuck!*"

A rock, dislodged from where Morg had kicked it, rattled down the slope. The axeman jumped on one foot for a moment, swearing.

"Gods! Doesn't this fucking forest ever *end*?"

After that came a moment of silence, as though he had run out of energy and needed to recharge. Melody used the opportunity to put in a quiet word.

"It's going to rain soon."

"What?"

She enunciated carefully. *Szandling* were notoriously bad at understanding those trained to speak the True Tongue. "It's. Going. To. Ra—"

"I heard you the first fucking time. How do you know?"

Melody took a deep breath through her nose. Her fingers, which were just inches from any number of potentially lethal objects, wouldn't stop twitching. Once she could trust herself she spoke again.

"Look at the sky."

She gestured to the southeast, where it was getting dark fast. The sun was already sinking behind the mountains, but she could still make out the approaching thunderheads through gaps in the canopy. Morg stared up, oblivious.

"We should find shelter."

"Yeah." His nose, which was oversized and red, twitched a little. "Just what I fucking need. Cold and wet in the middle of a fucking forest. Why am I even in a *fucking forest*?"

"There." Melody pointed up slope, where she could see the gray of bare rock. "There may be somewhere we can wait it out."

That would take some time, she knew. The storms carried on the westerly wind broke against the Shieldwall like a lancer's charge, spreading out to the north and south. She didn't bother to explain this to Morg, who followed her up the mountainside, still muttering softly. His voice was going, though, which reduced his curses to a barely audible trickle.

" . . . fucking . . . stuck-up . . . forest . . . Lord Adrian . . ."

It took nearly a half an hour to climb a few hundred feet, most of which Melody spent waiting for Morg to catch up. By the time he got to the bottom of the cracked ridgeline, she'd already found what she was looking for. There was a cave, only a few feet up and halfway along, really just a hollow where two boulders abutted, but it would do for keeping the rain off. She headed for it, opening the gap between herself and the axeman.

No one lives around here, but that doesn't mean it's empty. There could be a bear or an earth-spirit. Unlikely, but possible. Blood Angels lived by taking into account the unlikely. Melody waited by the entrance to the cave, staring into the darkness and waiting for her eyes to adjust. She didn't step out until she at least had a dim view of what was within, not wanting to be silhouetted against the light.

Finally, she put her head around the corner and nearly hissed with surprise. The cave was occupied after all. Two figures were sleeping around what remained of a campfire. *Careless.* They had relied on the same desolation that she had. She watched for another moment to make sure neither stirred, checked to see that Morg was a good distance behind her, then crawled in without a sound.

It turned out to be a pair of young women, short and well-muscled, curled up on opposite sides of the dying fire. Melody had a knife in her hand without even really thinking about it; after a bit of thought she reversed her grip and crawled closer.

She recognized the traveling uniform of a Khaev draekere at about the same time that the closer girl's eyes popped open. She took in the glittering knife a few inches from her throat, and nodded thoughtfully.

"If you're going to kill me," she said, "please get on with it."

KIT KEPT ONE eye on the knife while considering her options. She only had a split-second to do so while the stranger was surprised to find her awake, but that was long enough to get a basic read on the situation.

The strange girl blinked once, then apparently decided to take what Kit had said at face value. She thrust the knife toward Kit's stomach, hampered a bit by the low ceiling of the cave. There wasn't much else she could have done, so Kit was ready; she snapped one hand out and caught the other girl's wrist, pushing it up enough that the knife only lightly scored her side. The pain barely registered. She managed to crush the stranger's knife-hand against the ceiling and jam a boot into her ribs at the same time. Her attacker let out an 'oof', dropped the knife, and quickly backed out of the cave. Kit didn't blame her. In that position, her head was exposed. Kit followed her, on the general principle that leaving an enemy waiting outside a cave with only one exit is a bad idea, and scooped up the knife with her off-hand. She managed to get out of the cave before the stranger had quite regained her feet. Kit sprang up like a jack-in-the-box, tossing the knife to her right hand and smiling.

The other girl was her age, or maybe a little older, and wore wine-dark red leather from head to toe. Her hair was a washed-out red, tied back in two complicated braids, and she was absolutely festooned with weapons. Her eyes were pleasant as she retrieved two more, a short sword in her left hand and a knife in her right, both longer than the stiletto she'd left Kit.

There was a crash from downslope, as though someone had just fallen heavily into a thicket. A thick voice called up in Imperial.

"Hey, Mel! Where the fuck'd you go? I can see lightning!"

The stranger ignored it, so Kit did likewise. They circled cautiously, matching step for step.

Kei's got to be awake, but she's not in any shape for a fight. This girl doesn't know that, though, so she'll try to finish me fast and ambush Kei when she comes out. With a sword like that . . . Kit grimaced. Her options weren't particularly good; her opponent had a good foot of reach on her, and looked as though she was fast and well-trained. *Let me try . . .*

The stranger came in high and fast with the short sword, with the dagger lagging behind at waist height. The sane thing to do would be step back, out of knife range, and parry the long blade. Instead Kit held her ground, slamming her forearm into her opponent's hard enough to send the sword whistling over her head. She grabbed the other girl's shoulder with her empty hand, pulling her forward and off-balance. This let her drive the knife to the hilt into the underside of the stranger's jaw, with the disadvantage that it allowed the other girl to bury her knife in Kit's gut.

That was the plan, anyway. Something made Kit pause a moment before slamming the stiletto home; she flicked her eyes down and saw the stranger's knife poised at her stomach, its point pricking but not piercing the leather of her uniform. The other girl worked her jaw and felt the prick of Kit's knife on the soft skin underneath.

Thunder rumbled in the distance, like the growl of some great beast. Kit felt her heart racing, and a single bead of sweat traced a line just past her ear before getting lost at the nape of her neck. The girl's eyes, a brilliant sea-green, held her gaze unwaveringly. The moment seemed to last forever.

Eventually, Kit said, "Well?"

The stranger contrived to indicate with the muscles of her face that she would have liked to reply, but was prevented from doing so by the needle-point of the dagger just under her jaw. Kit nodded and shifted her grip so the knife pointed at the base of the girl's throat, just above the collarbone. The stranger took a long breath before speaking.

"What do you mean?" She spoke Khaev with a heavy accent that turned her 'W's into 'V's, so 'what' came out 'vaat.'

"You're dead."

"So are you, I think. More slowly."

"Why did you stop?"

"Where did you learn that?"

"Learn what?" Kit's hand was starting to ache, and her arm was trembling from the effort of holding the knife in such an awkward position.

"That, that . . . *tskel-t'vek* . . . self-sacrifice, perhaps?"

Where did I learn that? Knife-fighting was part of a draekere's curriculum, obviously, but their style focused on the defensive and responsive maneuvers, assuming that an opponent would always have an advantage of height or reach. But Kit had learned more than that, mostly from Zaneh. *And she learned them from . . .*

Her sleep-befogged brain finally caught up with events. *Red leather, the accent, the blades . . .* "You're a Blood Angel."

"Of course." She shook her head impatiently. "Answer the question."

"I learned it from a girl at Steelgod, who was trained by someone named Min. One of you."

The girl laughed. "I thought as much. You have *akusy'kyvya* written all over you."

"Aku . . ." Kit shook her head. "What?"

"*Akusy'kyvya.* Our philosophy, our motto. 'Victory is everything.'"

There was a moment of silence.

"So," Kit asked, "are we going to stab each other? Or what?"

"There would not seem to be much point," mused the girl. "We are a hundred miles from anywhere. Who would know?"

"So . . . I can put this knife down?"

"I think I will not kill you."

"Thank the gods." Kit let the knife fall to the dirt and stepped away from the girl's blade, massaging her palm. "I was cramping up really badly."

The stranger sheathed her sword and knife, then bent to retrieve the stiletto, looking at Kit curiously.

"You trust me not to kill you?"

"After we've become such friends?" Kit shrugged. "I'm Kit, by the way."

"My *szandling* name is Melody."

"Zand . . ."

"Call me Melody," she clarified hastily.

Another silence, broken by a much louder roll of thunder.

"You're a draekere?"

"Yes," Kit answered warily.

"One of the two that have been following Lord Adrian?"

Adrian? The sorcerer, presumably. Kit didn't see any point to denying it. "Yes. Do you work for him?"

"I'm attempting to rejoin him."

"That's great." She let out a heartfelt sigh. "Do I have to fight you after all, then?"

"No." Melody shrugged. "Not yet, anyway."

"Good."

At this point Kei, who had been quietly observing for a few seconds, poked her head out of the cave. She managed to get outside and on to her feet, moving with some difficulty and glancing quickly between Kit and Melody.

"What's going on?"

"This is Melody," said Kit, gesturing. "She's a Blood Angel, but she's not going to kill us."

"Yet," Melody added, grinning.

Kit nodded. "Yet. This is my Wing Leader Kei."

"Are you badly hurt?" the Blood Angel asked.

"I'll be fine." Kei gritted her teeth. "Kit, where did she come from?"

"She works for the sorcerer, apparently."

"The one we're . . ."

"Uh-huh. But she seems willing to be peaceful for the moment, and I figured we're hardly in a shape to be picking fights."

"A Blood Angel would not have hesitated to pick a fight," said Melody, with a touch of dry humor.

"I'm glad I'm not a Blood Angel, then," said Kei wearily. "We'd better get back under cover. It's going to pour in a second."

"How deep does that cave go?" asked the Blood Angel. "Will it hold four?"

"You have someone with you?"

Melody nodded wearily.

"It'd be tight." Kit looked at the other two women appraisingly. "Maybe if we were feeling really friendly."

Kit and Kei looked at each other, but Melody shook her head firmly.

THUNDER RUMBLED AGAIN, and the rain drummed on the earth, churning the thick soil into mud and covering the ridgeline with little waterfalls. Morg sat underneath a pine tree, which kept the worst of the rain off. Every now and then the wind would blow the branches apart and a heavy lump of water would hit his head and shoulders with a splat.

His muttered curses seemed to match the now-constant growl of the storm.

"Fucking Blood Angels . . . cave's not big enough . . . looked plenty big enough to me, just have to squeeze a little . . . wouldn't fucking mind squeezing with them, not that they care. Don't give a shit about me. I could catch my death out here, with them getting all toasty warm by the fire, takin' their clothes off to get dry . . ."

The sudden crash of thunder drowned the rest.

IT WAS DIFFICULT to miss an entire Blade on the march, particularly one the size of Kagerin Shuzan's. Nine hundred men and half again as many horses, plus a dozen wagons laden with supplies ordered up from the Palace storerooms. But Tashida Ikon hadn't made a move to stop them, hadn't even issued an official pronouncement, which Shuzan found quite puzzling.

He probably doesn't want to give me a direct order, because he knows I'll disobey and he's not willing to stop me by force. Letting everyone know I'm going against his authority would only undermine it. Shuzan wondered, privately, if the men of his Blade would back him against High Command. They were supposed to. Soldiers were supposed to be loyal to their Blade leader, first and foremost, willing to follow him into the jaws of Hell. And Shuzan would have trusted the men he'd brought from Khaevar to do so. They'd been Kagerin subjects, every one, and all from families with a long history of loyalty to their high lord.

Fewer than two hundred of his old guard remained. They'd been bled away, bit by bit, after the massacre in the Doomwood. Some had left for safer positions in other Blades, or to be trainers or instructors of new recruits. Others had simply gone home. Shuzan had been in the Empire nearly six years, and his men had been at his side the entire time. He'd replaced the losses as best he could; all Khaevs, of course, no Imperial could serve in a Blade, but they weren't all Kagerin men and were thus a bit suspect. All in all, Shuzan was pleased he didn't have to put them to the test by cutting his way out of the Palace and through whatever Blades Tashida Ikon chose to send against him.

django wexler

Shuzan's lieutenant was named Hiko Takei. He was short, bald, and filled to the brim with a fierce energy that made him invaluable. The lieutenant's task was to handle the day-to-day management of the Blade, leaving his lord to ponder important strategic questions. Hiko's family had been retainers of the Kagerins for generations, though, and Shuzan often went to his subordinate for opinions. Now he felt that he should introduce the Blade's guests.

"Hiko, this is Moriseki Hikari, Mistress of Draekeres for the occupation." He gestured vaguely in her direction. Moriseki bowed slightly, while Hiko gave her a deep bow in return. "The girls are Zee, Lin, and Aya."

The three draekeres bowed as well. Zee was the youngest, just out of Steelgod, with a long face and short, clipped hair. Lin was a little bit shorter, and wore a ponytail to her shoulders. Aya, the oldest, had a round, moon-like face and slightly wavy locks down to the nape of her neck. All three looked remarkably similar, slim and well-appointed in the gray draekere's uniforms.

"Will they be traveling in the wagons?" asked Hiko, ever eager to put everything in its proper place. Moriseki shook her head, smiling.

"I'll ride with Lord Kagerin, and these three will stay aloft, paralleling our progress."

"Very good." Hiko bowed again. "The Blade is ready to depart, my lord. We await only your command."

Shuzan nodded. "Ride. West on the road, for at least a few days. Then we'll see if we can pick up any trace of them."

"Very good, my lord. If you'll excuse me—"

"Of course."

Hiko bowed his way out of the chamber. A trace of a smile played on Shuzan's lips; he heard his lieutenant start to bellow orders as soon as Hiko thought his lord was out of earshot.

"If I might ask, Lord Kagerin," said Moriseki quietly, "what exactly is your plan? The mountains are vast, and the Valdiem are not always friendly. It's a big place to lose four or five people."

"That's one reason I'm taking the whole Blade. They may be able to find us. And if their draekeres are aloft, we'll certainly spot them."

"And if they can't find us?"

"We search." His face hardened a bit. "For as long as it takes."

THE SORCERER WASN'T even really aware of traveling anymore. His needs were met. Water and food seemed to appear when they were necessary, not that he paid much attention to such things. He slept when he was tired. In between there was Vaalkir, marching step by step into the mountains. The forest floor got steeper as they ascended, and, more and more, the oaks and maples gave way to hardier pines and razorleaves. When he glanced back, he could pick out the path of their ascent, since the spirit's footsteps left a line of burned and broken turf.

The sorcerer didn't get bored, or discontented. He just was, and walked, following his master.

When the Valdiem found them, there was no warning at all. One moment they were walking along what passed for an animal track, leading up a ridgeline in switchbacks. The next moment the trees and bushes had sprouted axe-wielding warriors.

The sorcerer looked them over without a trace of fear—his master would provide, as he always did—but with more than a little curiosity. For all his travels in the mountains, now only distantly recalled, this was his first time meeting the reclusive mountain people. They were shorter than the Diem, with the tallest of them only coming up to Vaalkir's shoulders, but they shared the sandy coloration of the highlanders. Dark hair was worn short, by both men and women, and their garb seemed to be mostly animal skins and woven grass. There were at least ten of them, ranged on both sides of the path, and each had at least three one-handed axes that looked as though they would serve for throwing or blade-to-blade combat.

Vaalkir stopped, his expression unreadable, and stared straight ahead as though waiting for something. The Valdiem were focused on him completely, ignoring the sorcerer; this was of course right and proper. The sorcerer waited patiently for something to happen.

Eventually, three more Valdiem emerged from the woods and planted themselves right on the path. Two strapping young men with axes in either hand escorted an older woman. Her neck was hung about with complicated silver amulets, and her hair swung in a silver braid well past her shoulder. She squared her shoulders, as though adjusting a great weight, and set to staring at the giant metal-clad spirit.

Finally she spoke, in a surprisingly normal tone.

"And what are you called, demon?"

Vaalkir answered in what the sorcerer assumed was the Valdiem tongue. The words were strange, but the meaning echoed heavily in his mind.

"Vaalkir."

The old woman switched to her own language. "Do you know this mountain is forbidden by the laws of Zemk?"

"It is forbidden by more than the dictates of your little god, sorceress."

If that bothered her, she didn't show it. "If you know this, why do you attempt to trespass?"

"Those rules do not apply to me," rumbled the spirit. "Get out of the way, or face the consequences."

She looked scornful. "Zemk has defended us against demons more powerful than you."

"No." Fire rippled across Vaalkir's armored form. "I don't think so."

The old woman grabbed at her necklace, muttering, and the sorcerer felt power surge through the clearing, a swirling mix of Ice and Shadow. Something started to take shape in front of the old sorceress, but before it could fully manifest Vaalkir threw up one gauntleted fist. The sorcerer felt the power shift as a torrent of cleansing Fire swept away whatever the old woman had been calling. She took a step back, aghast, and the spirit opened his hand, palm forward.

For a moment, nothing happened. The Valdiem warriors, glancing back and forth between their leader and the spirit, tensed their hands on their axes; Vaalkir held his position, and the old woman tottered a step forward.

Then she screamed, and smoke started to curl from her eyes. When she raised her head, the sorcerer could see that they were lit by an inner radiance. A moment longer and flames burst forth from her skin in a dozen places. Her scream choked off into a hoarse whisper, drowned under the fire's crackle. Her hair ignited, and her flesh melted and ran like wax, until all that was left was a blackened skeleton held upright amidst writhing tongues of flame. Vaalkir closed his hand, and the bones collapsed to ash.

The heat from the old woman's demise washed over the Valdiem in a palpable wave. Vaalkir simply waited, patiently.

Of the twelve, five found the courage to attack: the old woman's guards, a pair of young women from one side and a lanky young man from the other. The rest fled, either to warn others or to save their own skins. The sorcerer didn't blame them; he was impressed that any had remained. It made no difference, of course, one way or the other.

Three hand axes flew at Vaalkir in rapid succession, glancing off his armored carapace with showers of sparks. The old woman's guards reached him first, wincing at the heat, but swinging their axes two-handed regardless. Vaalkir ignored the weapons and touched each on the shoulder, then spun to engage the others.

The boy on the left shouted a hoarse war cry as he charged. The sorcerer's appreciation rose a notch. He hoped to distract the spirit so that the women on the other side might have a chance. Vaalkir rewarded him with a backhand slap that shattered his skull with a nasty crunch, sending him reeling. On the other side, the women aimed for the back of the armored demon's knees, landing heavy blows to no apparent effect. Vaalkir whipped around, grabbed one of them by the wrist and tossed her toward the forest, then took the other by the throat. He didn't need to squeeze; the spirit's metal hide was hot enough to melt lead, and the Valdiem girl screamed in agony as her skin blackened.

Once she had quieted, he let her corpse fall. The two guards he'd touched earlier writhed on the ground, coated in unquenchable flames. The boy he'd hit lay perfectly still, but there was some movement where he'd thrown the first young woman. The sorcerer, still curious, went to investigate.

The Valdiem warrior had hit the solid trunk of a razorleaf hard enough to shatter her spine. She lay on her side, scrabbling mindlessly at the ground and breathing in gasps, one hand blackened and blistered where the spirit had touched her. The sorcerer knelt beside her. He didn't feel anything, not really, but it felt as though there was a *gap* where feeling might once have been.

I should kill her. The thought came unbidden. *She's in agony.*

"Come," rumbled Vaalkir. "They will know better than to threaten us again."

The sorcerer nodded, and stood, leaving the girl behind.

KEI WOKE UP feeling as though she'd just finished a ten-mile march, which was a piece of cake for a draekere and worlds better than she'd felt the previous night. The ache in her shoulder had subsided to the point where it was almost tolerable, provided she didn't try to raise her arm above her head. That meant, she decided, that there were no broken bones from the crash, which was frankly a miracle. She muttered a prayer to whatever gods might be listening.

I'm surprised I got any sleep. It was a testament to exhaustion more than anything else. Between the thunderstorm and the sudden, unwelcome third presence in their little cave, Kei had felt too keyed up to sit still. Once the adrenaline had faded, though, she'd dropped right off. *I half expected the girl to slit our throats.* Although if the stories were true, a Blood Angel wouldn't have had to bother with the subterfuge. *If she wanted to kill us, we'd probably be dead already.*

Instead, she opened watery eyes as the morning sun crept across the rock. The warmth was paltry, but welcome. Between the rain and the altitude the cave had been damn near freezing overnight. A few embers still glowed in what was left of their tiny cook fire. Kit and Melody were gone, and Kei felt her heart skip a few irrational beats before she heard the conversation filtering in from outside. She rolled over and crawled out of the tiny cave, squinting against the sunshine.

"Do you think there's a trail?" asked Kit. She and Melody were sitting side by side on a boulder, facing west. Melody was pointing at something upslope. A few yards away sat the big axeman Kei had only caught a glimpse of last night, looking thoroughly wet and miserable. He was having breakfast—travel bread and dried meat, but it looked so good Kei suddenly realized she was ravenous—and muttering to himself in a sort of nonstop monologue, interspersed with sneezes.

"Damn Blood Angels . . . leaving me out in the" —he sneezed— "rain. She'll get mad at me for being loud, too, you'll" —he sneezed— "see. And now these damn Khaevs; we're supposed to be killing them, by the . . . all the . . . cold? gods. Fuck." He sneezed so violently he almost fell over and shuffled his sodden cloak closer around himself. "Fuck."

Melody and Kit paid him no attention. The Blood Angel nodded in answer to Kit's question.

"There has to be. Lord Adrian said the Valdiem considered it their sacred mountain, and performed rituals there. They have to have a way up."

"It'll be watched, though." Kit frowned. "I assume since it's sacred ground, they don't take kindly to trespassers?"

"No. Lord Adrian seemed to be of the opinion we'd have to fight our way through."

"How many of you were there?"

"Seven."

"Cocky bastard, isn't he?"

Melody shrugged; if the insult to her employer bothered her, she didn't show it. "He's a sorcerer."

"True." Kit looked down and noticed Kei. "Awake? How're you feeling?"

"Better." Kei worked her shoulder a little. "Though slightly disturbed to find you making plans with someone who's technically on the wrong side."

"We share a common goal, for the moment." Melody's eyes flicked between the two draekeres.

"We do?" asked Kei.

"I wish to rejoin Lord Adrian and request further instructions. Kit says she wants to rejoin Lady Tashida. Lord Adrian is headed to the Valdiem sacred mountain, and Lady Tashida is apparently following." She spread her hands, as though nothing could be more logical.

"So you'll help us get to the top of the mountain, meet your Lord Adrian . . ."

"And request further instructions."

"And if he tells you to kill us?"

Melody shrugged again, as though it made no difference. Kei nodded, thoughtfully, as though she understood. *Tellenna are crazy.*

"Do you also wish to rejoin Lady Tashida?"

Kei blinked. "Of course." *Of course?*

The answer seemed to satisfy the Blood Angel, who went back to studying the mountain. Kei sat down on a tree stump, shaking her head.

Of course? I was half-convinced that demon was leading Lady Tashida into the jaws of death, with the rest of us along for the ride. Whatever this Lord Adrian has done, it's not worth chasing him from here. He's a sorcerer. We wouldn't be able to take him down even if we caught up with him. So what am I following her for? It was a long way back to civilization even from where she was sitting, let alone from further into the mountains. Kei didn't doubt her ability to make it back, eventually; lower down the woods were full of game and edible plants, and she'd been well-trained for this kind of situation. *But the further up we go, the longer and harder the road back becomes. What I really want to do is get us* out *of here.*

So why 'of course'? Why should I go and get her? To pull Tashida Shiori out of the fire? *Not a chance. Let her precious uncle save her; he's the High Commander of the Occupation, after all.* Gota? The monk had been friendly, in a cold sort of way. *Not someone I'd die for. And*

Jyo-raku gives me the creeps.

Ultimately, of course, Moriseki told me to be here. Upslope was the way duty pointed. *But if I go back*—if *we* go back, she amended, since she had no intention of leaving without Kit. *No one will ever know. Lady Tashida isn't coming back this time. No one could possibly blame us . . .*

"What's up, Wing Leader?" Kei opened her eyes to find Kit smiling broadly. Her uniform was stained and her hair bedraggled, but, under the coating of dust, the girl looked as chipper as ever. "You look a bit lost."

"Just wondering what the hell we're doing out here."

"Having an adventure." Kit gestured grandly. "Aren't you having a good time?"

"Please tell me you're kidding."

The girl rolled her eyes. "Of course."

"Thank the gods."

"Still, you can't get so down."

"You know if we go up that mountain we probably won't come back?"

"Probably not," Kit said cheerfully.

"That Blood Angel will kill us, or else her boss and his demons will."

"Maybe."

"And Lady Tashida is probably already dead."

Kit frowned. "I hope not. I was looking forward to having more fun with her."

"So how exactly can you be so cheerful?"

"What's the worst that could happen?"

"We could die horrible deaths?"

"Okay." Kit shrugged. "And?"

Kei opened her mouth, let it hang for a moment, then closed it again. There was nothing to say, really.

"It's not all bad." Kit lowered her voice. "Look at Melody."

Kei looked. The Blood Angel was having some breakfast of her own, something she'd dug out of one of her pouches. From time to time she shot a look at the axeman, which was studiously ignored.

"What about her?"

"*Look* at her."

"You're not serious."

She was lithe, Kei had to admit, and attractive in a sort of wiry, thin-faced way. It didn't seem enough to justify the way Kit was staring.

"Come on, Kit."

"You didn't see her earlier, when she was stretching."

"Promise me you won't do anything stupid."

"Define stupid."

"You know what I mean."

"I have to release my tension somehow. Unless you're volunteering . . ."

"Damn it, Kit."

"I suppose there's always Morg."

Both draekeres looked over at the axeman, who sneezed again and hunched further under his cloak. Kei managed a weary smile.

"Point."

"I'll try not to compromise our mission goals."

"What were those, again?"

"Find Shiori and get the hell out of here."

"Right." Somehow, Kei suspected, it wasn't going to work out that way.

KATCH VETZ-KAL CONSIDERED guard duty to be among his worst assignments. It was a given for young men and women training in the ways of the Called, but that didn't mean he had to like it. It was simply boring. The only trespasser on the forbidden ground was the occasional lost easterling, who they gently directed home. A warrior on guard duty at a village had to be alert, since at the very least there were always the young warriors of nearby villages ready to play pranks and humiliate those on watch. But there was nothing *on* the forbidden mountain except the Vault, and no one dared play pranks on the Called.

Katch had chosen the way of the Called rather than the way of the warrior because it offered him a chance at real leadership. Those who showed the talent would be raised into the Called themselves, and even those who did not became Shields, the right hand of the Called and possessed of much power. He regretted his decision only occasionally, but this was one of those times; seeing the warriors marching off toward the pass, laughing and bragging about how many easterlings they were going to skin, had made him conscious of what he was missing.

He therefore stalked through the forest in a huff, forcing his partner to nearly run to keep up. Sem was short and well-muscled for a girl, with a shock of red hair she kept close-cropped. She had freckles and a pug-nose that was attractive, from a certain point of view, but she'd made her feelings about Katch quite clear from the outset, which added to his annoyance. She didn't bother to upbraid him for walking too fast, despite the fact that she had seniority, and that helped a little. *Maybe she's as anxious to be done with this round as I am.*

Katch put out a hand to steady himself as he padded around a boulder, moving through the woods with the unconscious grace of someone who'd lived there since birth. Sem followed as he picked his way across the rocks and dropped lightly to the ground on the other side, scanning for any signs of human presence.

The silhouette of a man in the tree line ahead made him grip his axe, but he released it almost immediately as he recognized Lan and Killik, another couple who were out on patrol. Who were *supposed* to be out on patrol, he amended. Killik had Lan's doeskin shirt pushed up over her shoulders and was nuzzling softly at her breasts, and neither looked as though they were getting much patrolling done. Lan's eyes were closed, and her mouth was slightly open. Katch felt himself color, and hated himself for it. He stepped heavily on a branch as he approached, sending a loud 'crack' echoing off the rocks.

Killik's head shot up, and Lan hastily covered herself and turned bright red. Her partner didn't seem nearly as embarrassed, though; he waved casually as Lan laced her shirt up again and sauntered over to meet Katch and Sem.

"Zemk defend, Katch."

"Defend, Killik," said Katch sourly. "I'm glad to see you're paying such close attention to your duties."

"Who's going to know?" Killik gestured at the empty forest.

"I would."

"Are you planning on informing the Called?"

That was a joke. Katch would never tell on a fellow novice, no matter how much he disliked him. He snorted. "Perhaps I'll just sneak up on you next time and teach you a lesson."

"Give it a try. You walk like a dying rhinoceros."

"I'm sorry, Katch," said Lan. "I didn't mean . . . we just didn't think it'd do any harm . . ."

"It's okay," said Katch gruffly. Lan looked as though she was about to cry—she usually did—and the red color hadn't faded from her face. "Just wait until you get back, next time."

Lan shot Killik a look, and there might have been further discussion, but Sem held up a hand suddenly. The other three quieted, and listened. Two sets of trudging footsteps were barely audible.

Katch kept his voice to a whisper. "Easterlings?"

"Probably," said Sem. "I'll go check. Wait here."

She was the quietest of them, but Katch objected to her assuming the position of most danger and therefore more honor. "I should . . ."

"It won't be necessary," hissed a new voice. All four Valdiem turned to find the shadows in the center of the clearing mounding up from the ground until they reached roughly man-height, then withdrawing to reveal a human figure cloaked in black.

A spirit of Shadow! Katch, standing right next to Sem, tried to find Killik's eye. *One of us has to warn the Called.*

"Begone from here, spirit!" said Sem. Her voice trembled only a little. "Your kind are not welcome, and Zemk defends his own."

"I'm sure he does. Therefore I think remaining hidden from him is the best choice." The spirit shifted, and Katch put a hand back on his best axe. "Since my human agents can't help blundering about, though, it falls to me to do a little reconnaissance."

Human agents? The footsteps, surely. A sorcerer and his demon?

"I warn you!" Sem put her foot forward. At the same moment, Killik drew his axe and swung at the back of the creature's neck, and Lan took off through the forest. *Going to warn the Called. Only spirits can fight spirits.*

The Shadow spirit whipped around, quick as darkness. The black aura that surrounded it hardened along its arms, and it blocked Killik's overhand strike with such force that it sheared through the axe haft entirely and sent the head spinning into the woods. Its other arm stopped Sem's blow and sent her staggering backwards with a push, spinning toward the fleeing Lan. The spirit gestured, as though tossing a ball, and a thousand darts of shadow flashed after her. Blood splashed, and Lan fell with a gurgling cry.

Katch had his own axe out by now, and he took a swing at the monster's back without realizing what he was doing. The spirit stopped the blow easily, countering with a cut that would have taken off his head had he not ducked just in time. Then it turned away to engage Killik, who'd drawn another axe; brushing aside his clumsy two-handed stroke, the spirit brought its arms down in a diagonal stroke that chopped the Valdiem's torso into three pieces.

Sem was back on her feet by now, hefting her axe and circling warily. She seemed unaffected as Killik fell, but Katch could feel his own gorge rising. The spirit turned toward her, and he edged closer, trying to catch her attention.

"Run!"

Either she didn't hear him, or decided there wasn't any point. Sem swung at the spirit's head. It parried easily, stepped out of the way of Katch's attack, and riposted toward Sem. Katch, once again acting without thinking, twisted into the path of the blow; whether he intended to block it or protect Sem he didn't know. It didn't matter either way. The cold energy of the spirit's weapon went into the small of his back, came out through his stomach, and pinned Sem through the chest to the tree behind her.

It didn't hurt. Katch felt glad that it didn't hurt. He was face-to-face with Sem, pressed against the tree, and he could feel the slickness of blood between them. She squeezed his arms to the point of pain and made a little surprised 'urk', then died with a convulsive shudder. The spirit pulled away, and Katch felt himself falling.

"I'd forgotten," hissed the spirit as Katch died, "how much fun it is being incarnate."

chapter 11

V EIL'S FIRST GLIMPSE of the Diem Highlands was not a particularly impressive one. It had been raining lightly but relentlessly for the past four days, and the sky was an unrelieved gray. The road reached a kind of knob, a high point in the pass from which it had to switchback down, and so, for the first time, presented travelers with a clear view of what lay ahead.

This turned out to be an endless vista of patchy woodland, interspersed with piles of rocks. Veil looked out at it dispiritedly and shifted uncomfortably in her saddle.

Veil had not taken to horseback riding. The Red Hills had no horses, and periodic attempts by traders to introduce them had never succeeded. The land simply wasn't rich enough to support them. Farmers hitched their plows to sturdy zoxen to break the dry ground, but nobody rode on a zox. There wasn't much point. It would be twice as fast to walk. So Veil had never ridden anything until her departure from Corsa.

Isobel and Zhin, raised in the riverlands, seemed to take horses as a matter of course. And Corvus, to no one's surprise, turned out to be nearly as good at riding as he was at fighting. Veil was convinced that at least part of that was fear: the horses tried things when she was riding them that they wouldn't dare attempt when Corvus was at the reins.

In any event, after a week of bruises, sprains, and a couple of near-serious mishaps, Zhin had put Veil on the best-mannered horse in the party and hitched it to the back of the supply train. The horse in question was old and docile, and Veil had nicknamed him Baldy. He wasn't used to having someone on his back. Zhin said he was really too old to be used as a riding horse, but he got accustomed to Veil quickly enough, plodding placidly behind the trio of big blacks that carried food and water.

After all the excitement and danger of Corsa, being on the road was deadly boring. Like the north road, the east road ran in between a pair of shoulder-high walls built of unmortared stone, with the fields to either side stretching into the distance. More walls divided one field from another. This late into autumn, many of the fields had already been harvested and were becoming infested with fast-growing weeds; others still bore rippling stalks of beans or corn.

And nothing changed, day after day. Hiking through the desert had been boring, Veil was fully prepared to admit that, but she'd spent most of her time in a catatonic stupor, trying to find the energy to put one foot in front of the other. Now, with adequate food, water, and clothing, she found her mind wandering.

I want . . .

She was unable to finish that sentence. *Something to do? I could have stayed in Corsa.* Admittedly, things had been getting a bit dangerous there. *And I couldn't stand the thought of letting Corvus leave.* That idea made her deeply, squirmingly uncomfortable, for reasons she couldn't or wasn't quite ready to articulate. *But what am I supposed to do?*

Corvus apparently has some reason to head this way, though he hasn't told me. Zhin's going back home, and he wanted me with him, again for reasons he hasn't bothered to disclose. Only Isobel seemed as lost as Veil was feeling. She kept attempting to ride next to Corvus, as though she wanted to start a conversation but didn't quite know how. He didn't like it much, and ended up spending a lot of his time riding ahead of the rest of the group, "'scouting." This left Veil without anyone to talk to. She was hesitant to approach Isobel, and couldn't think of anything worth discussing with Zhin. *Corvus, at least, I'm used to. Even if he's not very nice most of the time.*

All in all, Veil was feeling vaguely purposeless. The elation she'd felt at the dominion tournament had faded to a distant memory. She'd bought a capture board in Corsa, and occasionally tried to amuse herself with it; only Zhin agreed to play with her, though, and he was so bad it wasn't a fair contest, no matter how much Veil handicapped herself.

As a result of this boredom, by the time they started climbing the trail into the South Cloudrippers, Veil was positively looking forward to the Diem Highlands. By all accounts they were dangerous, filled with rogue spirits and wildlife and the Diem themselves, who, even Zhin admitted, were not to be trusted. Two months ago Veil would have blanched at the thought, but now she craved the break from the monotony of the banks of the Skelion.

A lot of that has to do with my company, she admitted. Riding by herself onto a plateau inhabited by hordes of ruthless barbarians was still not an attractive concept, but with Corvus riding on one side and Isobel on the other she didn't feel particularly afraid. For the first few days she kept looking over her shoulder, expecting to see spirits of pure light or possibly a flaming lion thundering up the path behind them; not only had these apparitions not appeared, Sybian hadn't said a word since the fight at the dominion parlor. It was as though the ice-spirit had abandoned her entirely, which in all fairness was possible. *She sounded like she had plans, though. Maybe something happened to her? She was fighting that other spirit—Saya. Maybe she lost?*

The South Cloudrippers were home to a gentle and agreeable sort of mountain, unlike the main spine of the range that ran along the edge of the High Desert. There were a dozen passes, some completely natural and others leveled from rough ground by the traders. Zhin led them toward one of the latter variety, passing under the eyes of a sentry tower sporting a couple of bored-looking archers, and with little or no fanfare they passed beyond the lands nominally under control of the Corsans and into the realm of the Diem. A few hours later they reached the top of the pass and began descending. It was almost possible to smell the change in watersheds; the air felt drier and stonier, and was certainly much colder than humid Corsa had been.

As THEY DESCENDED and the short, windswept trees of the highlands rose to meet them, Isobel pulled her horse alongside Zhin's for some kind of consultation. This allowed Veil to finally corner Corvus, who for the past week had been fairly elusive. It meant unhooking Baldy from the supply train, but she managed to keep him basically under control. The swordsman, still in his black-on-black attire, looked almost as bored as Veil felt. He perked up as she got closer, for which she was absurdly grateful.

"Hey."

Corvus acknowledged her with a nod, bobbing with the motion of his horse in a graceful way that Veil had yet to master. She managed to bring Baldy alongside Corvus' mount, a smallish Corsan silver who seemed totally cowed by her master.

"These are the highlands?" It wasn't great, as conversational gambits went, but Corvus went for it, possibly out of boredom.

"Yeah." He glanced at her sidelong. "Not what you were expecting?"

"I'm . . . not sure." She looked up at the sky. "At least it's stopped raining."

"Not much rain in the highlands. The Cloudrippers and the Shieldwall keep the storms out, so the Diem only get what comes up from the south."

"You've been here before?"

"I . . . yeah." Corvus jerked a nod. "I have."

"When?" Veil reflected, not for the first time, that she knew absolutely nothing about Corvus' past. He avoided the subject like the plague. It wasn't hard to think of a dozen reasons someone like him might not want to talk about it, but the way he avoided mentioning anyone or anything he'd known before meeting her was occasionally kind of creepy.

True to form, he dodged the question bluntly. "It doesn't matter."

They rode in silence for a moment.

"It reminds me of the cactus fields Jali used to keep. All those little trees. What do the Diem eat?"

"They hunt, I think."

The idea of surviving by hunting was as alien to Veil as the concept of a forest. The Red Hills and the desert that surrounded them didn't have enough game to support a hunter. Aside from lizards and chickens, animals were too valuable to waste by eating them. Kalil's family had eaten roast zox once a year, every Shadow. The festival marked the end of autumn and the beginning of winter.

"Huh," said Veil.

Corvus sighed. "What are you doing here?"

"Me?" She looked over at him, innocently. "Talking to you . . ."

"You know what I mean."

Veil rubbed the hair on the back of Baldy's neck with one hand. "Where else do I have to go?"

"You could have gone home."

"And had Kalil sell me again?"

"With the money you won at dominion you could've bought your own mansion, started your own clan."

The thought had honestly never occurred to her. Most of the six thousand—less what she'd spent on new clothes, and food, and a few other things—was still sitting in a bag on one of the supply horses. Veil tried to picture herself as a manor lord: ordering serfs around, fighting turf wars with other lords, having husbands—she colored at the thought of that—and children. It would be a scandal.

"They'd never let a girl be a manor lord."

"You could have stayed in Corsa. Played dominion, amassed a real fortune."

"They were trying to kill me."

"Money can buy a lot of things, including sellswords."

"Sellswords don't have a great reputation for being trustworthy."

"As long as you can outbid the other guy." Corvus gave her a small grin, which faded quickly under the weight of her stare. "What?"

"Are you trying to get rid of me?"

"Not exactly." He sighed. "I'm just wondering . . ."

" . . . what I'm doing here? Me too." She felt herself becoming a little irritated. "It seemed like a good idea at the time, all right?"

He threw up his hands in a conciliatory fashion. "Okay."

"What about you?" asked Veil, only vaguely mollified. "Is there any particular reason you felt like crossing the Diem

Highlands, or are you just a lunatic?"

She expected him to simply ride away after that, or at least offer a cool rebuff. Instead Corvus stared fixedly at the approaching horizon for so long Veil thought he'd nodded off in the saddle. Finally he reached to one side and drew his sword, long and gleaming. For one shocked moment Veil thought he was going to attack her; instead he flipped the blade around, carefully holding the blunt edge, and offered her the handle. Veil took it gingerly with both hands. This left Baldy free, but he continued to plod slowly forward.

It was lighter than she'd expected. The metal was thin, and tiny flecks glittered at the razor's edge. The pattern of light reflecting from the beaten steel was weirdly beautiful.

"Do you see the markings?"

Veil nodded. There were characters engraved down the length of the blade, starting from the hilt. They bore a vague resemblance to the Khaev alphabet, which she had at least a passing familiarity with, but she couldn't recognize any of them. She handed the thing back, gingerly. "What do they say?"

"The name of the sword, and its owner."

"Who was he?"

"I don't really know. That's what I'm going to the riverlands to find out."

"That's it?"

"That's it."

"Where did you get the sword?"

"I found it. In the desert."

"So why does it matter?"

He shrugged. Veil felt her irritation rising again, a week's worth of frustration and boredom behind it. "That's the purpose of this whole trip? Your stupid sword?"

There was a moment of silence; then Corvus spurred his

horse forward, leaving Baldy in the dust. Veil let out a sigh and slumped down in the saddle, feeling suddenly sore and aching.

Smooth, Veil. Very smooth. Part of her, the irritated part, still rebelled. *It's a damn sword. Corvus is nuts.*

"He may be nuts," said a long-silent, chiming voice, "but I happen to need him."

"Sybian?" Veil was so surprised she said it aloud, then hurriedly looked around to make sure no one had heard. Isobel and Zhin were still engrossed in their own conversation, so she lowered her voice to a whisper and continued. "I thought something had happened to you."

The spirit laughed, a sound like the chiming of crystal bells. "Happened to me?"

Veil burned with embarrassment. "I just . . ."

"I'm touched by your concern, but no. I've just been busy, and you haven't required my attention much. You did a fine job in Corsa, by the way."

"I didn't do anything." Other than win at dominion, she reflected, but that hadn't mattered much.

"You're alive. Corvus is alive. You're headed in more or less the right direction. It's good enough for me."

"I'm pretty satisfied with the first two myself, frankly. Though I'm beginning to have second thoughts about this trip."

"It's the only way to get where you need to go."

"Where exactly *is* that?"

"The riverlands."

"Why?"

Veil could almost see the spirit's cynical smile. "I'm afraid . . ."

" . . . I don't need to know?" Veil sighed. "I'll mention again that I could be a lot more helpful if you'd tell me what was going on."

"You're committed to being helpful?"

"Not unless you tell me what you're after."

"And therein lies the paradox." Another tinkling laugh. "I think we'll have to go on not trusting one another."

Veil felt that, as a relatively powerless flesh-and-blood girl rather than a bellipotent ice spirit, she was getting the raw end of that particular deal. Arguing was obviously pointless, however, and she set out trying to extract information out of Sybian while she had her attention.

"So is there anything we should worry about up ahead?"

"Maybe."

"Maybe?"

"It depends on whether Saya gets through to Ghael Rex or not."

"If she does . . ."

"If she does, we're in trouble. I've arranged an escort, but things could go sour."

"Great. Anything I can do?"

"If I come up with something," said the ice spirit dryly, "I'll be sure to let you know."

SAYA COULD REMEMBER a time when the iron fortress at Balkut had been one of the great miracles of the world. It had been built, of course, by sorcery; specifically by one of the first chiefs of the Diem, a sorcerer-king who'd supposedly had the place erected overnight by a horde of loyal spirits. Maintenance since then had been intermittent and not particularly skilled, so only one of the four main towers still stood at its original two hundred foot height. The new nickname for the place was the Palace of Rust, a moniker even more significant in the Diem tongue where rust was closely identified with failure and death.

This suited the current inhabitant just fine. Ghael Rex had a flair for the dramatic, and his people were easily impressed by portents and omens. No one dared live in the Palace of Rust except for the Smoke Lord and his priests, who had been granted special dispensation. The priests lived off the offerings of terrified Diem; Ghael Rex, by all accounts, lived by devouring the souls of those who displeased him.

At least, all that had been the case when Saya had last visited, two hundred years ago. She didn't expect things to have changed much. She flickered into being a few hundred feet from the main gates and walked toward them at an unhurried pace.

The guards, two humans and one Ghael, couldn't help but notice her approach. The humans eyed her complacently, but the demon was able to recognize what she was at a glance and pushed the gate open without even consulting his mortal colleagues. The guards, surprised, did little more than stare as she brushed past them, headed for the base of the surviving tower and the throne room.

Two more Ghael stood aside as she passed, which made Saya smile. *It's nice to see that someone remembers me.*

The throne room of the Smoke Lord was vast and, predictably, clogged with soot. Giant bonfires burned along the edges, day and night, throwing off not just the sweet scent of burning wood but the sickly smell of charred meat. A dozen Ghael lounged about, in crude chairs or on the floor, drinking or playing at dice. At the far end of the room sat Ghael Rex, looking just as she remembered him: nine feet tall and broad to match, with dark brown fur covering most of his upper body and huge bull-like horns curling up from his forehead. His cloak, draped over the throne, was woven entirely from the hair of men and women he'd personally defeated in battle; his belt, which was composed of interlocking horns, indicated he did not spare his own people when he waxed wroth.

Saya paused by the entryway and waited for the Smoke

Lord to notice her. He did, eventually, tearing off a huge chunk of flesh from a lump of unidentified meat sitting in a brazier next to his throne and washing it down with a long drink from a foaming flagon. She nodded, as one equal to another, and the lord of the Ghael narrowed his eyes and bellowed.

"GET OUT!" Smoke poured from his nostrils, but subsided to a trickle when he turned to face Saya directly. "Not you, of course. The rest of you. Out. Her Radiance and I have important matters to discuss."

The rest of the Ghael rose, grumbling, and filed past Saya. They were careful not to grumble too loudly, which spoke volumes. When the door finally clanged shut behind the last of them, Saya walked across the room toward Ghael Rex and raised an eyebrow.

"You don't have to use my title, you know. I gave it up long ago."

"There's only the two of us left now, Saya. If I don't remember, who will?" The Smoke Lord smiled, showing inch-long fangs. "It's been a long time."

"A few hundred years." Saya waved a hand dismissively.

"And no doubt you've come by simply to chat?" Ghael Rex snorted. "To catch up on old times, perhaps."

"Sadly, no."

"I thought not." He resettled himself on his throne and took another bite from the hunk of meat, dribbling juices in a hot stream down his chin. "Why, then?"

"I've come to call in a favor."

"Have you, now?"

"Corvus," she pronounced the name carefully, "is traveling through your domain, along with the upstart fireling's pawn and a few others. He must be stopped."

Ghael Rex stared for a moment, then guffawed, spraying

spittle. Saya took a step back.

"Corvus! Stop Corvus?"

"He must not be killed."

"I suspected as much. You know, Radiance, this is an unholy terror you've created."

"You know as well as I do what will happen . . ."

"Of course." Ghael Rex waved a hand—paw, actually—and shook his head. "Consider it done. But in return, I have a question for you."

"Ask."

"Why do you not seek the prize yourself?"

"The same could be asked of you."

"Me? I have everything I need right here. Mortals to worship me, my people to serve me, and many enemies to provide amusement. I am content for another few thousand years. Not like these young ones, rushing after every chance to become a god . . ."

"Let's just say I have interests to take care of."

"Interests to take care of!" Ghael Rex roared with laughter. "Well put, Radiance, well put. Now," he folded his paws, "let's see what we can do about stopping this runaway son of yours."

PITCHING TENTS WAS always something of a nostalgic exercise for Zhin, particularly because the tents they used were leftovers from the Imperial army—back when the Empire *had* an army—and they evoked memories of the old days. Zhin had joined a losing war, a terribly romantic concept for a sixteen-year-old with a rusty sword and a grudge against Khaevs.

The romance had evaporated pretty quickly. The Khaevs were not interested in fair fights or pitched battles, where one might make a heroic last stand. The remnants of the Imperial forces were ambushed, over and over, their positions reported by draekeres and their camps overrun by demons. Zhin had gotten out while the getting was good, and that had been the end of his personal patriotic war. Until Lord Valos, of course.

Between the pair of them, Isobel and Zhin could get the tent up in five minutes or less. It took another ten to get the spare they'd bought for Veil and Corvus up; Corvus was no-where to be seen, but Veil insisted on helping, which delayed matters somewhat.

Zhin was paying the camp set-up less than complete attention himself. The complete lack of contact from the Diem had him worried. *We should have heard something from them by now.* The tribes that counted the mountains as their western border were usually very careful about watching everyone who came through the passes, so they could swoop down on any group small enough to be easily overwhelmed. *Granted, Lord Valos negotiated safe passage—somehow—but last time they had someone here waiting for us.* Diem being Diem, it was entirely possible they were hiding in the shadow scrub-woods and simply not making their presence known. *I'm not sure whether that's more or less worrisome. If they have second thoughts about this safe-conduct thing—* Isobel seemed confident of her ability to cut her way free of any danger-ous situations, but Zhin wasn't sure he shared it.

Especially not lately. Isobel hadn't been the same since they'd left Corsa. She'd barely said ten words to him, which wasn't particularly unusual in and of itself, but her whole manner had changed. She gave the impression of being wrapped up in her own thoughts, rather than the usual feeling that she was care-fully observing everyone around her and deciding how best to kill them, should it become necessary.

On these long trips, they usually shared blankets as a mat-ter of course. It was a convenience for Zhin, and Isobel didn't seem to mind. He'd stayed away from her since Corsa, just because there were strangers in the group, and she didn't seem to mind that either. *She doesn't seem to mind anything. Or didn't used to, anyway.*

As though his thoughts had been a summons, Isobel pushed aside the tent flap and stepped inside. Zhin held up a hand in greeting before she let the flap fall and total darkness returned. He lay back on his blanket and listened to the sound of her routine, which he'd heard so many times he knew it by heart—faint clinks as she carefully laid out her knives by the side of the tent, four small ones and two big ones, followed by a rustle as she stripped and tossed her clothes into a corner.

Instead of what usually happened next, which was complete silence, Isobel spoke softly.

"Zhin?"

"Yeah?"

"I . . ." She hesitated. "I want to warn you."

"Warn me? About what?"

"About me. I'm not . . . I mean . . ." She took a deep breath and continued, with a trace of her old certainty. "There's something wrong with me."

"What do you mean?"

"I don't know." He heard her shake her head, violently. "I just don't feel . . . normal. I don't think you should rely on me."

That was unusual talk, coming from her. Zhin hesitated, then reached out across the darkened tent until he touched the bare skin of her shoulder. She flinched, shuddered, and took another deep breath; he ran his hand up to her neck. He could feel the tension in her muscles; the tendons stood out like wires.

"What's wrong?"

"I don't *know.*" She sounded irritated and terrified all at once. "I found him . . . I found Corvus. But it's not right. Something's still not right."

Zhin had long ago given up trying to understand Isobel's quest. She'd been looking for 'him'—a man who could beat her—since before they'd been partners, and as far as he could tell since she was old enough to walk. It went beyond an obsession. I t was the purpose of her entire existence. Working for Lord Valos was just a way to help pay the bills. *And now she's found him?* He'd watched them fight, briefly, and they'd seemed evenly matched. That alone made Corvus a swordsman of a caliber above anyone Zhin had ever met. *But she said he beat her, on the docks.*

He leaned forward, wrapping one arm around her. Her heart was beating like a jackhammer under the slight bulge of her breast, and her skin rose up in goosebumps.

"Isobel, are you okay?"

"I don't know. I don't think so."

He felt her hand cover his, her skin astonishingly warm. She pulled his arm a little tighter, and he felt her taut nipple under his fingers. Isobel flinched again.

"Isobel, are you . . ."

He cut off as she turned around and kissed him, inexpertly but with a great deal of energy. Zhin was too stunned to do anything for a moment; by the time he thought to put his arms around her, she was already pulling away.

"I'm sorry." He couldn't see anything, but he heard the faint rustle of bare feet on canvas. "Something's wrong with me. It's not right. I'm sorry—"

The tent flap opened, and he got a brief view of her against the moonlight. Tears glittered under her eyes, and one of her little knives was in her hand. Zhin started to his feet.

"Isobel!"

She was already running away, padding across the forest floor and lost in the shadows before he could hope to follow. He rushed out of the tent anyway, feeling like an idiot, and stared after her.

What is she doing? She'd taken a knife—that meant that she was either going to kill herself or, more likely, try to kill Corvus again. *What in the Aether is wrong with her?* It disturbed him more than a little. For four years, she'd been the one constant in his world; unemotional, incorruptible, invincible. Now something inside him flapped loose.

Zhin shook his head. *Forget that. I have to track her down before she does something stupid.* There was a light still burning in the other tent, but only one figure was visible inside, obviously Veil from its proportions. *Maybe she knows where Corvus went. Isobel obviously does.*

Isobel settled against a tree. The knots and whorls of the wood dug into the bare skin of her back, but she grabbed onto the pain as a real sensation, an artifact of the physical world she could rely on. She closed her eyes and dug her fingernails into her palms, trying to think.

I've gone insane.

It's the only logical explanation.

Her hands tightened as another wave of . . .what? Pain? Not exactly, but a close analogue swept over her. Corvus' face loomed behind her closed eyelids.

It's not right, *it's too soon, he's supposed to kill me and now it's gone wrong*—

It felt as though something in her mind had broken. Events had not gone as planned, and now one end of a tightly-wound string was whipping around loose, slashing everything else to pieces. *Corvus isn't the one I've been looking for. He's* not, *but he beat me, and now I don't know what to do.*

What the fuck *is wrong with me?*

Images—memories, really—flooded in uninvited. Limping home, age twelve. *I hurt myself, trying to outrun the guards.* Cornered in an alleyway by a pair of young nobles. *I didn't even fight them.* That seemed to disappoint the barrel-chested youths, who ripped the shirt from her back and hammered her to the ground with one heavy fist.

It wasn't the first time. Living in the slums of Crossroads, some things couldn't be avoided. But lying there, aching, naked but for scraps, and listening to the two laugh, she'd heard something else. A voice built from the roar of flames and the crackle of a bonfire, tempting and promising.

She'd mouthed the word through split and broken lips, spitting blood. "Agreed."

I'd almost forgotten that night. And with good reason. It wasn't something she liked to remember. For Isobel, memories were mostly a hindrance anyway. There was always the next fight, the next enemy, the bodies stacking up in her wake. *I was hurt. Hysterical.* It felt like another person who'd been lying there, another little girl, naked and bruised; she closed her eyes, and Isobel had opened them. She'd wandered home, covered in blood, and woken up feeling refreshed and more alive than she'd ever been.

A purpose.

It was my purpose. My reasons. Mine!

Something had gone badly, badly wrong.

After a timeless interval, the wave subsided. Isobel opened her eyes and her hands, ignoring the blood that welled from her palms where her fingernails had broken the skin. She retrieved the knife from where it had fallen, and stumbled on through the darkness.

Corvus . . .

The forest ended with a suddenness that took her breath

away, leaving her standing on top of a rocky outcropping covered with thick highland grass. Below was a valley, through which a narrow stream ran; across the gorge, the forest resumed. An endless carpet of stunted trees, stretching as far as the eyes could see. The moon was half full, and the soft light picked out a figure at the edge of the cliff, all in black.

Corvus.

Isobel reversed the knife, slipping automatically into the old patterns. She padded across the grass without a sound. Corvus' back was turned. He wore mail under his cloak, but it would be easy to stick the blade into the back of his neck. She felt suddenly calm, once again in control. *It won't last.* She moved.

That's impossible.

She hadn't made a sound. She *knew* she hadn't made a sound. *There's no way he could have known I was here.* But an instant before the knife plunged into his spine, the swordsman twitched to the side, letting it graze the side of his neck. At the same time, his hands gripped her arm at the wrist and elbow, using her own momentum to drive her headfirst into the grass. He twisted her arm behind her, applying enough pressure that she let go of the knife with a twitch.

There was a moment's pause.

"Isobel?"

"Do it." She felt him retrieve the knife. "The back of the neck. It won't hurt."

"No." He tossed the blade aside with a thud.

"Why not?" She squeezed her eyes shut. *This is* not *what's supposed to happen! It's wrong. It's all wrong.*

"Because I don't want to." He let the pressure up and sat back, and Isobel squirmed around to face him. His expression was unreadable in the shadows. "Why do you want me to kill you so badly?"

"I don't *know*." She practically screamed it. "I just . . . I . . ."
Isobel trailed off. Corvus shook his head silently.

"Something's wrong."

"Obviously."

Isobel clenched her hands again, feeling the slickness of blood on her palms. Another wave was coming, threatening to drown her consciousness in a tide of static.

"Iso . . ."

She leaned forward and kissed him, pressing her naked body against his. The links of his mail were cold against her breasts. Once she ran out of breath she sat back, and Corvus raised an eyebrow.

"Isobel?"

She clenched her teeth, fighting the onset of whatever-it-was. "It's okay."

"What?"

"I don't mind. Honestly."

He shook his head. Isobel clenched her hands again.

"Please?"

She kissed him again, dragging him to the ground.

Sometime later, her groping hand found the hilt of the knife in the grass. She grabbed it, quick as a viper, but Corvus was faster; he squeezed her wrist until she let the blade fall with a gasp of pain. This time, he tossed it over the edge of the cliff.

Sometime later, Isobel screamed. Her hands rubbed bloody trails across his back.

It's still not right.

VEIL WAS AWAKE by the time Corvus returned the next morning. She poked her head out the tent at the sound of footsteps. The swordsman was still in his customary black, but Isobel, following him, was totally unclothed and smeared with earth and blood.

It took a moment for this to sink in, and Veil managed little more than a surprised look at the swordsman as he ducked into the tent and started gathering his things.

She tried not to stare, thinking of a tactful way to broach the subject.

"Did you sleep outside last night?"

Corvus looked up, his expression unreadable. "I don't sleep, remember?"

"You have to sleep. Everybody sleeps."

He shrugged, shouldered his pack, and checked the sword at his side. Veil hastily grabbed her own pack and followed him outside, where he started uprooting the tent poles.

"I talked with Zhin last night."

"Oh?" Corvus pulled the last pole out of the ground with a grunt and set to rolling up the tent.

"He seems a little worried. Apparently the Diem usually contact him by now."

"The less we see of them the better, as far as I'm concerned."

"He was also a little worried about you."

"Me?" Corvus cinched the tent bundle tight. "Why?"

"He thought Isobel might try to kill you again."

Corvus chuckled. "He should relax."

"Did she?"

"What?"

"Try to kill you?"

"Aw." Corvus straightened up and looked down at Veil. "Were you worried about me, too?"

"Not . . . I mean . . ."

"You should relax, too. I can take care of myself."

"Did you see Isobel, though? I mean, we were wondering where she . . ."

He sighed. "Would you just ask the question you want to

ask already?"

"What?"

"You want to know if I slept with her, right?"

Veil colored. "No! I mean . . ."

"Sure." Corvus raised an eyebrow. "As you may recall, I get bored at night."

She looked at the ground, practically steaming. "It's none of my business."

"Nope." He shouldered the tent. "Shall we go?"

BY MIDDAY ZHIN was growing frustrated with the lack of conversation.

Veil appeared to be sulking. She kept her horse to the back of their little train, behind the supply horses, and said nothing to anyone. Isobel, after whatever outburst she'd had last night, was back to her usual silent self. If what had happened between her and Corvus—*whatever* that *was*, Zhin thought sourly—had affected her, it didn't show on the outside.

The swordsman in black was the only one who'd retained anything of his previous energy. He led the train, scouting a path into the little valley and leading them downstream, at Zhin's request. On all his previous expeditions, he'd had Diem guides, so his navigation was decidedly shaky; in the Highlands, all rivers ultimately led to Balkut. Head in that direction, he reasoned, and they were sure to meet Diem somewhere. Riding by the side of the little stream was quite pleasant, too. Judging from its banks, it ran much higher during the spring, so there was plenty of room for the horses and fresh, cold water to drink. If not for the unspoken tension between himself and his partner, and the equally obvious tension between Corvus and Veil, Zhin would have been enjoying himself.

It was well after noon when they stopped for another water

break. Zhin dismounted to fill his skin, and Corvus did likewise. Isobel knelt to fill hers, right next to Corvus; instead of fleeing, as had become his custom, he studiously ignored her. A little way downstream, Veil shot the two of them a fiery glare. Zhin sighed.

When a Diem war party burst out of the woods, axes waving, he felt sorry he'd wished for something to interrupt the monotony. But only a little.

"Veil . . ."

"Sybian?" Veil kept silent, in the manner she'd practiced. "I haven't heard from you—"

"I don't exactly have time to chat. Saya made it to Ghael Rex, which means we're in trouble. They're practically on top of you."

"Who are?"

"The Diem."

"I thought we had safe conduct from the Diem . . ."

"Saya met with their god and called in a favor, so I'm pretty sure that doesn't apply anymore. You should warn everyone."

"What do we do?"

"Head north. If you can make it to the mountains, I'll have some backup arranged."

"I'm not sure they'll listen to me."

"Corvus will."

She gritted her teeth. "Corvus seems to be taken with Isobel."

"Vaalkir's toy?" Sybian sounded taken aback. "What happened?"

"I'm not sure." *I'm not sure why I care, either.* Veil had spent most of the day trying to tease apart her own feelings. *She's crazy, anyway.*

"Do your best, or you're all going to get killed. The Ghael are coming."

"The Ghael? What . . ."

At that point, with ear-splitting whoops, six axe-wielding Diem crashed out of a stand of trees at the base of the cliff. Veil looked up, startled. They were dressed in leather and furs, four men and two women, each with a short axe in either hand. Physically they looked a lot like Red Hills people—dark skin, dark hair, but with an angularity to their features vaguely reminiscent of the riverlanders.

They covered the distance quickly, splashing through the little stream, and then a lot seemed to happen at once. Zhin spread his hands and shouted, Isobel reached for her weapons, and Corvus calmly corked his water skin and tied it to his belt.

"Wait—"

The Diem did not seem interested in waiting. They charged, water splashing around their ankles. Isobel's hands flickered, and the leader stumbled and fell, clutching his throat. The remaining five barely slowed, bearing down on Corvus, who had barely gotten a hand on his sword . . .

There was a spray of water from the stream, the hissing shriek of steel on steel, and the brief play of light reflecting from a blade. It was over in less than a second. Corvus straightened up, and five bodies crashed to the ground around him.

Zhin seemed a little bit stunned, his mouth hanging open in mid-shout. Veil didn't blame him. The Diem all lay still, except for one woman who rocked back and forth in the stream, clutching her chest and moaning. Corvus took a step toward her, thrust, twisted, and the moaning stopped. He stepped out of the water, running a black cloth along his sword and looking at the others.

"I take it," the swordsman said, "this isn't what you expected to happen."

"We're supposed to have safe passage." Zhin stared at the

bodies, as Isobel retrieved the knife she'd thrown. "Why would they just attack us?"

"Somebody wants us dead," Veil put in. Both men turned to look at her.

"How do you know?" asked Zhin, eventually.

"It . . . it's obvious, right?" Something made her reluctant to reveal Sybian's presence unless she had to. "Who granted you safe passage?"

"The Diem council of elders negotiated with Lord Valos." Zhin shook his head. "Maybe they're just an isolated band . . ."

"Veil's right," said Corvus. "Is there anyone who could overrule the council?"

"Only . . ." Zhin's eyes narrowed, and he stared at Veil. "Only the Smoke Lord."

"The Smoke Lord?" Veil felt herself wilting under all the attention.

"Ghael Rex. Lord of the Ghael, the Diem god. He lives in Balkut."

"Why would *he* want to kill us?"

"How should I know?" said Zhin, implying somehow that *she* should. Before Veil could answer, Corvus stepped between them, sheathing his sword with a hiss.

"Regardless, we need a new plan of action. What do we do if we don't have safe passage from the Diem?"

"Die?" Zhin suggested, then shook his head. "Sorry. But they control all of the Highlands. And if the Ghael come after us . . ."

"We could head north."

Zhin looked at her oddly. "There's nothing to the north but mountains."

"There might be somewhere to hide or . . . or something."

He shrugged again. "As good a plan as any. South is

Balkut, somewhere, and we won't be able to cross the river un-less we head north and find a ford. I'll get the horses together. Isobel!"

The girl fell in beside him. Veil followed, and was momen-tarily surprised to find Corvus joining her.

"What's going on?" he asked in low tones. "North? What's north?"

"It just seemed like a good idea."

"Since when are you having good ideas about navigation?"

She snorted and turned away, leaving him behind.

"The Ghael are coming." Sybian's voice echoed in her skull, suddenly loud. "You have to ride, now."

"We're going!" Veil almost said it out loud.

"Go faster."

The sound of a horn, long and low and mournful, echoed over the valley.

chapter 12

> "In my opinion, shadow spirits are th' worst o' the lot. When a big fire-dragon jumps out at you, at least you know where you stand. Where you stand is in deep shit, of course, but at least you *know*. Th' shadow spirits would rather talk than fight, and rather knife you in the back than talk."
>
> —Rosk Greentooth, Imperial Mercenary

B Y ALL THE dead fucking gods," Karl growled. "There's just no end to these guys."

He'd maneuvered to put his back to a giant razorleaf, holding his sword in a guard position. His arm was starting to tremble, though, from the sheer effort of swinging so much metal around; the top third of his blade glistened slickly in the early morning sunshine.

Four more Valdiem had emerged from the woods, weapons drawn. There wasn't much chance to parlay, since there were already two bodies lying at Karl's feet; wearily, he raised his sword. *Four on one. I've got reach on them, though, and armor.*

The barbarians spread out in a rough semi-circle at a gesture from their leader, a gaunt young man with deep-set eyes. He barked something in what was presumably the Valdiem language, which Karl didn't speak; he could answer only with a savage grin. *Let them attack all at once and I'm done for. Here goes.*

He pushed off the tree, aiming for the warrior on the far left and bringing his long sword around in a horizontal arc. The young man tried to parry but didn't make it; the weight of the blade chopped halfway through his torso and knocked him off his feet. Karl wrenched the weapon free and ducked as the next Valdiem came after him. A hand axe whistled over his head, and Karl bulled into the backswing, depriving the barbarian of the force he needed. The sharp edge of the axe scraped off the metal of the riverlander's shoulder-guard, and the barbarian got the full weight of the long sword under his arm. He dropped without a sound.

Next in line was the leader, who charged with an axe in either hand. Karl pulled his sword up to block, fatigue burning in his muscles, and didn't quite make it; the edge of the axe crunched against his forearm plate, and he felt a stab of pain. He backed away hurriedly, waiting for another charge; when it came, he thrust with the long sword and spitted the man.

The last Valdiem ran for it, headed for the tree line. He didn't get that far. A leather-clad shape emerged, arm extended at neck height, and the young warrior ran into it and flopped to the ground, clutching his throat. Erin drew her short sword and stabbed downward, gave the blade a casual twist, and removed it with a nasty wet sound.

Karl grounded his sword, too tired, for the moment, to even lift it back to its sheath. He eyed Erin, who wiped the end of her blade on one of the dead barbarians and slammed it home.

"I thought you'd gotten lost."

"I ran into some trouble," she said shortly. Karl noticed a cut and a damp spot on her leathers, on her right side, but if it troubled her she gave no sign. "You look like you've been doing pretty well for yourself."

"Right." Karl levered himself up, using his sword as a

crutch, and managed to get it back in its sheath. His forearm still ached from the force of the barbarian's blow. "These guys are everywhere, and they're not interested in asking questions."

"I've noticed. Someone's really stirred up a hornet's nest. Lord Adrian, you think, or that Khaev?"

"One or the other," Karl agreed. "Though I feel sorry for the Valdiem if they run into either."

"Can you walk?" she asked doubtfully.

"I'd better be able to. Or were you planning on carrying me?"

She snorted. "That's what you get for wearing fifty pounds of metal."

"It keeps me alive." Karl shook his head, wearily. "So where are we going?"

"Not much choice." Erin glanced upwards, at the looming slope of the nameless mountain. "Lord Adrian's up there, somewhere. If we try to walk down we'd never make it. We've got to find him and hope he's got some sorcerer's trick to get us out of this."

"Have you seen any of the others?"

"Sarth's dead, Aff's dead—"

"You're sure?"

"I found him afterward. Broke his neck rolling down the hill."

"What about Melody and Morg?"

"Morg's probably gotten himself killed by now. No sign of Melody."

"She'll be climbing, too. She could go through these guys without breaking a sweat."

Erin pretended to take offense. "So what am I? Arrow fodder?"

Karl smiled. "You're not a Blood Angel. Though if you wanted to put on that tight red leather they wear . . ."

She rolled her eyes. "I should really leave you for the wolves, you know that? Now come on. We've got a lot of ground to cover."

"And I was just getting bored."

TASHIDA SHIORI OPENED her eyes as the morning sun impinged on her hiding place. She took a deep, cleansing breath. Her back and shoulders ached abominably, from sleeping on rock and carrying the weight of her armor, but, otherwise, she felt remarkably calm.

Gota was already awake, sitting cross-legged on the rock next to her. The monk had been taciturn at the best of times, but since the ambush he'd been practically comatose, walking from place to place like a somnambulist. She was beginning to suspect that Jyo-raku had redefined the master/servant relationship between himself and his summoner. *If he was ever a servant.* Jyo-raku was obviously a lot more than the simple guardian Shadow spirit he'd pretended to be.

The spirit sat on the top of the rock pile, staring into the morning sun. The aura of darkness that always surrounded him boiled and churned in the light, but he seemed not to mind. Shiori climbed out of the hole between two boulders she'd been sleeping in and pulled herself up until she was on a level with him.

"Did anything interesting happen overnight? I heard noises."

Jyo-raku gestured absently at the bottom of the rock pile, where a half-dozen Valdiem bodies lay broken and bleeding. Shiori eyed them distastefully, then turned back to the spirit.

"We're still headed for the top?"

"Gota and I are."

"What about . . ." Shiori smiled as realization dawned. "You're sending me home?"

"I'm afraid not," hissed Jyo-raku. "You're no longer of much use, and it is bad form to leave one's tools lying around."

"But—"

Shiori gave a little gasp. It felt as though something had poked her in the chest, more irritating than painful. She looked down and saw that a spear of iron-hard shadow emerged from her skin. One hand brushed it and came away bloody, and her eyes were wide with disbelief.

"You . . . you can't do this to me. I'm a Tashida. My uncle . . ."

Shiori swallowed hard and slapped both hands on her chest as the spear twisted, and a moment later the breath rattled from her body. Jyo-raku let her slide down the rock pile with a clatter of armor, his expression invisible as always under his shadowy aura, then turned to Gota.

"We'll make for the top, and find those draekeres." He paused. "If she's gotten herself killed, I will be most irritated."

"KIT, DON'T BE an idiot."

"She's stuck up there!"

"Kit . . ."

"You'd do it for me, wouldn't you?"

"She's on the wrong side!"

Kit had decided to, once again, ignore Kei's advice and was already moving.

The Valdiem had chosen a particularly inopportune moment to attack. Their little group had run into a rocky ridgeline that stretched too far in either direction to detour around, so they'd been forced to climb. Melody had been the first one up; she'd made it almost halfway when Valdiem archers had emerged from the woods at the base of the cliff and started shooting at them. Their horn bows lacked the range of a Khaev greatbow, but under the circumstances it hardly mattered. The arrows they fired were barbed. The Blood Angel had taken one in the thigh before managing to swing to a position that afforded her at

least a little cover. Kei, Kit, and Morg had taken shelter in the
boulders at the base of the cliff, but a half-dozen axemen were
creeping slowly closer.

I wonder what's got them so cautious? The four of them certainly
didn't have any ranged weapons and nothing like the numbers
to justify this kind of ambush. *Maybe something spooked them.*

She occupied herself with these thoughts while working her
way to the edge of the boulder. There were three Valdiem on
her side—a broad-shouldered man, a hard-faced woman, and a
nervous-looking youth. Kit caught a brief glimpse of them and
pulled her head back just before a half-dozen arrows clattered
off the rock.

They're brave, but not very disciplined. Each warrior seemed to
be shooting on his own, not in cooperation with his comrades.
That gives me an idea.

She waited a few moments more. Kei, with a muffled curse,
crawled toward her.

"Kei . . ."

"You're *not* going out there."

"They're coming in here, so we don't have much choice.
Take out the rest of the axes while I distract the bowmen."

"Kit!"

"Relax," she said, and shot Kei a beaming smile. The Wing
Leader fumed as Kit poked her head out again and once again
drew fire.

This time, though, she didn't wait. *How long does it take them
to draw and nock?* Against a Khaev force, or even an Imperial
one, it wouldn't be an issue; a second rank of archers would be
held ready, waiting for targets to present themselves. But, as she
dashed out from behind the rocks, her suspicion was proved correct. There were only six Valdiem archers, and they'd all fired.
That left Kit in the clear for a precious second or two.

Melody had kindly lent her a brace of the short knives with which the Blood Angel was generously equipped. The Valdiem axemen were not expecting anyone to come barreling out of hiding, and she managed a nearly perfect throw while running, sinking the blade to the hilt in the eye of the leader. The big man crashed to the ground without a sound. Kit threw the other knife at the woman, but the Valdiem dodged and the blade stuck quivering in the tree behind her.

That left Kit without many options. She charged the third Valdiem, who hefted his axe above his head in a threatening but not very effective manner. Kit came in low and fast, slamming her shoulder into his chest and knocking the wind out of him. Another volley of arrows zipped past, going wide. Apparently the barbarians were unwilling to fire too close to their own man.

The youth backed up, gasping for breath, and Kit moved with him. She didn't acknowledge the woman behind her until the last minute, then ducked under her two-handed swing. The startled youth took the axe in the chest, and Kit faded past and buried her long knife in the woman's gut. She stumbled forward, onto her unintended victim, and the pair of them went down in a writhing, bloody heap.

Kit was left momentarily weaponless, sprinting in an effort to get to the archers before they got another volley off. It worked, mostly. The closest archer took careful aim but went down with a knife in her throat before she could fire. Kit didn't bother to look up, but the knife had come from the cliff. Apparently Melody had emerged from her hiding place. The rest of the archers fired and missed their rapidly-moving target; she reached the first one and flat-palmed him under the chin with all the momentum of her run, snapping his head back with a satisfying crunch.

There was a shout from behind her; it didn't sound like Kei, but she dared not look back. The next archer dropped his bow and reached for his axe; Kit grabbed the axe from the belt of the man she'd just killed and threw it at her new opponent. The Valdiem axes were not really designed for throwing, and her shot went wide, but it did a fine job of distracting the barbarian. He flinched backwards, and before he could recover Kit was on top of him, ramming her fist into his stomach and catching him on the back of the neck with her elbow on the way down.

That was enough. The other three archers had dropped their bows and were running for it. Kit turned around in time to see the last axeman still standing try to parry Morg's massive two-handed axe with his own comparatively tiny weapon; the blow took off his hand and wrist and half his chest. Kei was standing atop another body, retrieving her short sword. She jerked the weapon free with a vicious tug and waved it in Kit's direction.

"That was a terrible idea and you know it, Wing. Just because you think you're the reincarnation of Ebon Death is no reason to behave like an idiot."

"It worked, didn't it?"

"If they'd had any sense it wouldn't have. You deserved an arrow in the head."

Kit shook her head and looked up at the cliff. "Melody? Are you okay?"

"I will be fine," came her accented voice.

That turned out to be a little bit of an exaggeration, they found on reaching the top of the cliff. The arrow had gone cleanly through the Blood Angel's thigh without the barbs catching, so she was able to force it through without much pain. With the wound tightly wrapped, Melody could still walk, although it was with a pronounced limp.

Kei eyed the sun, which was beginning its slow crawl toward

noon. "Do you think we'll make the summit today?"

"Yes," said Melody. She pointed up the mountain. "That rocky area just below the summit is where Lord Adrian is bound."

"Shiori's probably going the same way," said Kit. "We can make that by nightfall, easily."

"Unless we run into more Valdiem," said Kei quietly.

"I was kind of hoping they'd learned their lesson."

"Lord Adrian said the Valdiem consider this mountain a sacred place," said Melody. "I doubt they take trespassing lightly."

"Great," muttered Kei, "just great."

"I'M SORRY, CALLED One." The girl—it was hard to think of her as anything but a girl, though she'd left the summit as a warrior training in the ways of the Called—spoke in a weak, feathery tone. "I'm sorry. I . . ."

She trailed off, gulping one huge breath after another. The old woman patted her hand, gently.

"It's all right, child. Tell me what you saw."

"A shadow." Her voice gurgled in the back of her throat. "It was a shadow. We had no warning. Zeiram was cut down from behind, and the rest of us tried to fight, but . . ." She gulped another breath. "How can you fight a shadow?"

The cave was thick with the scent of blood and decay. The old woman pressed the girl's hand as her thin body was wracked with shudders. She coughed, twice, and then lay still; her fingers clenched and then slowly went limp. The old woman sighed and muttered a prayer to Zemk, and the warriors standing around her echoed it. She let the girl's arm fall and straightened up.

"Called One," said J'tach, the leader of the guard, "we have failed. We cannot stop them. I have assembled all the warriors that can be found at the entrance of the Vault; they will enter only over our broken bodies." He raised his axe, and there was a cheer from the assembled guard. The old woman could hear the undertones of fear, though, and the sound stopped almost instantly when she held up her hand.

"No."

"But then . . ."

"Let them come."

He stiffened. "We have guarded the Vault since time before memory! Zemk himself has instructed us . . ."

"Zemk would not have us throw our lives away to no purpose." The crone smiled. "The Vault has been breached before. It can defend itself from intruders."

"Called One . . ."

"No discussion!" She raised her hand again. "Tell our warriors. We retreat. For now." She glared at the guard captain. "Understood?"

He hesitated for a moment, then lowered his eyes in defeat. "Yes, Called One."

THE MOUNTAIN HAD gotten rockier and less hospitable with every ridge, until they were climbing as often as hiking. Every ascent had to be agony for Melody, but the Blood Angel never showed it. Indeed, she was often the first one up the cliffs. Still, they all expressed relief when they stumbled upon a trail of sorts, a flat ramp carved from the rock that switchbacked up the slope.

"Valdiem," Kei murmured, and Kit nodded agreement. But there had been no sign of the barbarians since the fight at the cliff.

"Maybe they all gave up and went home," said Kit, cheerfully.

"More likely Lord Adrian found some way of dealing with them," said Melody. She glanced at Morg, who shrugged and snorted.

"You have a lot of confidence in him." Kit managed to

position herself right at Melody's side, somewhat to Kei's disgust, and was careful to offer her hand to the Blood Angel when they had to climb the occasional crudely-wrought stone stair. For the most part, Melody spurned these gestures, but it didn't stop Kit from trying.

"He's a sorcerer," said Melody, as though that explained everything.

"Even a sorcerer would be hard-pressed to get rid of an entire mountain full of Valdiem."

"He didn't have any trouble bringing us down," said Kei sourly. "Summoning seven demons of that caliber is no mean feat. I don't know anyone among the Maidens who could match it."

Melody gave Kei an odd look. "I've seen Lord Adrian perform far greater magic than that. You should count yourself lucky he did not burn you from the sky."

They rounded another switchback, and Kei groaned as the trail stretched out before them. "Does this damn mountain ever end?"

"We're only a couple of turns below the top," said Kit, encouragingly.

"And then what?"

"Wait for Shiori."

"And if her Lord Adrian shows up first and decides to broil us?"

"I will inform Lord Adrian that you two have made yourselves useful," said Melody. "If you offer no threats, he'll likely spare you."

Morg put in a rare word, since the conversation had turned toward his usual pessimistic tones. "I'm more worried about what these damn barbarians have waiting for us at the top. Probably a line of archers. They'll feather us as soon as we come 'round the bend, and our bodies will roll halfway to the bottom."

Kit and Kei looked at each other.

"I can see why you keep him around," said Kit.

Kei nodded. "He's so cheerful."

"It's not my decision," said the Blood Angel absently.

Morg glared. "Well, fuck the lot of you, then." He returned to his normal state of half-audible muttering. "You'd think with three of them . . .probably all sleeping together, nice and cozy . . . leave ol' Morg out to catch his death in the fucking rain . . ."

The next couple of turns passed in silence, or near-silence. Halfway up the last switchback, Melody waved the party to a halt, dropping her hand to the hilt of a knife. The two draekeres unconsciously dropped into fighting stances.

"Voices," mouthed Kit. Kei nodded.

They were speaking in the harsh tones of Imperial, rather than the liquid smoothness of Khaev or the gutturals of the Valdiem language. The words were inaudible.

"Now what?" Kei kept her voice to a whisper.

"It's most likely some of my companions," said Melody. "Lord Adrian may be up there already." She tilted her head, considering. "If you two wish, you may leave. I will tell Lord Adrian you're no longer a threat."

Kei looked as though she'd be fine with this plan, but one glance at Kit's determined face told her it wasn't going to fly. She sighed. "We'll go up, too. Our people might already be there, or be on their way."

"As you wish." Melody mounted the last switchback, favoring her injured leg only slightly. Kei looked at Kit again, shrugged, and followed.

Much to Kei's relief, there was no line of barbarian archers waiting for them at the top of the cliff. Instead she found what looked like the entrance to a natural cave, widened and cleared by human hands. Rocks lay everywhere, covered with lichen and occasional ambitious creepers, and a man and a woman sat together on a flat boulder near the cave entrance. They were both riverlanders, talking to each other in quiet tones; the man wore heavy steel armor, much dented and cracked, while the woman was in simpler traveling leathers. Both wore swords, and both turned as the draekeres arrived. The man's face went from surprised to hostile to surprised again in the space of a second.

"Melody?"

The Blood Angel nodded. "Karl, Erin. It's good to see you survived."

The man, Karl, blinked, as though not sure what to make of her matter-of-fact attitude. "L . . . likewise. I see Morg's with you," he added, as the big man rounded the bend. "Who are the other two?"

"Kit and Kei, Khaev draekeres."

Karl's hand dropped quickly to his sword; Kei held up her hands, hoping to placate.

"It's okay!"

Erin seemed a bit more ready to take this in stride. "Aren't they on the wrong side?" she said, addressing Melody.

"Given that the Valdiem seem to make no distinction, we thought it best to declare a truce. They have become separated from the rest of their party."

"I don't suppose you've seen them?" asked Kit, in what Kei assumed had to be a joke. Erin and Karl stared at her, and Melody ignored her completely.

"Any sign of Lord Adrian?"

Karl shook his head. "Nothing. This is definitely where he said to rendezvous, but we haven't seen him."

"He may have been delayed by the Valdiem."

"I have a hard time believing that," said Erin. "Unless they had a sorcerer themselves."

"So what now?" said Karl. His eyes were still on the draekeres.

"We wait." Melody shrugged.

"With them?"

Kei sighed. "We're not about to attack you. And if anyone is going to have *any* chance of getting off this mountain . . ."

"Ah," said a new voice. "Excellent."

Kei spun, recognizing the hissing tone. "Jyo-raku!"

THE SHADOW SPIRIT was standing behind the draekeres, hands crossed behind his back, his dark aura boiling in the afternoon sun. Behind him was the monk that Karl remembered from the ambush.

He'd drawn his sword without thinking, and heard Erin do likewise. Steel flashed in Melody's hand as well, while Morg grappled with his axe.

Damn. The two girls kept us busy, while he snuck up on us . . . That thought came and went; it didn't make much sense, since the spirit had sacrificed the element of surprise. The draekeres, in fact, looked as startled as anyone else by his appearance.

There was a moment's pause. Erin and Morg looked at Karl, waiting to see if he was going to attack; Melody kept her eyes on Jyo-raku as though gauging the odds. The spirit ignored the steel ringing him and walked toward the mouth of the cave, unhurriedly.

"I was wondering whether any of you would make it to the summit," he said, "given the Valdiem opposition. It's good to find you all gathered here. I have need of you."

"*Need* of us?" sputtered Karl. "You . . ."

"Are we talking to this thing or dicing it?" spat Erin, shifting her grip on her sword.

Jyo-raku raised one hand lazily, which gave Karl barely

enough time to move. He hit Erin in the side with the full weight of his armored body, knocking her sideways; at the same time, the dark aura around Jyo-raku speared outwards. It passed through the space Erin's head had occupied, punching through the metal on Karl's bicep and tearing a chunk out of his flesh. He and Erin hit the ground together, with him on top and her too stunned to move. Blood started to flow freely.

Jyo-raku lowered his arm. "I suggest you refer to me with more respect, mortal. As I am now fully incarnate, my need to tolerate your kind is greatly reduced." He half-turned toward Melody, who seemed to be on the point of jumping for him. "Are there any other demonstrations required?"

The Blood Angel shook her head, sheathing her knives, and the spirit nodded.

"If I may continue . . ."

Erin had recovered by this point, and was winding a strip of cloth around Karl's stricken arm. "Idiot," she hissed at him. He could only grin, shakily.

" . . . as I said, I have need of you."

"Why?" asked Erin. No one else seemed to have the presence of mind to ask questions. "If you're so powerful—"

"You should be thankful I haven't killed you outright, since you were in service to my enemy." Jyo-raku's tone was still casual. "But that is neither here nor there. This place" —he gestured to the cave— "was constructed specifically to keep my kind away from what it contains. At the moment, I cannot break the warding without expending much of my strength. Therefore, you humans will do it for me."

"Why?" asked Melody.

"Because if you don't, I'll kill you all."

Kei swallowed, hard, and estimated her chances of making it away.

Not bloody likely. I could run for the edge of the cliff and jump, and I might *survive the fall if I hit the trees . . .*

"I'll go in," said Kit, cheerfully. "I'm assuming it's dangerous, so everyone else can stay here."

Kei sputtered. "Kit . . ."

In some sense, though, she could have predicted exactly that
response. Jyo-raku turned toward the draekeres, expression unreadable under his black aura.

"As you wish. I do not care how many go and how many
stay. If you fail, however, the others will go in after you."

"I'll go with her," said Kei immediately. *What the hell am I
doing?* She rationalized it. *Better to go in together, and have twice the
chance to beat whatever's waiting in there, than to let it pick us off one at
a time.*

Melody had apparently been thinking along similar lines.
"I'll go as well." She exchanged a glance with the draekeres.

"You're hurt," said Kit. "And, Wing Leader . . ."

"Shut up, Kit."

"Yes, Wing Leader."

Morg spoke up, surprising everyone. "I'm goin' in too."

"You are?" asked Melody.

"Fuck if I'm staying outside with that *thing*," he replied in a
whisper that carried across the summit. If Jyo-raku noticed, he
didn't respond.

Erin glanced at Karl and shook her head. "I'd go . . ."

"Stay with him," said Melody. "His wound is severe."

"I'll be fine," muttered Karl.

"Kei will be staying outside as well," announced Jyo-raku.

"Why?" snapped Kei.

"Because I have further need of you."

"The hell if I will." Kei stuck out her chin. Jyo-raku hissed,
and it was all she could do to stand calmly. "And don't threaten

me. If you need me that much, you're not going to kill me."

"There are things short of death," hissed the spirit. "However, your point is taken. Go."

Kei let out a deep breath. *'Further need?' I don't like the sound of that at* all.

"What do you want us to do?" asked Melody.

"Find the warding and destroy it."

"What does it look like?"

"It should be obvious. A warding of this power is impossible to conceal. And, from the inside, it is quite fragile. Physical destruction should be sufficient. I will know when you've succeeded."

"You'll let us go when you're done?" said Kei.

"If I have no further use for you," said the spirit carelessly, "then, yes."

There was a moment of silence, which Melody broke, limping toward the cave entrance. Kit followed her at a jog. Kei exchanged a long-suffering look with Morg, checked that her short sword was free in its sheath, and went after them.

"LORD KAGERIN!"

Shuzan looked up from his evening meal as a soldier wearing Kurai colors slipped into his tent, followed by an apologetic-looking guard.

"He's come from the Anvil, my lord." The guard looked as though he expected a rebuke. "I told him you were eating, but he said it was urgent."

"Lord Kurai sent me," said the newcomer. "I beg your pardon, Lord Kagerin, but there's someone you need to see."

"You're from Kurai Morika's Blade?"

"Yes, lord." The newcomer bowed low. "He sends his regards."

Kurai Morika was commander of the Khaev forces at the Anvil. He was a good man, though from a minor family, one of the old guard who'd proved himself in the Conquest and had been rewarded with a position of responsibility. Shuzan stood from the low table, slid his sword into his belt, and nodded.

"Take me to him."

They didn't have to go far. Four more Kurai swordsmen waited in the clearing outside Shuzan's tent, accompanying a scrawny-looking riverlander in tattered black leathers. They all bowed at the sight of him, although the Imperial barely inclined his head. Shuzan felt his lip curl.

"Who are you?"

"Jon Grayleaf, my lord Kagerin," he said in heavily accented Khaev. "Best scout in Corsa, anyone'll tell you."

"Corsa?" Shuzan spoke Imperial, in which he was fluent. "You're a long way from home."

"Yes, lord. I'm on a contract. Got something for you."

"For me?" Shuzan raised an eyebrow. "From whom?"

"Gameh Lani. She hired me to deliver it. It's been a long ride, my lord."

"Gameh Lani?" *Father's spymaster.* He remembered, vaguely, being briefed on her position. *A good idea, having an eye in that city of thieves. They should all be destroyed.*

"Yes, my lord. She said to give you the letter—only you, mind—and that you'd understand."

"I see." Shuzan shrugged. "Let me look, then."

Grayleaf handed over a folded slip of paper, sealed with wax. Shuzan thumbed the seal open and found a letter, written in Khaev with an elegant hand.

Lord Kagerin Shuzan,

I hope this letter reaches you. I have been informed that this Jon Grayleaf is reliable and skilled. I hesitate to entrust too much to paper, but there are things you must know.

Yesterday, one of my agents spotted a man matching someone the Council had described as dangerous. Khaevs returning from the north are rare enough in any case, so I had him followed as a matter of course. I quickly learned that the man called himself Corvus, and was a swordsman of no mean ability.

Shuzan's eyes widened a bit at this, and he muttered to himself. "Corvus?"

In the spirit of investigation, I had a group of locals challenge him. I did not see the fight, but they were defeated easily. It should not have been possible, and a disturbing notion has taken root in my mind. This Corvus dresses entirely in black, and his skills are apparently considerable. Moreover, the weapon he wields bears a strong resemblance to the sword of the First, lost in the high desert for two hundred years.

You are Fifty-Fourth of Two Hundred, and you have read the secret histories. If there is even the possibility that Ebon Death has returned, the Hall of Two Hundred should be informed. Corvus is eastward bound, across the Diem highlands. I entrust this information to you, and hope that you will take appropriate action.

I hope you and your family are well, and that my suspicions prove unfounded.

Gameh Lani

Shuzan folded the letter again, carefully, and slipped it into his pocket. Grayleaf stared at him, anxiously; the Khaev lord appeared lost in thought.

"Lord Kagerin . . ."

That seemed to snap him out of it. Shuzan shook his head. "Pay him. Fifty eyes, on top of what Gameh gave you. That should be sufficient?"

"Absolutely, my lord. Thank you, my lord . . ."

"Then" —he waved vaguely— "take him wherever he wants to go. I have things to consider."

He turned on his heel, leaving the Kurai guardsmen behind him, and slipped back into his tent.

Is it even possible?

Ebon Death . . .

After two hundred years. He'd be dead three times over!

But if he wasn't mortal to begin with . . .

Shuzan pulled out the letter and went over it again, line by line.

Corvus!

chapter 13

CROSSING THE RIVER was not as easy as it had first appeared. Zhin had suggested they follow the river, both to throw the pursuing Diem off the scent and to look for a crossing place. They'd headed upstream, tending northward, only to find that the little valley divided and re-divided, with high cliffs rising on both sides. Corvus led the way, silent as ever. There was no conversation now, and the only noise was the gentle splash-splosh of the horse's hooves in the water and the ever-closer moans of the hunting horns.

"How can they be gaining on us?" Zhin listened to the horns with a growing unease.

"We have to follow the river. They must have ways up and down the slopes, private trails or something." Corvus guided his horse with one hand, keeping the other on the pommel of his sword. His eyes scanned the sides of the valley.

"I could probably climb one of those cliffs," said Isobel appraisingly. "Then I could lower a rope . . ."

"Unless you want to abandon the horses, I don't recommend it." Corvus shook his head. "I don't like this one bit. We could be riding into a dead-end and we'd never know it."

"There has to be a way out of this valley somewhere," said Zhin.

"It's probably got fifty Diem watching it." Isobel shrugged. "Hard to force our way through."

Zhin shot Corvus a look. The swordsman shrugged. "I'm more worried about the Ghael."

"Hopefully they're not after us—"

Corvus cut Zhin off. "They are. I can smell them."

"*Smell* them?"

Veil let them bicker. This close to the water, the temperature had dropped, and drifting tendrils of fog rose from the surface and filled the valley with mist. It was like riding inside a cloud. The edges of things were blurred, and the cliffs loomed out of the white with a vaguely terrifying suddenness. Veil sat on her horse, arms crossed and coat pulled tight, and let herself become the tiny warm core of a vast, cold universe.

She felt curiously passive. *I should be scared.* The Diem were coming, and the Ghael—*whatever they are*—and they had already demonstrated that they were not friendly. *Presumably they're out to kill us all or worse.* The possibility of being killed just didn't seem real, though. She couldn't imagine it happening without Corvus dying first, and try as she might, she couldn't picture the black swordsman going down. And all that Zhin and Corvus talked of battles and ambushes, the only evidence of barbarians' pursuit was the moaning of the horns.

Maybe, Veil mused, *it's that there's nothing I can do. I can't fight, and there's nowhere to run. All I can do is follow and hope that one of them comes up with something.*

Another fork in the canyon loomed ahead. The right side seemed wider and Corvus guided his horse that way, until the shattering blast of a horn broke the stillness. The swordsman's horse reared, and he fought to get it back under control.

"They're right on top of us!" spat Zhin, and cursed. To the right, the fog swirled menacingly, as though it concealed dozens of figures. Corvus looked between the two branches, hesitating.

Something prickled at the back of Veil's neck. *Too easy. Why leave us an out instead of confronting us earlier?* But Corvus was already riding to the left, with Zhin and Isobel following. Veil was pulled along helplessly behind the supply horses.

"Corvus!" Shouting was an effort as she was jostled back and forth. "Stop! This is a trap!"

He either didn't hear her words, or ignored them, and their headlong flight continued. The canyon twisted around them, shrinking, and Veil devoted all her effort to holding on to the saddle until Corvus pulled up short. Zhin skidded to a halt with a muffled oath, and Isobel brought the pack horses to stop just after. Ahead lay a rock wall sixty feet high, with a trickle of cold, clear water emerging from its base. The canyon walls remained high on both sides.

"Dead end," said Zhin, who had a penchant for stating the obvious. "Now what?"

"Trap," gasped Veil, trotting up to them. "It's a trap." She caught her breath. "They force us into a dead-end path, and then plug it up. Much easier than catching us on a straight-away."

"Climb the walls?" mused Corvus, still apparently unafraid. "Or . . ."

A sinister hiss announced the arrival of a flight of arrows, which rattled down a moment later. There was a metallic sound from Corvus' direction and a curse from Zhin's, followed by a terrified whinny from one of the horses.

"Get down!" Corvus splashed into the stream, ducking behind his horse. Veil needed no prodding to follow his example. Zhin, whose horse had apparently been hit and bolted, picked himself up out of the water, and Isobel drew a long knife in either hand.

"They can't hit anything in this fog." Corvus kept his voice low. "Once they close, I'll charge them. The rest of you try to slip past, and I'll break out and join you. Then we can find somewhere to hide."

Zhin shook his head. "In these canyons? Where?"

"Got a better idea?"

He bit his lip, but said nothing. Corvus turned to Isobel. "You stay with Veil." The girl nodded.

The mist swirled, parting slowly around more than a dozen shadowy figures. Corvus nodded and drew his sword, then bellowed.

"Come and get me, demon-worshipping whorechildren!"

The Diem emerged from the mist, cold water condensing on the blades of their drawn axes. They made no move to attack, though. Veil wondered for a moment if they actually wanted to talk, or if they had merely seen Corvus cut down their comrades and were understandably reluctant to approach. Then a larger figure shouldered its way past the barbarians, and she understood.

The Ghael stood more than eight feet tall, and it steamed in the damp. Most of its body was covered in thick black fur, though it wore a breastplate that covered its chest, and its upper torso seemed grossly out of proportion with its comparatively tiny legs and head. Huge hands gripped the center of a massive double-ended battleaxe. Its face was a horrible combination of animal and human, with disturbingly intelligent eyes staring out from under a heavy brow, which was adorned with two curled horns. When it spoke, Veil could hear the snap and crunch of wood as it crumbled in a bonfire.

"I am Baron Vildsvarung, outlanders," said the Ghael.

"Throw down your weapons, and you shall be spared."

Corvus didn't even blink, and Isobel apparently wasn't intimidated. Zhin definitely looked taken aback, though.

"You've never seen a Ghael before?" Veil whispered to him.

"Never." Zhin glanced at Corvus. "Now what?"

"New plan," said the black swordsman out of the corner of his mouth. "I take the demon. The rest of you are going to have to cut your way out."

"Now!" shouted the Ghael, smoke billowing from its nostrils. It lifted its axe threateningly, spinning it end over end until the blades merged into a circle of flashing steel. *That axe must be taller than I am*, Veil thought with a touch of detachment. She wondered what it would be like to get hit with something like that. *It would just chop you in half.*

Corvus stepped forward, sword raised. Drops of water ran down the blade and pattered off the cross guard in a steady rain.

The Ghael did not look disappointed that its threat had failed to cow the intruders. It barked something short and guttural to the Diem, and there was muffled laughter from the fog-shrouded figures. Corvus endured it silently, and after a moment the laughs tailed off. There was only the steady drip-drip-drip of the water and the heavy swishing of the Ghael's axe. Then, tentatively, Zhin drew his sword. Knives appeared in each of Isobel's hands. Veil felt spectacularly useless, and shivered.

Both sides moved at once, as though on some unheard signal. The Ghael's charge was a slow and lumbering thing, but the axe wove a nasty pattern of dancing steel in front of it. Corvus stood his ground and thrust, but the iron-plated haft of the weapon batted his sword aside and he was forced to jump out of the way as the demon lumbered past, its bulk making it slow to stop and turn. He seized the advantage, dashing in behind it, but just before the point of his blade scored the Ghael whipped around faster than it had any right to, swinging its axe in a vicious horizontal arc. Corvus ducked under the blade and sprang backwards to avoid the other end, backing away from the demon with an expression of concentration, as though trying to solve a knotty problem.

The barbarians, in the meantime, charged the other three. They'd apparently been instructed not to interfere with the demon's battle, as they ignored Corvus completely. Three of them closed on Zhin and four on Isobel, with another heading for Veil. Isobel's hand's flashed and steel sprouted in two throats, leaving Zhin facing only one opponent; he caught the man's stroke on his sword and disemboweled him on the backswing.

That left Isobel unarmed, though, and facing four axe-wielding Diem. She ducked to one side, away from two and under the swing of a third, and came up inside the grip of the last barbarian. The Diem, a short-haired woman with a scar on her forehead, grunted in surprise as Isobel slammed into her full-tilt. She didn't have time to do much else; the dark-haired girl twisted, producing a stiletto from somewhere and sinking it into the soft spot under the woman's jaw. The Diem sagged, and Isobel sagged with her, pulling the body so that another barbarian's hand axe bit into its back instead of her shoulder.

Veil backed away from the Diem who'd come charging at her. He gave up, about half-way there, as his comrades went down. The barbarian turned to engage Zhin, much more effectively than the other; the soldier was quickly driven to the defensive, barely checking the powerful strokes the Diem delivered with an axe in either hand.

Isobel had killed another of the Diem with her long knife, and looked to be more than a match for the remaining pair, who gave ground steadily. Veil trotted after them, afraid of losing track of the girl in the mists. She glanced over at Corvus, who was still facing off against the Ghael. The demon feinted at a couple of charges, but the swordsman wasn't fooled. He leaned out of the way of the axe and waited for his opportunity.

It came a moment later. The Ghael, apparently deciding to crush its opponent by sheer strength, raised the axe over its head in a two-handed grip and brought it down with inhuman power. The sane thing to do would have been to get out of the way, but Corvus stayed under the blow, lifting his sword as if to parry. Veil barely had time to shout as the descending axe met the much lighter blade andstopped, with a scream of metal on metal. Sparks flew from where steel scraped on steel, but Corvus checked the Ghael's swing with a casual strength.

Veil almost couldn't believe it; it certainly surprised the demon, which provided Corvus the opportunity to step forward and hack off one of its arms with a beautiful upward stroke. The Ghael screamed in pain, and smoke poured from the wound.

It kept enough self-control to ward Corvus off, though, swinging the heavy axe with its remaining hand while it backed away. Once it had gained enough distance it turned and lumbered into the mist. Corvus whipped around and followed it like a man possessed.

Veil's attention was occupied by more immediate matters. Another six barbarians had emerged from the mist, intent on the three of them. She shouted after Corvus.

"Get back here, damn it!"

"I'll get him!" Zhin edged forward, but the barbarians were intent on Isobel. Even as they watched, she separated the head of one of their number from his shoulders, then backed up, a long knife in either hand. Zhin shot her a look, which she ignored, He took off running after the black swordsman.

Seven against one. The last of Isobel's original opponents had joined the other six, spreading out into a rough semi-circle.

Isobel backed up until she was against the wall of the canyon; with her back to the rock, she flipped the knives over and smiled a death's head grin. *She's going to die.* Veil felt like she should dash forward and . . . *Do what?* Damn *it!* Tears of frustration appeared at the corners of her eyes.

Even seven against one, Isobel wasn't giving up. She rushed for the space between a pair of Diem a heartbeat before they attacked, ignoring the axes that whistled toward her and burying her knives in a pair of stomachs. One of their blades opened a bleeding line on her shoulder, but she was already turning to the next in line, blocking his strike and lashing out at his throat. He danced out of range, and she was forced to dodge a blow from behind and then dodge again as another pair of barbarians bulled forwards. Isobel spun back up against the wall, parrying strokes from the right and left, but a third Diem buried his hand axe in her ribs, just below her right breast. The black-clad girl folded silently, splashing face-first into the stream.

"Isobel!" Veil knew the shout would only attract attention to her, but she couldn't help it. She raced forward; an unseen but half-expected blow from behind knocked her into darkness.

KETSCHYA, PRIESTESS OF the Zan'diem, knew that she was dreaming.

Since becoming a priestess, she'd learned to pay more attention to her dreams. Fragments of thought, cut loose and drifting from the spirits of the world, embedded themselves in receptive minds. For every dream that was consequential, though, there were a thousand that were nothing more than the nonsense of her own mind. Learning to tell the difference had been an important part of the lore that Jikova Zan'diem had passed on to her, before he grew old and died.

Now Ketschya herself was growing old. She could feel it in her bones, with the coming of autumn; a weary ache that presaged the day she would be allowed to leave the world and be at peace. Before then, of course, she had to train an apprentice of her own. That day was years away, though, and in the meantime she'd learned a dozen ways to tell if a dream was real, or simply a figment of her imagination.

This one was definitely real. Its very sparseness told her volumes. She found herself standing on an endless white plain, under a vaulted, empty sky. It was *cold*, bitterly cold, and as Ketschya crossed her arms she found that she was naked. That was not too unusual, in dreams, and she held no false modesty before spirits. She simply waited, breath turning to steam in the chill air. After a while, a swirling mist arose from the sandy ground, coalescing gradually into the translucent figure of a young woman, carved from ice. The statue moved as though it were alive, accompanied by the distant sound of chiming crystal.

"I am Ketschya Zan'diem." The priestess inclined her head, showing proper respect for a spirit. "Who are you, creature of ice?"

"Sybian." The spirit's voice was the groan of ancient, tired ice, the grinding of glaciers.

"Sybian." The name was unfamiliar to the priestess, which was also not surprising. There were a huge number of minor spirits in the world, and more came into existence all the time. "And what would you have of me?"

"Everything." The ice-girl smiled, showing tiny icicle teeth that narrowed to fine points.

The priestess backed away, making a protective gesture with her hands. There was little fear in her face; her profession, after all, was the summoning and binding of spirits. Sybian barely flinched at the ward, though, walking right up to her despite her frantic gesticulations.

This is no minor spirit! The thought flashed through Ketschya's head, too late. Sybian was on top of her, icy hand plunging *into* her breast as though flesh was no more substantial than mist. The priestess felt a deep wrench, at the core of her being, and had time for a despairing scream before her soul was torn from her body and cast loose to dissolve in the Aether.

KETSCHYA OPENED HER eyes and found herself in a warm bed, with a heavy arm around her shoulders and her loins still aching from the earnest attention paid to them earlier. Her mate, Dikorik, was fast asleep. He was first among the warriors of the Zan'diem, tall and muscular, with a rakish smile and a mop of dark-brown hair.

She poked him in the ribs, in a spot she knew would tickle. He grunted and hugged her a little closer; she poked him again, and he opened his eyes, sleepily.

"What is it, beloved?"

"How many warriors does the Zan'diem tribe have, lover?"

He blinked. "Almost a thousand. Ketschya, what's wrong?"

"I have had a vision." She sat up in bed, letting the sheet fall to her midriff. Dikorik sat up next to her.

"A vision?"

"A command, from the Smoke Lord."

The warrior's eyes went wide. Of all the spirits, the Diem owed loyalty first to the Smoke Lord and his Ghael, who protected them from outlanders and demons. "The Smoke Lord? What did he say?"

"Assemble the warriors. We must leave at once."

He looked at her for a moment longer, as her lover; then his face hardened into a warrior's. Dikorik nodded. "As you wish, priestess."

Before leaving the bed, though, he hesitated. "Ketschya? Are you all right?" He hugged her a little tighter. "You feel cold."

"I'm fine, lover." She pushed him away, gently. "I'm fine."

VEIL AWOKE WITH a throbbing spike driven into the back of her skull. When she opened her eyes, the pain was so bad for a moment she almost returned to the welcoming darkness. She gritted her teeth and clung to consciousness, and gradually the pain subsided to a throbbing ache and a numbness at the back of her head.

She lay still for a moment, sensing that movement would further aggravate the pain, and tried to parse her surroundings. The floor underneath her was hard and gritty, like unswept wood, and there were a number of familiar smells: earth, first and foremost, combined with the distant smoke of roasting meat and baking bread. There was conversation all around her. It seemed to be in the deep-throated Diem language, though, of which she could not make out a word.

An interval passed, during which Veil concentrated on breathing. Afterwards—it felt like minutes later, but she couldn't be sure—her head no longer felt as though it would explode if she jostled it, and Veil sat up.

For a moment she thought her head *had* exploded, but the sudden, stabbing pain subsided almost immediately. Veil blinked and looked around. She was in a wooden building, about the right size and shape for a simple hut, no windows and a single hole in the roof which let in a slanting ray of sunlight. There was a door, a simple wooden board that could be slid out of the way, and a block of wood that might serve as a small table or chair. In one corner, curled into a tight ball, lay Isobel.

Veil crawled over to her as quickly as she dared, dreading what she might find. But Isobel's black coat and shirt were missing, and someone had cleaned her wound and bound her chest with rough brown bandages. She was breathing, if a little shallowly. Veil sat back on her haunches and gave a little prayer of thanks—to whom, she wasn't sure—and shook her head.

So what in the Aether happened? They took us prisoner, obviously. For some reason. She didn't understand why they'd bother, but she didn't understand why they'd attacked in the first place. *Did they get Corvus and Zhin, too?* That they weren't here proved nothing, since Corvus would obviously merit closer confinement than anyone else. *Though if Isobel were healthy I'd keep an eye on her, too.*

She'd shuffled over to the door while having these thoughts. A quick shove confirmed that it was immobile—*probably barred from the outside. I could probably break through the walls eventually, but there have to be guards.*

"Sybian," Veil subvocalized. "Are you there?"

The answer took a moment to come. The chiming voice of the ice-spirit was softer than usual, as though coming from a greater distance. "Of course."

"Things aren't going well."

"I'm perfectly aware of the situation." Sybian sounded irritated. "Things are proceeding satisfactorily."

"I thought you wanted me to stay close to Corvus!"

"He'll come and rescue you, which will cement him to you further."

"He's still alive?" Veil had been pretty sure of this, but hearing it from Sybian quieted hitherto-unacknowledged doubts.

"Of course he's still alive." Sybian sniffed derisively. "If Saya could have stopped him that easily she'd have done it a long time ago."

"Saya?" Veil remembered Sybian mentioning the name before the demons had attacked in Corsa, and then again before the Diem showed up. "She's behind this?"

"She called in a favor with Ghael Rex, the Diem god. She's

got half the tribes looking for him."

"Why? Why does she hate him so much?"

"Not important." Sybian's voice got a little louder. "What *is* important is that you stay put. Don't try anything silly. They won't kill you, not quickly anyway, and Corvus will be back before long."

"Not *quickly*? Sybian . . ."

"I'm busy securing our route to the riverlands."

Veil felt the spirit move away, and further entreaties received no reply. She sank down against the door, disappointed. *What did I expect, though? Sybian's not my private genie. She made it clear from the beginning that she's just using me to get to Corvus. He's the one that matters.* She sat against the door, thinking gloomy thoughts, until a wooden sound from outside announced the arrival of her jailers. Veil scrambled away from the door and stood up in the center of the room, feeling a twinge of fear for the first time since she'd left Corsa.

Three Diem entered. Two were young men, in the fur-and-leather of warriors and wearing axes at their belts. The third was older, dressed entirely in soft leather and carrying a gnarled walking stick he didn't appear to need. He said something to one of the others, and the warrior closed the door behind him. Then he turned to address Veil, first in a liquid language she assumed was Khaev and finally in the familiar Imperial.

"Do you understand me?"

She contemplated pretending ignorance for a moment, but decided there was nothing to be gained by it. "Yes. I speak Imperial."

"Good." The man chuckled. "My Khaev is not so good, truth be told." He spoke with a heavy accent, coming down too hard on his hard consonants, but managed to make himself understood.

"I . . ." Veil stopped. *What does one say, in this situation?* She decided to go on the offensive. "Why did you attack us?"

The man shrugged and spread his hands. "The Ghael demanded it. When the spirits demand, what can we do but obey? Besides, we do not allow outlanders to roam our lands freely."

"Zhin had safe conduct from the Council . . ."

"It is no longer valid." He snapped the words off. "Ghael Rex has instructed us."

Veil blinked, and much to her embarrassment she felt a little fear creep into her voice. "What are you going to do with us?"

"Present you to the Ghael."

Those demons. She shivered. Sybian's promise of rescue was starting to seem quite attractive. "And what will they do with us?"

"I do not question the spirits."

While they'd been talking, the two warriors had been looking with some interest at Veil. One of them had wandered to the other side of the room to poke at Isobel, who remained soundly unconscious. He said something to his companion, which provoked raucous laughter from both of them.

"What did he say?" asked Veil automatically.

The older man glanced at the warriors, then shrugged again. "He says that he is looking forward to having your companion tonight. Apparently he believes his attentions will revive her." He followed this with something in Diem, which made the two warriors laugh again.

"Have her?" Veil had a lurking suspicion about what that meant.

"It is their right, their battle-right. She will be shared among those who had a hand in her taking."

She felt her anger flare. "If you lay a finger on her . . ."

"I would advise not struggling overmuch. Kulkareth, who captured you, has something of a temper." He stood up and gestured to the warriors, who opened the door again and stood outside it. "You will be fed and watered soon."

"Wait just a—"

The door slammed shut on her words, and Veil sank back down to the floor, hands curling helplessly into fists.

"Veil."

She turned around, quickly. Isobel had opened one eye. "Isobel? Are you . . ."

"Help me sit up."

Veil grabbed her arm and pulled her into a sitting position. It couldn't have been pleasant, and Isobel grimaced a little, but didn't otherwise betray any pain. Once that was done, Veil sat down opposite her.

"Are you feeling . . ."

"Okay?" Isobel raised an eyebrow. "No. I'll live. Axe glanced off a rib."

"Oh." Veil clenched her fists, and released them again. "Did you hear what he said?"

"Yeah." Isobel leaned her head against the wall and closed her eyes.

"We have to do something!"

"What? They've got to be watching us closely."

"So we just sit around?"

"Until Corvus or my partner manages to come rescue us. Or until an opportunity comes along that we can take advantage of."

"That doesn't help us for *tonight*, Isobel. You heard him?"

"Yeah."

"He said we're . . . you know . . ."

"Going to be raped." Isobel still had her eyes closed. "I've heard the word before, you know."

"So how can you be so calm?"

"It's happened to me before. It'll happen again. One of the hazards of our profession." She opened one eye. "Just lie back and it'll be over soon enough."

Veil blinked. For a moment, she tried to imagine it. Some husky Diem warrior tearing her shirt off, forcing her . . .

"No." She bit her lip. "There has to be something we can do."

"Got a sword somewhere I don't know about?" Isobel looked almost eager. "We could fight our way out."

"They took all your weapons?"

She shifted uncomfortably and withdrew a stiletto from inside one of her socks. The blade was barely four inches long, and as thin as a needle. Isobel tossed it casually so that it stuck in the floor by Veil's foot, shivering. "Not quite all of them. But that little thing's not going to do us much good."

"I could kill one of them when he tried to . . ."

"Maybe. Even if you did, the rest of them would chop you into hamburger."

Veil closed her hand around the hilt of the little dagger. *There has to be* something.

RUMORS WERE STARTING to spread among the Diem.

"He's a monster." Gendi snuggled closer into the crook of Makep's arm. "A monster left over from the Godswar, unleashed on the world."

They were on sentry duty. On any other day, this would be something to take seriously. Other tribes were always ready to raid Rel'diem land for game or women, and at the very least the honor of the tribe could be seriously compromised if a rival snuck in and out without being noticed. But now, with practically every able-bodied warrior engaged in the hunt, there wasn't much point.

But tradition was tradition. At least, thought Makep thankfully, the priestess had been kind enough to give him sentry duty with Gendi. That they were lovers was common knowledge in the Rel'diem camp, and it meant that spending several hours away from prying eyes was not entirely a waste of time. He squeezed her shoulder as she shivered.

"They say he killed a Ghael lord. And that if he even glances at you, your heart stops on the spot." She pressed his hand to her breast, and he could feel her rapid heartbeat. "He's a monster."

"He's just an outlander." Truth be told, Makep's relief when he wasn't chosen to be part of the hunting party had been palpable. But now was not the time to be admitting weakness. He gave Gendi's breast a squeeze, and she squeaked playfully and batted his hand away. "One of the Khaev Two Hundred, they say. The greatest swordsmen in the world."

"You know what I heard." She sat up, suddenly serious. "Pori was listening to one of the priestesses . . ."

"You know she shouldn't be doing that."

Gendi waved a hand. Controlling her little sister was beyond her power, and might have been beyond the Smoke Lord's. "The priestess said it was Ebon Death. That he'd finally returned, like he promised."

"Don't be ridiculous. The Smoke Lord killed him two hundred years ago."

She settled her head on his shoulder again, lowering her voice. "What if he came back? As a spirit?"

That was a frightening thought, certainly. Makep did his best to put certainty into his voice. "I'm sure Ghael Rex wouldn't let that happen. Besides—they'll catch him, and kill him. He can't fight the Ghael."

"Yeah." Gendi did not sound convinced.

"Isobel," said Veil eventually. "Can I ask you something?"

The sun was sinking below the mountains to the west, and

what light remained stained the hut crimson. A bar of red came from the crack by the door and painted the wall just above Veil's shoulder. Isobel sat on the other side of the hut, curled around her wound, eyes closed, perfectly still. If not for the gentle rise and fall of her chest Veil would have thought she was dead.

"What?"

"How long have you been doing this?"

"Doing what?"

"You know. Riding around. Sword fighting."

"You mean mercenary work?"

"Yeah."

"All my life."

"Really?" Veil felt a hint of pity. "What about when you were little?"

Isobel was silent for a moment. "I was raised by an old woman who took care of orphans. Never met my parents."

"And what happened?"

Isobel opened her eyes to slits. "You really want to know?"

"Yeah." Veil shifted uncomfortably.

"There was this other kid. Bernar." She shook her head slightly. "Why I remember that name, I don't know. He used to boss around all the others. He was the biggest and strongest. You know how it is with kids."

"Yeah." Veil thought back to her old life. It felt like it had been lived by another person.

"Well, he tried to pull it on me one day, and I killed him."

"You *killed* him?"

"Yeah." Isobel fixed Veil with a penetrating gaze. "Snapped his neck."

"How old were you?"

"Nine."

Nine years old. Veil shook her head. "And since then?"

"Kicked around. I was a bandit for a while, but by then it was pretty obvious I was a girl, and most of the bandits had this idea that just because a woman rides with them they get to fuck her." Isobel sighed. "That's the thing about men. They get these idiot ideas, and most of the time you have to kill them. And that doesn't help."

"How'd you end up with Zhin?"

"He recruited me after a bar fight. He works for Lord Valos." Veil remembered hearing the name, but didn't recognize who it belonged to. "And he offered me a steady income and decent companions. I've been with them ever since."

"Why?"

"Why?" Isobel chuckled. "It's a living."

Veil stayed quiet. The other girl caught her eye, and after a moment she shrugged. "You really want to know, don't you?"

Veil nodded silently.

"I can't really tell you, because I don't really know. But I'm looking for someone. A man, a great warrior."

"Corvus?"

"I thought so, but I'm starting to doubt it." She shook her head. "When I fought him at the dock, and I thought he was going to kill me . . .it felt so *right*. I knew he was the one. But afterward . . .no. I don't think so."

"But why? Why are you looking?"

"Fuck if I know. Ask the gods. I can't *help* it."

"Oh." Veil fell quiet again. "I used to live in the Red Hills."

"I can tell." There was a touch of sarcasm, which Veil ignored.

"I lived in Kalil's mansion, with all his other kids. It was . . . pretty bad, I guess, but I didn't know any better. I was going to grow up and get married and have a normal life. Have some kids of my own. Help run a house. Make friends with my husband's other wives."

"And?"

"Kalil lost a war. He sold me to some slavers."

"You should be grateful not to have to go through with that life. It sounds awful."

"I don't know. Maybe it would have been." She sighed. "It would have been nice to give it a shot, you know? I wish I could've have tried being normal."

"Trust me. You're better off."

"How would you know?"

"Hang around a town and get married, and you're stuck. When things go wrong—husband starts drinking, crops don't grow, whatever—there's nothing you can do."

"And that's not true if you're a mercenary?"

"At least you can fight. As long as you've got a sword, you've got a chance."

"We're locked in a room, probably about to be gang-raped at nightfall."

Isobel raised her eyebrows. "That's not the end of the world."

"And if they slit our throats afterwards?"

"Then we die." She shrugged. "What are you so afraid of?"

"I don't *want* to die." Veil blinked and rubbed her hands against her eyes. "Is that so strange?"

"Don't ask me. I've been told I'm not exactly normal."

"I want to see what the riverlands are like. I want to" —Veil groped for meaning— "I want to play capture, and eat interesting foods, and watch the sun set."

Isobel chuckled. "That's an odd list."

"It's the best I could come up with at the spur of the moment."

There was another pause. The sun had slipped almost completely below the mountains, leaving a single, fading spark of red on the wall.

"Veil," asked Isobel, "why are you telling me this?"

"I don't feel like getting raped. Or dying. So I'm about to do something incredibly stupid. And I just . . .felt better, I guess." She smiled a little, and blushed. "Silly."

Isobel's eyes were hooded. "Yeah."

"I'm okay now." *I'm okay now. Really.*

"Let me know before you try whatever it is." Isobel leaned back against the wall. "I hate surprises."

"I think you'll know. If it works."

Isobel closed her eyes. Veil wrapped her hand around the hilt of the little knife, tightly.

"Sybian." She whispered the word, inaudibly. "Sybian!"

"What?" snapped the ice spirit. She sounded annoyed, with a hint of ice crunching creeping in to her normally melodious voice.

"The Diem are planning to rape us tonight."

"They do that." She sounded as though she didn't consider it of any consequence. "They believe it's a warrior's right to do what he wishes with captives."

"I don't plan to stand for it."

Sybian chuckled, a faint tinkle. "You don't exactly have a choice."

"I do if you help me."

"I already told you, it's better if Corvus rescues you. They've given us a great opportunity here, and I'm not going to waste it."

Veil took a deep breath. All this she'd been expecting. "I demand that you rescue us."

"Oh?" Sybian still sounded amused. "And what makes you think you're in a position to demand anything, little girl?"

"You need me to get to Corvus. Rescue us, or I'm not going to cooperate."

"I don't need you to cooperate."

"You need me alive." Veil pulled the little dagger and pressed it to her throat.

That seemed to give the ice spirit pause. "You're bluffing."

Am I? She wasn't sure. *But I need to do* something. "I'd rather die."

"That's not logical."

"Humans are strange about things like this." She pressed the knife until the point dug into her skin. The pain brought home the reality of what she was doing.

Gods preserve. I've gone insane. Her hand started to shake. *I can't do it. It's not going to work. She can read my mind, she knows I'm bluffing. I can't do it.* She wanted to cry, and forcing herself to maintain a straight face took most of her attention. *I can't.*

"Come on, Sybian. What have I got to lose?"

"Your life?" The spirit's voice quivered, like distant bells.

"My life isn't worth spit in the Aether." *It is, it is.* Veil felt an unpleasant clenching in her stomach. *It's the only one I've got.* "Especially not if you let me get raped and tortured whenever it suits your plans."

There was a long moment of silence. The hand that held the knife was starting to cramp. Veil caught Isobel's eye, across the room; the girl was watching with interest. *I must look like a lunatic, standing here with this knife, muttering to myself.* The idea made her laugh, though her throat was raw.

"Interesting," said Sybian finally. "Interesting."

Veil held her breath.

"You can put the knife down. I get the point. I do need you, and I suppose that means I need to treat you a little bit better."

Veil breathed out. "So you'll help us?"

"I'll do my best. I can't guarantee your safety once things get nasty."

"Good enough for me." Veil let her hand fall, shaking, to

her side. "When?"

"When they show up. Get ready to run."

"Right."

She felt Sybian's presence depart. Veil slumped back against the wall, breathing hard. Isobel raised one eyebrow.

"Are you okay?"

"I'm fine." She forced her hand open, letting the knife clatter to the floor. "Just doing a little negotiating."

"I see." Isobel apparently saw no point in pressing the matter further. "I assume this relates to your 'something stupid'?"

"Yeah." Veil thought suddenly of Isobel's wound. "Can you run?"

"Probably. Not very far."

"When they show up, things are going to happen."

"Things?"

"Yeah." Veil shook her head. "So get ready to run for it."

"Can I have my knife back? I'll probably be able to do more good with it than you will."

Veil kicked the knife over to Isobel, who picked it up and flipped it delicately, testing the balance.

"Isobel . . ."

"What?"

"I'm sorry if this . . . wasn't what you wanted. I mean, we could get killed trying to escape. I don't want to . . ."

"Don't worry about it." She tossed the knife in the air and caught it by the hilt as it fell. "This is more my style anyway."

They didn't have to wait for long. A delegation of Diem arrived just after sunset, smashing the door open and crowding into the room. There were five of them, strapping young hunters in fur and leather, plus another pair who stayed outside as guards. The five had apparently spent the day celebrating their triumph. They stank of alcohol, and at least one of them was having serious trouble standing up. Veil looked at them with what was almost pity. *They have no idea what's about to happen.*

The Diem chattered back and forth in their own language, looking at the two girls. One of them pointed at Veil and said something that sounded decidedly uncouth, provoking general laughter. Finally, one of the less-inebriated warriors stepped forward and spoke in heavily accented Imperial.

"You are our prisoners." He belched hugely. "You know the prisoner-rights?"

"Are you Kulkareth?" asked Isobel.

"Yah." The Diem smiled. "I captured you. I get first choice."

Isobel also smiled, pleasantly. "You're dead."

The tiny stiletto sprouted, as if by magic, from Kulkareth's throat. He staggered backward with a gurgling scream, into one of the other Diem. The rest of the warriors didn't quite grasp what was happening, and Veil sprang to her feet. *Damn! What if Sybian's not ready? We're both going to get killed . . .*

Then the air started to sparkle, and a pale form took shape in the hut.

Veil recognized it from Corsa: a reptilian ice-spirit, curled in on itself. A crest of jagged ice crystals ran from the top of its skull down the length of its back, and sky-blue eyes flickered open and focused on the dumbfounded Diem. Kulkareth was still dying noisily, but his companions let him slump to the floor in their haste to draw weapons. The spirit extended its head toward them on a long, flexible neck and exhaled a cloud of frost with one lazy breath. The two Diem on the right were instantly crystallized, covered with an inch-thick layer of frost. Behind them, the wooden wall of the hut cracked and exploded.

Veil scrambled out of the way as the spirit got to its feet, separated from Isobel by the bulk of its body. It was far too large for the hut. The walls splintered and gave way, and the roof crumbled as the thing shrugged. The two Diem who'd been guarding backed away, terrified, but the two that had been inside the hut had nowhere to run. One of them managed to get his axe out, but his wild swing glanced off the ice-like armor on the lizard's flank. It shifted, uneasily, and crushed him under one foot. The other Diem just cowered until the great head swooped down at the end of its flexible neck and scooped him up. There was a brief spatter of blood, and Veil caught a glimpse of dozens of needle-sharp icicle teeth before the poor barbarian disappeared down the monster's throat.

"Veil!" Isobel had to shout over the mayhem. "Get this thing out of here before we get crushed!"

Veil pointed to the door, unable to summon the breath to scream. The temperature in the room was falling rapidly, and she could see frost forming on the ground around the lizard's feet. It lurched forward, whether in obedience to her commands or in search of more food she didn't know, and took most of the wall and roof of the hut with it. The remainder collapsed, showering Veil with rubble and splinters. A broken board twice the size of her head hit the ground a few feet away. Thankfully, it was a small building, and a moment later the lizard was striding away into the Diem village, leaving Veil and Isobel standing in a pile of rubble.

Isobel got to her feet, one hand on her wound. "That was impressive. I didn't know you were a sorcerer."

"I'm not!" Veil stared after the lizard, which had run down one of the Diem who'd been guarding the hut and torn him in half with a swipe of its paw. She looked back at Isobel and shook her head. "It's complicated."

"Okay." The black-clad girl seemed to accept this. She had already gathered a couple of hand axes; Isobel thrust one through her belt and tossed the other to Veil. "Here."

Veil barely caught the axe. It felt large and alien in her hand. The grip was wood, lovingly polished to a fine sheen after years of use. She swung it experimentally with one hand, and found that she could barely control it. *Still, better than nothing.* "So we're escaping?"

"It would seem to be a good idea, while we have a distraction."

Veil took her first real look around. They were in the middle of a Diem village. She could see a dozen huts ranged around the edges of a central clearing, most of them larger and more elaborate than the one she'd been imprisoned in. It was dark, but the village was lit by a bonfire in the center of the clearing and dozens of flickering torches, many of which were on the move. Shadowy figures converged on the ice-lizard, which had wandered unconcernedly over to another hut and broken it open with a powerful blow from its claw. Veil heard a woman's scream, high-pitched and shrill, carry across the clearing, followed by the crunch of massive jaws. The scream was abruptly cut off.

"So where do we go?" Veil, still clutching the hand axe, picked her way carefully from the rubble.

"You didn't think this plan through very well, did you?"

"It wasn't much of a plan. I just didn't feel like getting gang-raped."

"You weren't first in line." Isobel shook her head.

"You might be a *little* more grateful."

Veil started as someone shouted in Diem. Three barbarians, two women and a middle-aged man, pointed and started running across the clearing. Veil raised her axe, feeling more pathetic than scared, and Isobel stepped in front of her.

The Diem were apparently not looking to recapture the escapees, and came in with weapons drawn. Isobel stood her ground as one of the women charged, then stepped to the left at the last minute, leaving the blade of her axe at neck level. The barbarian flew into the air and landed heavily on her back. The other woman, momentarily startled, got a kick to the side of the head and went down like a sack full of bricks. Isobel looked up just in time to parry an overhand stroke from the last Diem, and steel rang on steel for a moment as the axes flashed back and forth. Then he was backing away, clutching the stump where one of his hands had been, and Isobel turned back to Veil as though nothing important had happened.

"Grateful isn't something I do very well," she said irritably. "Now where in the Aether do we go now?"

Veil's eyes widened, looking over Isobel's shoulder. "Away!" Isobel caught the cue and dove aside and the ice-lizard came thundering in. It ignored her completely, bearing down on Veil with a lumbering intensity. It breathed in, and Veil leapt to one side as freezing breath blasted the spot where she'd been standing. She landed badly, rolling over some rubble that left inch-long tears in her arm, but Veil didn't even feel the pain.

"Sybian!" She screamed it aloud as the lizard turned toward her, icicle teeth flashing at the end of its long, snaky neck. The only reply Veil got was a distant, tinkling laugh. Her thoughts whirled frantically.

Why? Why is she trying to kill me? I thought she needed me. Maybe Corvus died, or she found some other way to get to him . . .

Isobel was shouting something incomprehensible over the screams of the Diem and the sudden roar of the lizard as it bore down on her. Veil felt rooted to the spot, unable to dodge or even raise her axe in a pathetic attempt at self-defense.

I can't stop her. I'm just a little girl I can't fight, or . . .

A blur to one side caught the spirit's attention, and it twisted suddenly away, blasting another stretch of clearing into frozen turf. There was the hiss of a drawn sword, and the screech of metal. Veil stood perfectly still as the lizard's bellow dwindled; after a moment, its head fell from the end of its long neck and hit the ground hard enough that it broke into a thousand icy fragments.

Silhouetted against the bonfire was a familiar figure in black. Veil felt her breath catch.

"After all," said Sybian quietly, "he has to rescue you from something."

As Corvus walked over, Veil managed a shaky smile.

GHAEL REX HAD lost his sense of humor.

"I am not pleased with you, Count."

The Ghael groveled on the floor, head pressed against the rusty iron plates that were everywhere in the palace. Ghael Rex stood with one foot inches from the demon's head, smoke trickling from his nostrils. Saya stood a step behind him, more amused by the display than anything else.

"I'm sorry, Lord. He . . . that is, the quarry . . . has proved more elusive than we expected. And your directive not to kill him . . ." The Count looked up, pleading. Ghael Rex kicked him angrily to one side. The demon flew through the air until he hit one of the iron walls with an almighty clang, then slid to the floor and lay still.

Probably lying low, thought Saya. Ghael Rex's anger was a terrible but transient thing.

"Radiance," said the demon lord in what was almost an ingratiating tone. "Your monster is being difficult."

"He's not my monster."

"You created him." The Smoke Lord raised his massive eyebrows. "And you seem to take responsibility for him."

"And he's evaded you. All your pet humans, even your

own people."

Ghael Rex held up his hands. "Now, Saya. He hasn't gotten away yet."

"Once he crosses the mountains he'll be beyond your sphere of influence. And now you tell me that the Zan'diem are marching to *help* him?"

Fire bloomed in the demon's eyes. "They are. And they will be disciplined accordingly. An entire tribe of Diem defying my will . . ."

"You've got these humans well cowed. I suspect the involvement of one of the others. Most likely Sybian. The frigid bitch has been dogging my every step."

"You should destroy her."

"She's cautious. I haven't had an opportunity. Besides, some of these younglings are more powerful than you realize."

"More powerful than you and I, Radiance?" The Smoke Lord laughed. "I think not."

Saya gritted her teeth. "In any case, my Lord, I take it you intend to stop them before they reach the passes? Despite their new allies?"

"Of course." The corner of the demon lord's mouth quirked in a smile. "The Zan'diem need to be taught a lesson about obedience to the will of the spirits."

METAL SCRAPED ON metal as three gauntleted hands were raised to breastplates in salute. Lord Justin Valos waved a hand dismissively as he ducked into his command tent, his sodden cloak hanging heavily behind him.

"Good evening, Lord Commander," said Michael, removing his lord's cloak and spiriting it away. "An evil night. Would you like something warm to drink, to take the chill off?"

Justin nodded, and Michael imperceptibly bowed his way

out. The servant was from a family that had been retainers to the Valos' for generations, and Justin's personal body servant had chosen to follow him into exile when the rest of the clan turned everything over to Tashida Kuron's armies. Over the years, Justin had come to rely on him to run the non-military aspects of the camp. Somehow he still found time to fix his lord a hot drink.

"Be seated, gentlemen." Justin took his seat—a cushion, really—at the head of the table. "Time is short, so we'd best get right to business. Tayla, what's the latest?"

Tayla Barschef, chief of scouts, was a former horse thief who'd turned to scouting when the Khaevs invaded. Somehow she'd wound up attached to Justin's forces and hadn't abandoned the fight like so many others. She was a thin, hard woman, all skin and bones, with her hair cut barely an inch from her skull. The perpetual scowl she wore was generally considered fair warning; a scout who failed in his or her duty got the sharp end of her tongue and usually regretted it. Even Justin got a warning swat now and then, which he tolerated in relatively good humor.

"Somethin's goin' on there, m'lord. Shuzan had his men spread out all over the face of th' Aether, as if he were lookin' for something."

"Us, perhaps?" said Lord Benham Cartwrite. He was chief of cavalry: round, red-faced man with more courage than imagination. Justin kept him around because courage was the primary qualification for a cavalry leader, and because the Cartwrite forces were among his staunchest supporters. Their estates had been burned to the ground during the invasion, and most of them still wanted revenge. "I can't think of anything else worth rousting a whole Blade out for."

"There's obviously somethin'," Tayla snapped. "Shuzan's outriders were makin' no attempt at concealin' themselves.

They were lookin' for someone who wanted t'be found. My people had no trouble wrigglin' around them."

"And what did you discover?" asked Justin.

"Shuzan himself an' the hard core of his Blade are camped here." She pointed to a spot on the map, west of the Tsel and near a smaller river called the Moth. "They ain't makin' much progress. He's got as much as half the Blade out scoutin'. Even had some of his heavies drop their armor and join the lights."

"It sounds like a perfect chance," said Benham eagerly. "We should strike. Shuzan's scouts are mostly to the north and east, correct? If we swing around to the south, we might be able to overrun his camp before he even knows we're there."

"It sounds like a trap to me," said the last member of the council. Fyder Gunson, chief of infantry, was a lean, many-scarred man who'd spent years as a mercenary before Justin had convinced him that the Khaevs wanted to put him out of business for good. He freely professed to having survived due to his inclination to trust nothing and no one. "Doesn't make any sense. Why would Shuzan give us a chance like that?"

"He obviously has something else on his mind," retorted Benham. "We should take advantage of his mistakes."

"If I might *continue*," interjected Tayla acidly. "This was Shuzan's disposition as of about two days ago."

"It's changed?" Benham looked embarrassed.

"Yes." The chief scout drew a line on the map with her finger. "He's pulled in all the scouts and is ridin' the whole Blade, hard, for the mountains. Whatever he was looking for, I think he found it."

"Looking for something in the mountains," Justin mused. "A bandit gang, perhaps?"

"It seems unlikely that they'd send Kagerin Shuzan himself after a measly gang of bandits," said Fyder.

"Whatever he found," said Tayla "It's a problem for us. Shuzan's headed right for us, more or less, with almost a thousand heavy cavalry. He's got draekeres with him, too, so it's safe to say he'll find us if we don't move out, and soon."

"We should swing around him," said Fyder. "Let him go chasing his will-o-the-wisps. We'll snipe at his flanks and rear, and if he's not careful we'll cut him off completely and trap him against the mountains."

Justin shook his head. "Unlikely. He could always fall back on the Anvil, and we have neither the men nor the time to take that place."

"We should meet him head-on," declared Benham. "We have more men than he does. " "But we're not nearly as mobile," interjected Fyder. "Shuzan's Blade is entirely mounted, and he has those damn draekeres. He could avoid our main strength and chop our infantry to pieces."

Justin wasn't paying attention anymore. He was staring at the map, and thinking.

Move south. Run away, like we have so many times before, and live to fight again. Shuzan's Blade closing like a hammer against the aptly named Anvil. It certainly looked like a recipe for disaster. *We could make a stand of it. But if they break our line, we have nowhere to retreat to—the Khaevs will sortie from the Anvil and hunt us down.*

But . . .

There was another factor, something none of his subordinates were aware of. *If we move now, we abandon the hidden passes of the Diem. Isobel and Zhin will be cut off when they arrive.* Normally, Justin wouldn't have hesitated to make that decision, despite his long friendship with Zhin. *The fortunes of war. But this time, if the Prophet is to be believed, they have the girl who will be the key to our ultimate victory. Can I abandon them?*

Fyder and Benham continued to squabble, a melody that was

all to familiar to Justin. Tayla sat quietly and watched her lord; he wondered if she had discerned the nature of his struggle.

Do I trust the Prophet, or not? That was what it came down to. *The old man has never led me false before. But can I bet my entire command on one of his ideas?*

It was the thought of Ethan, back in Crossroads, that ultimately decided him. Another old man, putting down his sword. *And there's no one to pick it up again. Surviving isn't enough. If something doesn't change, the Empire will truly have fallen, and it will take another thousand years to put it back together again.*

Her face rose again in his inner vision. *Mika.* Justin's hands curled into fists and he cleared his throat.

"We stay." Benham looked delighted. "At least until the arrival of our team from Corsa."

"My lord," protested Fyder. "We don't know when Zhin will return. Or even if he will. There are rumors of unrest amongst the Diem . . ."

"He'll return. It'll take more than a few unruly barbarians to stop him." *And the Prophet said he would.* "He's bringing something crucial to our cause, and I won't let it fall into Khaev hands."

"So we'll be taking the battle to Shuzan?" said Benham eagerly.

"We can hardly sit here in our camp while he descends on us, can we?" Justin forced a smile. *Hurry up, you old fox. Even if we beat Kagerin Shuzan, others won't be far behind.* "Tayla, have your men find out the exact position of Shuzan's main body. I want you to start picking off his outriders, too. Try to keep him blind to the south."

"What about his draekeres?" asked the scout. "If they fly free, he'll find us anyway."

"We'll deal with that when it comes. Benham, assemble our

cavalry. Outfit as many of the heavies as we can."

"Yes, sir!" The cavalry chief was practically vibrating with excitement.

"Fyder."

"Yes, sir?"

"Have your men find some woods in his path, and set up the light infantry there. We may be able to bleed him enough that he thinks better of a frontal assault."

"Yes, sir." It was clear the infantry chief didn't think much of the plan. *Neither do I, frankly. Kagerin Shuzan's Blade is one of the strongest in the Occupation. But it's the best chance we have.*

If the old man is right.

chapter 14

> "The older something is, the more reasons there are for leaving it alone."
>
> —Diem proverb

K IT HUNG BACK as the group of five entered the cave. Gota, who'd joined them at the shadow spirit's unspoken command, took the lead. Kei went second, glancing at Kit but not commenting, followed by a very nervous-looking Morg. Melody brought up the rear, limping slightly, and Kit dropped back to her side.

"Are you all right?" she asked in a low tone.

Melody looked at her with cool, haughty eyes. "You have a lot of concern for your enemies."

"I've always had a soft spot for you Blood Angels." Kit scratched the back of her neck. "Something about your quest tugs at the heartstrings, you know?"

"No." Melody half-smiled, leaving Kit uncertain whether she was amused or not. "In answer to your question. I will recover, and the pain is quite bearable."

"You can leave most of the fighting to Kei and I. We can handle things."

"If there is any fighting to be done," said Melody, "I worry that it might be beyond all our abilities. If the Valdiem are to be believed, no one has entered this tomb for hundreds of years.

Any guardians would have to be spirits. And if they were powerful enough to ward the place against a demon of Jyo-raku's
caliber . . ." She let the thought trail off. Kit considered for a
moment, then shrugged.

"I've killed spirits before."

"As have I. It's not a task to be underestimated."

Melody picked up her pace before Kit could reply, catching
up with Morg. The draekere watched her from behind, shaking her head. A distant part of her couldn't help but admire
the sleek lines of the Blood Angel's body. *Now*, Kit told herself
sternly, *is* not *the time for that.*

It quickly became apparent that whatever natural cavern
had once existed here had been vastly expanded. The tunnel
that stretched from the cave entrance looked to have been *bored*
into the mountain. Sets of grooves spiraled from the walls to the
floor at regular intervals, and the ground under their feet was
only marginally flat. It was as though someone had cut a perfectly circular tunnel, and someone else had provided a surface
for walking on.

"Sorcery." Morg sniffed the air and wrinkled his nose. Kit
was forced to agree. The wind that blew from the depths of the
cave had the taste of decay. *And only a demon could have carved this
tunnel so perfectly.* A demon was what was likely waiting for them
up ahead, too. Truly powerful sorcerers, according to legend,
could bind demons with agreements that stayed in force even
after the sorcerer's death, so that their sanctums would remain
eternally undisturbed. The tales Kit had grown up with had
been full of heroes charging in to such haunted tombs, inevitably
doing battle with the guardian spirits and being rewarded with
great wealth, or even a Bound Blade. Kit felt her spirits lift a
little bit. *I wonder what it'd be like to use a Bound Blade.*

"The tunnel widens ahead." Gota's voice had lost all trace

of personality, as though Jyo-raku wasn't bothering to conceal his control anymore. "Some sort of chamber."

Morg put a hand to his axe as the five of them crowded together. The light from the tunnel entrance was dim and failing, so Gota produced a torch from his knapsack and lit it, bathing the rock in a flickering orange glow. Kit could vaguely make out an oval room, perhaps forty feet wide, with the darkness of an exit tunnel on the other side.

"Could the ward be in there?" asked Kei. She didn't sound optimistic, and Gota shook his head.

"No. It must be further on. We should proceed."

"I smell a trap." Kei peered out by torchlight.

Melody nodded, slowly. "Why have a room?"

"It's a little obvious for a trap, isn't it?" said Morg. "If there are demons about to come crawling out of the woodwork, why not ambush us in the corridor?"

"Search me," Kei replied quickly. "I'd just as soon not go in there, though."

"It's not like we have a fucking *choice*," said the axeman. "That demon's waiting outside for us, and if we don't smash this ward thing he'll shred us."

"So we've got to cross." Kit fingered the knife at her belt. "Who's going first?"

Kei immediately looked at Gota, who in turn looked at Morg. The axeman stared at the priest, opened his mouth to say something, and thought better of it. He muttered darkly under his breath.

"Might as well. This whole thing is fucking crazy anyway." He unslung his axe and held it in both hands. "Here goes nothing. Come on out, beasties. I know you're fucking there. You don't scare me . . ."

Morg strode into the room. Melody had produced a pair

of knives from somewhere, ready to throw, and both draekeres were a bare instant from drawing their weapons. The emotionless Gota was, of course, unperturbed. He pushed the torch forward, to give the big man a little more light.

"Okay." Morg had reached the center of the room, and turned slowly in a full circle. "I don't see anything. It . . ."

"Look out!" Kit and Kei shouted almost simultaneously.

With barely a rumble for warning, a huge stone block dropped from the ceiling, directly over Morg. He tossed his axe down and dove to one side, getting out of the way just in time; the heavy cube crashed to the ground and filled the cave with thunder. Morg ended up on his stomach; he pushed himself halfway up and managed to turn back toward the rest of the group when a second stone block came barreling down, crushing him from the hips up. Blood splattered from underneath it, like the juices of a cockroach squashed underfoot, and his legs kicked and twitched pointlessly. Kit barely blinked, and had to make a conscious effort to keep from grabbing Melody's shoulder.

"Interesting," said Gota.

"Dear gods," said Kei. She rounded on the priest. "You knew that was going to happen!"

"It was likely there was a trap of some kind," Gota said calmly. "We needed to find out what it was. He was by far the most expendable."

"Who's next most expendable?" Kei's blade was suddenly in her hand, pressed against the priest's throat. "I should . . ."

"Kill me if you wish. It's of no consequence. Jyo-raku is still waiting outside."

Kit couldn't take her eyes off Morg's legs, which were still shivering reflexively. She jumped half an inch when Melody cleared her throat.

"The priest is right. Whether or not he is Jyo-raku's creature now does not change our fundamental problem."

"This doesn't make any sense." Kei hadn't moved her blade. Gota still stood calmly, even with steel an inch from his jugular. "If the place is warded, why have traps?"

"To keep humans out, of course," said the priest. "The ward is only effective against spirits."

"Why not just bury the whole thing under the mountain?"

"Undoubtedly the designers had some pass phrase or trick that would get them past the dangers." Gota shrugged. "Since the designers are thousands of years dead, that isn't of much help."

"Look!" Kit pointed.

Two creatures—spirits, obviously—had emerged from the gaps in the ceiling. They resembled bumblebees, but grossly oversized and with a clay-red color instead of yellow and black stripes. Each bee-thing attached itself to the top of one of the stone blocks that had fallen and started to lift, ludicrously under-sized wings beating furiously. The blocks shifted, ascending inch by inch back toward their places in the ceiling.

"Setting it up again," said Kei sourly. She glanced at the ceiling. "There must be dozens of them up there."

Steel glittered in Melody's hands. "Then a solution presents itself."

Knives flashed across the room, into the flanks of the two bee-creatures. They lost their grip on the blocks at once, letting them drop a few inches to the floor with a thunderous crash; Kit averted her eyes as more of Morg was splattered across the floor. The two bees followed the blocks down, fluttering to earth and lying still, apart from the occasional feeble wing beat. Within a few seconds they started to dissolve, and a few seconds after that there were two little mounds of mud atop the stone blocks.

"That's two," said Kei, "out of how many? How many knives do you have?"

Melody frowned. "I think that coaxing them from the ceiling is the larger problem."

Kit took a deep breath. "I can help with that."

"You're not going to do what I think you're going to do."

"How long have you known me, Wing Leader?"

"You'll get crushed!"

"Little bits of me spread all over the room," Kit agreed. "Probably. Got any better ideas?"

"Let her try." Melody had produced her long fighting knives. "Or we'll never cross."

"Kit . . ."

Kit cut her off. "Here goes nothing."

She dove out into the cavern, landing lightly next to the block that was already there. Ignoring the slick of blood, Kit grabbed the edge of the block and vaulted on top of it, just as another mammoth stone came thundering down, shaking the cave with its impact. Kit hopped lightly forward, waited just a moment, then jumped back up on the stone in time to avoid yet another plummeting monolith.

The three stones which had fallen, lined up neatly edge-to-edge, were wide enough to cross most of the room. Kit stood atop the center one and smiled at Kei and Melody.

"Look out!"

The shout came from the Blood Angel; Kit dropped instantly to her knees. One of the bee-spirits, whose stinger had been aimed at the back of her neck, drew a bloody line across her back. The razor tip of its inch-long sting sliced through leather as though it were paper. Another one came diving in like a raptor. Kit rolled over and caught it with one foot, sending it flying against one of the walls with a sickening crunch.

Unfortunately, the roll sent her halfway over the edge of the block. Kit ended up on her back, staring upwards, at another massive chunk of stone that started to descend . . .

She felt someone tug at her hand, hard, and pull her back onto the block just in time. The room shook with yet another impact, and Kit was so close she could feel the wind of the block's passage. She looked up and found Melody holding on to one of her hands, while Kei faced down the charge of another of the bee-spirits. The creature was unsubtle. It dove at the draekere, stinger extended, and Kei coolly waited until it was almost on top of her before stepping aside and chopping it in half. Another bee emerged from the ceiling, headed for the block that had just fallen, and dropped with one of Melody's daggers in it before it had gotten a few feet.

"By all the *fucking* gods, Kit." Kei sheathed her sword. "Are you all right?"

"Fine." Kit got to her feet, or tried to. Her knees were wobbly with adrenalin backwash. She fingered the long cut down her back and winced. "I'll be fine."

Gota calmly pulled himself up onto the block and looked around, nodding. "Excellent work. We should be able to proceed."

"We were all nearly killed!" Kei shouted.

"He doesn't care," said Kit weakly. "Don't you get it?"

"Shut up, Wing." Kei threw her a sideways glance. "I'm allowed to be a little hysterical, under the circumstances."

"*You're* not the one who was nearly crushed." Kit crawled to her feet and made it this time, shaking her head to clear a sudden dizzy feeling.

"Only because *I'm* not an idiot," Kei retorted.

"If we might get on with it?" said Melody. "I personally plan on getting out of here alive, and that means not standing around all day."

"Agreed." The priest pointed down the exit tunnel. "Onward."

Once again, the tunnel widened. The four that remained paused, letting the torches' light dimly illuminate the room. Kit brought up the rear. As soon as they stopped, she leaned against the wall, pressing her forehead against the cold stone. It felt wonderful. The rest of her body felt like it was on fire. Her heart still thumped double-time in her chest, absurdly loud.

"What now?" Kei asked Gota.

"A final line of defense. The spirits who built this place most likely imprisoned one of their number to guard it. Without his consent," he added, "so he's probably quite angry by now."

"How long has it been?"

"Six thousand years."

"Maybe he's had time to cool down," volunteered Kit, from her position against the wall.

"We can always hope." Kei peered into the semi-darkness. "I don't see an exit."

"I expect it's behind the dragon," said Melody calmly.

Kei blinked and looked harder, and Kit looked up. As Gota moved the torch, a large patch of shadows and rocks on the other side of the room resolved into a curled, reptilian form. The darkness was suddenly broken by a baleful red glow, emanating from a narrowed pair of eyes. The shape started unfolding itself with a heavy slither.

"Mortals," came a voice like the hiss of nearly-extinguished coals. "It has been a long time."

"We—" Gota tried to interject a word, but the spirit cut him off.

"Save your pleas. I am bound, and in any case I am hungry. You servants of the doomed gods will never reach what you seek."

"The gods are dead," said the priest. "You have won the war."

A wide, reptilian grin, also outlined in glowing red, joined the eyes. "Good news indeed. You have earned yourself a swift demise."

The dragon unfolded itself. It was thirty feet long and moved on four legs, like some giant scaled cat. Torchlight glinted off armored flanks of green and gold, and tiny tongues of smoke leaked from its mouth. It walked surprisingly lightly, padding closer on the balls of its feet.

"Someone must draw its attention," hissed Gota.

"Who's next most expendable?" snapped Kei, nastily.

Kit pushed herself away from the wall and reached for her sword. Melody had a knife in each hand. Gota raised his staff.

"On my signal," said the priest, "break."

Even Kei didn't argue with that. The spirit approached slowly, as though savoring the terror of its prey. Gota waited, calmly.

"Wait . . . wait . . ."

The dragon lunged.

"Break!"

Kit and Kei sprinted to the right, Melody to the left. Gota stood his ground, staff leveled at the approaching beast like a spear. It ignored the weapon completely and struck, viper-fast. The priest angled his staff so it would go directly down the dragon's throat, and didn't make a sound as its jaws closed on him.

Steel flashed from Melody's hands once again, one knife digging into the thing's shoulder and the other glancing off a scale and ricocheting into the darkness. The dragon whipped its head into the air and thrashed back and forth, obviously having trouble with the six feet of heavy ash shoved down its throat. It closed its jaws with a horrible crunch, chopping Gota in half just above the hips; part of his body crashed to the ground, trailing the glistening snakes of his intestines, while the other half disappeared down the dragon's gullet.

Kit didn't have time to retch. She slashed at the first available piece of the creature, which happened to be its right foreleg, and drew a gleaming line through its scales. Something liquid and white-hot welled forth, covering the blade of her sword. A moment later she had to drop the weapon as the metal began to glow cherry-red and sag. Kit staggered backward, against the cavern wall. Further down, Kei failed to find the correct angle and drew sparks as her sword slid from a scale.

The dragon's head whipped back and forth, trying to swallow. Gota's blood seeped from between its teeth. Finally its cleared its throat with a horrible bellow and opened its mouth again, more of the liquid fire dripping from its jaws. *Gota's staff must have cut its throat*, Kit thought, and then frantically threw herself to one side as a paw the size of man swiped past, claws digging into the rock wall of the cavern.

Kei ran at the thing, driving her sword to the hilt in its hindquarters, and the dragon bellowed. A moment later the draekere jumped back, holding only the hilt of a weapon whose blade had melted in the dragon's flesh. It whirled to face her, tail whipping back and forth, and she ducked just underneath the snapping jaws. Kit muttered a curse and reached for her dagger.

Melody, who'd been quiet up to this point, drew her two long fighting-knives. Her eyes found Kit's, even across a room filled with raging dragon; the Blood Angel nodded solemnly before rushing forward.

The beast was occupied with Kei, trying to corner her between its forepaws. The draekere dodged, nimbly, and slipped underneath one of the claws. The spirit turned to follow, and presented its side to Melody just as the Blood Angel dove underneath it, her twin blades raised. She slid across the floor, knives carving two giant rents in the dragon's underbelly. Blood sprayed and the beast bellowed; Melody managed to roll out from underneath it before it collapsed twitching to the floor.

"Melody!" Kit rushed to the Blood Angel's side. Melody had fallen to her knees, and as she looked up the draekere saw she hadn't entirely escaped the spray of white-hot elemental blood. Her face was black from the nose over, and her left eye was nothing but a charred mass, leaking blood. The leather had protected the rest of her body, mostly, but it had burned to a crisp in the process. Angry red skin showed through in places, flaking off a crust of black char.

The Blood Angel gritted her teeth, but, almost unbelievably, managed not to scream. Kit hovered, not sure whether throwing a helpful arm over her shoulder would do more harm than good. The obvious pain in Melody's features hit her like a punch to the gut, and her dizziness resurged. Kit staggered a bit to one side, then straightened out.

"Kit?" Kei picked her way past the fast-dissolving dragon. She sounded concerned. She'd obviously seen her friend wobbling. "Are you all right?" She came into view of Melody and stopped with a startled gasp. "Dear gods."

"Melody . . ."

The Blood Angel waved a hand. "Necessary." Opening her mouth too far was obviously painful for her, so she kept her teeth together and growled the words. "All dead otherwise. Too strong."

"We have to get you out of here," said Kit, trying to achieve a brisk tone.

"No. Break ward. Or Jyo-raku will kill us."

"She's right." Kei swallowed hard, glancing at the remains of the monk. "He said this was the last guardian. We have to move on. Melody, can you . . ."

Slowly, the Blood Angel pulled herself to her feet and nodded, bits of charred skin flaking off her like dandruff. Kit stayed a step behind her, ready to catch her if she fell, though given the way she was feeling that might lead to both of them ending up on the floor. Kei led the way, groping for the exit tunnel by the dying light of the dragon's carcass.

"AWAKE AGAIN, ARE we, Princess?" said Erin. "I was wondering if you were going to sleep all day."

Karl blinked and tried to focus. There was an edge to the swordswoman's voice; when he tried to sit up, the stabbing pain from his right arm reminded him that a big chunk of it was missing. Karl's head hit the ground hard enough that he heard an audible thump. He was lying full-length, with Erin crouching by his side, her back to the rocks of the mountainside.

Karl struggled to find the voice to speak. Finally he cleared his throat.

"Princess?"

Erin smiled. "It seemed appropriate."

"Call me 'Princess' again and I'll poke your eyes out with a blunt stick."

"You know, that threat is somehow less credible now."

He said nothing. Erin shook her head, a little sadly.

"What in the Aether came over you, anyway?" she asked.

"Is that any way to talk to someone who saved your life?"

"I knew what I was doing."

"Fuck if you did." A rare cursed slipped past Karl's lips. "You would have been shish kebab and you know it."

"Even so, it was my affair." She blushed, a faint red tinge only. "You had no call to meddle in it. If I wanted to piss off some bastard son of a god, you had no right to deprive me of the appropriate consequences."

"You sound like you wanted to get killed."

"Not exactly. But I hate being grateful."

"You'll forgive me, someday."

"I doubt it." She pulled her knees in and wrapped her arms around them, staring at him. Karl blinked uncomfortably.

"Are you okay?"

"Yeah." She blinked, and he thought he saw tears at the corner of her eyes before she wiped them away angrily. "I'm just . . . frustrated."

She wanted to talk about it, he thought. "Frustrated?"

"That *thing* is playing with us like dolls, and there's nothing we can do. How am I supposed to fight something like that?"

"You're not. That's why I . . ."

"But I can't just do nothing!"

"How long have you been working for Lord Adrian?"

She looked taken aback. "Six months or so. You remember, since that battle at Cardavon Manor. Why?"

"I've been with him a long time." Karl stared at the sky, which was a steel-gray fading slowly toward black. "Five years, I think. It seems like longer. Long enough to know that there are some times when you just have to keep your head down and stay out of the way."

"But . . ."

"No buts. Staying alive is always first priority."

Erin sighed, her moment of vulnerability gone. "Speaking of which, where in the name of the dead gods is Lord Adrian? This sort of thing is his responsibility."

"I have no idea. Maybe he already went inside."

"I suppose. You think Melody and the others will run into him?"

"It's possible."

"Those poor Khaevs." Erin gave a mock shiver. "So do you think he'll be along in time to rescue us?"

"We can always hope."

Erin sighed again, turning from him to look out across the

mist-shrouded plain. Karl stayed quiet, trying to ignore the pain from his arm.

"You know," she said finally, "my policy on romantic entanglements with fellow soldiers."

He nodded.

"If we get out of this alive, I think I'm going to have make a special one-night-only exception." She turned back to him. "So start getting better."

"I'll work on that."

Jyo-raku whipped around with a satisfied grunt.

"The warding is down."

He stalked toward the entrance, and Erin called out to him before he crossed the boundary.

"Hey!"

Jyo-raku turned. She did her best to appear diffident, while inside she fumed. "What about us?"

"I have no further need of you." The shadow spirit shrugged. "I imagine the Valdiem will return soon enough."

Erin stared blankly as the shadow spirit disappeared into the darkness of the cave.

MELODY COULD TASTE bile at the back of her throat. I t tasted of failure, and impending death.

The death she didn't mind. She was *mantacor,* a "Blood Angel," named both for their crimson armor and for the blood they inevitably shed. Only half the Blood Angels that passed through the *tesngat* on the way to the lands of the Empire returned, and, of those, only one in a thousand survived to reach the ranks of the Eternal Guard and be granted life unending. She had never dared dream she would be one of them, had never consciously given the thought room, but somehow that hope had always been there. Now it was snuffed out, and it left a yawning hole in the center of her being.

Failure was worse. The *mantacor* were expected to return to Tellen having fought against the most skillful warriors the mainland had to offer. They imparted that knowledge through combat, and, as they died on one another's swords, the ultimate victor, who joined the Eternal Guard, would be the greatest warrior on Tellen. Thus had the True Land defended its borders for thousands of years, ever since the fall of the gods.

But I will not get even that far. The knowledge I have gathered will go to waste. I will die here, in this cave, and in half a year's time a scribe in the Floating Garden will draw a red line across my name with a zoxhair brush, and that will be the end of me. A funeral had been held already; her family mourned her as though she had already passed on. She'd attended, as was the custom, and though no one there would speak to one who was as the dead, her youngest sister had managed a curious glance. Melody was grateful for that.

She waited, wearily, with her back against the wall. The two draekeres were arguing again. They'd found the ward, a delicate tracery of silver inscribed onto one wall of the tunnel that glowed with its own faint light. Ahead, the tunnel widened again into another cavern. Without Gota's torch, though, it was pitch black. The tunnel was lit only by the slowly fading light from the body of the dead dragon.

Kit had taken the jagged remains of her sword and scratched deep lines through the ward, and its light was fading in fits and starts. The younger draekere wanted to proceed into the cavern, while they could still see; Kei refused to move.

"We wait for Jyo-raku."

"But . . ."

"Like it or not, Kit, our best chance of getting out of here is to do what he says."

"We could try to ambush him . . ."

"With what? He's a demon. You saw what he did to that Imperial when he got mad."

Karl, Melody mused silently, *and Erin. I didn't think they'd survived the demons the monk unleashed at the ambush.* Strange that Gota hadn't called anything up to defend himself in the cavern. *Perhaps the warding prevented it? Or perhaps Jyo-raku was hiding inside him, all along.* The Eternal Guard defended Tellen from wandering spirits and demons, but they were all too common in the gods-forsaken lands of the Empire. The people thought nothing of letting them wander around *loose.* Even the Khaevs didn't seem to care.

The Khaevs. That was the news the latest tide of *mantacor* would bring back to Tellen. The strange warrior people from the north who had felled the Sixth Dynasty before it had had time to flower. Melody had heard that the Khaevs considered their best warriors the finest swordsmen in the world. *I would have liked to have fought one of the Two Hundred.*

She closed her eyes—*eye,* she thought forlornly—but it seemed to make little difference. The right side of her vision was black as night, and where liquid fire had burned out her left eye the blaze still seemed to burn, white-and-red flames dancing endlessly. The pain had subsided to a dull, numbed ache, which she suppressed using the skills that were taught to all *mantacor*; still, Melody was aware that her body was on its last legs.

I might live. The sudden, animal instinct surprised her. *If I get these burns cared for, so that they don't fester.* She didn't delude herself, though. The chances of that were slim to none, and there was a mountain full of angry Valdiem between the three women and anything resembling civilization. *We will all die here, or go with Jyo-raku if that is his pleasure.*

She found herself hoping that it was. *So that I can continue my mission, of course.* Melody tried to breathe deep, to suppress the uneven drumbeat of her heart. *My mission.*

"We could go back," said Kit, "and find one of Gota's torches."

"Where are you going to look? The dragon's belly?"

"Maybe. It should be falling apart by now . . ."

"Thankfully," hissed a familiar voice, "that will not be necessary."

Melody opened her eye to find Jyo-raku standing at the entrance to the cavern, dark aura flaring around him. There was no sign of Erin or Karl. Kit and Kei snapped around, as though springing to attention.

"Is there anything nasty waiting for us in there?" said Kit.

"No." The spirit raised a hand, and a shadowy twilight radiance began to emanate from the top of the cavern. "Just the object of our little adventure. A Bound Blade."

ERIN DOVE FOR the bushes at the sound of approaching footsteps. Karl was out of sight, well-hidden amongst some rocks a bit downslope; she'd gone back to survey the tunnel entrance, waiting for someone to reemerge. This sound, though, was coming up the path, and as it got closer she realized it was far too loud to be a single person.

Must be a whole damn regiment, she thought, *or . . .*

A demon crested the hill. It was more than seven feet tall, and sheathed in metal from head to toe. Flames spurted from its joints as it moved, and in its footprints the ground bubbled and fused. Its face was featureless, a blank metal visor that nonetheless seemed to stare with a particularly penetrating gaze. A man follow it, emaciated and hunchbacked, dressed in the remnants of what had once been fine clothing . . .

Lord Adrian! Something kept her from calling out, his decrepit state or fear of the steel giant, she wasn't sure. The pair didn't see her, in any case. They barely paused in the clearing, proceeding directly into the tunnel. Erin stared after them, uncertain of what she should do next.

What in the Aether is going on here?

PROPPED AGAINST THE wall where Kit had left her, Melody had an excellent view of the proceedings.

"A Bound Blade?" asked Kit. She backed out of Jyo-raku's way as he entered the cavern. "What's that?"

Ignorant szandling. Somewhat to Melody's surprise, Jyo-raku answered.

"A weapon. Forged by the gods in the last days of their final war, designed to destroy my kind. Once the war was over, the alliance of spirits fell to pieces. One of their last acts was to seal the weapons away forever, each afraid the others would use the power to become overlord."

The light brightened, little by little. This cavern shared the hemispherical shape of the others, and was empty but for a rough pedestal of stone in the center. Over that pedestal hung a sword, a straight-bladed Imperial design. It stood vertically, as though impossibly balanced on its point, and although it didn't move the patterns of light reflected from its surface shifted and swam, giving the impression that the thing was revolving. The hilt was made of the same silvery not-quite-steel as the blade, and reflected Jyo-raku's shadowy light with an odd brilliance. All in all, it was both beautiful and disturbing, like a flawed crystal that twists light in strange ways.

The shadow spirit stepped up to it and spread his arms, as though feeling his way around an invisible barrier. He hissed, more or less to himself, "It is bound to this place. Breaking this ward will require much effort." Jyo-raku threw a glance over his shoulder. "You may want to stand back. But none of you may leave."

Melody would have laughed, had it not been so painful. *At the moment, I lack the strength to escape.*

Jyo-raku's dark aura gathered itself, waited a moment, then pounced. It completely encircled the sword and pressed inward, as though crushing something invisible and resisting. Occasionally it fell back, but little by little the vise closed around the Bound Blade. The spirit himself stood perfectly still, surrounded by only the faintest of shadows.

There was a heavy footstep from the back of the cavern, but Jyo-raku either didn't notice or was preoccupied. The shadow aura pressed inward, faster and faster, until it outlined the sword itself. There was a rapid feeling of suction, as though the entire room were falling inward, and a sound like the shattering of fine crystal. Then the Bound Blade toppled from its pedestal and rattled to the ground as though it were an ordinary sword.

Jyo-raku, aura much diminished, paused to catch his breath. Before he could reach for the Blade, the ground underneath him burst into flames.

THE WHOLE MOUNTAIN shook, solid granite ringing like a bell. Birds took off from the forests of the lower slopes, hundreds and hundreds of them at once, streaming away from the peak like clouds of dark smoke. On the plain below, a top-knotted Khaev outrider pointed and called out to his companions. Messengers were swiftly dispatched, commanders consulted, and within the hour Kagerin Shuzan's Blade was headed into the mountains.

The steel-clad giant lowered his hand, faceless visor sweeping slowly across the room. The smoke was gradually clearing, revealing that the entire center of the cavern had been reduced to red-hot bubbling rock. The Blade was on one side of the pool, Jyo-raku on the other; Kit and Kei had pressed themselves against one of the walls. Melody had fallen to her knees, coughing and choking until the air cleared.

Scuttling behind the new spirit was an emaciated, weather-worn man that Melody nonetheless recognized instantly as Adrian. His posture toward the demon made the situation clear at once. *He's summoned something beyond his ability to control. Sorcerers always do.* It was one of the major reasons they were not permitted on Tellen. *Now he has become its creature.*

"Vaalkir," hissed Jyo-raku, backing away.

The metal giant spoke with a voice like a roaring bonfire. "Predictable to the end. You knew it was a trap, but the prize was simply too tempting. With a Bound Blade, even you would have a chance at transcendence."

"You speak as though the prize were not already mine." The words were Jyo-raku's usual arrogant banter, but the tone was different, with a slightly pleading edge.

"I think I will put an end to you." Vaalkir took another step forward, and the floor of the cavern quivered. "You are incarnate, and therefore vulnerable."

"As are you."

"And you are weakened from breaking the wards."

It must have been true, Melody thought, because Jyo-raku reacted at once. "We will see how weak I am!"

His dark aura flared, and spears of shadow darted out toward the fire-spirit. Vaalkir ignored them, and they glanced off his heavy plate. He advanced on Jyo-raku steadily, implacably, and the shadow spirit kept backing away. Blossoms of fire began to sprout around the pair of them, more and more of them clustered around Jyo-raku. Before long no more dark tongues lashed out, and wave after wave of flames battered the shadow spirit toward the wall. Vaalkir walked still closer, massive arms crossed over his chest, seemingly unconcerned.

Failure, thought Melody. *And death.*

The mission of a mantacor *is to confront the most powerful threats on the mainland and eliminate them, ensuring the safety of the True Land.* Her body understood what was happening before her mind did. By the time Melody realized she'd decided something, she was already in motion, lurching to her feet with reserves of strength she hadn't known she'd possessed. She stumbled forward, ignoring shouts from the draekeres who were beating a hasty retreat toward the entrance, and walked along the side of the pool of fire.

A shabby figure blocked her way. Lord Adrian had once been a powerful man, tall and well-muscled and fond of the finest fabrics money could buy. Now he was a shadow of his former self, so thin that his ribs showed and clad in little more than rags. His face had a little of his old imperiousness, though He held up his hand as he stepped into her path.

"Stop!"

Melody barely spared him a glance. *If I stop moving, I'll never get up again.* She pushed past him, but the sorcerer grabbed at her sleeve. Without quite realizing what she was doing, she swung him around by ingrained reflex, flipping him over her shoulder. Adrian flew through the air, let out a horrible shriek before he landed, and hit the pool of molten rock with a liquid plop. There was a brief gout of flame as he was consumed.

The Blood Angel used the momentum to stumble into a run, circling the pool and heading toward the battling spirits. Jyo-raku was all but invisible now behind a curtain of fire, and the booming cracks of Vaalkir's laughter shook the walls. Melody leaned down and opened her hand, scooping up the Blade by the hilt; the weapon began to hum, as though it anticipated carnage.

Vaalkir didn't hear her coming. Her charge was perfect, swinging the Blade in a neat arc through the spirit's waist.

Instead of the hard contact she'd been expecting, it cut through solid metal as though it weren't there, accompanied by the horrible shriek of twisting steel. There was once again a feeling of suction, and for a moment Melody heard Vaalkir's bass voice blended with a thousand others, crying out in agony and demanding release. Then the spirit's metal body clattered heavily to the floor, and Melody fell once again to her knees. Blood ran freely from her mouth, pattering quietly on the rocks.

The flames cleared. Melody couldn't move, couldn't do anything but take one massive breath after another. The hilt of the sword was warm under her hand.

"That was . . . unexpected," hissed Jyo-raku. His dark aura was almost gone, revealing a humanoid figure entirely wrapped in black cloth.

"Leave," Melody gasped between breaths. "Leave this place. Never come back."

"Oh?" It was amazing how quickly the shadow spirit regained his mocking, sarcastic tone.

"Or you'll be next."

He eyed her hand, which could barely wrap itself around the Blade's hilt. "You're bluffing."

"Come. Find out."

All of a sudden her strength was gone, and Melody toppled forward. She felt the heat of the ground on her skin, through the tattered leather of her armor, and she could hear the shadow spirit's footsteps as he walked over to her. Her head was facing the wall, and she didn't have the strength to turn it.

KIT PULLED AT Kei's grip on her arm as Jyo-raku walked behind Melody, trying to break free. Not too hard, though, because she knew it was already too late. The dark aura around the shadow spirit lanced downward like a spear, punching through the side of Melody's skull with a horrible crunch. Her body jerked, and one of her arms waved in the air, slowly, until it sank to the ground. Then the Blood Angel was still.

"I thought not," hissed Jyo-raku. He pulled the Bound Blade from her nerveless fingers and hefted it, as though testing the balance. Stepping over her body, he gestured Kit and Kei to one side with the tip of the sword. "We're leaving. Various unfriendly people will no doubt be here soon. Kei, you're coming with me."

Kit was still too shocked to answer, but Kei shook her head violently.

"Enough! What do you need me for?"

"Questioning me will get you nowhere." The shadow spirit gestured with the Blade. "Now are you coming along, or does your friend need to lose an arm?"

Kit got to her feet suddenly, dragging Kei with her. "Come on."

"But . . ."

Kit tore her eyes away from Melody's silent corpse with an effort. "Come *on*, Kei. Let's go."

"What about Kit?" Kei directed this question at the shadow spirit, who shrugged.

"She's free to go, as far as I'm concerned."

Kei rounded on Kit, but her friend's expression told her all she needed to know. "Don't even think about it, Wing Leader. We're in this together."

"Where are we going?" Kei asked, as they passed the spirit.

Jyo-raku raised the Blade in front of his face in a mocking salute. "Godsdoom," he said.

By the time they stumbled out of the cave and into the morning sunshine, the color had not yet returned to Kei's face.

chapter 15

"One of the tenets of good play in capture is to sacrifice stones that have served their purpose. The spirits do the same with the lives of men."

–Miika Kanoe, Maiden

THE REST OF the escape was a confusion of fire and blood in Veil's mind. Diem warriors loomed out of the night like ghosts and were chopped down like wheat before the reaper. Once the adrenalin began to wear off, Veil realized how exhausted she was, stumbling along behind Corvus in an effort to stay on her feet. Eventually Zhin had to lend a hand to keep her upright. H e offered his other arm to Isobel, but she waved him away and slogged onward. As the night wore on, even Zhin's pace began to flag, and his huffing breaths filled Veil's world, which had contracted to the weight of his arm on her shoulders and the ground directly under her feet.

Only Corvus was unaffected. If anything, he appeared to gain strength as the horrible night wore on. Veil's thoughts were blurred. He seemed to be less of a man and more of an elemental force of destruction. Time after time, torchlight and the glitter of steel enveloped them, and eventually Veil could do nothing but wait, dully, for the screams and spatters of blood.

And then, suddenly, there were no more Diem. The four walked for half an hour or more, threading their way in the dark through the intermittent tree-cover, until Zhin gasped out a word to Corvus.

"Rest."

The swordsman looked back, his steel a shimmering line in the moonlight. Not for the first time, Veil could have sworn his eyes glowed with their own light.

"We . . . need . . . to rest. Corvus. I think we've lost them."

"More likely they've given up." Corvus straightened, and sheathed his blade with a rasp. Suddenly he seemed closer to human. "A blind child could follow the trail we've been leaving."

"Either way." Zhin slid his arm off Veil, letting her slump against a tree trunk. "I can't run any farther, and the girl's just about done. And Isobel, this can't be doing you any good."

"I can continue," she protested. Veil could see by her pinched expression, though, that her wound pained her.

Corvus shrugged. "Then we stop, for now. I hope the confusion we've created prevents them from regrouping before dawn."

Veil closed her eyes as soon as she heard those words. Somewhat to her surprise, she did not drop off to sleep on the instant. Her body was screaming for rest, but her mind wouldn't stop running in circles.

The dragon . . . a woman's scream, truncated by a crunch . . . blood gleaming slickly on icicle fangs . . .

They were going to rape me. Kill me!

She shifted, uncomfortably. *They deserved it.*

All of them? asked an irritating internal voice. *The ones in the village? The children, too?*

I didn't know what Sybian was going to do. I didn't care. She gritted her teeth. *I had to do it, to save myself. That's all that matters.*

Is it, now? asked the voice. Veil turned over and pressed herself against the tree trunk, trying to banish it.

"Thanks, Corvus." This was Zhin's voice, and Veil's ears

perked up, eager for a distraction from her self-remonstration.

"For what?"

"For going back for Isobel."

"I went back for Veil."

Veil felt herself blush, but kept silent.

"Thanks anyway." Zhin sighed, and settled back against a stone. Veil could feel his gaze on her. "She's amazing, isn't she? How old do you think she is? Thirteen? Fourteen?"

"Something like that." Corvus sounded bored, as he often did.

"Not many girls her age could take this."

"No."

Veil's blush deepened.

"Where'd you find her, anyway?"

"She followed me across the High Desert."

Zhin whistled. "Damn stubborn."

"It's kept her alive so far."

"That and having the greatest swordsman in the world for a bodyguard."

Corvus grunted, and Zhin continued, a bit foolhardily in Veil's opinion.

"Honestly, Corvus, you're unbelievable. I've never seen anything like it. I can't believe someone with that kind of skill could exist without someone having heard of it.."

"You wanted to sleep, didn't you?"

Zhin was taken aback. "Y . . . yeah."

"Then sleep. I'll keep watch."

That's my Corvus, thought Veil with a sleepy smile. *As soon as the conversation turns to him, he clams right up.*

I wonder if he did something awful, and doesn't want anyone to find out? It'd have to be pretty bad. Maybe he murdered a lord, or betrayed someone important, or . . .

Veil drifted off before she'd thought of a third possibility.

SHE WOKE UP the next morning feeling, surprisingly, much re-freshed. Her limbs were only a bit stiff. Veil sat up, shivering at the morning chill, and stretched. Her legs were a little wobbly and had a deep, pleasant ache, but on the whole she felt more human than she had any time in the past couple of days.

Zhin was still asleep, head tilted all the way back and snoring from his open mouth, and Isobel was curled up in the hollow of a tree a few feet away. Corvus sat where he'd been last night, on top of a rock, but facing the other way. His sword was balanced across his knees, and he might have been a statue clothed in black if not for the little movements of his hair when the wind blew.

Veil climbed up the rock gingerly. It was wet with the morn-ing dew, which was freezing cold. Corvus glanced down at her, but said nothing as she made her way to the top and sat down next to him, staring out at the forest. The sun was hidden behind a thick layer of clouds, so it was difficult to tell how late it was; the dew dripped from the leaves of the trees, leaving the ground sodden. In the distance, birds hooted and screamed their deri-sion at one another. Veil listened, fascinated. She hadn't had much opportunity to pay attention to birdsong, and it took her a moment to realize the calls were all different than she remem-bered. *Of course they are. We're not in the Red Hills anymore.* She put her chin in her hands and rested her elbows on her knees, swing-ing her legs against the rock.

"You came to rescue me."

He didn't look at her. "I did."

Veil thought for a moment, then carefully leaned her head against his shoulder. She felt him start, almost imperceptibly, and then settle down again. It wasn't a particularly comfortable pillow. Chainmail shifted under the cloth of his shirt, digging

ango wexler

into her cheek. She ignored it.

"Thank you."

They sat in silence as the sun rose higher, slowly burning through the clouds. The forest began to lighten, and the birds got louder, as though encouraged.

"You'll probably get mad at me for saying this," said Veil eventually, "but you really are amazing."

Corvus grunted, but didn't immediately reproach her. Veil forged on, encouraged.

"I know you don't like to talk about it, and that's okay. But if you ever did want to, you can talk to me. You know . . ." She sighed. "I just want to feel like I'm helping."

"What's the first thing you can remember?"

The question came out of nowhere, and Veil had to think for a moment. "It's hard to be sure. I remember sitting in a playroom with some of the other children, and being really upset because somebody wouldn't let me touch a toy soldier."

"How old were you?"

"Six or seven, maybe?" She looked up at him and found his eyes hooded. "Why?"

"My earliest memory is the desert."

"You lived in the desert?"

His lips twisted into a slight smile. "No. I remember walking through the desert, a day or so before I ran into that slaver. That's it."

"But . . . where were you before?"

He shrugged. "I wish I knew."

Veil sat back, stunned. "You don't remember *anything*?"

"Some things, obviously. But not who I am."

"Your name?"

"I don't know if it's my name. It's engraved on my sword."

Veil shook her head. "Sorcery, do you think? Were you

possessed by a spirit?"

"How should I know?" He leaned back against the rock. "The sword's all I've got. It's got Khaev writing on it, so I'm going to find some Khaevs."

There was another awkward silence as Veil parsed this. Finally, she ventured onward. "Why tell me this now?"

"Why not?" He looked down at her with a sarcastic grin. "You're my oldest friend, right?"

"I . . . guess." Something inside her glowed at the word friend. "But you haven't told Zhin or anyone."

"I don't trust Zhin. There's something in this for him, and he's not telling us what."

"And Isobel? I thought you two were . . ." Veil trailed off, her cheeks heating. To be honest, though, Corvus had barely given the girl a look after that night. Isobel had stopped chasing after him, and returned to her usual place at Zhin's side.

"That girl?" Corvus rolled his eyes. "There's something wrong with her. I thought you were jealous, anyway, so shouldn't you be happy?"

"I . . . no, I mean . . ." Veil sputtered to a halt, took a deep breath, and started again. "I . . . talked with her, a bit. While we were with the Diem. She's not as bad as she seems."

"She's still crazy." Corvus looked away. "I've been meaning to ask you about that. Are you . . . okay?" Now *he* seemed almost embarrassed. "They didn't hurt you, or . . ."

"I'm fine." She leaned against his shoulder again. "Just fine."

"You're just the only one I can be sure is honest, right?" Corvus shrugged again. "Not working for anybody, or trying to use me for anything."

"Veil," said Sybian, in a voice like the tinkle of crystal bells, "you're a genius."

Veil went stiff, like someone had run a spear through her

gut. Corvus looked down at her, concerned.

"Veil?"

"It's nothing." She shook her head quickly. "I have to . . . you know . . ." She laughed, feigning embarrassment. "I'll be right back."

She could feel his narrowed eyes on the back of her head as she walked away. Sybian continued, blithely.

"The man would kill for you, and that's exactly what I need him for. I really didn't expect you to get so far."

"I'm not doing this for you," hissed Veil under her breath, once she had reached a safe distance.

"That's not a nice thing to say," said the ice spirit mockingly. "After I saved you last night."

"Thanks." Veil gritted her teeth. "But you only did that because I threatened to kill myself."-

"True. And its an interesting philosophical question, isn't it? If I tell you to do something you were going to do anyway, are you doing my bidding or not?"

"I'm not doing your bidding."

"You weren't nearly this irritated before. Corvus must have struck a nerve."

"And may I add that was a particularly poor time to interrupt us. Now I'm sure he's suspicious."

"It doesn't matter. We're almost done with the hard part, Veil. Once you get over the Shieldwall, we'll be in the hands of my people all the way to the end."

"And where is the end?"

"What do you care? Just keep your wits about you and try not to end up dead."

Veil bit her lip, deep in thought. "What if I told Corvus about you?"

"Then you'll definitely end up dead." Sybian laughed.

"I'm not afraid of you."

"No? You should be. Even now I could have you killed in a dozen different ways, and once I incarnate I could bury you in so much ice that even good old Corvus couldn't dig you out in a hundred years."

"You still need me."

"Don't overestimate your own importance, Veil. It's true that you're of some use to me, but if you start actively destroying my plans, that goes downhill rapidly. Understand?"

"I understand," said Veil, as defiantly as she could.

"Besides, I'm not asking anything particularly onerous. Just stay close to Corvus. He trusts you. Maybe sleep with him, if you get the chance."

Veil's blush returned. "I . . ."

Sybian cut her off with a laugh. "Whatever you want. You've been doing a fine job so far."

Veil took a deep breath. "Was there some *point* to this conversation?"

"Just letting you know where matters stand. I've done my best to clear you a path, but you'll have to keep moving. I assume you already knew that."

"Clear us a path?"

"If you haven't noticed, pretty much everyone west of the Shieldwall wants you dead. Saya's work, as I mentioned. So I hijacked one of her messengers and set them to watching the passes. That should keep you from getting trapped again. You may run into the occasional Ghael they haven't been able to stop, but I'm sure Corvus can handle them."

"I'm sure he can." Veil didn't like the sound of what Sybian was saying, but there didn't appear to be anything she could do. "The passes?"

"The Diem have some semi-secret ways through the

mountains. Not good enough for an army, but more than sufficient for four people. That's where Zhin's been heading, but it
looked like you needed a little help. He obviously didn't plan on
Saya's interference."

"Why does this Saya want to kill us so badly?"

Veil could almost see Sybian's mocking smile. "That's also
irrelevant, for the moment. Just think of her as the bad guy."

"Girl."

"With spirits that's a matter of choice anyway."

"Are you finished?"

"For now. Keep up the good work, little pawn. Your big
day is coming. Pretty soon you get to do what you do best."

"What's that?"

There was no answer. Veil waited for a long moment,
watching her breath turn to frost in the chilly morning air, then
stomped back toward the rock where Corvus was sitting, her
mood thoroughly ruined.

BREAKFAST WAS SUBDUED. They'd lost most of their supplies with
the horses when the Diem had attacked, but since Corvus appeared to require no fuel whatsoever Zhin said their stock would
last at least through the mountains, if rationed properly. That
meant a smaller portion of stale trail bread and dried meat for
everyone, which didn't upset Veil particularly. She fell into the
pleasant rhythm of walking, behind Corvus and ahead of Isobel,
who was acting as rear-guard. Zhin led the way, though the
general direction at least was obvious. The Shieldwall was visible from any clearing now, a remarkably uniform set of peaks
taking semi-circular bites out of the eastern sky like a massive
fence. The thought of trying to cross it seemed ludicrous. Veil
hoped there really were secret passes, and that Zhin knew where
he was going.

Just after midday, Zhin pulled up short. For a horrifying moment Veil thought he was going to announce that they were lost, but he seemed more wary than disoriented.

"What's wrong?" asked Isobel. Since their rescue from the Diem, she seemed to have regained a bit of her initiative. If anything, she was more talkative than she'd ever been, at least since Veil had known her. Something had changed; despite their moment of clarity while imprisoned, though, Veil was too timid to ask what.

"Too quiet." Zhin shook his head.

Veil rolled her eyes and started to say something about looking for trouble, but Corvus cut her off.

"I agree. The Diem have been following us closely this far. Why would they give up now?"

"Maybe they're tired of getting killed?" suggested Veil. It was meant as a joke, but Zhin seemed to take it seriously.

"As far as we can tell, the Ghael are driving them, and I can't see the demons getting upset because Corvus has killed three or four dozen barbarians."

"A trap, then?" asked Isobel.

"That doesn't make any sense," said Veil. "They must know we're running for the mountains. It doesn't look like there's anything between here and there but more forest, so what does leaving us alone gain them?"

Corvus gave her an odd look before continuing. "It's true. If anything, they should be testing us constantly, trying to run us ragged. They have manpower to spare."

Isobel had wandered off during this conversation; now she waved for attention. "Look at this!"

Zhin turned on his heel. "What?"

"The ground cover's been beaten down. Here, and here. And over there as well."

"Animal tracks?" suggested the old soldier weakly.

Corvus shook his head. "Men, and lots of them."

"Recently, too." Isobel looked a little irked at being up-staged. "Last night, maybe."

"Which way were they going?" asked Veil.

"That way." Isobel pointed east, in roughly the direction they'd been traveling. "They must've been just ahead of us."

"So we're walking *in*to them?" Veil raised an eyebrow. "That doesn't seem terribly bright."

"Not much choice," said Zhin. "We have to get out of the highlands, and unless you want to make for Crimson Pass and try to get past the Anvil, this is our only shot."

Corvus knelt and fingered a patch of ground, running his hands along a patch of moss that looked burned and dead. He shuffled forward a few steps and found another, similar patch. Veil looked at him curiously.

"Find something?"

"Ghael. Or a fire demon, at any rate. Probably more than one."

"Great." Veil rolled her eyes.

"Relax," said Zhin. He clapped Corvus on the shoulder. "Nothing you can't handle."

There was a long moment of silence.

"Zhin?" Corvus' voice was soft.

"Yeah?"

"I appreciate your guidance on this journey."

"Thanks."

"We would certainly be in dire straits without you."

Zhin smiled. Veil wasn't sure whether or not he could see it coming.

"But you should remove your hand from my back. I'd hate to have to see if you could guide us with no arms."

"I'd point with my tongue," said Zhin jovially. Veil noticed, however, that he pulled his hand back rather quickly and kept a step farther away from Corvus.

"So what now?" asked Isobel impatiently.

"We push on," said Zhin, suddenly the team leader again. "What else can we do? But be careful."

Not exactly a useful injunction, thought Veil. *Am I not going to be careful on purpose?*

They continued on as the sun sank to the west and the day wore into evening. Veil spotted the first body, a young man who'd been driven into a tree trunk so hard the tree had folded in half around him. They gave him a wide berth, which meant they practically walked over a young woman whose body lay spread-eagled in the dirt and whose head was nowhere to be found. Veil found herself remarkably unaffected; she stepped over the pool of congealing blood with something approaching equanimity, and only a little churning in her stomach.

They rounded another copse of trees to find another little clearing, and Veil's stomach suddenly gave up the fight entirely. She leaned into the shadow of a pine and let breakfast and lunch well up. By the time she was done, her eyes were watering, but she felt a little bit better. Rising, she found Corvus behind her. He kept his voice low.

"Are you all right?"

"Fine." She wiped her mouth and tried to smile. "It just took me a little . . . by surprise."

He nodded solemnly and turned back to the clearing. The swordsman was unperturbed, of course, and Isobel seemed similarly unaffected, but Zhin was definitely looking a little bit queasy, which made Veil feel slightly better. She forced herself to look. *It's nothing. Just dead bodies. There's nothing left here that can hurt you.*

The clearing was covered in bodies, in many places two or three deep. All were Diem warriors, who had apparently been engaged in a vicious battle with one another. The charnel stench was such that Veil was forced to clap her hands over her face, and her mind gave up as it tried to take in the magnitude of the carnage. She was left with a succession of tiny details: two dead women, holding each other like sisters, or a young man who'd managed to crawl quite a way from the battlefield despite not having any legs.

Zhin led them around the edge of the clearing, and ultimately Veil had to look away. The bodies were covered with carrion birds, who jumped and squawked at the human intruders on their feast. Insects crunched underfoot from time to time. After the first nasty squishing sound, Veil stopped looking down to see what she'd stepped in and locked her eyes tightly on a tree on the other side of the battleground.

"Ghael," said Corvus quietly, once they'd passed. Zhin nodded, and even Veil could see what he meant. The path of the fire demons was horribly clear: a gauntlet of bodies literally torn limb from limb, intermixed with intact skeletons seared down to the bone.

"This was a final stand," commented Isobel, unemotionally. "The Ghael and their followers were coming from the west, and they ran into these other Diem. They never had a chance, not against the Ghael, but it doesn't look like any of them ran for it."

"Odd," said Zhin. "I'd have run for it."

Isobel shot him an amused look. "Of course. I wonder what they were protecting."

"And why are the Diem fighting each other?" asked Veil. "I thought the Ghael were in charge of everything."

"Apparently not." Corvus glanced at one of the burned bodies. "Though they look like they will be again before long."

They came upon the answer to at least one of those questions a few moments later. Corvus was back in the lead, following a narrow animal track. He halted on coming to a thin defile, cutting down to the bottom of a small cliff.

"Good place for an ambush," the swordsman muttered. Veil agreed with him. The defile's walls provided an excellent shot for waiting archers, and anyone at the bottom of the cliff would have no cover at all.

Isobel, stepping around Corvus, pointed downslope. "Somebody beat you to it."

"More?" Veil swallowed.

Another group of Diem lay at the bottom, riddled with arrows. They lay mostly face-down, and had obviously been descending the defile when the archers had sprung their trap. A few had gotten farther, even shot full of arrows, and trails of blood led to a number of bodies that lay just short of the tree line at the bottom of the cliff.

Corvus descended first, ignoring the bodies and keeping his attention on the top of the cliff. When hordes of Diem archers failed to materialize, he gestured the rest of the group forward. Veil hung back, trying hard to keep her eyes from the piles of bodies. Where the defile leveled out they were so thick they actually blocked the path. Corvus gave one woman's corpse an absent-minded kick, rolling it onto its back and out the way. Veil couldn't help looking as she passed; the Diem's hands were pressed to her stomach, from which poked the point of an arrow that had gone into her back. The expression on her face made Veil's hands twitch, longing to reach out and grab someone's arm; since the closest person was Zhin, she restrained herself with some effort.

It's okay. She repeated it to herself, over and over, like mantra. *It's okay. It's o-*kay. *It's* o-*kay. Everybody's dead. Nothing's going* *to hurt you, Veil, get a hold of yourself! I thought I was tougher than this. These are the bad guys. They're the ones who wanted to rape you and kill you. They deserve it!*

She caught sight of more corpses ahead, dragged into a rough line. They were all young women, lying naked on top of the remains of their leathers.

Gods. Veil closed her eyes. *Oh gods.*

"Looks like they weren't in that much of a hurry after all," remarked Zhin sourly. Veil heard his comment distantly, as though muffled by thick cloth; she took another wobbling step and sank to her knees, unable to banish the images from behind closed eyelids.

They left her shirt on. Apparently the Diem had been interested in getting down to business as quickly as possible. *And afterwards, they killed her.* A hand axe was buried between the girl's breasts, handle pointing upwards like some obscene flag. Her face was contorted in agony. *Oh gods.*

This isn't me. Veil felt distanced from herself. *Someone else is on her knees, crying like a little girl. Not me.*

". . . Corvus . . ." She choked the word out, between tight, controlled sobs. *He won't bother.* The swordsman in black, who carved men down like they were wood. *Why should he? Come on, Veil. Up. You have to get up, walk through this. Cry later.*

She felt the touch of a gloved hand on her shoulder. Veil grabbed it and clung to it as though it were a lifeline, pulling herself to her feet. She pressed herself against him, feeling the regular pattern of the mail under his shirt. Corvus stood awkwardly, as though not quite sure what to do, so she reached back and pulled his arm around her shoulders. Her tears soaked into his shirt, until it lay damply against the mail beneath.

Isobel and Zhin stood by quietly, apparently unable or unwilling to say anything. Veil found her sobs eventually dried up.

Corvus pushed her away, and stared down at her gravely.

"Are you all right?"

"Yeah." Veil wiped her eyes. "I just . . . I couldn't . . ."

She expected a sarcastic retort, but he said nothing. Veil shook her head.

"Let's go." She started walking forward, with Corvus behind her. Isobel and Zhin exchanged a quiet glance, then followed without a word.

THEY WALKED PAST more bodies, more battlefields; Veil stuck to Corvus' side and kept her eyes firmly ahead. The mountains loomed ever larger, and despite local dips and valleys the general trend was definitely upward. As the sun set, they broke out of the forest and found themselves on a scree-covered hillside. Further up there was nothing but bare rock, rising in a long series of near-vertical cliffs. Veil didn't see the entrance to the pass until Zhin pointed it out: a nearly invisible cleft in the stone wall that the old soldier assured her led to a relatively mild valley running all the way through the mountains.

As he spoke, a flurry of motion near the pass caught her eyes. There were figures there, locked in desperate combat in the fading twilight. Corvus shaded his eyes to get a better look and stiffened as fire bloomed, bright and clear.

"Ghael." He put one hand on his sword. "Stay here."

"What if there are more of them in the woods?" snapped Veil.

"True." Corvus put his head on one side, considering. "Follow me, then. But not too close."

He led the group up the hillside at a jog, threading his way past the waist-high piles of rocks and jumping over the occasional patch of brush. Isobel stayed close behind him, while Zhin and Veil stayed further back.

It became apparent, as they got closer, that the Ghael had

beaten whoever they were fighting. There were two of the fire-spirits, sitting on either side of the pass; they both rose as Corvus approached, lifting their heavy axes with hands the size of Veil's head. There was another pile of bodies at their feet, and pieces of barbarian were strewn here and there.

"I am Count Jaerkyvik," said the one on the left as Corvus approached. "This is Baron Morgenstrahd."

"Corvus." His hand dropped to the hilt of his sword.

"I know," rumbled the count. "Many brave men and women have died today, fighting for you."

"I don't need anyone to fight for me."

"They died for you nonetheless," put in the baron. "The Zan'Diem are no more."

"You will tell us how you managed to deceive them," said the count.

Corvus rolled his eyes. "Is it all right if I just kill you instead?"

The count chuckled. "He's brave."

"He'll tell us," said the baron, "once we pull his arms and legs off."

Despite herself, despite all the horror she'd witnessed in the last few hours, Veil found herself smiling. *I almost feel sorry for them.* The twisted faces of the dead Diem, rank after rank of them, rose in her memory. *Almost.*

Corvus spread his feet slightly and lowered his head. The Ghael, apparently annoyed that he had the gall not to be intimidated, lowered their heads like a pair of bulls and charged, bellowing a savage war cry. Smoke poured from their nostrils, and they raised their double-ended axes. The count broke left and the baron right, intending to prevent Corvus from dodging; both axes came whistling around at waist-height with demonic strength behind them, a pair of blows that would have shattered stone.

Veil heard Zhin gasp. She only kept smiling.

Corvus toppled to the left, free-falling backward. His sword rasped from its sheath as he did so, and he planted it in the count's path. The blade bit into his leg, driven by the force of the Ghael's charge, cutting through fur and bone with ease. The count toppled before he could take another step, one leg severed at the thigh; Corvus ended up on his back, but twisted lithely and sprang back to his feet before the baron could get turned around. The Ghael barely spared a glance for his fallen companion, who was roaring in agony and clutching the stump of his leg. He charged Corvus again, this time feinting left with the other end of his axe.

The swordsman bulled into the feint. Veil heard a shivering 'tzing' as his blade made contact with the axe handle and slid along it until it jammed against the head. The Ghael, attempting to pull back from his feint, found himself unable to, all his momentum going the wrong way; Corvus ducked a shoulder and let the force of the Ghael's charge flip him completely over and land heavily on his back. The ground shivered, and before the stunned demon could get its bearings Corvus whipped around and brought his sword down in a single vertical stroke that bisected its head.

The other Ghael was still screeching, so the swordsman withdrew his sword, walked over to it, and gave it a couple of vicious thrusts until it stopped moving. Both corpses started to dissolve into smoke and ash in the stunned silence that followed.

Veil broke it first.

"Are you all right?"

"Hmm?" said Corvus, cleaning the ash from his sword with a black cloth.

"You didn't get hurt, did you?"

He looked at her as though the question was the most idiotic thing he'd heard all day. "I'm fine."

Zhin came out of his paralysis, too. "That . . .that was un-believable. You just . . ."

"There may be more of them." Corvus sheathed his sword decisively. "That's the pass, correct?"

"Yeah." Zhin nodded.

"Then, let's go." He turned and headed for the crack in the rock. Veil followed, and Zhin and Isobel were forced to hurry to catch up. By the time they did so, Corvus was even with the pile of barbarian bodies; he stepped around them and walked into the narrow-walled pass without a second glance. Veil tried to keep pace, but a tiny movement caught her eye.

"Wait a minute."

Corvus stopped and half-turned. "What?"

"One of them's still alive." A hand had twitched; Veil located the body it was attached to and rolled the corpse of a burly warrior off it. He'd been run through, and his blood had totally soaked the woman lying underneath him; it took Veil a moment to realize that she was wounded, too, her other hand pressed tightly against a gash in her stomach. She was breathing, though, shallow and fast.

Isobel came up beside Veil, looked down, and sniffed. "Gut wound." The girl shrugged. "She's as dead as the others, she just hasn't stopped moving yet." She moved on, following Corvus into the pass.

"Wait. Wait a minute." Veil grabbed Zhin's arm as he walked past. "We can't just leave her."

"We're not going to be able to carry her through the pass." Zhin, at least, had the decency to look a little downcast. "Besides, Isobel's right. She's not going to make it, not without sorcery. And unless you've got a tame demon you're not telling us about . . ."

"But . . ."

"Come on." He gestured. "We need to be well away from here by nightfall."

Veil watched the woman's chest rise and fall. She was dressed differently from the rest—no armor, just brightly painted leathers and an elaborate necklace made from the claws of some forest animal. *A priestess, maybe?* Veil got to her feet, sadly, and turned to follow Zhin.

"Veil."

The voice was so quiet that she thought she'd imagined it at first. Veil turned around, carefully, and looked down at the dying woman. Her lips moved, ever so slightly.

"Veil . . ."

Zhin was already vanishing into the pass. Veil glanced over her shoulder, then knelt down next to the Diem.

"You know my name?"

The woman's eyes popped open. They were a cold, pale blue, and seemed perfectly focused, despite her pain. "Of course."

"But . . ." Veil looked around, at the bodies and the decomposing demons. "Who are you?"

"I told you I was getting backup . . ." The voice trailed away into a wheeze. *Backup. But . . .* There was something familiar about the woman's voice—not the tone but the cadence, somehow . . .

"Sybian?"

The Diem smiled, weakly. "For the moment."

"You did this?" Veil's voice shook. "All of this?"

"The Zan'diem were on the point of rebellion against the other tribes anyway." The priestess gave a painful-looking shrug. "I just assisted matters. Told them you were the key to everything."

"You wiped out a whole tribe of Diem?"

"Not yet." The woman closed her eyes. "Though I imagine the other tribes will be arriving at the Zan'diem villages any time now. It'll be a bit of a massacre." She smiled slightly. "I wonder if they'll take the women and children as slaves, like they usually do, or if the Ghael are mad enough to just slaughter everyone?"

"But . . ." Veil blinked, unable for a moment to fully understand what had happened. "Why?"

"So you could get away, of course." The priestess coughed, once, and drew a wheezing breath. "Even Corvus couldn't carve his way through that many Diem. I needed a distraction."

"For us?" Veil's voice was tiny. "You did this for us?"

"You should be grateful. I saved your lives. The Ghael aren't inclined to mercy, not after you escaped once already."

"I . . ." The words caught in her throat.

"Now you need to go and catch up with the others. Can't have you getting lost." Another wheezing laugh. "Not now. But can you do me a favor first?"

"Favor?" Veil blinked.

"This body is almost done. Could you finish it? Its pain is becoming annoying."

Veil shook her head, reflexively, and got to her feet, backing away.

"No?" The woman closed her eyes as Veil's footsteps faded into echoes. "Pity."

SAYA ARRIVED AT the scene an hour later, appearing in a column of the purest white light. She strode quickly amongst the bodies, not waiting for Ghael Rex, who materialized in a flash of flames a moment later.

"Sybian!" Saya cast about, heedless of the blood that spattered on her with every step. "Where are you?"

"Over here."

The weak voice came from a young woman who'd managed to prop herself up against one of the rocks. She raised a hand, shivering as though the effort pained her, and then let it fall.

"You . . ." Saya stormed over to her. "What have you done?"

"Didn't see this coming, your Radiance?" said the woman, mockingly.

"You . . . you . . ." Saya struggled to find the words. The priestess lay there, but Sybian watched from behind her eyes, amused.

"What is it?"

"All these people are dead!"

"They're humans. That's what they're for." The priestess smiled, bubbles of blood on her lips. "It was caring too much about humans that got you into this mess, your Radiance. And you, Smoke Lord," she addressed the fire spirit, who had moved up behind Saya, "you've gone coward. So desperate to protect what you have that you won't take risks."

"No one calls me coward." Ghael Rex snorted tiny tongues of flame.

"So why send your pets to kill Corvus? Why not confront him yourse—"

Enraged, Ghael Rex put one heavy foot between her breasts and pushed. The woman's ribcage gave way with a nasty crunch, and he ground her vitals against the rock. Her hands grabbed the fur on his leg, twisted tightly, then flopped to her sides; the icy chill faded from her eyes.

"And what purpose did that serve, exactly?" Saya regarded the demon lord with her hands on her hips.

"You heard her. I do not tolerate . . ."

"She was right." Saya looked up at the much taller Ghael. "You are a coward."

Smoke trickled from between Ghael Rex's gritted teeth. "Your Radiance, I would not say such things."

"Then why not fight him? Are you afraid of my little monster, Smoke Lord?"

"This is nonsense." The fire spirit snorted. "Consider my favor to you discharged."

"Incompetently." Saya brushed her hair back over her shoulder where it had gone astray, rapidly regaining her calm demeanor. "If I somehow manage to stop these upstarts from Transcending, you can be assured I'll return here to discuss matters."

"I'll look forward to that day," said Ghael Rex, his voice low and dangerous.

"For now, though, I have more important matters to attend to." *Like figuring out what the hell to do next*, she thought but didn't say.

"Farewell, your Radiance." Ghael Rex dissolved into a spinning cloud of ash, then vanished entirely. Saya slid back into the realm of pure light like a woman returning to her lover's well-remembered embrace, relishing the feeling of being free of the dead weight of pure matter.

Now what? She flickered through the mountains, watching the little party trudge glumly through the narrow pass toward the riverlands. In the distance, across leagues of mountains and forests, the Trap at Godsdoom glowed like a beacon.

Only two of us left that remember the war. There were probably a few more, here and there, but if they cared they hadn't shown themselves. *And now they want to start it all over again.*

Damn *Sybian*.

THEY MADE CAMP at what Zhin said was the pass's mid-way point. As promised, the narrow valley had opened up in a gently sloping canyon that zigzagged between two precipitous peaks. Periodically, sections of it had been obliterated by rock-slides, but never enough to completely block their progress. Zhin mentioned that the Diem would come through, after the winter, and clean it up; they safeguarded their secret route past the Anvil zealously.

Veil's body walked along behind Isobel, but her mind was somewhere else entirely. She found herself floating freely above a plain of corpses. There were thousands of dead Diem, of course, and the women and children whose tortures she could only imagine. But it was more than that—dozens, hundreds more, a trail of bodies and blood leading back to the oasis in the desert, and Bali's slavers.

My fault. His fault. Sybian had set the Diem against each other because of her. The thugs in Corsa had died because of her. The Diem in the village she'd killed directly, forcing Sybian to summon a dragon to rip their peaceful little town apart. She remembered how triumphant she'd felt at the time, and felt bile rise in the back of her throat.

So many bodies. She wanted to curl into a little ball and wait for her heart to stop beating. *And for what? To keep me alive? What in the Aether am I worth?* Sybian obviously had some use for her, but Veil had never been able to fool herself enough to think that the spirit was on her side. *She needs me for something, and then she'll throw me away.*

And what am I going to do, when this is all done? I've been running ever since Corvus cut up the slavers, from one place to the next, from one fight to the next, drowning in blood. There was no way out that she could see. No way out except death, no end except darkness.

Am I ready to die? She'd considered the question once before, in the desert, and had come up with an unconvincing answer. *Why not? With all else being equal, why not make the effort to live? Sure, it's futile.* Although, as it had turned out, it had worked. *So I'm alive. But all else isn't equal. All those people are dead because of me.*

Gods. Veil shook her head. *Listen to me. This is ridiculous.*

So I'm selfish. I want to live and be happy. I accept that, all right? Wanting to live is not a bad thing. I'm not going to blame myself for whatever some crazy ice-spirit and an amnesiac sword master do.

Why should I care, anyway? Practically everyone I've met has wanted to rob me, kill me, fuck me, or some combination of the three. So what if they keep ending up dead? Not my fault. Not my *fault.*

"Sybian." Veil whispered the name under her breath, and felt the ice-spirit's chill in her mind. There had been stories, back in the Red Hills, about demons who came when you called them by name. Mostly they had been scary stories.

"Yes, Veil?"

"In your infinite wisdom I assume you've got some plan for us after we get to the other side of this pass?"

"Of course."

"Feel like letting me in on any of it?"

"I've got a few tasks for you. Nothing major."

"Such as?"

"To begin with, I need you to win a war."

Veil blinked.

"LORD VALOS." METAL clinked on metal as the soldier saluted.

"Report." Justin sat in his chair, chin in his hands, brooding over his map table by the light of a dying cook fire. Slips of paper, weighted down with stones, marked the last reported position of his men and the Khaevs. It was not an easy map to read, marked over and over again with the latest information arriving from Tayla's scouts and outriders, but Justin had been reading maps for a long time. It looked like catastrophe.

"Elizabeth's cavalry have reformed on the other side of the ridge, here." The soldier moved a marker a short distance.

"The messengers have had to take a fairly roundabout route, because the main body of Kagerin Shuzan's Blade has advanced to here"—paper rustled again—"with a little detour around the woods here. Fyder's infantry report some skirmishes, but nothing major. They're still sitting tight."

"What about Benham?"

"His men are ready, he says."

What's left of them. Benham's cavalry wing, half of his mounted forces, had gone head-to-head with the Khaev elites on the first day and had come off much the worse for it. That had been the start of a panicked retreat; Justin had struggled to find ground in his favor, and had finally settled for positioning a third of his infantry behind a narrow stream. Kagerin Shuzan had declined the invitation to attack, since the water would most likely foul his charge; instead he'd cut sideways, looking for a good crossing place. *If I had twice as many men, I could stop him.* With Fyder's infantry trapped in a forward position, though, there were simply too many possibilities to guard against. Shuzan had encamped his men on the other side of the brook at nightfall, but by morning he'd be across.

And once he is, he'll have my men flanked, and all I have to stop him are Benham's precious heavies. The cavalry commander had sworn his unit would die to the man before breaking. It was even possible he was telling the truth. *Even if they do, Shuzan'll have five hundred lances to throw at me.*

You tossed the dice, Lord Valos, and you lost. Fyder warned you to run. But you put your trust in the old man.

"Another thing, my Lord. The unit you sent on that special expedition has returned."

Speak a demon's name, thought Justin grimly, *and you shall see his horns.* He'd detailed a dozen men to escort the Prophet to his camp; the old man wanted to greet his genius personally when she arrived. *If any of us are around by then.*

"My Lord!" Another soldier burst in to the tent. "I've just had a report from one of our patrols. You wanted to be informed immediately . . ."

"What?" snapped Justin, still staring at the map.

"We've just picked up Zhin and Isobel, my Lord."

Justin didn't turn. "And with them?"

"A swordsman in black, and a young girl, my Lord."

He was right. Justin kept himself from smiling. *It's too early to tell, yet. And it may be too late for us. But still — the old bastard was right!*

FOR ISOBEL, IT felt as much like coming home as anything ever had.

Home was not a concept she was particularly familiar with. Most of her life had been spent on the move, from job to job, from fight to fight. She'd learned from anyone who would teach her, and afterward she'd mostly killed them. She'd been *driven*, searching for something she couldn't even define. A swordsman without equal. Someone she was supposed to kill, or die trying.

I thought it was Corvus. The black-clad warrior certainly met that description. But he hadn't killed her, and later, on closer . . . examination . . . she'd concluded he was not the one. *He's just* wrong, *somehow. He shouldn't be here.* There was something about him that set her teeth on edge.

She'd been working for Valos longer than she'd worked for anyone else. That was partly because his was the first job she'd taken simply to make ends meet, and not to learn how to fight. Great swordfighters had become scarce, and action had become even scarcer as the Khaevs tightened their grip on the land, bottling the rebels up in their castles and taking them, one by one. Only Lord Valos evaded them, time after time, slapping the hands of such eminent commanders as Kagerin Shuzan and Kurai Morika when they tried to corner him. Rumors had started to spread, and one day Isobel had shouldered her pack and gone looking for the last of the Imperial armies.

After that, she'd been content, or at least as content as she ever was. Valos took care of mundane matters like food and lodging, and having to occasionally kill someone unworthy of her talents was a small price to pay. He turned a blind eye to Isobel's solo expeditions, and even provided support when her targets were Khaevs.

Though not always. She'd presented Valos with a plan to sneak into the Kaiune Palace and fight a duel with Gefura Suron, the High Commander's personal bodyguard and Thirty-Seventh of Two Hundred. He'd turned her down, for what on reflection turned out to be good reasons. So she'd restrained herself, except during her trips to Corsa, and tried to ignore the fiery worm that twisted in her gut, telling her that every moment not searching was a moment wasted.

But something has changed.

She'd ridden into camp before, many times. She'd even returned from long expeditions before, although admittedly none quite as blood-soaked as this one. But before, she'd always been planning her next trip, her next fight. She'd barely noticed the sights and sounds of Valos' army. This time, though, she found herself sighing contentedly at the smell of baking bread, and smiling at the familiar ring of blacksmiths' hammers on steel. She even found a kind of comfort in the way the ordinary infantry took one look at her and scrambled to get out of her way.

Valos' aides immediately pounced on Zhin and dragged him off to the command tent to be debriefed. Isobel was glad, frankly, that she avoided that fate. Nobody expected her to observe, or report, or plan elaborate strategies. *All I have to do for Valos is kill.* She was quite satisfied with that arrangement.

Still, it left her at loose ends. Tugged by her stomach, she drifted in the direction of the mess tent. *After trail bread and dried meat for gods-know-how-many weeks, anything else is going to taste like a feast.* And Lord Valos' army was generally well-provisioned. His foragers were still met with generosity, since anyone who fought the Khaevs had sympathizers everywhere. She ducked under the tent flap and found the usual arrangement, a half-dozen long tables with a single larger one at the front, laden with steaming bowls of soup, loaves of bread, and a mostly-empty platter of roast zox. Isobel grabbed a wooden plate and started filling it, taking absent note of the stares she collected. There weren't many soldiers up at this hour, but there were always a few late-night snackers or unlucky scouts who had drawn the night shift.

With a plate of meat and a flagon of pure water, she picked a table at random and sat down. The others who'd been sitting there—two women in scout's uniforms and a bleary-looking sub-commander of infantry—hastily got to their feet and shuffled away. Isobel smiled. Everything was as it should be.

So why don't I feel happier? Something's wrong with me. It felt like something was missing. She'd awakened, the night after the rescue, with a searing pain at the base of her skull, as though someone had pressed a hot poker into her flesh. It had passed after a moment, and she hadn't told any of the others. *But ever since then . . .*

She tore a chunk from the roast beef with her fingers and devoured it, juice running from the corner of her mouth down her chin. It was good. She'd never noticed before, but the meat Valos' kitchen served usually was. *I wonder who cooks it?*

The tent flap opened and closed again. Isobel didn't look up until she heard the scrape of the bench opposite her. Veil set down a bowl of soup and a loaf of bread, looking at her nervously.

"Do you mind?" Veil's voice was small. "I can move to

another table . . ."

In the past, a glare had sufficed to get rid of anyone who acted too familiar. It would certainly have worked on Veil. She looked as nervous as a rabbit in a wolf pack. Isobel swallowed her meat and muttered, "Go ahead."

"Thanks." Veil settled in and tore the loaf in half, dipping it in the soup for flavor. "They didn't seem to have much use for me at the moment, so Lord Valos' servant said I might as well go get something to eat."

"Mmm." Isobel washed the beef down and tore into her own bread.

Veil paused a moment, searching for something to say. "So . . ."

"Mmm?"

"This is your army?"

Isobel swallowed. "Well, it's not *mine*. It belongs to Lord Valos. I just work for him."

"Right." Veil stirred her soup idly, and Isobel shrugged.

"It keeps me fed, and he doesn't demand too much. Mostly I've been playing bodyguard for Zhin."

"Just going to Corsa and back?"

"Going to all kinds of places. I've been to T'Bach, and up to Steelgod. There are people everywhere who hate the Khaevs."

"Why?"

Isobel blinked. "Why? They conquered the Empire. They conquered your people too, didn't they?"

"Kalil used to say he didn't care whether the tax collector was blond or dark-haired. And the Khaevs never really bothered us."

"You didn't fight them. Here in the riverlands, things are different." Isobel tore off a hunk of bread. "There've been massacres."

"So you hate the Khaevs?"

"Not really."

"So why . . ."

"I have to eat." She shrugged. "That means I have to fight for someone. Lord Valos is understanding."

"I guess." Veil looked down. "You've never thought of just not fighting?"

"What else am I supposed to do?" The idea of not being able to fight had once inflamed the worm, practically doubling her over in agony. Now she didn't even feel a tickle. It was an odd sensation, being able to think about something she'd always avoided before. "It's the only thing I really know how to do. You want me to marry some farmer and become a fat housewife?" Isobel gestured at her body, blade-slim and barely curved, and Veil chuckled.

"You're right."

In the silence that followed, Isobel became aware of the murmurs that surrounded her. The other soldiers were too far away for her to hear, but she could guess their content. *She's actually talking to someone!* It made her want to giggle, which was another decidedly unfamiliar sensation.

Veil noticed it too. "Everybody seems kind of scared of you."

Isobel nodded. "I think it's because I have a tendency to kill people without warning."

"Really?"

"No." She shrugged. "But you know how rumors get around. I'm surprised you're not scared of me."

"I've been hanging around with Corvus too long, I suppose."

Isobel laughed. "I guess you don't get to be squeamish."

She laughed!, went the murmurs. Isobel ignored them. *It's not like I've never laughed before. Just not . . . often. What's wrong with it, anyway?*

What's wrong with me?

"So what are you going to do now, Veil?"

"I don't know." She rolled a bit of bread between her fingers. "Follow Corvus, I guess."

"And where is he going?"

"Further into the riverlands, I guess. I'm not sure he knows."

"And you're going to keep following him? Forever?"

"What else am I supposed to do?" said Veil, parroting Isobel's words so exactly that they both dissolved into giggles for a moment. "Honestly. I'm fourteen. What am I good for? Playing capture?"

"You can make money playing capture."

"I suppose." She put her chin in her hands. "I don't know. Maybe I will, someday."

"The longer you stay with him, the more likely you are to get killed."

"I know. I've gotten used to it." She shivered. "That's a scary thought—that that's something you can get used to."

"So are you in love with him, or what?"

Veil blinked, as though she'd taken a crossbow bolt right between the eyes. Isobel watched with dry amusement.

"I . . ." Veil's mouth hung open, as though she wasn't sure what to say, then shut with a clop. She stared thoughtfully into the distance. "I don't know."

"You don't know?" Isobel was skeptical.

"Seriously. I've never fallen in love before. Why? Does it look like I am?"

"Sort of. I mean," Isobel shrugged, "it's the kind of thing you read about in stories. Women following their loved ones across the world, enduring all kinds of hardships for their sake, and so on."

"You'd think they'd wise up after a while."

Isobel smiled. "Maybe. Does the thought of being alone with him make your heart beat faster?"

"Not that I've observed." Veil put one hand to her breast, and counted silently.

"When you're alone at night, do you imagine him sliding his hands over your naked body, caressing supple young flesh in . . ."

Veil had turned bright red. "Isobel!"

"Sorry." Her smile widened. "That's also the sort of thing that goes on in stories."

"Apparently I've been reading the wrong kind."

"Or I have."

They laughed again, harder. Isobel wiped a tear away from the corner of one eye as they settled down.

"I never did thank you, did I?"

"For what?"

"Saving us from gods-know-what, when the Diem took us prisoner."

"Oh." Veil nodded uncertainly. "Don't mention it."

"And I don't suppose you'd like to tell me *how* you did it?"

She shook her head stiffly.

"I thought not. To each her own, I suppose." Isobel popped the last of the roast beef into her mouth and leaned back. *There's something about the flavor,* she thought. *Not even the restaurants in Corsa get it quite right.*

Veil had gone quiet, and Isobel looked over at her.

"What?"

"What happened to you?"

Isobel looked down at herself. "To me?"

"You're different. I guess I hadn't known you very long, but . . ."

"You're right." Isobel shrugged again. "I have no idea.

Maybe I have brain fever and this is dementia."

"It's nice, for dementia."

"Thanks," said Isobel, and to her surprise she meant it.

"Veil?" said an official-sounding voice with a thick Sithan brogue. Both girls looked around; an officer was standing by the tent flap, so ramrod-straight that Isobel's back ached in sympathy. He seemed to be extremely uncomfortable calling Veil in such familiar terms. Addressing someone with no rank or even last name was apparently an affront to his military dignity. Isobel didn't recognize him. *Must be someone Valos picked up since I left.*

"Yes?" said Veil.

"Lord Valos wants to see you."

"Me?" She pushed her plate away and stood up. "Of course. Isobel . . ."

"I'm off to get some sleep." She pushed away from the table as well. "I'll see you in the morning."

"Right."

"Word is there's a battle coming." Isobel put on her best grin, which Veil matched. The girl turned back to the officer.

"Lead the way."

After Veil had gone, the murmurs returned to the mess tent in full force. Isobel ignored them, dumped the two plates in the dirty bin for the stewards to take care of, and went in search of the tent she'd been assigned. Isobel got her own half of a two-person tent, like an officer. She hadn't asked for it, but she got it all the same. *Respect,* she thought, as she flopped down on the mattress, *is a good thing.*

She would have liked to fall asleep on the spot, but her leathers were much too stiff. Isobel rolled out of bed, stripped down to cloth, and flopped back down again, twisting the Imperial-issue blanket on top of her. It quickly became a warm little cave in a huge, cold night; she closed her eyes and sighed.

It had been a good day. If she'd thought about it, she would have expected good dreams. Instead she dreamt of a black, burnt plain, and a steel giant whose body was alive with fire. Isobel twisted in her sleep.

chapter 16

> "You sit there, in your silk robes, and speak of necessity?
> "Is there one among you who realizes what they've done? We've spent centuries in terror of the Empire. We formed the Council to repel the Empire, built an army to defeat the Empire. We created central orders of Maidens and draekeres, to defeat the Empire.
> "Now the Empire is gone. And what . . . will the army disband? The draekeres return to their rightful place underneath the lords of land? The Council dissolve?
> "Of course not. There is still 'necessity'. We need to govern our new possessions, after all. And there are threats to our new borders to be dealt with.
> "We are like the terrified lord who turned over the keys to his castle to the sellsword. We've given the Council all the weapons they need, and no one will be able to take them away."
>
> —Kuroda Yami, in his last speech before his execution for treason by order of the Council

*G*ODSDOOM.

The word echoed through Kei's head, repeating with every step. Her blistered feet complained where her riding boots had rubbed them raw, her thighs were clenched bundles of agony, and what Jyo-raku had said would not stop repeating itself.

Godsdoom. Godsdoom.

It was like the beat of a drum, low and deep.

Doom. Doom. Doom.

There had been a Khaev expedition to try and reach Godsdoom. Only one. Kagerin Semike had taken every Maiden the High Commander could spare, every monk she could get her hands on, a dozen draekeres. *And Kino.*

And nothing, *nothing* had come back. The Doomwood had swallowed them all, as though they had never existed. Since then, High Command had followed the Imperial example and pretended that there was no bastion of killer spirits right on their doorstep. There was a war to fight, although it was winding down, and those who'd had friends in the expedition cried and moved on.

She'd always known it was a silly love affair, with Kino. He was a swordsman sworn to the Kagerins, and she was a draekere. Their meetings were short-lived things, separated by long months of campaigning. She'd had other lovers in the meantime, and she assumed that he had, too. But he was always something to look forward to when she returned to the draekere base at Steelgod. And he always seemed happy to see her.

Afterward, she'd found herself having nightmares, imagining his last moments. Alone, in the dark of the Doomwood, surrounded by amorphous shadows. Screams all around, as his comrades were dragged down one by one. Drawing his sword in a useless gesture of defiance, slashing wildly at the tide of darkness as it crashed over him.

She'd awakened every night for months in a cold sweat. Eventually, it had faded into the background of her life: one more regret, one more thing to fear, but no worse than anything else. She'd even managed to keep the thought at bay while dealing with Jyo-raku, who moved under a shroud of liquid darkness, but his naming of their destination had brought it all crashing back.

Doom. Doom. Doom.

Kei spent her days walking, eyes fixed on the trail ahead of her, forcing herself to take each step despite the pain. Jyo-raku set a murderous pace; Kit seemed to be able to cope, but Kei lived in fear of not being able to keep up. *He'd just kill me, 'further need' or not.* Her mind replayed the awful crunch of Melody's skull giving way. *There's no way out.*

At night, she curled up under her blanket and sobbed.

Doom. Doom. Doom.

Awake or asleep, the visions came to her. Only now she was the one in the darkness of the Doomwood, listening to the screams and waiting for the cold touch of the dark. Behind her, the glowing archway, glittering obscenely with arcane promise. And always the horrible hissing voice in her ear. She woke every morning with a gasp, dully confronting the knowledge that she had another day to live. But, every day, the Doomwood drew closer. *And Heaven's Gate is in the Doomwood.* She felt certain it was a real place, now. Her steps seemed to be leading her there, slowly but inexorably.

It was three days before Kit broke the silence that had fallen over the little group, matching her stride to Jyo-raku's. Kei walked sullenly behind them.

"Jyo-raku," Kit said, finally. "Are you going to spit at? me if I ask you a question?"

There was a long pause, during which Kei held her breath.

"It would seem to be waste of effort," hissed Jyo-raku finally. One hand caressed the hilt of the Bound Blade that rode on his hip. "Unlike Tashida Shiori, you are a competent fighter and thus have some value to us."

"So she's dead, then?"

"Oh yes." Jyo-raku glanced at her, or at least turned his head in her direction. "Was that the question?"

"No."

She honestly doesn't care. What, if anything, Kit cared about was a mystery to Kei, but it certainly wasn't the noble she'd had a crush on. *I don't understand her at all.*

"So? Ask."

"What's so important about Kei? Why did you bring us along?"

Kei's breath caught again. Kit had a way of cutting right to the heart of the matter, usually by ignoring things like tact. Somewhat to her surprise, Jyo-raku answered.

"Kei is an oversight. The fact that she is alive at all is a testament to her brother's love and skill at arms."

"Brother?" Kit glanced over her shoulder. "You never told me you had a brother."

He knows. Kei felt only a dull surprise. Jyo-raku was a spirit, after all. That he knew her little secret was only to be expected.

"So I expect that her brother is following us as we speak. Once he catches up with us, I have a favor to ask of him." The spirit made a choking hiss that might have been a chuckle.

Shuzan! The idea that he might follow her had never occurred to her. *Wait. Nobody knew where we were going, except for Lady Tashida and . . . Moriseki! Jyo-raku must have gotten to her somehow. I wondered why she let us go so easily.*

"So you dragged her out here just so this guy would follow?"

"Partly. She has another function as well."

"Oh?"

"You'll see once we arrive."

The younger draekere sighed. "So who's this brother of hers, anyway? What makes him so special?"

"His name is Kagerin Shuzan, and he is the Fifty-Fourth

of Two Hundred." Jyo-raku touched the Bound Blade again. "And I have someone I need him to kill."

IT WAS FOUR years before the draekeres-in-training got their first honest-to-gods leave.

There was a vacation at the end of every year, of course, but that was only for the girls with families. Kei, along with quite a few others, ended up spending the Ice holidays at the fortress. Some of the instructors obviously felt sorry for them, and there were only a few drills and more food than usual to sustain them through the coldest stretch of winter. Even so, it hardly counted as leave.

Which means, Kei thought, *this is the first time I've set foot outside these walls since I got here.* She paused, right outside the gate, to look up at the fortress from the outside. Sora was built into the side of a mountain, a central keep and various subsidiary build-ings surrounded by a massive curtain wall. The rock itself was honeycombed with tunnels, as Kei well knew. She'd explored a goodly portion of it herself, but the maze beyond the well-lit halls was endless. Far above, rising from the roof of the main keep, stood the huge towers that served as the "stables," with tiny specks of draeks circling around them like oversized ravens.

The instructors had decided that, once they were fourteen, it was safe to turn the girls loose on an unsuspecting world. For most of them this didn't mean much change. In previous years, the families had been forced to send a carriage to Sora to collect them, and many still did. Another, smaller fraction were using the opportunity to descend on the nearby town of Zhakuri like a swarm of locusts, where they'd sleep on warm beds instead of cold slabs and drink wine and stay up until the small hours of the morning. The instructors turned a benevolent, blind eye to all of this, secure in the knowledge that, given the training they'd already received, the girls were capable of laying the average grown man out in a couple of seconds, armed or not.

For all of them, the fourth-year leave was a treat—maybe a little nicer than the usual Ice, but nothing terribly special. For Kei, it was something she'd been fantasizing about ever since her arrival.

I finally get to see him again. Finally!

She'd gotten an anonymous letter, nearly a month ago, which had informed her that her brother would be waiting in the Silk Fang Inn in Zhakuri on the first day of her leave. So now she was riding in a carriage pulled by a pair of fine black horses, hired for the occasion by Kei and three of her classmates. The others had their heads together, talking in low tones and giggling; occasional hand gestures revealed that they were back onto the subject of boys, which was a perennial favorite. There were no boys at Sora, aside from the instructors. Kei had no ear for their gossip. She stared out one rain-streaked window, eyes on the stone-walled fields that rolled gently past but not really seeing them.

What should I say to him? Try to play it cool with a joke? *'Fancy meeting you here!' or something like that.* She didn't want to ruin the moment, though. And she didn't know if she could keep a straight face long enough to pull it off. *Will I even recognize him? Will he recognize me?* Kei's memories of her brother's face were distant, blurred by time. She thought of him as a hawk-like nose and a pair of bright, shining eyes. *And I've changed a lot, obviously.* At fourteen, her figure was just beginning to fill out, and her long braid had been clipped military-short. She'd thought about wearing her uniform, but in the end had decided on civilian dress—a skirt that modestly covered her knees and a matching top. The fabric felt odd as she walked, swishing back and forth. Draekeres-in-training wore tight fighting outfits that wouldn't get in the way while riding or flying.

"Zhakuri, ladies." The voice of the driver jolted Kei out of her reverie. He'd stopped in the town square and opened the door, treating them all to a horrible gap-toothed smile. "Is there anything else I can do for you?"

Kel flipped the man a pair of copper coins, which he caught adroitly before stepping out of the way. The four draekeres stepped down to the cobbled square and looked around with wide eyes. Kei wasn't the only one who'd lived most of her life within the fortress walls. There were people everywhere. The square was lined with merchants, sitting behind painted paper signs proclaiming the goods they had for sale. A young noble-man was perusing the wares of a bronzesmith, while a pair of guards in his family colors watched suspiciously. Another pair of draekeres were looking at jewelry; Sev recognized one of them and waved a greeting. And commonfolk were everywhere, modestly dressed in blacks and grays, hurrying across the square on errands of their own.

The other three conferred briefly, then turned to Kei.

"We're going to meet up with Kal and Ren, over at the noo-dle shop," said Kel. "Do you want to come?"

Kei shook her head, to the other girl's evident relief. They were acquaintances rather than friends—Kei didn't have many friends—and it was only out of politeness that she had made the invitation. With another backward wave, the three rushed off, pointing and giggling. The young nobleman gathered more than his share of stares, of course.

Kei giggled to herself. *I've got someone better.* She stepped in front of a gray-clad old man and bowed, preemptively, before asking directions to the Silk Fang Inn. He was only too glad to oblige, and before long she stood before the building. It was marked by a massive silk banner, hung from the second story, depicting a stylized wolf. Kei took a deep breath, straightened the shoulders of her blouse, and walked up to the door.

Somewhat to her surprise, it opened before her, revealing a bowing footman in gray. She bowed in return, uncertainly. Kei realized, belatedly, that she had no idea what the proper protocol was for entering an inn, especially a fancy one.

Luckily, the servant didn't seem to notice. He stepped silently out of the way and gestured her in. The anteroom was mostly empty, draped in more expensive-looking silk hangings, and a single desk was flanked by a pair of staircases. The woman behind the desk favored Kei with a bright, empty smile.

"Can I help you?"

"I'm looking for" —she almost said Kagerin Shuzan, before remembering herself— "Kemula Ayumu." The name had been in the letter.

"Of course." The woman nodded. "Room four, on the right. He's expecting you."

"Thank you." Kei bowed again, feeling ridiculously formal, and restrained herself from sprinting up the stairs two at a time. *Shuzan, Shuzan, Shuzan!* There was a hallway filled with doors, with painted numbers. She padded up to number four, then stopped.

Now what?

What's really behind this door? My brother? Her former life mostly receded into a half-remembered haze. The clearest memory she had was of her escape, which haunted her dreams almost every night. *Is this really where I want to go?*

A barely-acknowledged thought squirmed its way to the surface. *If I don't go in, I'll just be Keimani Shia forever. No mystery, no cloak-and-dagger meetings, nothing to worry about. The Army will take care of me.*

She took a deep breath, and knocked on the door.

It was answered almost immediately. Kei stared, and wondered how she could have possibly forgotten what Shuzan looked like. His features were burned into her memory, as clear as day.

Shuzan blinked, obviously not sure what he was seeing. "S . . . Shia?"

Then Kei stormed into the room, wrapping him in the tightest hug that she could manage and squeezing as though she never intended to let go. She barely had the presence of mind to kick the door shut behind them.

KIT BROKE THE quiet, dropping back from where Jyo-raku walked to plod along next to Kei. They walked together for some time, saying nothing, until Kit finally cleared her throat.

"Wing Leader . . ."

"Kei."

"Kei." Kit paused. "Are you all right?"

Am I all right? She wanted to giggle, to laugh at the monumental idiocy of the question. *Am I all right? I'm on a march to certain death with a shadow spirit ready to spit me if I make a false move, and you're completely insane! Do you fucking* think *I'm all right?*

Anger bubbled up inside her, and she snapped off a reply. "I'm fine."

"Ah." Kit paused. "You just haven't seemed—"

"I'm fucking fine. What about you and your buddy up there?"

"Jyo-raku isn't saying much anymore."

"Oh, too bad," said Kei savagely. "Why don't you offer yourself to him? You've never fucked a spirit before, I imagine it would be an *enlightening* experience."

"Wing Leader—"

"I told you to call me Kei. It's not like we'll ever fly again."

"Kei. Calm down."

"No." Something inside Kei had snapped, and she found herself lashing out at that oh-so-calm face. "I think I deserve to be a little bit upset. In fact, I'm starting to wonder if you're human or not. Your last little crush got her head smashed in. Or have you forgotten her already?"

"I haven't forgotten." Kit's voice was quiet.

"No, of course not," Kei continued. "You've just moved on. Shiori disappeared, Melody got killed, and Jyo-raku isn't interested, so you've come back to talk to me, is that it? You want to fuck me, Kit?"

Kit raised an eyebrow. "Sure, but this is hardly the time or place—"

"*Fuck* you." Kei stomped past her, forcing Kit to hurry to keep up with her. "You have no right to be so fucking cool."

"Why?"

"Because we're all going to *fucking die.* Have you not absorbed this concept somehow? Jyo-raku's marching us to Godsdoom."

"I know."

"So can't you be just a little bit upset?" Kei could feel tears coming to her eyes, and she wiped them away angrily. "By all the fucking gods. Is it so wrong for me not to want to die?"

"Of course not." Kit put her hand on Kei's shoulder, but Kei swept it away.

"Then what the *fuck* is wrong with you?"

"What I cared about died a long time ago," said Kit quietly.

"Bullshit." Kei wiped her eyes again. "That's bullshit."

Kit walked quietly while Kei regained her composure. Kei noticed a couple of curious glances from the younger draekere, and finally shook her head.

"Look. I know you want to ask, so go ahead and ask."

"You don't have to tell me."

"I don't suppose it matters now."

"So is Kagerin Shuzan really your brother?"

"Yes."

"So you're . . ."

"Kagerin Shia." The name sounded odd, as though it belonged to a stranger. She hadn't heard it spoken out loud for more than a decade.

Kit shook her head. "So what happened?"

"I never really understood. Shuzan snuck me out of Yamika when I was ten years old and gave me to the draekeres. I've only seen him a few times since then."

"And you never asked him why?"

"I asked. He never answered, aside from what he told me to start with — that my family wanted to kill me, and I had to hide."

"They wanted to *kill* you? But . . ."

"I know." Kei sighed. "It doesn't make any sense. I can't tell you how many times I've wanted to just go to the Kagerin estates, find my father, and ask him what happened."

"Why don't you?"

"I trust Shuzan, I guess," Kei said, and glanced at Kit. "And as foreign as this may be to you, I'm actually happy. Or I was, until all this started."

There was a long pause.

"Do you hate me now?" Kei asked. "I know you and nobility . . ."

"Relax." Kit leaned her head back to look at the sky. "You're still the same person you used to be."

And Kei did, a little. A knot of hitherto unrecognized tension released. "I'm sorry I snapped at you. I'm just scared out of my fucking mind. Don't take it personally."

"It's okay." Kit put her hand on her Wing Leader's shoulder, and they walked in silence.

"You know . . ." said Kei eventually.

"Hmm?"

"Never mind." She shook her head. "So now what?"

"We're still alive, Wing Leader." Kit smiled broadly. "There's always a chance."

ERIN AWOKE TO the sound of conversation in the fluid Khaev tongue. It took her only a couple of seconds to go from *Thank the gods, someone found us!* to *fuck, the* Khaevs *found us!* Eyes still closed, she groped carefully at her side for a weapon.

It wasn't there, of course. She'd been holding it in her hand, since she was supposed to be guarding. She patted the ground desperately, hoping that the Khaevs had been stupid enough to leave it where it had fallen when she'd nodded off, but there was nothing there but rock. Karl's head resting on her arm was romantic, but it also trapped her other hand behind him.

So, in summary, I'm screwed. Erin opened her eyes. *Maybe if I can grab one of them . . .*

There were four Khaevs, which put an end to that idea. They were obviously cavalrymen, with riding boots and spurs, wearing a pair of short swords each. One of them had been watching her intently, and rattled off something in Khaev too fast for Erin to follow. Another of the soldiers took a step closer, his hand on the hilt of his weapon, while the others stayed back.

"Do you speak Khaev?" he snapped, slowly enough that Erin could barely understand him.

She nodded. "Speak slowly."

"You're a soldier. What are you doing up here?"

She thought about denying it, but between the armor and the short sword she could now see lying a few feet away, there wasn't much point. Karl, too, was armored, and obviously wounded.

She gave him a quick check to make sure he was still asleep, and wouldn't contradict her story. *Now I have to come up with a story.*

"I'm a mercenary." She took a deep breath. "We were guards, on a caravan heading though Crimson Pass."

"Crimson Pass is a hundred miles south of here," said the Khaev warily.

"We were attacked by bandits well short of the pass. They broke up the caravan . . ."

"Bandits broke up a caravan?"

"There were a lot of them. Fifty, sixty."

"There's no . . ."

One of the others said something, too quietly for her to hear, but she caught the word 'Valos'. The leader nodded slowly. "Go on."

"We fled, once the battle was lost. My companion was wounded, and we didn't have a map. We wandered into Valdiem territory and we've been running away from them ever since."

"This is an inconvenient place to run to."

"We hoped that would discourage them. Since I'm still alive, it may have worked."

He smiled. "I think the presence of a cavalry Blade has scared them away."

A whole Blade out here? She looked closely at the colors on the Khaev's arm. There were a lot of Blades, and she didn't even know all of the house colors, but . . .*Kagerin Shuzan!* That particular combination was burned into her memory. Erin could remember the first time Lord Valos' army had gone up against Kagerin Shuzan; only the grace of the gods and Valos' enigmatic Prophet had let anyone come out of that disaster alive. *What in the name of all the gods is he doing out here?*

There was only one answer, of course. *He's hunting Lord Valos. Again.* Last time, he'd ended up running off into the Doomwood, for reasons no one was quite sure of; rumor said he'd come out with less than half his men, and his Blade had been licking its wounds ever since. *Now he's back.* While Lord Valos had no personal antipathy toward the man, the Khaevs were the sort of people who took even minor setbacks personally.

"How long have you been here?" said the Khaev, breaking in on her private thoughts.

Erin glanced at the sun, which was climbing toward noon. "Since last night."

"Since last night?" There was some more chatter in quick, quiet Khaev. "Have you seen anyone else?"

She wondered whether lying or telling the truth was more likely to get her skewered. In the end, she decided on the truth. *If I say I haven't seen anyone, they have no incentive not to kill us. If we know something they want, maybe they'll help.*

"Aside from the Valdiem, you mean?"

He gave a curt nod.

"Yeah. A lot of people, actually. There were a couple of the other . . . mercenaries I worked with . . ."

The Khaev waved his hand impatiently. "And?"

"Three Khaevs. Two draekeres and a monk, plus what I assume was his spirit." She kept the second spirit to herself, just to have something to bring out later.

The Khaev stepped closer. "What happened to them?"

"They went into the cave, stayed for a while, and then came out again—only the draekeres and the spirit. Then they headed down the mountain."

"When was this?"

"Last night."

The leader turned to his subordinates and shouted, gesturing wildly. Two of them bowed and started trotting down the path. Erin was considering making a grab for him when he turned back. "Can your companion walk?"

"Probably." She poked Karl and switched to Imperial. "Wake up, or we'll have to carry you."

"That would be tragic," said Karl, eyes still closed.

"You were awake?" She rapped him on the head. "Why didn't you help me out?"

"You were doing such a good job." He yawned and sat up, wincing as he moved his injured arm, and switched into Khaev as well. "Good morning, gentlemen."

"You're both coming with us to see Lord Kagerin."

"Lord Kagerin?" Karl raised an eyebrow, and glanced at Erin. "We're moving up in the world."

"Stand up and get rid of the armor," said the Khaev, ignoring him. "We'll be riding double, and the horse won't take the weight.

Karl grumbled, but did as he was told. Erin once again weighed making a dive for her sword, but the Khaevs were between it and her, and moreover had taken a careful step back when Karl got to his feet. *These guys are good.* Kagerin Shuzan's cavalry had always been elite, but she'd hoped their quality had suffered somewhat after the losses they'd incurred. Apparently they'd been keeping busy.

Karl's half-plate clanked to the ground, piece by piece, until he was left shivering in his leather pants and thin undershirt. Erin got to her feet and moved closer to him, protectively. "He'll freeze."

"It'll warm up. We're headed down the mountain." He nodded to the path. "You two first. Just follow the path until we get to the horses."

Karl caught Erin's eye, and an unspoken communication passed between them. *So I won't try anything funny.* She swallowed. *Yet.* Meeting Kagerin Shuzan was an honor she'd hoped to avoid.

"I'm holding you to it, you know," said Karl, as they started down the path.

"To what?"

"To what you said last night, about an exception to your rule."

Erin fought a blush. "I thought we were going to die!"

"What makes you think that's changed?"

She glanced back at the impassive Khaevs and winced. "Not much."

"Lucky for you that you probably won't have to follow through, then."

He would *remember something like that,* thought Erin furiously. *Now is not exactly the time.*

"AH," HISSED JYO-RAKU, "our messenger has arrived."

He was staring up at the sky, inasmuch as it was possible to tell where the spirit was looking, and stroking the hilt of the Bound Blade that hung at his side. Kei shaded her eyes against the sun and looked up as well; it was just possible to make out a tiny circling dot, winging back and forth as though weighing the idea of coming down for a closer look.

A draekere! Her heart leapt for a moment at the thought of rescue. *But if she comes too close, Jyo-raku will just kill her.* She tried to focus on the dot. *Don't come down. We're not worth checking out. Don't bother!*

Kei's attempt at telepathy was evidently a failure. The dot circled closer, until they could make out the slowly flapping wings of the draek. Having been in this position many times herself, Kei knew what was going through the girl's head. She couldn't quite make out the figures on the ground, but from that altitude could probably tell they weren't carrying any bows. Therefore, it was safe to come lower and take a good look.

Don't! She knew she should shout a warning, but the spirit was watching out of the corner of his eye; any attempt to signal the incoming rider would result in a swift death. Kei glanced at Kit, who appeared nonchalant. *I hope she doesn't do anything stupid.*

The draekere circled even lower, close enough now that they could see the girl riding on the beast's back, her long ponytail flapping in the slipstream. The draek swooped past, pulled up sharply, and made a lazy turn right over their little party.

This gave Jyo-raku plenty of time. He extended one hand just as the draek reached apogee, and a silent lance of solid darkness speared out. It hit the drake in the head, twisting enough to saw the creature's skull in half in an explosion of blood and bits of bone.

The girl shrieked and hauled uselessly on the reins as the draek flipped over and spiraled toward the ground. More darkness billowed outward from the shadow spirit, this time engulfing the rider; her shriek was cut off as she was surrounded by liquid shadow.

Only a few seconds had passed. Kei's mouth hung open. She'd expected something to happen, but nothing quite that spectacular. The draek hit the ground with a crunch, and the ball of shadow that contained the rider drifted over to Jyo-raku, touched the ground, and dissipated, leaving the girl lying down but apparently unharmed. She shrieked again, reflexively, and backpedaled from the spirit, scrabbling for the sword at her side.

"That would be unwise," said Jyo-raku, in his usual hissing tones. The girl managed to reach a knife and toss it at him; the spirit's dark aura slapped it aside and sent it spinning away. "I suggest you remain calm."

Kei spoke up, despite the fear that gripped her throat. "May

I speak with her?"

Jyo-raku nodded, apparently pleased with her deference. "Go."

Kei hurried to the girl's side. She was breathing hard, unable to take her eyes from Jyo-raku's rippling form. *Young*, was Kei's first thought, *younger than Kit, even.* She put her hand on the girl's shoulder and whispered rapidly.

"Calm down. It's okay. You're okay. Look at me." The draekere didn't respond, and Kei let a bit of forcefulness creep into her voice. "*Look* at me, Wing!"

The girl turned, military reflex triumphing over terror, and her eyes gradually focused. Kei kept talking, to hold her attention.

"Just stay calm. You'll be fine." She felt a twinge about saying that, since it could easily be a lie, but it was effective. "I'm Wing Leader Keimani Shia. Who are you?"

She blinked. "Lin." Then, recovering some of her composure, "Wing Linaya Suun."

"What Blade are you attached to?"

"K . . . Kagerin Shuzan's."

There was a satisfied intake of breath from Jyo-raku, which made Lin glance in his direction; Kei grabbed her head and dragged it back. "Look at me, Wing. Look at me."

"W . . . What's going on?"

She looks like a scared little girl. Kei reprimanded herself. *She's a draekere, one of the elite. I'm sure she can handle herself.*

"It's hard to explain. I don't really know myself. But your mission has gone to hell in a handbasket."

"Who . . ." She paused, and lowered her voice. "*What* is that?"

"I am Jyo-raku," hissed the spirit, "and you may address me directly, but with respect."

"J . . . Jyo-raku?" She turned to look at him, a bit more appraisingly.

"He's a spirit of shadow," said Kei quietly.

"So there's a sorcerer around here?" There was a note of hope in her voice. While an Imperial sorcerer would be bad news, at least he would be human. Kei shook her head grimly.

"Jyo-raku is in charge here. I suggest being respectful."

"What do you want with me?" There was still a tremble in the draekere's voice, but at least she was looking right at the spirit now. Kei had to give her credit for a quick recovery. *Getting yanked out of the sky can't be fun.*

"I plan to use you as a messenger to Lord Kagerin." Jyo-raku's face was invisible under his aura of darkness. "For now, you will accompany us, but eventually I will set you free."

"Wait a minute. Why do you need to send a message to my brother?"

Jyo-raku turned to her, apparently undecided whether to gloat or punish impertinence. He settled on gloating. "If I didn't tell him where we're going," he hissed, "how would he know where to come and rescue you?"

"You won't get him to kill for you."

"We shall see."

"Shuzan is far too smart for you."

"We shall see," the spirit repeated. Jyo-raku snapped his gaze back to Lin. "Until I release you, you follow us and do not attempt to escape. Is that understood? You can end up like that" —he indicated the carcass of the draek, still spurting blood from its ruined neck— "quite easily. Behave, and you will survive."

Lin looked up at Kei, and then back at Jyo-raku. She nodded, jerkily. The spirit turned to Kei.

"Take care of her until then. We're moving on."

Bile rose in Kei's throat at being issued an order, but she nodded. "As you wish."

IT WAS A few minutes before Shuzan was even able to separate himself from his little sister. Kei found herself, inexplicably, on the verge of tears. Eventually she pulled back and wiped them away with the back of her hand.

"Shuzan," she sniffed.

"It's good to see you, too," he said dryly.

Kei laughed, uncertainly. There was an awkward silence.

"Shia . . ."

She shivered, deliciously. "Nobody calls me that anymore."

"Should I say Kei?"

Kei shook her head. "It's fine."

"Do you want to sit down?"

She took in the room for the first time. It was well-appointed, in her limited experience. There was a sleeping mat rolled up against the wall along with a table, chairs, a chest, and a well-stocked sideboard. A single white vase, filled with a brilliant spray of flowers, provided a centerpiece.

"Sure." Kei pulled one of the chairs back and sat. She was uncomfortably aware of how she had to cross her legs—another irritating deficiency of skirts. Shuzan, apparently just as ill at ease, bustled around the room for a moment.

"Would you like a drink?"

She nodded, jerkily, and he went to the sideboard, relieved to have something to do with his hands. For a moment there was only the gentle splash of liquid in glass.

Kei cleared her throat. "It really is good to see you."

"You, too."

"You look . . ." She was at a loss—he looked about the same as she remembered, tall and strong and handsome. " . . . well."

He turned and set two glasses down on the table, smiling broadly. Kei's heart flopped as he ruffled her hair with one hand.

"And you don't look like a little girl anymore."

"It's been four years."

"Somehow I still never expected you to grow up." His smile widened. "It looks good on you."

Kei smiled, too. She could feel the ice of four years of separation slowly melting. "Thank you." She sipped at the drink, which was flavored with raspberry and had the bite of hard liquor, somewhat to her surprise. Draekeres were not allowed to drink, and she was proud she managed to swallow without gagging.

"So." Shuzan pulled back a chair and sat down. "Are things at Sora really as hard as they say?"

"How hard do they say they are?"

"I heard they only feed you once a week, and that you only get to drink rainwater." He grinned, and she chuckled.

"Not quite *that* bad. There's a lot of running and training and so forth, but the food's good enough. You get used to it."

"Are the instructors really nasty to you?"

"Sometimes. It's only to help us in the end, though. And we work together a lot."

"Great." Shuzan leaned back and sipped his own drink. "Gods, I missed you. Not having a little sister around the house was awful."

"I thought I was always underfoot."

"That's what I missed."

They both smiled. Kei took another sip of the drink and felt the warmth spreading through her body.

"So." She shook her head. "Did you get in trouble? For what you did?"

"I'm sitting here, aren't I?"

"I guess . . ."

"Nobody ever found out. I think Father suspects, but he won't risk investigating. I've done well for him."

"That's good to hear. Not that I had any doubts."

"Hold on." Shuzan got up and rummaged in the chest for a moment, then came up with a sheathed blade. He set it on the table between them. Kei ran her fingers over it, pausing to feel the embossed characters on the hilt.

"Seventy-Fifth of Two Hundred?" She looked up. "Really?"

"I'm the youngest ever." He said it proudly, and she could see an echo of the slightly gawky older brother she'd grown up with in his smile.

"That's amazing!"

He shrugged, modestly, and changed the subject. "You must have a lot of questions for me, though."

"Questions?"

"About what happened."

"Oh." Kei sipped her drink and swirled the liquid in the glass, looking down. "I suppose I do."

"I don't know much. It's hard. I can't investigate, it might look suspicious . . ."

"It's okay! You don't have to . . ."

"It's not okay." Shuzan's face had gone hard, and a little scary. "The family records have been altered. There never was a Kagerin Shia. She died in infancy. Nobody talks about you. It's as though you never existed. They were going to kill you that night, Shia."

"W . . . Why?"

"That's what I don't know. Father won't discuss it. But it's happened before. If you look back through the records you can get a hint of it. Portraits of children who never existed, nurseries built by couples with no babies. I think it's been going on for a long time."

Kei recalled her thought, outside the door. *If I'd turned away, Kagerin Shia would have been gone forever.* "As long as you remember me."

"I," he said solemnly, "will always remember you."

Kei downed the rest of her drink and sighed. "I never got to thank you."

"For what?"

"For saving my life, dummy! You smuggled me out of Yamika."

"I couldn't let them kill my cute little sister, could I?"

Kei smiled. "Thank you."

Shuzan nodded, formally. "Don't mention it."

There was a moment of silence, and then they both broke down giggling.

IT WAS IN the hours just after dawn that they crested the last rise and saw the Doomwood spread out ahead of them.

It looks normal from here, thought Kei, trying to suppress a thrill of atavistic terror. And indeed the legendary forest, from a distance, looked like nothing more than a loosely packed bunch of oaks, maples, and the occasional conqueror pine jutting up through the canopy like a watchtower. It was huge, though, spreading both east and west as far as the eye could see. The only other remarkable feature of the wood was the lack of human habitation. Anywhere else, there would have been logging villages at the edges, and the grasslands before the forest would have been cultivated fields. Here there was nothing.

Not nothing, she noticed. Every so often a fire-blackened stone wall marked the remains of an ill-fated attempt to settle near the woods. *The Imperials built a whole fortress somewhere along the border, a few hundred years back.* That endeavor had ended like all the rest, destroyed by the relentless spirits of the forest.

And it was easy enough to see the truth of another rumor,

too. Some of the ruins were *inside* the border of the forest. Since no one would be foolish enough to build a home inside the Doomwood itself, that meant that what the old men claimed was true. The cursed place was *growing*, inch by inch, year by year.

"Lin," whispered Jyo-raku. "The time has come for you to leave us."

"L . . . leave?" said the young draekere. Jyo-raku had mentioned that she'd be released, but she'd obviously considered that too good to be true.

"Yes. You are free to go."

Lin shot a glance at Kit and Kei. "What about them?"

"They must come with me, I'm afraid. I'll need Kei, and Kit apparently won't leave her side."

"I . . . I won't leave without them!"

Quavering or not, Kei had to admire the girl's courage. *If not her sense.*

"You will leave without them," hissed Jyo-raku, "or you will not leave at all."

Lin looked back at Kei, in agony. Kei sighed.

"Go."

"But . . ."

"Go."

"And tell Lord Kagerin what has happened here." Jyo-raku's expression, as always, was unreadable, but Kei got the sense that he was smiling. "Tell him where his sister has gone."

"I . . ." The draekere's face twisted in confusion. *And no wonder. Kagerin Shuzan has no sister. I've been written out of the history books.*

"Now go." Jyo-raku turned away. Lin hesitated only a moment, and then ran for it.

I can hardly blame her. Kei turned back to her study of the Doomwood, pausing briefly to look over her companions. Kit

432

seemed almost eager. *It figures. She probably thinks this is going to be fun.*

"As for us," said Jyo-raku, "we proceed."

"Into the Doomwood?" asked Kei.

"I will keep you safe," said Jyo-raku. That eased her fear a little bit, until he added, "If I can."

"Thanks for the reassurance."

Kei caught Kit's eye. As one, they checked their blades.

chapter 17

> "You can keep your plans and strategies. War is about sticking pointy things into other people and watching their guts get your boots all dirty; and anyone who claims otherwise is deluding herself."
>
> –Joy "the Butcher" Carver, mercenary captain

ISOBEL, NAKED BUT for a few small strips of cloth, twisted and turned on her bed. She'd kicked the blanket off long ago. Despite the cool of the night air, she was sweating, her pillow already damp. The morning sun's rays snuck in, through the tent flap, and caressed her slowly until they got to her face. Isobel's eyelids fluttered, and she awoke with a start, sitting up and grabbing spastically for weapons that weren't there.

A monster.

The image was already fading, but she remembered a metal face-plate, like a helmet but utterly featureless and surrounded by flames. The heat she'd felt faded rapidly, and before long she was shivering. She dressed quickly and in silence, wincing a little with every move. Her head didn't so much hurt as feel heavy, like there was a stone somewhere at the back of her brain that shifted a little every time she turned. That sensation, too, was fading, and by the time she'd strapped on all of her knives Isobel felt ready to face the day.

And a good thing, too. There'd been no orders from the

commander's tent, of course, but the gossip around the camp was not good. *Half the infantry stranded on the other side of the river, most of the heavy cavalry wiped out, and we're facing close to a thousand of the Khaev's best chargers.* She frowned. Isobel had a distaste for cavalry. Horses were *big*, and messy, and all in all just cluttered up a battlefield. *Once they get bogged down they're as vulnerable as anyone else.*

She fingered the well-worn hilts of her long knives lovingly then ducked out through the tent flap into the bright morning sunshine. Valos' camp was full of the sounds of soldiers waking up, strapping on armor, moaning and wondering what they'd eaten the previous night; it was as familiar to Isobel as the cock's crow was to a farmer.

I wonder what happened to Veil.

VEIL, AS IT happened, was waiting in a sort of anteroom in Lord Valos' tent, created by a couple of folding screens that separated the entrance from the rest. She'd been brought there last night by his guards, but the lord had been deep in consultation with someone who was apparently too important to even name, and she had been left to wait. Eventually, she supposed, she must have fallen asleep. She woke in the morning, after a gentle prod from one of Valos' attendants.

"Miss Veil?"

Veil sat up a little straighter in the cushioned chair she'd nodded off in. "I . . . I'm sorry. I didn't mean . . ."

"No need to apologize." The man smiled gently. "Lord Valos was talking with the Prophet until late last night, and he instructed us to let you sleep. Apparently you've had a busy few days."

Busy does not begin to describe it, thought Veil, but she merely nodded. A few moments later, the name registered. *The Prophet?*

"Are you ready to see his lordship now?"

"Now?" Veil looked around frantically. "I wouldn't want to keep him waiting, but I just woke up . . ."

"I can have breakfast and water brought in, if you'd like."

"Thanks." She paused. "Then, I guess so."

"Come with me."

She followed the servant around the screens and into Lord Valos' tent proper. It was remarkably spartan. Veil hadn't pictured gilded statues and harem girls, but here there was no luxury whatsoever. A table covered with maps and another smaller one, probably for eating, that had been carefully set with a capture board. A camp-bed, and three more padded chairs. A chest of drawers.

That was all. Nothing special to mark that this man was the leader of an army, and that everyone for a mile around would live or die by his command. Veil wasn't sure what she'd been expecting, but this wasn't it.

Two of the chairs were occupied. One held a man she assumed was Valos. H e was tall and hard-looking, with an unpleasant face and a square jaw that had been designed for teeth-clenching. The rebel lord was in his mid-thirties, if she had to guess, and had the look of someone who had seen a great deal of hardship but was determined not to be affected by it. A sword, unornamented, hilt worn with use, leaned against the side of his chair.

The other man was much kindlier-looking, but something about his stare made Veil feel uneasy. His eyes were ice-blue, and, despite his friendly smile, seemed somehow cold. He was much older than Valos, buried in a fur coat that dwarfed his shrunken body, and the bald dome of his head rose up through the remains of his hair like a mountain rearing above the tree line. He also seemed somehow *familiar*, in a way that Veil couldn't articulate; she found this intensely annoying. *He must be the Prophet.*

"You must be Veil," said Valos. He had exactly the kind of voice she'd been expecting: a voice used to barking out orders and having them instantly obeyed. "I'm sorry I kept you waiting last night."

Veil nodded, uncertain of how she should address a river lord. She decided to play it safe. "It's fine, Lord Valos. Your chair was probably the most comfortable place I've rested lately."

"Excellent." Lord Valos smiled, just a little. It didn't change his face much, but it helped. "And you must have many questions for me."

"Actually, only one, sir . . ."

He held up a hand. " 'Sir' is not necessary."

"Only one, then."

"Which is?"

"Why did you call me here?"

Valos glanced at the Prophet, who nodded slightly. "Why do you think I did?"

Veil took this question at face value, rather than rhetorically. "I came here following Corvus, and Corvus was following Zhin. Zhin told us he wanted Corvus to come work for you" —that had been back in Corsa, in what felt like another lifetime— "but now you've asked to see me. And it must be important, since everyone seems to think there's a battle coming, and I doubt you'd be wasting your time."

"Very astute." Valos stood up. "I can answer that question, but there's a formality to be taken care of first."

"A formality?"

He indicated the capture board. "Shall we play a game?"

Veil blinked. "A game of capture? Now?"

"Yes."

"Against you?"

"If you don't mind?"

"Of course not, I just . . ."

"Humor me." Valos' smile thinned.

"Okay." Veil stepped over to the table and took one of the pots, which turned out to contain the red stones. "You're first, my lord."

Valos took the top off his own pot and clicked a stone onto the board. Veil followed suit, and soon the only sound in the tent was the steady click-click of ceramic on wood.

Standard opening, Veil thought, *but he's giving me too much room to maneuver on the left.* She tossed a stone into one of his corners, and the resulting altercation revealed much. *He's too ambitious in a fight. Overextends. And his tactics need work.* She felt confident she could win the game . . .

. . . hang on. Do I want to win the game? It might not exactly be politic.

The only thing to do, she thought, was ask. Valos clicked down another stone, and Veil looked up at him.

"My lord, you'll have to forgive me for asking you this . . ."

"Go ahead."

"Do you want me to win this game?"

He raised an eyebrow. "Why wouldn't I want you to try?"

"I don't . . ." She realized what she'd implied. "I just don't know you, my lord. Some nobles don't like . . . to lose, or . . ."

"I assure you, Veil," said Valos patiently, "my ego is not at stake here. I want you to try your best."

"Of course, my lord."

Veil fished out one of her stones, thoughtfully spun it in her fingers for a moment, then slammed it on to the board on the left side in an absurdly overexposed position, much too close to Valos' corner group. The noble quirked an eyebrow and countered with a pincer.

Veil threw herself into the fight that followed, which grew like an amoeba to engulf the entire left-hand side of the board in a tangle of red and green stones. Valos started taking longer and longer for each move, while Veil's stones still clicked down in quick succession. Finally his lordship was left staring at a hopeless position. While the stone that had instigated the fight had long since been sacrificed, Veil had cut the groups attacking it to ribbons. Valos dropped his stone back in his pot, admitting defeat. He shook his head.

"Marvelous." He turned to her. "If I may ask, how did you do it?"

She shrugged. "I knew I could out-fight you. So the surest way of winning the game was to draw you into a fight big enough that you couldn't afford to lose it."

Valos again glanced at the Prophet, who again nodded. Veil looked from one to the other, confused.

"I'VE BROUGHT YOU the Imperials we captured, my lord."

Kagerin Shuzan pulled a leather riding glove onto his left hand, then shook out the right glove with a crisp snap. "Escort them in. They've been searched?"

"Of course, my lord." Hiko looked vaguely scandalized at the idea that he would let someone into his lord's presence without assuring that they were harmless.

"Good." Shuzan pulled on his other glove and started checking the buckles on his armor. It was an automatic motion for him, as natural as breathing. Meticulous preparation was what kept a man alive during battle, he'd always felt, and there was certainly going to be a battle.

Lord Valos. Shuzan's lip curled. *If he had anything to do with this disappearance, I'll have his head on a platter.* The man would die anyway, of course. No more merciful punishment could be imagined for those who rebelled against Khaevar. But death in battle or by the headsman's axe would be quick compared to what Shuzan was planning. The fact that Kei was involved made it personal. *And if he's hurt her . . .*

He had to calm himself. *She'll be fine. She's always fine.*

"The Imperials, my lord."

Shuzan smoothed his expression and turned to face the tent flap. A couple of bedraggled-looking Imperials were standing in front of Hiko. The man looked like a warrior, wounded fairly badly in one arm and dressed in the remnants of under-armor padding. The woman also looked tough, nursing a couple of minor cuts but still glaring daggers at anyone who met her gaze. There were two cavalry troopers in the tent, and Shuzan himself was well-armed, but neither of the two appeared intimidated.

"I am Lord Kagerin Shuzan." Shuzan inclined his head the slightest bit. "I understand you two were mercenaries in the employ of a merchant caravan."

The woman glanced at the man, who shrugged and let her speak. "That's correct. I'm Erin, and this is Karl.

Just Erin and Karl, eh? "You're here because you told the guards you'd seen a pair of draekeres."

"I didn't know it was important, but they certainly reacted to my description." Erin smiled, insolently. Shuzan had to restrain himself.

"When?"

"The night before your people found us."

"Were they healthy?"

"As far as I could tell. They were in the company of a monk and a shadow spirit. All four went down into a cave in the mountains, and all but the monk came back."

"A shadow spirit?"

"Jyo-raku," said Karl, "was his name. I think."

"Jyo-raku." Shuzan kept his expression deadpan.

"It was a nasty one, too," said Erin, apparently irritated at being interrupted. "Karl's missing a chunk of his arm because of it.""I see." Shuzan's mind was whirling. *Jyo-raku is still with her. Or was.* "The spirit . . . and the draekeres . . . they came out of the cave together?"

"And left together." Erin nodded.

"Which direction?"

"Down the east slope of the mountain."

"East?" Shuzan frowned. "Not south?"

"East. Though they might have turned south later . . ."

He held up a hand. "I've heard enough."

Erin looked annoyed at being cut off, but held her peace. Hiko cleared his throat, gently.

"What should I do with them, my lord?"

"Hmm?" Shuzan looked up from his thoughts. "Oh, let them go."

"Let them go?" Hiko seemed taken aback.

"They've brought me valuable information. If we killed them, it would discourage others from doing the same."

"As you wish."

"And on your way back, bring me the mistress of draekeres."

"Yes, my lord."

The two Imperials were escorted away, and Shuzan sat down and thought in silence.

East. Why would they be going east? He'd assumed, once his scouts had detected the presence of Lord Valos' forces, that the rebel must have had something to do with this. *But if Jyo-raku is still running things . . .*

But then, why hasn't he gotten word to us? If they've slipped past us to the east, even by accident, they've had plenty of time to stop at a town, send a rider. We've made no secret of where we were going. And why would Valos stand and fight otherwise? The Imperial commander had deployed like someone unable or unwilling to retreat to better ground. Khaev reinforcements were already on their way from the Anvil to cut off his retreat, so he was now likely to be destroyed wholesale. *Not that I'd protest that outcome, but it doesn't make any sense.*

Moriseki Hikari edged past the tent flap, and bowed. Shuzan nodded back. "Mistress."

"Lord Kagerin."

"Has there been any word from Lin?"

"No." Moriseki's mouth was a tight line.

"An accident, perhaps?"

"Unlikely. My draekeres are highly trained."

"So you believe something brought her down."

"It seems to be the only logical conclusion."

"And she disappeared on patrol to the east?"

"Yes." Moriseki looked at him curiously. "Is something wrong, Lord Kagerin?"

He closed his eyes and shook his head. "I'm having to entertain a most unpleasant possibility."

"Which is?"

"That Jyo-raku has betrayed us."

She thought about that for a moment. "Possible, of course. Spirits are inscrutable. But why? The Bound Blade is of no use in the hands of a spirit."

"So the legends would have us believe. Jyo-raku may know more than we do."

"But in that case, why involve us at all? And why take my people with him? He must have known we'd come after him."

"A trap, perhaps."

"For an entire Blade?"

Shuzan shrugged. "Either way, we may have to turn around once the battle's done."

"We're going ahead with the battle? I thought you came out here to find Shiori and my draekeres."

"Of course. But we're too deeply committed to disengage now. Lord Valos' infantry, behind us, would make a retreat quite difficult. So our only option is to break his front and crush him against the reinforcements from the south." Shuzan rose. "I want you and your draekeres with my command section. Lord Valos has a sorcerer, though we haven't seen any evidence of him yet, and I may need you to deal with whatever tricks he conjures up."

"Understood." Moriseki nodded. "Unless there's anything else . . ."

"Go and get ready. In three hours, we ride."

"CHILD," SAID THE old man eventually, "I am the Prophet."

"I gathered." Somehow winning the game had given Veil a bit of her confidence back. She no longer felt quite as intimidated by Lord Valos and his companion. "I'm not 'child', by the way. My name is Veil."

"Veil." He said the name slowly, as though he were tasting it. "Veil, have you ever met me before?"

That put her on guard. "No," she answered warily.

"Would it surprise you to learn that I had warned Lord Valos of your coming more than a year ago?"

"Not really. They wouldn't call you 'the Prophet' for no reason, would they?"

"Indeed." The old man smiled, showing teeth that had not survived the rigors of age unscathed.

"What confuses me," Veil continued, "is why you bothered.

I'm as self-important as the next person, and I'm grateful to you for the hospitality and so forth. But why did Lord Valos need warning? Why do you care if I live or die?"

The Prophet took a long time to answer. After a moment of silence he stood up, creakily, and walked over to the table, studying the patterns on the capture board. He picked up one of Veil's dead stones between two fingers and spun it, as though admiring the pattern of cracks in the ceramic. Finally he said, "Do you know this was a Khaev game, originally?"

"It is?" Veil was genuinely surprised. "We've been playing it in the Red Hills as long as I can remember."

"It was imported by traders during the First or Second Dynasty, and spread all over the continent during the Third and Fourth. That was a few thousand years ago, so it's no wonder no one remembers. But while in the Empire it's generally considered a pursuit of the lower classes, the Khaev nobility takes it quite seriously. Do you know why?"

"No," said Veil, who had gotten the sense that it was a rhetorical question. "Why?"

"Historical precedent." He dropped the stone back into the pot with a click. "Generals play capture, girl, generals and kings. The best of them play it brilliantly."

"My name is Veil," said Veil, but the Prophet kept right on talking.

"We needed a general. The Empire needs another Maximillian Senar. We're losing our soul to the Khaevs, piece by bloody piece. The people chafe, but they have no one to unite them. No leader to rally behind."

"Wait a minute." Veil did not like where this was headed.

"It is given to me to see the future, in fits and starts and little glimpses of what is to come. I saw the rise of a general, a girl, but I didn't know what she looked like. So I had Lord Valos send

Zhin and Isobel to keep watch on the west, as my other agents kept watch elsewhere."

"So Zhin spotted me playing *capture*, and he thought . . ."

"He knew you were the general we've been looking for."

"Wait, wait, wait." Veil held up her hands. "Capture is a *game*. I don't care what you've seen in the future. I've never even been in a battle! Well," she amended, "not until recently, anyway. I certainly don't know how to be a general."

"Your ability to play capture," cut in Valos, "is a side effect of tactical genius."

"If I was a tactical genius, don't you think I'd have noticed by now?"

"Girl . . ." began the Prophet.

"Veil."

" . . . listen to me." He knelt, bringing himself roughly to her height, and put his hands on her shoulders. Veil found herself trying to avoid staring directly into his eyes, which were blue and somehow *cold*. Even just looking into them seemed to drain the warmth from her. "We have been looking for you for a long time." He lowered his voice, until it was a bare whisper that even Lord Valos couldn't overhear. "It's all bullshit, of course. But it keeps them entertained."

Veil barely stifled a gasp as the Prophet *winked*, smiling a wrinkled smile that didn't reach his frozen eyes.

"*I need you to win a war for me.*" And the old man looked somehow familiar . . .

"Sybian?" she whispered. The Prophet nodded, infinitesimally.

"Trust me," he said, and pulled away from her. Veil sat perfectly still, staring into space. Valos looked at her, concerned, and then over at the Prophet.

"What did you do to her?"

"She is confronting her true destiny," intoned the old man. "That takes its toll on anyone. She needs to be allowed to rest."

"She can't rest too long." Valos shook his head. "It's past dawn. Shuzan will be crossing the river as we speak. Her trial by fire is coming."

"She will be ready."

What? Veil wanted to scream. Only the recollection of the devious look in the old man's eye kept her silent.

Valos held a long breath, then blew it out. "I've trusted you so far. I don't think I have anything left to lose."

"You will not be disappointed."

"I've got preparations to make. She can rest in my bed until our scouts make contact with the enemy."

"I will look after her."

Valos nodded curtly and stalked from the tent, his cloak swirling behind him. The Prophet waited until he was gone, then turned back to Veil, grinning like a hyena.

"You can speak freely now."

"Are you *really* Sybian?" Veil blurted.

"Is this better?" The spirit's tinkling, crystal voice issued from the old man's mouth. Veil gulped. The effect was disturbing. "A more precise answer to your question is that this is a human body I happen to be borrowing."

"Like the Zan'diem priestess." Veil's stomach turned at the memory.

"You're learning."

"And all that stuff about seeing the future?"

"Lies, of course. No one can see the future."

"But why . . ."

"The great Lord Valos is unlikely to do what I want him to do if I just came down and said, 'Hello, I'm a malevolent spirit,' now is he?" The Prophet laughed, deep and hearty, but at the edge of hearing there was a hint of Sybian's crystal chiming. "I needed Valos and his Diem contacts to get you across the highlands. He's still suspicious enough to demand something out of the deal. After we win the battle, though, he'll be ready to believe. Then he'll let us go where we need to go."

"Where . . ."

"You don't need to know that yet."

That was becoming a depressingly familiar snippet of conversation. Veil turned to another topic. "But how am I supposed to win a battle?"

"Ah," said the old man, "*that* part of what I said was true."

"Which part?"

"About generals. You're the second coming of Maximillian Senar, Veil. Maybe the greatest military leader who has ever lived."

"Is that supposed to be a joke? I don't even know how to use a sword!"

"You think old Max Senar went out there and defeated the enemy in personal combat? A general *commands*. You look at little pieces of wood on a map and give orders."

"I won't do it." Veil shook her head violently. "This is crazy."

"It's no different from capture."

"Capture is a *game*, where you might lose a few eyes if you mess up. In real life people *die*."

"People are going to die anyway. We just have to make sure they're the right ones." The Prophet's voice had acquired a slight edge of pleading. "I'm not asking you to start a war, Veil. Just finish one."

"I thought you wanted me to rally the Empire and defeat the Khaevs. That sounds like starting a war . . ."

"Please." The Prophet waved a hand. "I told you all that was bullshit for Valos' sake. Why should I care about the Empire, or the Khaevs? All you have to do is fight this battle, so we can get out of here."

"But . . ."

"Look. The Khaevs are coming. Kagerin Shuzan has eight hundred heavy cavalry across the river, and Valos doesn't have much left to stop him. If it comes down to a line battle everyone here is going to die, do you understand? They need you. Not to mention that the Khaevs aren't likely to be too concerned with civilians when they overrun this camp."

"But I can't do it!"

"You can."

"How do you know?"

"Trust me."

"How am I supposed to do that?"

"You don't have much of a choice, do you?"

"Gods be damned," Veil cursed. "This is ridiculous."

"Maybe a little."

"They won't even do what I tell them to."

"They will if Lord Valos orders them to. And Valos trusts the Prophet."

"What if I screw it up?"

"You won't."

"Valos would kill me!"

"The Khaevs are going to kill you once they get here. Besides," the Prophet showed his ghastly grin again, "Corvus will be here to defend you."

Corvus. Somehow the thought was calming, though Veil's heart was still pounding. "I still think this is ridiculous."

"But . . ."

She took a deep breath. "But it looks like I don't have a choice."

The feeling was oddly familiar. *Sometimes I feel as though I've been walking on a path someone else mapped out, ever since I met Corvus in the desert. When was the last time I had a real choice?*

"When you're done," said Veil, cautiously, "you'll let me go?"

"Absolutely."

"No more fucking around with my life?"

"On my word of honor as a completely untrustworthy spirit." Sybian's laugh tinkled again, in the distance.

I suppose that's the best I'm going to get. "Then I guess I'll give it a shot."

"Good. Lord Valos will be back in a moment."

"What do I do?"

"He'll set up the maps with the latest reports from the scouts. I'll get him to explain what everything means. Then you just tell us who should go where."

"Absurd." Veil rolled her eyes. "And you actually think I can do this?"

The tent flap opened, and Lord Valos swept back in and started talking, without preamble.

"Shuzan has crossed the river. He's reordering his troops on the south bank. Best guess is that we've got an hour until he rides."

A swarm of soldiers followed him, descending on the map table. A set of wooden blocks was produced from somewhere, black and red, and there was a sudden flurry of paper-reading as the men set up the table. Valos turned to the Prophet.

"Is she going to help us?"

"Of course she is," said the old man gravely. "It is her destiny."

Veil smiled uncertainly. "I'll do what I can . . ."

"We need all the help we can get."

They walked, together, to the map table. Veil stared down at the confusing welter of colors and blocks, and tried to think.

"So what does all this mean?"

Valos eyed the Prophet silently, and began to explain.

"Let me through!" The young female voice was just barely audible on the hilltop where Kagerin Shuzan had set up his command post. "I must see Lord Kagerin!"

"Lord Kagerin is preparing for battle . . ." began one of the guards, but Moriseki cut him off as she caught sight of who the newcomer was.

"Lin!" She gestured frantically at the guard. "Let her go."

To his credit, the guardsman looked first at Shuzan, who nodded silently. The draekere, her fine uniform now covered with dust and mud, practically sprinted the rest of the way up and stopped next to Shuzan's horse, out of breath.

"Wing Lin." Shuzan inclined his head, which was as much as was possible while mounted. "It's good to see that you've returned."

"He let . . . he let . . ."

"Take a deep breath," said the mistress of draekeres. "You're safe here."

Shuzan waited as the girl gulped air. "He let me go," she said finally. "He said I was supposed to come and tell you . . ."

"Who said?"

"The shadow spirit. Jyo-raku."

Moriseki and Shuzan glanced at each other, but said nothing. Lin went on.

"He has Kit and Kei, my lord!"

"Is she unharmed?" 'She' instead of 'they'. It just slipped out. *Damn it, Shuzan, you have to be careful.*

"I . . . I think so. I didn't get the chance to talk to them."

"Where?"

"To the southeast." She hesitated. "My lord, he let me go at the border of the Doomwood. It looked as though he planned to go inside!"

"The *Doomwood*?" said Moriseki, incredulously. "Why?"

"I don't know, mistress. But he said to make sure Lord Kagerin knew where he was going."

"This has to be a trap." Moriseki turned to Shuzan. "He's trying to lead us in to the Doomwood. Even an entire Blade would have difficulty . . ."

"Believe me," said Shuzan, "I know. We may not have a choice."

"You don't mean to go in *after* them."

"I thought you were concerned for your people."

"Of course!" Moriseki hesitated, then plunged onward. "But marching into the Doomwood is *suicide*, Shuzan. Remember Kagerin Semike."

"Kagerin Semike planned to take Godsdoom. We only need to rescue a couple of errant draekeres."

She took a half step backward, as though regarding him in a new light. Shuzan watched her eyes and realized he'd finally run past the end of his credibility.

Can I trust her? There was no reason to think that he could. As Mistress of Draekeres for the Occupation, Moriseki Hikari was ultimately responsible to the Council and thus to the Tashidas and Kagerins. *But without her tip-off, I wouldn't have known Shia was in danger until it was too late. I owe her something for that.*

"Lin. Thank you for the information. Go find Zee and Aya."

"Yes, mistress."

Moriseki waited until the girl was gone before turning back to Shuzan. "Lord Kagerin. I am beginning to suspect your concern in this matter."

"Oh?" He raised one eyebrow. *Let us play this to the end.*

"Since your goals are the same as mine, I haven't questioned you until now. You obviously don't care about Tashida Shiori . . ."

"Isn't the matter of the Bound Blade enough for concern?"

"If it even exists. The ramblings of spirits are not to be trusted."

"I'm convinced it exists, or something like it. Jyo-raku came into these mountains looking for *something*, and when he found it he turned around and headed southeast." *Which is true, if entirely beside the point.*

"Even still. I've begun to suspect you have a . . . personal . . . relationship with Keimani Shia or Kitsu Meru."

Ah, so that's *where she's gone with it. Bad enough.*

"And if I do?"

"Taking an entire Blade in pursuit of your lover, against the High Commander's explicit orders, will be a black mark on your record. The story about the Bound Blade might balance that. But marching that Blade into the Doomwood is treason, no matter what."

"I . . ." Shuzan stopped, and let out his breath. *Enough. It's time for the truth.* "As you wish, Mistress Moriseki. You want to know?"

"I do."

"I must swear you to secrecy."

"You have my word, of course." It was her turn to raise an eyebrow. "You think me that indelicate?"

"It's not what you think." Shuzan sighed. "Shia is my sister."

"Shia?" Moriseki blinked. "Keimani Shia . . ."

"Her real name is Kagerin Shia, of course."

"That's not possible. You were the only child of Kagerin Sendoh. His wife died . . ."

"She was erased." His hand tightened on the hilt of his sword. "The servants who'd raised her for ten years refused to acknowledge her existence. My father's orders. She was to have been killed."

"Then why . . ." Moriseki's eyes widened. "You. You gave her to the draekeres."

"Of course."

"That's . . ." She shook her head. "That explains much."

"Then you understand."

"A little better. You still cannot take this Blade into the Doomwood."

"If he's taken Shia in there, I must." He shook his head. "This is a discussion for another time, though. My sister is unharmed for the moment, and before I can go after her I need to extricate myself from this situation." He waved vaguely at the lines of horsemen getting ready for battle. "We may well be able to catch up with Jyo-raku before he gets too deep into the cursed forest, but first Lord Valos must be crushed once and for all. Tend to your wounded girl. I have a battle to win."

"Yes, my lord." Moriseki bowed, but the look in her eyes said, *This isn't over.*

Kagerin Shuzan's Blade was divided into three subsections, with a little over two hundred horsemen each. He referred to them as White, Black, and Red. Every Blade commander had his own system of accounting for sub-units, which could be confusing in a large battle. From the hilltop, Shuzan could see that all three were almost ready. The horses, having been stripped of their armor to swim the river, had been re-equipped; the men were armored and mounted with weapons ready. The morning sun glinted on nearly a thousand steel-clad soldiers, arranged as three twisting snakes of wood, steel, and equine flesh.

As he watched, the soldier in charge of Black—Kagura, Shuzan vaguely recalled—raised his lance in the air, signaling that his section was ready. The other two followed suit soon after. Shuzan shaded his eyes against the sun as he looked east. Valos' camp was not quite visible, concealed behind a small ridgeline, but his scouts assured him it was there.

"White cleaves to the river and anchors the flank. Black makes the primary assault, over the ridgeline. Red swings around south to hit from another direction." It was simple, but the best plans were always simple. Valos had his back to the wall. He couldn't withdraw without abandoning anyone on foot to the tender mercies of Shuzan's horsemen, and, in any case, there was nowhere to run. East was open ground where he'd be run down, and south were the Blades from the Anvil, marching as fast as possible to close the gap entirely.

At least, Shuzan mused, *it's a nice day.* He hated fighting in the rain.

He drew his sword and raised it above his head, and the steel flashed in the morning sun.

"Advance!"

VEIL STARED AT the map.

This is some kind of test. Valos doesn't want to hand over command of his army unless he knows that I'm minimally competent. Real life can't be this easy.

She fingered one of the black blocks. "How long can your infantry hold out against one of Shuzan's groups?"

Valos raised an eyebrow. "We've got spears, but with only light armor, casualties would be awful."

As I figured. "And Shuzan knows this."

"Of course."

"Then it's obvious, right?" She looked around at the assembled command staff, nervously. "I mean, it's kind of a gambit. But when you're the underdog you've got to hope for a mistake. Right?"

There was a long pause. Valos knelt down and said, gently, "Veil. Would you like to explain what you're talking about?"

She took a deep breath. *Here goes nothing.*

"Infantry engages here, against the unit coming in from the front. We break quickly and run, they follow. The enemy flankers are going to take a while to get here. In the meanwhile, there's a gap. We send our cavalry up the center. The river group can't wheel in time, so our cavalry hits the enemy command section here." She tapped a red block that had been painted with a gold star. "Our scouts keep the river group pinned down. Our infantry across the river heads to the ford, blocks the escape of the enemy command. Once they get turned around and head back to save their command group, they charge right into our infantry and the cavalry hits them from the side." Veil laughed nervously. "Right?"

There was a long pause.

Valos closed his mouth with an audible click.

"Right?"

"I don't like it," said one of the soldiers to whom Veil had never been introduced. "Too risky. If their front group restrains itself, there won't be a gap, and our cavalry will run right into them . . ."

"Do it."

"My lord!" There were a number of gasps from around the table.

"Do it." Valos shook his head. "She said it herself. We're the underdogs, so we have to gamble."

"Kagerin Shuzan is not going to take the bait!"

"But he's not leading the charge, right?" said Veil. "He's with the command group, here. What about his sub-commanders?"

"He'll have messengers . . ."

"Not one that can keep up with charging cavalry," said Valos. "Give the orders. Shuzan is already moving."

Valos' camp was bustling with activity. Veil, who'd wandered out of the command tent as Valos started barking orders at his subordinates, watched the men and horses frantically assembling and began to have second thoughts.

This is crazy. I'm not a genius. The pattern had been obvious. *Tempt the enemy into advancing too far, then take the cut.* Valos had to have seen it, too. *Is he just humoring the Prophet?*

Even more disturbing was the possibility that Kagerin Shuzan had foreseen it as well. *I should go back in. Tell him to call it off. If it's this obvious to me, Shuzan will counter. All he has to do is keep his troops from advancing too far, and our cavalry will run right into them.* She turned around, and had almost worked up the nerve to head back into the tent when she realized someone was calling her.

"Veil."

She turned to find Corvus and Isobel. The swordsman's expression was as grim as ever, but Isobel was actually smiling, her hands already resting on the hilts of her twin long knives.

"I hear you're running this army now." The ghost of a smile passed over Corvus' face.

"It's ridiculous." Veil shook her head. "They've got some Prophet who's convinced that because I'm good at capture, I can be a great general."

"I've heard crazier things," said Isobel.

"Are you two going to fight?"

Isobel shrugged. "Valos is my boss, after all. I've got to do my best to keep him from getting killed."

"We're riding with the cavalry," said Corvus.

"You're fighting, too?" Veil shook her head. "I thought you just came here to find out . . ."

"Lord Valos got us through the Diem. I feel like I owe him something."

"*You* got us through the Diem, Corvus!"

Corvus was silent a moment. "Kagerin Shuzan," he said

finally, "is Fifty-Fourth of Two Hundred. One of the greatest of the Khaev swordsman." Isobel licked her lips in anticipation. Corvus continued. "If anyone knows where this sword came from, it will be one of the Two Hundred."

"So you're planning to take him alive?"

"If possible." Corvus smiled grimly.

"Gods." Veil squeezed her eyes shut, her voice small. "Ridiculous. This is ridiculous."

"Relax," said Corvus. "If anything goes wrong, I'll take care of it."

KAGURA MEDIN RODE at the head of a twisting column of steel and horseflesh, advancing deceptively slowly across the open ground that separated the Blade from its enemies. To his left, he could see White, riding alongside the river; Red had already disappeared around the ridgeline.

The only question, he thought, *is whether they're going to stand and fight.* He hoped they did. There was nothing quite like the shock of a cavalry charge. Riding down fleeing infantrymen didn't compare. *Unlikely, though. They must know they haven't got a chance.*

The enemy camps were in sight now. Tents were being hurriedly pulled down and loaded onto packhorses, as though they could outrun the Khaev cavalry. More importantly, though, a block of spearmen was being drawn up to the south of the camp, their hedgehog formation bristling with spearpoints.

There aren't enough of them, not nearly enough. And with light armor they'll go down fast. Being a leader of cavalry took a certain amount of daring, and Kagura Medin had that in plenty. *All that matters is who breaks first.* An infantry formation was a threat only so long as it *was* a formation. Once it became a confused mass of separate fighters, it stood no chance against heavy cavalry.

Medin raised his sword, then swept it downwards in a decisive gesture. He bellowed his orders in a commanding voice.

"Group Black will prepare to attack!"

A clanking audible even over the pounding of his horse's hooves went up, as two hundred men readied their lances. The infantry block drew closer and closer. Medin could see the frightened looks on the faces of the soldiers, some of them barely more than pimply-faced children. The riders spread out slightly, choosing targets. Medin snapped his visor down and lowered his own lance. For himself he picked a girl in the front rank who looked a little less afraid than the rest, holding her spear with a fierce determination.

"Group Black will *charge*!"

Two hundred horses lumbered into a gallop, each one concentrating the energy of half a ton of man, beast, and armor on the razor-sharp point of a fourteen-foot lance. Medin watched his target until the very last moment; her spear never wavered, but the point was just slightly too low . . .

The moment of contact, as ever, was indescribable. The sound alone was overwhelming—a sudden chorus of screeching metal and screaming men and horses. Medin was suddenly aware of the *smell* of the battle: blood and sweat and mud. His view contracted, and there was only the spearman directly before him. She tried to thrust the spear as he came in—a common mistake, since it loosened one's grip—and Medin felt the spearhead impact hard on his side, scraping away from his plate mail and bouncing upward. His lance point caught the woman square in the chest, punching through leather and bone as though it were paper and lifting her off her feet. She kicked feebly until he shook her free, and then she disappeared under the hooves of the cavalry.

They're breaking. He could *feel* it, a moment before it became obvious. The infantry were dropping their spears and running for their lives. He thrust his blood-slicked lance into the air and slashed downwards.

"After them! Victory!"

VEIL, SAFELY IN the command tent, couldn't see the awful moment of impact. She could hear it, though. Even a half a mile away, the screams of humans and horses and the triumphant clang of metal were faintly audible. And in her mind's eye she could see a confusing tangle of steel and blood.

None of the soldiers seemed to be affected, at least openly. More than one expression was a little more nervous than it had been, though, especially when she caught them out of the corner of her eye.

Servants moved the blocks on the map, bringing one of the red ones into contact with a smaller black unit. Valos paced impatiently, waiting for further messengers. As soon as one of Tayla's scouts raced in, he practically jumped on her.

"First infantry has engaged the enemy, my lord. They've taken heavy casualties from the initial shock, and are retreating toward to the east."

Heavy casualties. Veil wondered how many lives had been snipped short, behind that simple phrase. *My fault. I used them as bait. Gods.* She started to shake, but still listened with half an ear to the scout. *If the Khaevs don't pursue, it's all for nothing.*

"What about the Khaevs?" asked Valos, echoing her thought.

"Pursuing," said the scout shortly. "First infantry is attempting to reform in the trees behind the camp, but I'm not sure how many of them we'll be able to gather up."

Pursuing. The servants moved the blocks on the map again, sliding the Khaevs eastward past the camp. As planned, a gap opened up between the slower-moving river unit and the galloping chargers. Valos stared at it, impassively.

"Give Benham my compliments and tell him the word is go."

"Yes, my lord." The scout nodded and left. Valos looked over at Veil.

"They appear to be dancing to your tune thus far."

"Y . . . yes." Veil closed her eyes, trying to banish the screams. "If Benham can get their commanders . . ."

"Kagerin Shuzan is one of the Two Hundred." Valos frowned. "I do not expect him to go down easily."

"Corvus will take care of him."

"I know he's a good swordsman, but . . ."

"He'll take care of him," said Veil wearily. "Don't worry about it."

"Lord Kagerin, Black reports contact with enemy infantry. Kagura says they've broken, and he's giving chase."

Shuzan stared pensively at the battlefield. There was movement in the enemy camp; his river unit was getting closer, but hadn't covered the distance yet, and Red, which he'd sent south, had not yet reappeared.

"Tell Kagura to leave the infantry alone and turn to deal with the enemy camp. I want their leaders taken, alive if possible."

"Yes, my lord. Getting a messenger to the Blacks will be difficult."

"Try."

The movement in the enemy camp was increasing. It looked almost like another detachment getting ready to move out. *They wouldn't dare leave themselves unprotected. I've been up against this Lord Valos before, and he's nothing if not cautious. In the worst case, he'll take his heavy horse and flee.* Not that it would do him any good, this time, but Valos was not the kind of man to surrender. He'd play the game through to the end.

It really does look like those cavalry are moving. Shuzan blinked as the whole squadron lumbered into a trot, lances high in the air. In a few moments they had passed through the area Black had vacated. He could see mass confusion in the ranks of White, as half the riders tried to turn to engage the enemy that had calmly ridden past them, while the rest kept to their assigned objectives.

They're coming this way. It was insane. No commander would risk his own life that way. *And in any case, we simply have to retreat to the ford.* Losing operational control of the battle would be a nuisance, but it couldn't be helped.

"Those cavalry are coming this way," he said. Moriseki, standing by the map table with her draekeres, looked up in alarm. "Pack everything up and withdraw toward the ford. They won't be able to swim their horses across in armor. You and you," he pointed to two of his personal guard, "go on ahead. You, go to White and tell them to turn around and take these cavalry in the rear."

There was a chorus of agreements and three of the two dozen or so guards peeled off. Hiko and the other adjutants had already started folding up the map table and mounting it on the back of the pack horses.

"My lord . . ." murmured Moriseki.

"It'll be close, but we'll make it out."

"Once we cross the river, I'll get my draeks in the air. We should be able to get an idea of what's going on that way."

Shuzan nodded. There was a moment of peace. He watched the enemy cross the field, trying to close the distance before their target fled.

"My lord!" The cry was accompanied by rapid hoof beats as one of the guards galloped back into the camp. Shuzan whirled. "There are spearmen at the ford!"

"Spearmen? Where did they come from?"

"The woods, undoubtedly," said Moriseki.

"There was only a thin skirmish line in the woods."

"There are at least two hundred of them, my lord," said the rider. "And on the other side, the remnants of the Imperial cavalry we routed yesterday. Eighty or more."

"We can't break through two hundred spearmen." Shuzan's mind whirled. "We'll have to split up. Scatter, until White can turn around and deal with these cavalry."

"There's no time, my lord!"

The enemy cavalry had broken into a gallop, lowering their lances. Kagerin Shuzan found himself staring at a forest of razor-sharp points.

"CHARGE!"

Lord Benham Cartwrite was in his element. The pennants on his lance snapped and waved gaily in the wind of his passage, and he gestured triumphantly with his free hand. His cavalry was spread out in a rough delta behind him, with Isobel and the strange swordsman she'd brought along near the center. Neither had a lance, and thus they were fairly useless in a cavalry fight. Lord Valos had said to bring them along, though, so he'd put them in a position of safety.

Charging up a hill was less than ideal. It would cut the horse's speed and reduce the shock of impact. *Still,* thought Benham, *when we outnumber them five-to-one it's not likely to matter.* He could see Khaevs on the hilltop, twenty or so horsemen and a few on foot. *Those will be the commanders. We'll deal with them afterward—probably need to take them alive.* Only the mounted enemy were a real threat. They had lances of their own and looked to be preparing a counter-charge down the hill. *They're brave, I'll give them that.*

Less than a minute till contact. Benham took a deep breath. *Wait . . .*

There was something else, on the hillside. He couldn't imagine how he'd failed to notice it before. A young woman, with silver hair and skin the color of burnished gold. *Dear gods, she'll be crushed—*

The woman raised one hand, and white light streamed forth.

VEIL HEARD THE shouts from outside.

"What the . . ."

"What's going on?"

She ducked out the tent flap before Valos could stop her and blinked in the brilliant glare. As best she could tell, it was on the hill the Khaev commanders had camped on. It was as though a tiny white sun had descended.

"Saya." Sybian's normally melodic voice sounded almost grating. "She must be getting desperate."

"Sybian?" Veil shook her head. "What in the Aether is going on?"

"She's intervening directly." Sybian's voice had acquired a grim humor. "Don't worry, I'll take care of it."

"But . . ."

"Veil!" Valos and one of his men had finally followed her out. "Get back inside!"

"But . . ."

ISOBEL GOT ONLY the barest glimpse of the brilliance; something hit her, hard, and she flew from her horse. Old instincts forced her into a tuck-and-roll, which meant the impact with the ground didn't break anything important, but a spike of pain still went through the shoulder she landed on.

What in the Aether? She looked up in time to see her horse galloping forward, terrified. A beam of almost solid light slid across its chest and then vanished; the horse collapsed in a spray of blood, chopped into two pieces. Where the light had touched it, it was just *gone*, flesh and bone blasted into vapor.

Sorcery!

She rolled over onto her stomach and looked up at the top of the hill. Lord Benham and his vanguard had vanished in the first explosion of light, and now the cavalry was scattering in all directions, desperate to escape the deadly beams. Armor was no defense; a spear of white light slashed across one fleeing cavalry-man from shoulder to hip, and his torso fell into two pieces.

For a moment Isobel stared, uncomprehending, stunned by such wholesale destruction. Then she felt a hand grip her shoulder, and winced in pain. Corvus was lying beside her, pointing. She could barely make out his words under an explosion of sound so loud as to be inaudible.

"Stay here!"

"What?"

"I'll handle it!"

"Are you crazy . . . we have to run . . ."

He was already moving.

Corvus sprinted up the slope, rapidly closing on the gold-skinned woman. He had one hand on his sword.

I have to finish her quickly. Spirits were dangerous, and this one was evidently quite powerful. *If I can get there, I can cut her down.*

The woman noticed him a moment too soon, turning toward him and raising her hands. Corvus tensed, ready to dodge the beams of liquid fire, but they didn't come. Instead, the woman just lowered her hands and stared.

He closed the remaining distance in an eye blink, but something kept him from drawing his sword. When he got a good look at her face . . .

Saya? The name surfaced out of nowhere. There was something in her eyes he couldn't identify—sadness—*more like resignation. She expects me to kill her.*

And . . .

She knows me! The realization hit him, suddenly. *She might have the answers I need.*

All this passed between them in the space of a moment. Corvus skidded to a halt, his sword still sheathed. In the next moment, the world was filled with a deep growl, the distant rumbling of an impending avalanche. Saya—he was sure that was the woman's name—spun as something huge and fast bounded down on her. It was a dog, if a dog could be the size of a horse and be made entirely of pale blue ice, with an icicle mane that ran halfway down its back and massive, jagged fangs. Saya raised her hand, but the new spirit moved too fast. It bit down on her shoulder with a crunch, and Saya screamed.

Corvus found his body moving of its own volition. His sword flashed from its sheath and carved a deep groove in the spirit's foreleg. The dog shook Saya violently, as though she were a toy, and something gave way; the woman flew to the ground, and the ice-spirit rounded on Corvus.

The swordsman spared a glance at Saya. Her entire left arm was missing, along with most of her shoulder; she lay curled up around the wound, her other hand pressed to it. *If she dies . . . but she's a spirit, too . . .*

The dog glared at him, but seemed unwilling to attack. It kept looking over its shoulder at Saya, and Corvus got the feeling that only his presence was keeping it from savaging her. They stood in silence for a moment, until the woman finally broke the stalemate; she gasped out a few words that Corvus didn't understand and vanished entirely. The dog gave Corvus a last, baleful look and turned away, bounding down the hillside at a fantastic pace.

What. The hell. Was that?

"Charge!" This was in Khaev. Corvus turned again to find a score of armored Khaev lancers bearing down on him.

"Gods damn him," said Sybian.

"Who?"

"Corvus!" It was a shout, loud enough that Veil cringed. "I had her this time."

"Is he okay?"

"Of course he's okay. Saya just barely escaped."

"What about the battle?"

"I imagine Corvus is handling it."

KAGERIN SHUZAN HAD no idea who the strange spirit was, or why she'd seen fit to decimate the approaching Imperial cavalry. He was not a man to pass up an advantage, though, even an unexpected one. As soon as the spirit battle had concluded, he threw his guards down the slope, spreading out to engage the routed Imperials. Only a few of the enemy stood and fought. Mostly they were galloping back across the field or unable to control their own mounts.

Four of Shuzan's personal guard bore down on the one Imperial who'd managed to stay on the hillside. He'd been dismounted, and wasn't wearing armor. *Should be easy prey . . .*

Something tickled the back of Shuzan's mind just as his guards charged. The man waited, calmly, as four lance-points bore down on him. An instant before they reached him, there was a sudden blur of glittering steel. Then two of the horses were down, and one was galloping away with its headless rider. The last guard wheeled, clutching the stump where his hand had been. The swordsman in black stood perfectly still, blood dripping from the end of his blade.

Moriseki gasped. "That . . . he . . . that's not possible!"

Corvus. Shuzan felt numb. *Ebon Death.* It was the most logical explanation for what he'd just witnessed. *He's returned. The man must be two hundred years old!*

His hand dropped to his sword. "I'll handle him."

"But . . ."

"I am Fifty-Fourth of Two Hundred. I'll handle him."

CORVUS ADVANCED, SPORTING a death's head grin. He still wasn't sure what had happened between Saya and the ice-spirit, but more pressing concerns were distracting him.

This is where I belong. Another rider cantered toward him, having discarded his lance and drawn a heavy two-handed sword. Corvus feinted to the left, then slipped under the horse's head as the huge blade whistled down. He thrust his own sword upward, slipping through the rider's heavy armor where the legs met the torso and punching through the thin chain mail skirt. The Khaev slumped, and his horse trotted away.

Elation ran through Corvus, a feeling of power that grew stronger with every step. His body felt weightless, his movement effortless. The sword of the First of Two Hundred was a part of him, like an extension of his arm.

Another Khaev stepped in front of him, this one on foot. Corvus swung at him absent-mindedly, a wickedly fast cut at head height that would have decapitated most men. The Khaev drew and parried the stroke in a single motion, and the ringing impact made Corvus' arm shiver.

He's fast. Corvus' grin only widened. *Perhaps I should pay attention to this one.* He backpedaled a few steps, instinctively, and raised his weapon back to a guard position. The Khaev did likewise.

Neither moved.

"Do you speak Khaev?" asked the stranger, after a moment.

"Yes." *Damned if I know why, but I do.*

"I am Kagerin Shuzan, Fifty-Fourth of Two Hundred."

Speak of the demon. Corvus looked at his opponent in a new light. Shuzan was tall for a

Khaev, and broad-shouldered, with a thin build that indicated speed rather than brute strength. His stance was open, almost inviting Corvus to attack. *Interesting.*

"Do you wish me to know your name, before you die?" There was something behind the question, an almost burning desire.

Corvus laughed, once. "I'm Corvus."

"Corvus is dead."

He knows! "You'll tell me what you know about him."

"It's generally a waste explaining things to the dead."

Corvus shrugged. "Be that as it may."

He pushed off, sweeping in low and fast. Shuzan's blade met his with a metallic rasp. The two parted and clashed again, and again, flickering back and forth too fast to follow, until the sound of steel on steel had risen to a steady scream.

ISOBEL GOT TO her feet and looked around the battlefield.

After the blinding light had vanished, she'd gotten up just in time to nearly be trampled by a Khaev horseman. After getting out of the way and planting a dagger in his eye slit as he came around for another pass, she finally had a chance to see what had happened.

The Khaev counter-charge had done a marvelous job of scattering the Imperial cavalry, but there weren't enough of them to completely rout what was left of Benham's unit. A large group of Imperials had reformed, just in time to meet a charge from Shuzan's river group. From *part* of Shuzan's river group, she amended. It looked as though fifty or sixty riders were headed for the hilltop at a gallop, intent on rescuing their commanders. This left the river group in disarray, which in turn meant the Imperials might have a chance. The momentum of both charges had already been expended, and the two units were embroiled in a swirling melee of men and horses, discarding their lances and hacking at each other with swords.

On the hilltop, there were only a few people left. Three girls and an older woman, who seemed to be headed in her general direction along with another Khaev in servant's guard, and —

Is that Corvus?

The swordsman was easy to pick out, dressed entirely in black. He was fighting another Khaev, blade slamming against blade at an unbelievable speed. *I've never seen anyone move that fast.*

The Khaev—*that must be Kagerin Shuzan!*—was getting the worst of the duel, giving ground fast in an attempt to avoid Corvus' flickering steel. The four women were running toward him, and Isobel broke into a run herself.

If they get behind him, he's in trouble. Corvus was almost preternaturally fast, but Kagerin Shuzan was the Fifty-Fourth of Two Hundred; the Khaev was matching him stroke for stroke and *almost* keeping up. Four more Khaevs would probably overwhelm him.

Isobel racked her brain to come up with a suitable insult, and failed. *I should work these things out in advance.*

"Over here, you Khaev bastards!"

Not original, but it does the job. She drew her twin blades and pulled up just short of them. The girls—she recognized the uniform that marked them as draekeres—turned to face her, their own weapons coming to hand.

The woman made a fast decision. "Aya, help Lord Kagerin. Lin, Zee, with me." She drew her sword and advanced on Isobel, the two girls flanking her.

"Corvus, there's one more headed your way!" The swordsman didn't acknowledge the warning, and Isobel lost track of him a moment later, embroiled in her own problems.

Draekeres were good, Isobel knew that from personal experience. And these two had obviously worked together before. The one the woman had called Lin shifted right, and the other went left, while their commander pressed straight in. Her blade licked out, testing Isobel's defenses. She parried first with her right hand, then with her left, giving ground to avoid being surrounded.

Now what? Something crazy, obviously. *It's hard to win a three-on-one by fighting fair.* Isobel had the distinct advantage that the draekeres didn't scare her in the least; Lin, on the other hand, was breathing hard already, and Zee's eyes were a little wide. *I wonder how many actual fights they've been in on land?*

Isobel waited until the woman attacked again, a cheap little feint to the left, and instead of parrying she threw herself forward. Only a quick twist of her shoulders kept her from getting skewered, but her opponent was obviously not ready for such an aggressive response and couldn't get her blade around in time. Isobel spun past her, opening her left side in passing with a quick slash. Zee spun and thrust at her, a moment too slow. Isobel parried and brought her other blade around at head height, catching her on the side of the head and sliding across her face. Blood spurted, and the girl dropped her sword and screamed until Isobel ran her through and she fell with a gurgle.

"Zee!" The other came at her, anger winning out over fear. But alone she was no match for Isobel, who parried her initial charge and then drove her backward with a furious rain of blows. The draekere was on the defensive, and took a half-dozen cuts in quick succession—on her forehead, both arms, and a deep one over one breast. Lin didn't stop fighting until Isobel trapped her blade against her side and put the point of her other knife through the girl's throat; the draekere jerked for a moment, then sagged.

Isobel rounded on the woman, who had gotten back into something like a fighting stance, one hand on her bleeding side. She caught the Khaev's gaze. There was no fear there, just a heavy resignation. Both of them started at a sudden clatter from the other side of the hill.

"The Imperial infantry." The woman staggered forward. "They're coming. My lord, please . . ."

Isobel half-turned. Shuzan had paused for a moment and was looking at Corvus. "I . . ."

"*Flee*, my lord." The last of the girls was shaking, but her eyes were resolute. She was bleeding liberally from a wound that left her right arm hanging useless. "Now."

Kagerin Shuzan's eyes went hard, glaring at the black swordsman.

"My lord," said the woman, "think of Shia."

Isobel didn't recognize the name. It seemed to decide the Khaev noble, though. He sheathed his sword, carefully, and bowed to Corvus.

"What makes you think I'll let you get away?" The swordsman raised his blade, and then everything happened at once.

Corvus lunged, and the girl named Aya stepped in front of the blade, taking the stroke clean through the vitals. Shuzan turned and sprinted for a string of horses tied to a tree further down the slope. The woman lunged for Isobel, who side-stepped and drew her blade neatly across the Khaev's belly. Blood and entrails fountained forth, and the woman coughed once and collapsed.

Corvus jerked his blade backward, but the girl had grabbed

it and clung to it with both hands. Isobel winced as she saw blood leaking from between Aya's fingers, but the draekere only smiled wistfully until Corvus gave the blade a twist. Then her mouth opened, as though she'd just realized something surprising, and she became a dead weight that dragged the sword to the ground. The swordsman put a boot on her chest and finally dragged his weapon free, but by then Kagerin Shuzan was already galloping across the field toward the remains of his cavalry.

Then there was only silence, broken by a faint moan from Lin that trailed off into a rattle as she expired. Isobel wiped her weapons clean on the woman's leathers and slid them back into their sheathes; Corvus cleaned his with a black cloth and slammed it home, irritated. He gave Aya's limp body a kick in the side of the head.

"A victory," said Isobel, "is a victory."

"He knows." Corvus stared after Shuzan, his eyes gleaming in the sun. Something about him made Isobel shiver. "Shuzan knows."

"Knows what?"

"The answer I need."

"So you're going to chase him?"

"To the end of the fucking earth." Corvus strode down the hill, stepping over Zee's twisted corpse. Isobel looked around the hilltop-turned-charnel house one last time, shrugged, and followed him.

chapter 18

"The Doomwood lulls you into a sense of complacency. Everything looks harmless and normal, up until the point it bites your arm off."

—Max Goran, Imperial Explorer

I'M GOING AFTER him."

Outside, the party was in full swing. Valos' men had captured most of Kagerin Shuzan's supplies intact, and they were making the most of it. The drink was flowing freely, and someone had decided to display their not-so-prodigious talent on the pipes. There was a tune in there, somewhere, but Veil heard it as a kind of mournful wail, like a lone off-key wolf in the night.

She sat in the command tent, hugging her legs to her chest, not really listening to the conversation that swirled around her. *It's not like anyone notices. Why should they? I hardly know these people.* Veil fought down a surge of bitterness. *They'd all be dead now if it wasn't for me. They'd all be fucking dead.*

But it was unreasonable, she felt, to expect more. She'd performed on demand, and they'd thanked her profusely. *What else do I want? What else could they give me?*

She couldn't help thinking of the field beyond the camp, sown with corpses. *Not my fault,* she thought adamantly. *I just made sure it was a bunch of Khaevs instead of a bunch of Imperials.*

"Sybian?" she asked, silently.

"Yes?"

"Did everything go okay?

Sybian chuckled. "Yes, Veil. Except Saya getting away, but I didn't really expect her to intervene in the first place. Not directly."

"So now what?"

"Oh? You're cooperating whole-heartedly now?"

I'm lonely, Veil thought. *And you're someone to talk to, someone who cares whether I live or die.* "As you've mentioned repeatedly, I don't have much of a choice. And what else is there for me to do, really?"

"Very logical."

"So where do we go now?"

"Pay attention."

"I'm going after him," said Corvus again. Veil perked up and started listening in.

"Why?" asked Valos. The senior staff were ranged around the commander's circular table; Corvus had been given pride of place. The story of what he'd done on the hilltop was slowly seeping out, and in the camp outside he was already something of a legend.

"The dispute between Kagerin Shuzan and me is a private matter," said Corvus stiffly. "I'd like to finish it."

"Shuzan is headed south," said Tayla. She'd taken a wound in the battle, and had one arm in a sling. "Away from Crossroads, away from the Anvil, away from anything that matters."

"He's headed for the Doomwood."

"You believe that story?"

Veil would have been skeptical herself. One of Shuzan's personal guard had been captured alive, and had eventually described the return of the draekere Lin. Tayla was of the opinion that it was a trap: that there were Khaev forces to the south, or that Shuzan hoped to lure Valos within the Doomwood and atone for his failure in death.

Sybian had assured Veil that neither was true, but hadn't bothered to explain why a Khaev lord would be riding hard for the most dangerous place in the world.

"You said yourself there's nothing that matters south of here."

"He could be swinging wide, planning to turn east toward Crossroads . . ."

"Why? Why not just ride directly there?"

"The swordsman is right," said the Prophet. "Kagerin Shuzan rides for the Doomwood."

Even though she knew it was an act, Veil couldn't help but be impressed by the Prophet. Producing Veil had given him more authority than ever, and he wore it like a cloak. Veil had to admit it suited him. Even Valos hesitated to contradict his pronouncements The chief scout settled back into her place, looking chagrined.

"And?" Valos addressed the old man. "Should I follow him?"

"*We*'re going to follow?" snapped Tayla. "That's absurd. We're far too slow. The Khaev Blades from the Anvil would run right into us!"

The Prophet, somewhat to Tayla's surprise, nodded agreement. "No, Valos. This is a task for Corvus alone."

"Alone?" Veil mouthed, alarmed.

"Relax," Sybian said. "You get to come, too."

"I'm not sure if I should be happy about that or not. Are we actually going all the way to the Doomwood?"

"We're going all the way to Godsdoom."

"Godsdoom?" *The tomb of the gods, where they came to rest at the end of the great war. The center of the Doomwood. The end of the world.* "We're going to *Godsdoom*?"

"Didn't I just tell you to relax?"

"It's just that I've heard some bad things about that place. Such as: Everyone who goes there is horribly killed."

"'Everybody' doesn't have me helping them. Now be quiet for a second."

"You're set upon this?" asked Valos. "We would be honored if you joined our company. I can offer you . . ."

"I need to find Kagerin Shuzan, before he slips away." Corvus waved a hand. "Perhaps afterward, I can consider your offer."

Valos sighed. Clearly the thought of letting a warrior like Corvus go did not sit well with him. "Very well. You'll have a mount and provisions."

"Thank you." Corvus dipped his head.

"Now," said Sybian. "Tell him you're going, too."

"Um," said Veil, out loud, and instantly hated herself. *Um? Who starts with 'um'? Idiot!* "Corvus? I think I should go, too."

Corvus' face was blank, but Valos looked distraught. "Absolutely not! You . . ."

"This girl's destiny," the Prophet intoned, "does not lie here. It is entwined with the swordsman's. She must accompany him."

Valos looked as though he were about to voice an objection, but a glare from the old man silenced him. He slumped backward and shook his head.

"Very well."

"I'd like to go as well."

There was a wave of cold air as Isobel slipped in through the tent flap. Everyone at the table turned to her, and she bowed respectfully. "My lord. I'd like to go with Corvus."

"Why?"

"I . . ." Isobel stopped, uncertainly.

She doesn't know. "What's wrong with her?" Veil asked Sybian.

"Possession. Some spirit is trying to run her."

"But . . ." Veil shook her head. "Can she come with us?"

"The more the merrier, as far as I'm concerned."

"You are under contract, Isobel," said Valos. "I'm afraid . . ."

"Valos." The Prophet cut him off, and the nobleman rounded on him.

"Her, too?"

The old man nodded, eyes twinkling.

"You're having fun with this, aren't you?" mouthed Veil.

Sybian gave a chiming laugh. "Being a Prophet has certainly come in handy."

Isobel bowed again. "Thank you, my lord."

Valos was not a happy man. "Prophet. I must speak with you alone."

"As you wish, Lord Valos."

"Ah," said Sybian in Veil's ear, "it looks like I'm in for a scolding."

Veil suppressed a giggle. Valos stormed out, with the Prophet trailing behind him, leaving Corvus, Veil, and Isobel alone in the room. There was a moment of silence.

"Corvus . . ." Veil began.

"Veil . . ." Isobel began.

"Isobel . . ." Corvus began.

There was another moment of silence. Veil sighed.

"I suppose there's no talking you out of this, Corvus?"

"Why would you want to talk me out of it?"

"I'm just not sure that chasing one of the world's greatest swordsmen into one of the world's most dangerous places is such a great idea."

The swordsman shrugged. "He knows the answer I need."

"But you could wait until he comes out . . ."

"He could be killed in there. I can't come this close and let it slip away."

"There must be others," Isobel put in. "Maybe any of the Two Hundred."

"Maybe." Corvus shrugged. "I'm not taking the chance."

Veil hadn't expected that to be a battle she could win, but she was surprised when Isobel spoke up. "What about you, Veil?"

"Me?"

"You don't have to go with him. Valos would be happy to have you. He'd keep you safe."

"And all I'd have to do is fight his battles for him?" Veil shook her head. "It doesn't appeal to me."

"And walking into the Doomwood does?"

"Not especially." Veil sighed. *Not being able to tell them about Sybian is awkward.* The spirit had been quite firm on that point, though. "But . . ."

"It's obvious," said Corvus. Both girls turned to stare at him.

Obvious? Veil's thoughts sped in circles, in a panic. *Does he know about Sybian? She said she'd kill me if I told him. What if he found out on his own? He might not let me come along; he probably doesn't want some spirit hanging around . . .*

"She's in love with me." The swordsman shrugged.

Veil felt herself turning crimson under Isobel's eyes. "Veil?"

Now what am I supposed to say? The swordsman had handed her a perfect excuse, but . . .

"I mean . . . it's not . . ." *Why can't I say it?*

"See?" said Corvus. Isobel nodded solemnly. "So I'm not going to stop her from coming along."

"Speaking of which," said Veil, anxious to change topics, "what about you?"

"Me?" said Isobel.

"What do you care about Kagerin Shuzan?"

"Nothing," she said promptly.

"Then why . . ."

"It's just something I have to do."

"Possession," put in Sybian. "She can't help it."

"Can you help her?" asked Veil silently.

"We'll see."

"I won't object to having another sword along," said Corvus, "but don't expect me to bail you out if you get into trouble."

"Don't worry about me." Isobel flashed them both a quick grin.

There was another slightly awkward pause, which Corvus broke by getting to his feet.

"We need to get ready."

"We're leaving *now*?" said Veil.

"Shuzan isn't getting any closer." The swordsman shook his head. "I'll go see if Valos has gotten our supplies ready."

"I'll go get my stuff." Isobel stood as well, and followed the swordsman through the tent flap.

"I'll . . ." Veil stopped, since they were already gone. "I'll just wait here, then."

After a while, she put her head down on the table and sighed.

KEI KNEW IT was unrealistic to expect the Doomwood to be as her imagination had painted it, filled with old, dead trees and fragments of human bone. Still, she managed to feel vaguely offended as Jyo-raku led the way down the slope and into the forest. *It's too normal.* The trees were perfectly healthy oaks and maples, broken by the occasional conqueror pine or a grove of thorny sinbush where an old tree had fallen. It wasn't even dense enough to be uncomfortable to walk through. The shadow spirit led the way, following an old animal track, and Kit and Kei stuck close behind.

"So where are all the ghouls and goblins?" asked Kit brightly.

"Please don't say things like that."

"What's the matter, Wing Leader? Scared?"

"Of course I am! I thought we established this."

"Sorry." Kit managed to put a touch of human feeling into her apology, which left Kei feeling vaguely mollified. "I just expected the Doomwood to be more . . . I don't know . . ."

"Gloomy?"

"Yeah."

"I know what you—"

Something fast and green flashed in front of Kei's vision. She heard Kit yelp at the same time as something struck her heavily from behind, sending her stumbling forward. Somehow, she managed to keep her feet. Kei whipped around, sword flashing from its sheath, in time to see something swinging toward her. It was almost humanoid, if a human had arms with two elbows that were longer than the rest of his body and was completely covered with green fur. Tiny black eyes glared above a pig-like snout, while the creature's ludicrously undersized legs were tucked under its body, out of the way. It moved by swinging at her from a nearby tree limb, bringing its other arm around in a long sweep.

Kei reacted instantly. Instead of backing away, which given the length of the demon's arms was bound to fail, she spun inside its reach and brought her sword down just below its shoulder. Something went *crack* and the spirit screeched and fell to the ground, writhing. Kei kicked it aside and looked for Kit.

Two more of the things had attacked the other draekere. One of them had managed to get her by the throat, but Kit had apparently spitted it from beneath and tossed it aside. Blood flowed in frighteningly large amounts, soaking the front of her uniform, but she was still fencing with the other one. It swung round and round the same branch, whipping its free arm out; Kit deflected each blow with the flat of her blade, but was unable to close and attack.

Kei resolved the situation by stepping up beside the demon and stabbing it in the back of the head. It twitched and let go of the branch, collapsing to the ground and beginning to dissolve rapidly into green glop. Kei looked around for more, didn't find any, and rushed to her friend's side.

"Are you okay?" Kei grabbed Kit's head and stared at her neck, trying to wipe away the blood. "Hold still."

"I'm fine."

It was true. By some kind of miracle, the demon's claws had dug into the fleshy part of Kit's neck, just missing her throat and the artery that pulsed there. Kei shook her head.

"You're luckier than you have any right to be."

"Absolutely." Kit raised her sword and found the blade coated with green stuff; she made a face. "Yuck."

"Are you both alive?" hissed the shadow spirit.

Kei looked up at Jyo-raku. Three of the creatures lay dead around him, chopped into several pieces.

"Yes, no thanks to you."

The jab apparently did not bother the spirit. "These are the border guards of the forest. Their death will draw others, so we must keep moving."

Without another word he turned and started walking. Kei shook her head.

"See?" said Kit, who was pressing a cloth to the side of her neck. "Things are getting more interesting."

"Good." Kei rolled her eyes, trying to fight down bile in her throat. "Because I was getting bored."

The sky was a deep, crystal blue. A tiny pack of clouds was clustered at one point on the horizon, huddled together as though intimidated by the vast depths of the vault. Aside from that there was nothing to get in the way of the sun, which beamed down on the hidden meadow with everything it could muster.

It wasn't really hot, since autumn was already well-advanced, but the air was nearly motionless. Lying still, Saya was coated in warmth as her skin drank in the rays of the sun. The grass underneath her was frigid, still wet with dew, and since her body didn't give off any heat it would remain so.

Not that she cared what the temperature was. All that concerned Saya was the sun, and the power that slid down from the sky.

That, and self-recrimination, of course.

Careless. Her whole left side was tingling, an echo of the agony she'd been in earlier. *Too damn careless. I knew Sybian had to respond, somehow, but I never thought . . .*

She gritted her teeth. *I never thought she was this strong.*

Ordinarily, Saya considered herself above any of the spirits of the world, with the possible exception of Ghael Rex. They were the only ones left of the old order, the alliance that had been forged in desperation to defeat the bellipotent beings who'd called themselves gods. The thought that any spirit created since that time could challenge her seemed laughable. After all, Saya had had six thousand years of building her power, and experience that no young demon could match.

Careless. I've been careless. Ghael Rex had taken the safe route, carefully husbanding every resource, building his power base. *While I wandered the world feeling sorry for myself.* And now there was a spirit—an *ice* spirit—who was almost . . . quite possibly . . .

Admit it. Saya felt like a bit of self-flagellation. *She's stronger than I am. Anyone strong enough to keep something like that demon she sicced on me in thrall . . .* She shivered.

For a spirit, admitting that someone else was stronger was not an easy thing. *But there's nothing else to do. Quite frankly, I wouldn't care how strong she was, if not for Corvus. Let her become a god.*

After six thousand years of life, Saya had lost faith in her cause. *The world is no better because we banished the tyrants.*

But I cannot allow Ebon Death to be unleashed again.

You should have killed him. The mocking voice danced around her mind, a miniature tormentor. *You should have ended him when you had the chance. You never should have created him.*

I should have killed him.

She shook her head. *Enough.* Wallowing in self-pity, as attractive as it was, was not useful. *What can I do now?*

The answer was depressing. *Sybian has Corvus, and she's headed for Godsdoom. Certainly nothing in the forest will be able to stop her. So she has to convince Corvus to fight the Guardian, somehow, and hope that he wins.* If he did, the seal Saya had helped bring into existence after the death of the gods would be released, and Sybian would have what she wanted so badly.

So what can I do about it?

Attacking them directly was no longer an option. While Corvus' resolve was questionable, Sybian had been unwilling to endanger her position by intervening too openly. As the battle had shown, though, that stage of the game had passed. *I'd only get myself killed.*

The forest spirits will attack, though. And if Sybian's pawn is killed, she may have to at least rethink her plans.

And if all else fails, there's always Corvus. Sybian had some lever, something to convince him into undertaking her final battle. She'd never have come this far without one. *But if I can reveal her plot, I might be able to turn him against her.*

Saya sat up, and raised her hands. One of her arms consisted only of sparkling motes of light. She twisted, carefully, testing the range of motion. *Not perfect, but it will suffice.* She desperately wanted to disincarnate and spend a few years as an unconscious cloud, sucking up power from the sun, but that seemed to be out of the question.

There was a flash of light, and then the meadow was empty. The grass stirred a little with the wind of Saya's passing.

"Isobel."

She'd left the tent flap open, and the setting sun painted the tiny space red. Now the light was blocked, and she turned to find Zhin standing in the entryway. The old soldier was still in full leather armor, with a sword at his side. A tiny golden cross trailing a blue ribbon was pinned to his chest.

Isobel raised an eyebrow. "Valos gave you another medal?"

"For some reason."

"What happened?"

Zhin shrugged. "You've got to have heroes. Our southern infantry was damn near wiped out. My squads were among the few that survived. So we get medals."

"Good for you." Isobel turned back to her packing. She had a pair of saddle-bags in front of her and was trying to figure out what she could afford to leave behind. Large stacks of pointy metal objects sat on either side of her. "Did you get a pay raise, too?"

"Ha, ha." He looked around the nearly-empty tent. "Mind if I come in?"

"Go ahead." She put one of the seven-inch stilettos in her pack, stared at it for a moment, then took it out again and replaced it with a pair of shorter throwing daggers.

"I've heard," said Zhin, after a few moments of listening to the rasp of metal on leather, "that you're going south with Corvus."

There wasn't much point to denying it, so Isobel nodded.

"Can I ask why?"

"You can ask." Frankly, Isobel was fed up with trying to

explain it. *I just have to. I have to stay close to him.* She'd thought the nameless desire, the urge to find the person she was supposed to kill, had been burned out of her. *Apparently I was wrong.*

"I figured." He sat down, heavily, on the camp bed. "Are you coming back?"

"Probably not." She felt a lump in her throat, which she quickly dismissed. "He's waiting for me."

"The person you've been chasing all this time? The one you're supposed to kill or die trying?"

"Yes," she said shortly.

"I see."

Zhin sat quietly while she packed a few more weapons. She could feel his eyes on her, which she steadfastly ignored. In the end, he sighed and shook his head.

"I hope you do make it. You've been a very useful person to have around."

"Even if I do come back," Isobel said, "I have no idea what I'll be doing." The idea of life beyond her final confrontation hadn't even occurred to her.

"I know. Still," he ran his hand through his hair, "I hope to see you again."

"You always were an optimist."

Zhin chuckled. "I'm glad to see that you've regained your cheerful temperament."

Have I? The crack had been almost a reflex. Underneath, though, Isobel *felt* different, as though something had broken open inside her and was now flapping around loose. It was wonderful and awful, all at once.

"I guess," said Zhin quietly, "I should say goodbye, then."

"Goodbye, Zhin," she said, levelly.

"Goodbye." He got up off the camp bed and walked to the entryway. Isobel turned back to her packing. After a moment, she became aware that he hadn't gone. "Was there anything else?"

"I don't . . ." He sighed.

"What?"

"I don't suppose I could kiss you again? For old time's sake."

Isobel hesitated a moment, then shrugged and stood up. Zhin threw his arms around her, gripping her so tightly it was hard to breathe, and press his lips to her. She stood, quietly, and let him do what he wanted, let him chew on her lower lip and his tongue play with hers.

When he finally stepped back, she wiped her mouth and said, "Is that all?"

There was a long pause.

"Yeah," said Zhin. "I guess it is."

He turned and ducked out through the tent flap, the setting sun stretching a long shadow behind him. Isobel turned back to her pack, running her hands lovingly over the hilt of each sword or dagger before assigning it to its proper place.

THE NEXT DAY dawned bright and clear, though dark clouds to the south marked another round of storms making its way over the Doomwood toward the mountains. Lord Justin Valos' army was leaving, too. By the time Veil had shouldered her pack and joined her little group, soldiers were already tearing the camp apart. Before too much longer, all that would remain were the latrine pits and the rows of graves, plus the rotting bodies of men and horses in the field. The Imperials had buried their own dead, and left the Khaevs where they lay.

This was clearly a routine the army had done before. Everyone knew their assigned places, and which tents went on which supply wagon, so there was a subtle order to the hustle and bustle. Veil felt like a solid ghost. For the most part, the soldiers ignored her, aside from the occasional curious glance. Since she'd decided on leaving, Valos hadn't popularized her part in the battle. It made her feel lonely, but also a little smug. *I saved your lives,* she thought as a crowd of men and women passed, manhandling a massive load of supplies. *You and you and you. You'd all be dead if it wasn't for me.*

Corvus appeared, silent and dark as always, leading a stallion he'd acquired from Valos' stables. Veil had taken a long time choosing a horse, and had settled on a mare that seemed the least likely to gallop or rear or do anything else distressing. She kept looking at the horse out of the corner of her eye, as though expecting it to make a sudden move; Corvus laughed after he saw her do it for the fourth or fifth time.

"Still not a fan of horses, I take it?"

Veil made a face. "They're handy, but they're big and ugly and don't smell very nice."

"You get used to it."

"I figured."

They stood together, and watched the churning activity. Without knowing the plan, it had the same sense of frantic pointlessness as the scurrying of ants.

"Corvus," Veil said quietly.

"What?"

"Last night, you said . . ." She stopped.

"I said?" He looked over at her and took in her blush. "Oh, that. You don't have to worry about it."

"I don't . . ." Veil took a deep breath. "I just wanted to know. If something like that . . . were true, you know . . . what would you think of it?"

There was a long pause. Finally, Corvus sighed. "It's hard."

"What?"

"Obviously I don't mind you tagging along, or I'd have killed you long ago."

"Thanks a lot," Veil muttered.

"But I have no idea who I really am."

"I've only known you for a month or so, but I think I have a pretty good idea."

"I'm dangerous."

"Obviously."

"So . . ."

"Those are just circumstances." His hesitation seemed to give her strength. "How do *you* feel about it?"

"They're pretty important circumstances."

"Answer—"

"Good morning!" Isobel arrived at exactly the wrong time, leading her dark gray mare. She'd put on a fresh suit of armor, rough cloth and leather with metal studs, and was wearing a short sword on either hip. Behind her was another pair of horses, tied to hers and loaded high with water skins and bags of food. Corvus surveyed them approvingly. "How are the two of you?"

Corvus shrugged.

"A bit on the tired side," said Veil. "You?"

"Fine, fine. I'm glad I escaped being conscripted for manual labor."

"Riding into the Doomwood to get out of a bit of lifting seems like a poor trade."

"This is bound to be more exciting, though." Isobel smiled, and Veil felt her spirits lift a little. *Ever since she . . .changed . . . Isobel's been a lot better company.*

"Is everything ready?" asked Corvus.

"Should be. I checked it myself."

"How long before we reach the forest?"

"Two days, if we ride hard."

"And Shuzan?"

"He'll have reached it by now."

"We may have a hard time catching him then."

"Thankfully," Sybian whispered in Veil's ear, "I don't think that will be a problem. We're right on schedule."

JYO-RAKU, SOMEWHAT TO Kei's surprise, slowed his pace considerably once they were inside the forest. Part of this was from necessity. Despite his protection, both Kei and Kit were worn nearly to exhaustion fending off the attacks from the forest spirits, who regularly charged out of the underbrush and attempted to tear them limb from limb. The wound on Kit's neck kept breaking open, blood seeping through the crust of dirt and scab, and Kei was starting to worry about infection. Kei had thus far escaped serious injury, mostly because Jyo-raku seemed to be more concerned about her than about her Wing. *He still needs me. Though gods only know why.*

But even that did not account for how slowly they were traveling. Frequently, he would stop and wait for no apparent reason, staring off to the north as though he could see through the clustered oaks and pines. It gave Kei the impression that someone was chasing them. From his earlier comments, she had some idea who it might be.

Shuzan. She felt sure the shadow spirit was wrong. *He's not that stupid.*

Stupid enough to sneak his little sister out of a fortress at midnight, with all the power of the Kagerin family arrayed against him. She sat heavily on that traitorous voice and the even more traitorous feeling that wanted to be rescued. *No. No chance.*

The shadow spirit paused again once they'd gained the top of a rocky ridgeline. Kit and Kei collapsed onto a reasonably safe-looking rock; they'd learned not to ask questions and simply use the rest breaks as best they could. This time, though,

Jyo-raku seemed to be doing something unusual. He walked back and forth at the edge of the ridgeline atop a massive granite outcropping, and his shadowy aura reached out to the rock in the form of a thousand feather-light tendrils, as though probing it for something.

Kit's curiosity finally got the better of her.

"I'm going to ask him what's going on."

"Careful."

Kit rolled her eyes. "Relax, Wing Leader. If he planned to kill us, he would have done it by now."

There was something to that, Kei had to admit. Jyo-raku had certainly had plenty of opportunity to simply let his two human companions die. *He still scares the hell out of me.*

"So are we waiting here?" said Kit, who'd gotten to her feet.

"For a time." Jyo-raku glanced at the sun. "The rest of the players must arrive."

"What are you doing?"

"Quiet."

Curious or not, Kit shut her mouth and stepped back. Jyo-raku drew the Bound Blade from its scabbard and held it aloft. As always, the god-forged weapon played tricks with the senses. There was a subtle feeling of suction, as though everything around it was being imperceptibly drawn inward, and sometimes she felt as though a horrible cacophony of voices was babbling just too quietly to make out.

With a sudden, vicious motion, Jyo-raku thrust the sword into the rock. The Bound Blade pierced the granite as easily as if it were flesh, and stood upright with only a few inches of steel showing.

"And now," muttered Jyo-raku, apparently to himself, "a little inviting touch."

His dark aura launched itself at the cliff, fountaining

skywards until it had shaped itself into a rough cylinder; then it faded without actually changing in any way, so that it became one with the background. The shadow spirit looked at it, apparently satisfied, and the Blade glittered invitingly.

"You're just going to leave it here?" asked Kit.

"The wards will keep the forest spirits away," hissed Jyoraku, "and they don't have to hold long. We'll rest here for a few hours, then continue on. We should make it to Godsdoom before tomorrow night."

"You hear that, Kei?" said Kit. "Only one more day to go."

"Do I finally get to die then?" said Kei, exhaustedly.

"Very funny."

"I wonder."

KARL WAS STUMBLING through a patch of dead brush when he heard the most welcome thing he'd heard in days.

"I've got an arrow aimed at your head. Go for that sword and you're a dead man."

The aggressor spoke in Imperial—after speaking Khaev for so long, Karl was starting to wonder if he'd forgotten his native tongue—and, as she stepped slowly into view, appeared to be dressed as a scout. She was slim, with short hair and no armor to hinder her movement. The cloth and cloak she was wearing had been dyed to blend in with the dead and dying browns of the plains in autumn. A sword swung at her side, and, as promised, she had a short bow nocked with an arrow pointed at his head.

"I . . ."

She cut him off with a sharp motion of the bow, and he raised his hands wearily. "Who are you?"

"My name is Karl Halter. I'm in service to Lord Justin Valos."

The scout glared at him, suspiciously. "I've never seen you

before."

"You must be new. I'm the commander of Lord Adrian's personal guard."

"Is there anyone else out here with you?"

"One. Can I call her?"

"Yes. But tell her to be slow."

"Erin, dear? Come over here. Slowly."

It was a few moments before Erin appeared, her hand hovering above her sword. She flicked her eyes from the scout to Karl, taking in the expressions of both. The scout kept her bow on Karl, turning only her head.

"And you are?"

"Erin Torem."

"You work for him?"

"Yes." Erin shot him a scathing glance that, Karl sensed, meant he would pay for 'dear'.

"So you're also in service to Lord Valos?"

"You work for Valos?" Erin's face lit up. "Thank all the dead gods. We've been looking for you people . . ."

"Quiet! We're going back to camp."

"You'll get no objections from me," said Karl.

"You first."

"Of course. Just point the way."

She did, and he started in that direction. Erin followed, then the slim scout, her weapon still drawn. *Her arm must be hurting.* Luckily for her, the camp was close by. *Another few hours and we would have walked right into them.*

The familiar sight of Lord Valos' caravan of soldiers and wagons came close to bringing a tear to his eye. A second glance, though, told him that something major had been happening. The cavalry, in particular, wasn't anywhere near the numbers it had been when he'd left. *There must have been a battle.*

Another scout rode over to them, leaning down from his horse to converse with their escort.

"Good to see you, Jill! What have you got?"

"A couple of mercenaries who claim to work for his lordship."

The scout looked Karl over, and squinted. "Hmm. What's your name?"

"Karl Halter." Karl racked his brains, trying to think if he'd seen the man before. "I don't think we've met."

"That doesn't prove much." He spat in the dust. "Take them over to Valos, see if he knows them. If he doesn't, throw them in with the prisoners."

"Right."

Karl suffered himself to be prodded in the direction of a knot of heavily armed soldiers. Lord Valos rode in their center, looking as discontent as ever; he glanced at the scout, then did a double-take when he saw Karl.

"Karl Halter!" Valos sounded genuinely surprised.

"My lord." Karl gave the best bow he could manage. Erin, beside him, did likewise.

"I take it they're on our side?" said the scout. She sounded disappointed.

"Of course." Valos swept off his horse. "What happened to you? Where's Adrian?"

Karl sighed. "Adrian is dead."

"Dead? But . . ."

"As for what happened," Erin put in, "that's a very long story."

"We'd best get you mounted, so you can tell me without slowing us down too much."

The pair looked at each other and nodded.

"As you wish, my lord."

Shia.

The giant centipede reared up, lifting dozens of its legs off the ground. A cold mist emanated from its mouth, and in place of pincers it had two jagged icicles. Shuzan stared at it, one hand on his sword, waiting for his moment.

"Lord Kagerin!" One of the soldiers disobeyed his lord's commands, apparently feeling the spirit had drawn too close; he charged, sword over his head. The centipede twisted its body casually, slamming sideways into the unfortunate man and crushing him against a massive conqueror pine. The rest of Shuzan's men stayed well behind their leader, who remained firm as the spirit wound toward him.

Almost . . .

The centipede lunged, and Shuzan stepped forward to meet it. He slipped under its head as it went for him, bringing his sword around in a lightning-fast overhead arc. Then he was dodging to the side to avoid the thing's body as it crumpled, head severed entirely. Its legs continued to twitch, spasmodically, until the spirit began evaporating into freezing mist.

Shuzan barely had time to sheathe his sword before his men had moved up to surround him, alert for further dangers. He turned to Hiko, who had assumed his usual place at his lord's side.

"Well?"

"We're getting closer, my lord." Hiko consulted his map. Inasmuch as anyone could map the Doomwood, the Imperials had tried. The problem was that everything they had done was hundreds if not thousands of years old, so reading anything beyond the basic lay of the land could be dangerously misleading. *Godsdoom should be in the same place, at least.* That was where the shadow spirit's trail was leading. He was sure of it.

Damn him. Shuzan cursed Jyo-raku, cursed Moriseki and Shiori for falling into his trap, and most of all cursed himself. *I should have known. I should have kept better tabs on what Shia was doing, I should have investigated the woods more thoroughly. But I was too damn eager—worried that Valos might slip through my fingers, again. Damn, damn, damn.*

He was down to three dozen men, more or less. At the border to the Doomwood, he'd sent most of the three hundred or so who'd survived the battle home. *Someone at Crossroads needs to know what has happened.* Tashida Ikon would not take the destruction of one of his elite Blades lightly, even if that Blade was acting against orders. The knowledge that Justin Valos' army would not long survive his did little to revive Shuzan's spirits.

Besides, having an army is worthless in here. It only draws more of the damned things. So far, the Khaevs had been holding their own surprisingly well, making it most of the way to Godsdoom in only a day and a half and losing less than a quarter of their men. *Something's different.* On his first attempt to penetrate the cursed forest, the spirits had contested his advance every step of the way; now the attacks were sporadic. *Maybe it's something Jyo-raku has done. Or maybe, since he's here, they have bigger fish to fry.*

In any case, the shadow spirit was rapidly approaching the point where he'd have nowhere left to run. *Unless he can fly, there's nowhere to go once he gets to Mortalcliff.* The storm-wracked shore marked the southern edge of the Empire. Nearly every day, ocean squalls whipped the water at its base into a deadly froth.

But he's not going to the cliffs. Jyo-raku is going to Godsdoom. Shuzan was sure of it, for some reason he didn't quite understand. *It's only logical. Why go south, once he'd slipped past us, if not to reach Godsdoom?*

And I will follow him. That no human had ever reached the tomb of the gods and returned Shuzan considered unimportant. *If it comes to that, I'll be the first. And when I catch up with him . . .*

"Over that ridge, my lord," said Hiko gently, interrupting Shuzan's winding thought. "Then it should be a gradual descent until we can see the tomb."

"Good. Have we found a route up?"

"Yes, my lord," said one of the soldiers. "Follow me."

They made their way up, one at a time, wary of an ambush. None came. Shuzan went first, as had become his custom, and was the first to reach the top of the ridge.

It was quiet, preternaturally quiet. He stood on top of a knuckle of rock, thrusting out through the fabric of the forest; Shuzan blinked in the direct sunshine and looked around. There was a gleam, as of light on metal, and he shaded his eyes. *That looks almost like . . .*

"My lord?" Hiko spoke just behind his ear.

"Is that a sword?"

"A sword, my lord?" Hiko also shaded his eyes. "It certainly looks like one, my lord. Half-buried in the rock. I . . . my lord, where are you going?"

Shuzan strode across the clearing. The sword was buried in the rock, as though it had been thrust cleanly into solid granite. *That's not possible, though. But . . .* There was something off about the blade, too. The longer he stared at it, the more he felt as though it was on the verge of sucking him in, sucking in the entire clearing and possibly the world. There was a sound, too, which would have been inaudible if not for the absolute silence—many voices babbling, screaming, shouting nonsensically at each other.

What in the seven hells is that thing?

"My lord." Hiko touched his arm. "This is a trap."

Shuzan nodded, slowly. "That is a weapon of power, Hiko."

"We're in the Doomwood, my lord. The spirits have left it to beguile you."

"They've succeeded." Shuzan took another step forward. The pattern of light and shadow undulating just under the surface of the metal was almost hypnotic.

Even if we catch up with them, what am I going to do? This was the tiny voice of doubt he was finding it more and more difficult to silence. *Jyo-raku is a spirit of immense power. Can I really kill him?*

If I lose, all of this has been a waste.

Shuzan stretched out one hand and grabbed the sword. A faint but persistent hum emanated from the weapon, and he could feel the vibration in his bones. The voices redoubled, a shouting cacophony that was somehow not only tolerable, but pleasant. A gentle tug and the weapon slid free of the rock.

He smiled.

"What is it, my lord?"

When Shuzan Kagerin spoke, there was a slight resonance to his voice, a tiny atonal buzz. "A Bound Blade."

"But . . . the Bound Blades . . ."

"Onward." Shuzan gestured with the tip of the sword, which hummed as it cut the air. "To Godsdoom."

CORVUS PAUSED, ON the edge of the forest.

It was getting on toward evening and the shadows of the trees stretched across the ground like living things, trying to escape their tethers. Veil shivered. There was a cold breeze blowing from the south. It was colder than it ever got in the Red Hills, cold enough to make her glad she'd borrowed a leather coat from Valos' stores before they'd left.

So this is a forest.

It wasn't quite how she'd pictured it. She'd seen little woods, of course, on the road from Corsa and across the highlands, but she'd always thought the Doomwood would be bigger, that the trees themselves would be different. Instead, there were the same four or five varieties that were slowly becoming familiar, broad-leaves interspersed with pine. But it went on and on and *on*; from where she was standing, the forest was an unbroken sea stretching away to the south and east, broken only by particularly huge trees that stood out like islands in the surf.

She could smell it, too, she realized—the accumulated earthy scent of countless generations of plants that had lived and died and grown again. In the hills, decent soil was a precious resource, quickly covered with low-growing plants like beans or potatoes. But this forest had been standing for thousands of years, and the trees had never felt the axe. The age of the place was imposing.

Corvus was focused on something else. There was movement in the trees. He waved Veil and Isobel back, hand dropping to his sword.

"There's something in there."

"I brought some of my friends along," said Sybian, "to make sure everything goes smoothly. See if you can convince Corvus not to fight them."

Veil nodded, her mouth hanging open, as she watched the spirits emerge from the trees. There were two of them, vaguely resembling dogs, albeit dogs the size of horses and made entirely of ice. A mane of crystals ran from the top of their heads down to the small of their backs, and Veil could hear the wood snapping underfoot as they padded forward. When they panted, their breath instantly flashed to steam; their mouths were filled with row after row of needle-sharp teeth.

"The one on the left is Kuul, and the other one is Kaal. They'll take care of you on the way to Godsdoom." Sybian sounded a little smug.

"Corvus . . ."

"Veil, now is *not* the time."

"No, Corvus, listen. I don't think they want to fight."

Corvus looked down at her. Veil put on her best innocent expression.

"They're spirits of the Doomwood, Veil," said Corvus, as though explaining things to a small child. "They don't want us to enter."

"I don't think they are. Watch." Before he could stop her, Veil ran forward, toward the dog-things.

"Wait . . ." Corvus took a step, and his sword flashed from its sheath. By that point Veil had already reached the spirits and taken up a position between their icy flanks. Neither so much as twitched.

"See?"

Corvus kept his hand on his sword. "I still don't think . . ."

"Come on, Corvus. It's cold over here. Just trust me on this."

The swordsman finally straightened up and shook his head. "If you say so."

Kaal and Kuul padded away from Veil, and she rejoined Corvus and Isobel, who'd just returned from tethering the horses. The girl eyed the two giant dogs mistrustfully, but said nothing; neither Corvus nor Veil seemed inclined to mention it.

"So we're on foot from here." Corvus pointed southeast. "As far as anyone knows, Godsdoom is a day and a half that way, assuming we can keep up a good pace."

"We know Shuzan is going to Godsdoom?"

"The Prophet told us so," said Corvus sourly. "And Veil seems sure."

Veil smiled, lamely, and nodded.

"I like this less and less." Corvus shook his head. "There's too much going on that we don't know about."

"We could always turn back." Isobel didn't sound as though she expected that suggestion to be entertained, and she was correct.

"No. If Shuzan's in there, I'm going in as well."

"Let's get moving, then!" Veil tried to inject some cheerfulness into the situation, which fell on deaf ears. Nevertheless,

Corvus shouldered his pack and started for the edge of the forest, and Isobel followed. Veil hurried to catch up with them, the two huge spirits loping easily on either side of her.

The Doomwood seemed the same as any other forest, in Veil's limited experience. Every so often they'd come to a truly gigantic tree, which Isobel said were called conqueror pines. The ground was covered with bushes, ferns, and other under-brush, and while there was a slight upward slope it wasn't steep enough to bother them. Veil started feeling a bit better. The surroundings were downright pleasant.

"You know," Corvus said after a while. "What you did be-fore was really stupid."

"With the dogs?"

"Yeah." Corvus glanced sidelong at Kaal and Kuul. "Don't try that kind of thing again."

She looked at him, fighting a grin. "Are you worried about me?"

"It'd be a shame for you to die after following me this far."

He moved up to the front of the group, and Veil stayed where she was, but she smiled for an hour thereafter.

chapter 19

> "Godsdoom!
>
> "Could anything be more romantic? The final fortress of the gods, the fortress that became their tomb. From there, it is said, they worked their last great magic, that protects us even today.
>
> "It's all bunk, of course. But it makes for a good story."
>
> —Joy Kenth, Imperial storyteller

KEI WAS TIRED enough that, when she finally got to the top of the ridge, she didn't really understand what she was seeing.

What rest she'd managed to grab in the Doomwood, under Jyo-raku's watchful glare, had not been refreshing. Every time she closed her eyes she found herself standing in front of the carved arch, surrounded by the horrible spirits that had killed Kino. Every time, she woke up with her heart in her mouth and her leathers soaked with sweat. The only reason she'd been able to keep going was that the demon attacks had abated, as though the creatures of the forest had recognized their superior in Jyo-raku.

Well, that and Kit. The younger draekere seemed prepared to walk until she dropped from blood loss and exhaustion. Somehow, Kei felt like she shouldn't fall behind.

Now Kit stood on the spine of the ridge, shading her eyes

against the sun and staring down the other side. "Kei, come and take a look at this!"

Kei lumbered over. She'd somehow stopped worrying about the end of their perverse quest. It seemed as though there had never been anything but the endless walk through the gods-forsaken woods. Therefore, it was a moment before she realized what Kit was pointing at.

The ridge was roughly circular, as it turned out, a giant ring of stone surrounding a central valley. The center was marked by a grove of massive conqueror pines, the smallest a hundred feet if it was an inch. And, in the center of the grove . . .

What in the name of the gods is that?

That was a stone spire, towering above the conquerors. The tip of it was higher than the ridgeline, and glittered like a single giant diamond; it was ludicrously thin, as though a needle had been thrust up through the quilt of the landscape. *That's ridiculous. The first storm would topple it.* A second part of her mind chided *her* for being ridiculous. *This is the Doomwood, so the whole place was built by sorcery. Obviously.*

Then her exhausted brain clicked into action.

Godsdoom!

It has to be. There were no other structures in the Doomwood, certainly nothing as impressive as this. *The tomb of the Imperial gods. The end of the world.* She blinked. *We made it?*

"Unbelievable." Kit shook her head. "Do you know no human has ever seen this before?"

"Seen it and lived," said Kei, with a touch of her old dry humor. "A lot of them never came back."

"It's still amazing."

She's genuinely happy. Kei shook her head and turned. Jyoraku was approaching. The spirit looked at the spire, and his sibilant voice held something like satisfaction.

"Finally."

"I was beginning to think this forest would never end." Kit rolled her eyes. "Is this where we've been headed?"

"It is indeed." If her attitude annoyed the spirit, he didn't show it. "Now we must move quickly."

"*Now* we must move quickly?" muttered Kei. "Why did we wait for half a day before, then?"

"A trap," said Kit quietly, after the spirit had started downhill.

"What?"

"Jyo-raku has someone following him, who he intends to lure into a trap. Ten to one it's Kagerin Shuzan. He mentioned him earlier. And why else bring you along?"

Shuzan. Would he follow me, all the way to the tomb of the gods?

"I don't know."

"So the question is why?" Kit shook her head again, trying to clear out the cobwebs. "I know Shuzan is Fifty-Fourth of Two Hundred, but this is a bit complicated just to assassinate him."

"Obviously."

"Don't fall behind," hissed Jyo-raku. "We'll be at the tomb in less than an hour."

THAT PROVED TO be more-or-less accurate. The descent to the valley floor was surprisingly easy, and approaching the tomb even easier. Kei had expected to be hacking through underbrush the whole way there, but the high canopy of pines apparently kept the bushes down. Once they got close enough, she could see that the base of the colossal spire was a small stone hemisphere, in what appeared to be the exact center of the valley.

As they got even closer, she realized perspective had been playing tricks on her. The stone hemisphere was, in fact, rather large—it could have swallowed a dozen Saido townhouses comfortably—and utterly featureless. It was slate-gray and perfectly smooth; if six thousand years of wind and rain had had any effect, it wasn't obvious.

So this is the tomb of the gods. Kei felt a little bit disappointed. While the scale of the place was impressive, the architecture left something to be desired. *A few statues, maybe, or some nice bas-relief at the base of the wall.* She felt herself giggle.

Jyo-raku angled their path slightly to the left, and they walked almost a quarter of the way around the giant monument before he found what he'd been looking for. Kei went pale as they rounded a stand of conquerors. Kit stopped a moment later, looking back at her.

"Kei? Are you all right?"

"Y . . . Yes." Her voice was a whisper. Kei had literally stepped into a nightmare. She'd never seen the dome, or the spire, but the arching gateway was perfectly clear. The symbols—she'd memorized every unintelligible loop and whorl—were identical. The space under the arch was filled by a ghostly purple gleam, which obscured whatever lay beyond.

"Kei?" Kit peered at her closer. "You don't look okay."

"I've seen this place." Kei's hands curled into fists, her nails digging in to her palms. "I've seen it."

"Nobody's seen this place." Kit waved her hand. "At least, nobody who lived to tell about—"

"I've seen it!" Kei put her hand on Kit's shoulder. "This is wrong, Kit. We shouldn't be here. I shouldn't . . ."

"We don't have a choice, unless you've got a way to get past Jyo-raku."

She glanced at the shadow spirit, who was a good twenty paces ahead. "We could try to jump him."

"We could slit our throats, too. It's likely to be a good bit less painful."

"I thought you didn't care?"

"I'll admit the thought of days of whatever awful tortures he can dream up doesn't appeal." Kit shifted uneasily. "I thought you *did* care?"

"Do you really think we have a prayer of getting out of here alive?"

"We always have a *prayer*, Wing Leader."

"Kei." Jyo-raku half-turned. "I have need of you."

Kei hurried to his side with Kit behind her. She felt like a dog, coming when called. *But what else is there to do?*

"We've arrived." Jyo-raku pointed, unnecessarily. "This is . . ."

" . . . Heaven's Gate," whispered Kei, at the same time he said it. The spirit didn't seem to notice.

"It's a part of the ward designed to trap the remnants of the power of the gods," hissed Jyo-raku. "A small part, created by the alliance of spirits after the war."

"Will it stop us from going inside?" asked Kit, ever curious.

"Ordinarily, yes." Under his black aura, Kei was sure the spirit was smiling. It wasn't a pleasant sensation. "But we have a key."

"A key?" Kei took a step back. "What do you mean?"

"There were six keys to Heaven's Gate." Jyo-raku took a step toward her, and Kei kept retreating. "After the war against the gods, the six most powerful spirits wanted to seal this place forever. But since no one of them trusted the others, each fashioned a key—a way to get past the binding. Out of the six, Lady Light and the Smoke Lord still hold theirs. The Frost King vanished, and though many searched his key was never found. Those belonging to the Dark Queen and Lord Flame were lost when they removed themselves from the affairs of this world."

He tilted his head. "And the Crystal Lady, for reasons I will never understand, made a deal with a mortal to suppress her key forever. She intended to end her life, of course, and the key itself is impossible to truly destroy. I think she was worried about what would happen if one of the younger spirits like me got hold of it." He followed this with a nasty hissing cough that might have been a laugh.

"I don't know what you're talking about," said Kei, still backing up.

"I don't expect that you do. But your family knows. The key surfaces, every few generations, but up until now it has always been suppressed."

"Stay away from her!" Kit drew her sword, though what she intended to do with it wasn't clear. Jyo-raku didn't bother to reply.

"Are you saying I have this key, somewhere?" Kei shook her head violently. "I don't . . ."

"It's not so much that you have the key," the shadow spirit hissed. "It's that you *are* the key. It's not a physical *thing* so much as a spell, a binding, wrapped like an anchor-chain around your family line. It was your ancestor, you see, who made a deal with the Crystal Lady. I imagine that has something to do with the success of your family—her blessing, her power, in exchange for a promise to keep the key secure. It follows you through history, and in every generation it binds itself to a newborn child. According to the ancient agreement, such children are suppressed once discovered, but, thankfully, you managed to slip through the cracks. It was some work tracking you down, I must admit. I was lucky in my choice of Shiori. She proved to have the wherewithal to recruit exactly the draekeres I needed."

"This is ridiculous . . ." *Suppressed? They wanted to kill me— would have, if not for Shuzan. I would have been erased from history . . .*

"Please," said Jyo-raku, with what was almost a sigh. "I don't expect a human to understand. Just go stand under the arch."

Kei gritted her teeth. *The danger's not from the arch, but from what's inside.* Her dreams were clear enough on that point. *Is there something horrible in there? Or maybe Jyo-raku entering will cause some disaster?* "What if I refuse?"

"You'll do it." His aura expanded menacingly. "Whether or not you have any limbs left at the time is up to you."

Kei sighed, defeated. *It's not like there was much doubt. I'm the coward.* Kit would have made him kill her, if she were really convinced.

"Go." Jyo-raku gestured sharply. Kei went, trudging toward the purple radiance of Heaven's Gate.

KAGERIN SHUZAN LOOKED at the mammoth spire with an unreadable expression. Hiko waited patiently, just behind his master; the twenty or so riders that were left of Shuzan's command had simply collapsed exhaustedly to the rocky ground at the top of the ridgeline.

"This is where the trail leads." It wasn't a question, but Hiko answered it anyway.

"Yes, my lord. Down into the valley. They are no more than an few hours ahead of us."

Shuzan pressed his lips together and stroked the Blade that rode on his hip. Its hum was ever-present now, at the back of his thoughts. It was composed of the nearly muted buzz of a thousand voices, all screaming madly. He had to concentrate to maintain his train of thought.

There was never any doubt. He'd known for some time now that Jyo-raku could only be heading for Godsdoom. *There's nowhere else to go. The forest exists to protect the tomb.*

"Hiko," said Shuzan finally. "I am presented with a choice."

"Yes, my lord?"

"I must go into the tomb. Alone."

"Alone, my lord?" Hiko sounded shocked. "But . . ."

"Alone." *Anyone else would only be killed to no purpose.* Carrying the Bound Blade gave Shuzan some hope that he might prevail against Jyo-raku or whatever horrors lived inside the tomb of the gods, but he had no illusions regarding his men. "You can either wait here for me, or attempt to return to the outside."

"We will wait here, of course." The adjutant seemed offended that the other course had even been suggested. Shuzan smiled, teeth bared.

Into the jaws of hell. My men. He was half-tempted to order them to return anyway. All that stopped him was the knowledge that his skill and the Bound Blade were their only halfway reasonable chance of escape.

"I may not return."

"My lord . . ."

"If you have had no word from me by morning, make for Crossroads. That's an order."

Hiko nodded, slowly. "As you wish, my lord."

"So what do I do?" asked Kei.

Up close, Heaven's Gate was awe-inspiring enough to shock even Kit into a moment of numb silence. It was *huge*, the top of the arch easily fifty feet off the ground, and the purple curtain that cloaked whatever was beyond was even stranger up close It was composed of thousands and thousands of tiny purple sparks, all whirling around each other in an intricate dance with a fine structure just slightly too small for the eye to resolve. Kit kept trying to follow the little sparks through their courses. Kei looked at the whole thing with a sick anticipation, and Jyo-raku, as usual, was unreadable.

"Can I touch it?" said Kit. They were all bathed in the purple glow of the Gate, and Kit, in particular, looked slightly unearthly.

"I wouldn't recommend it," hissed Jyo-raku. "The wards were not placed by the kindest of spirits."

Kit looked disappointed. "It's beautiful, though."

"It has survived for six thousand years, feeding off the energy of the Trap. For a ward of this potency, that is quite a feat." Jyo-raku put his hand on Kei's shoulder His touch was icy cold, with a bit of slimy moisture. "And now it is time for it to be opened."

Kei had gone past the stage where she bothered protesting. "What do I do?"

"Step into the curtain."

"That's it?"

"Assuming I'm right, and you have the key. It will create a hole in the ward and we will pass."

"And if you're wrong?"

"You'd be disintegrated. But I'm not wrong."

He's not. Kei took a step toward the curtain. *I almost hope that he is. One quick flash, and then I'm done. Like Kit said, better than whatever he has planned.* Her hand moved almost of its own volition, and she took another step, until her finger was mere inches from the curtain. The purple sparks swirled, altering their dance so that, while still continuously in motion, they formed a whirlpool in front of her.

"Kei . . ."

"Please don't burden me with any last-minute confessions, Wing."

"Oh." Kit stood back, smiling. "Go ahead then."

Kei took a deep breath and touched the curtain. As her fingers passed through the purple sparks, she cringed, expecting a killing heat. Instead she felt nothing. The sparks jumped away from her fingers, as though her very presence repelled them. She took another step forward, until she was standing directly under the curtain, and spread her arms. The sparks cleared a space around her, creating an archway-within-an-archway with room for someone to duck through on either side.

Kit was the first to follow, ducking past Kei into the semi-darkness beyond, and then Jyo-raku stepped in front of her. Kei felt a tiny flaring of a resentful spirit.

"This is it? This is what you dragged me halfway across the continent to do?"

"Indeed."

"I feel like something's missing."

"The best plans avoid drama whenever possible. I intend to do what I came to do as quickly and efficiently as I can."

"Do I have to stand here the whole time?"

"No, you come inside with us. The ward is one-way. We should be able to leave whenever we wish."

"Great." She gestured inward, the corona of sparks mirroring the move. "After you, then."

Jyo-raku ducked and passed through the barrier. Kei followed, letting Heaven's Gate close behind her like a waterfall.

THE DEMON ATTACKS had abated as they'd climbed the ridge, as though the creatures of the forest had realized they were outmatched. That implied an intelligence that, when Veil gave it a moment's thought, was more frightening than all the toothy apparitions they'd witnessed thus far.

Not that they'd had many problems. Between Corvus, who'd taken the lead, and the giant ice-hounds Kaal and Kuul, few of the swarms of forest creatures came anywhere close to her. While Veil still jumped every time some horror blundered out of the underbrush, she wasn't really afraid. Even Isobel, who had taken a position next to her, barely had to dirty her blade.

The swordsman, of course, was in his element. Corvus chopped his way through the Doomwood with a savage glee. It was a faint echo of what she'd felt from him the night of her escape from the Diem. With every fight he seemed to get more energetic, rather than wearier, until all she could see of him was a black-and-steel blur that occasionally spat out dismembered demons.

"We're almost there," whispered Sybian. It was just past noon, and they'd been crawling up the rocky, coverless ridge long enough that Veil could feel the weak heat of the sun on her back. It was pleasant. She hadn't felt really warm in a long time. *And Isobel says this is just the beginning. Not even winter yet.* For a girl from the Red Hills, that was a horrifying thought. It was already colder here than it ever got in her homeland.

"Almost where?"

"Godsdoom."

Veil shivered, superstitiously. *The tomb of the gods.* The holiest place in the Imperial pantheon, where no one had visited and survived. *And we're just walking in the front door? It seems a bit ludicrous.*

There was a spark of light on the horizon, almost bright enough to be a second sun. Veil shaded her eyes and stared and was just able to make out the impossibly thin tower on which it balanced. "Is that it?"

She said this out loud, and Isobel nodded. "I assume so. I've never seen the place."

"So are we going down?" Corvus half-turned to speak to Veil.

"You're asking me?"

"You're the only one who seems to know anything about where we're going. Shuzan definitely came through here, and recently. He's headed for that thing"—he gestured—"whatever it is. If you know where there's an entrance . . ."

"Angle to the left," whispered Sybian. "Kaal and Kuul will lead you. We need to pass through Heaven's Gate."

"Follow the dogs," said Veil aloud. "They'll lead us to something called Heaven's Gate."

"That sounds promising." Corvus rolled his eyes. "When I've caught up with Shuzan and we have a moment to rest, Veil, you're going to have to tell me how you know all this."

"I hope I get the chance."

The ice hounds were already loping down the slope, and three humans followed.

"SO NOW WHAT?"

Kei stood still, one hand on Kit's shoulder, letting her eyes get adjusted to the semi-darkness. The purple curtain of Heaven's Gate blocked all light from the outside, but the hall they'd passed into was filled with a strange, sourceless radiance that gave it a gloomy, twilit feel. It was ideal for Jyo-raku, and the shadow spirit stretched luxuriantly.

Kit repeated her comment. "So? Now what?"

"I don't know," said the spirit.

"You don't *know*?" Kei rounded on Jyo-raku. "What the hell does that mean?"

"I have never been inside the tomb before. No one has. At least no one who's willing to talk about it. So we are, as you humans say, off the map."

"But what are we doing here?" asked Kit, reasonably.

"We're looking for something called the Trap."

"And once we find it?"

"We wait for Shuzan."

"Shuzan?" asked Kit. "What does he have to do with this?"

"There's someone," hissed Jyo-raku, "that I need him to kill."

"Shuzan isn't going to kill anyone except you," Kei retorted.

"It depends on the proper application of leverage." There was the definite hint of a smile behind Jyo-raku's shadowy aura. "Now. Let us be on our way."

Kei's eyes had adjusted by this point, and she found herself standing in a nearly featureless hallway. Heaven's Gate, behind her, was an all but solid curtain of purple. The arch was smaller on this side, somehow, barely taller than a man. Floor, walls, and ceiling were constructed of the same perfectly smooth flagstones, polished to a fine sheen; bits of mica sparkled and glittered as she moved. Ahead, the corridor bifurcated, with passageways going in either direction.

"Well?" She looked back at Jyo-raku. "Which way do we go?"

"If the old stories are to be believed, the tomb is in some sense a spiral. All roads lead to the Trap. Thus, one way is as good as another."

"Fine." Kei started walking, determinedly. Kit hurried to stay by her side, while Jyo-raku followed, amused.

"Are you in a hurry, Wing Leader?"

"I'd like to get this over with and get out of here as soon as possible, if that's what you mean."

"You're worried?"

They'd reached the junction. "Of course I'm worried. There's no telling what kind of things live in a place like . . ."

Whaum. They came from all directions at once. Purple sparks gushed from the walls on both sides, congealing rapidly into humanoid shapes. Once the mist had cleared, there were four of them on either side—vaguely female parodies of the human form. While the gross details were correct, the skin was pure white and featureless, with no hair, eyes, or mouth breaking the flat oval of the face. Each figure had a weapon, a golden two-handed sword as plain as the creature that bore it.

Kit and Kei backed up, in unison, toward the shadow spirit.

"And who might these be?" Kei asked, as she drew her sword with a rasp. It was notched, and pitted, and looked pathetically small compared to the massive golden great swords of the newcomers.

"Guardians of the tomb, obviously." Jyo-raku extended his hands, and the shadowy aura that surrounded him extended and hardened into a pair of blades. "I was expecting as much."

"Excellent." Kit drew her sword as the guardians closed in. "I thought this was dull."

Kei couldn't tell if she was being sarcastic or not, and didn't have the chance to ask before the caryatids attacked. They charged, all at once, and Jyo-raku surged forward to meet them. The shadow spirit laid about with his blades, frighteningly fast, and chopped the center four guardians to pieces in the space of an instant.

That left two each charging Kit and Kei, which, from Kei's point of view, was two too many. She ducked away from their initial rush—the great swords clattered off the stone behind her, drawing sparks—and pulled a cut across the stomach of the guardian on the left. This had distressingly little effect—the creature started to leak purple sparks. But the zeal with which it came after her was not reduced. Kei was forced to parry desperately, backing toward the center of the corridor, and then dive out of the way as the guardian forced its way past her guard with an overhand chop. This time she twisted toward it and ran the thing through, which staggered it somewhat, and, when she pulled the short sword out, the caryatid dissolved completely—weapon and all—into a purple mist.

She spared Kit a glance. The younger draekere was facing only one opponent, and was doing a reasonable job of keeping it at bay. And Jyo-raku . . .

Kei felt the icy touch on her arm just as she turned. She found herself stumbling forward, pulled by an irresistible strength. A moment later she was standing next to the shadow spirit, her body clammy-cold and wrapped in a shadowy projection of Jyo-raku's dark aura.

"Kei!" Kit pushed the guardian aside and sprinted forward, but at that moment another *whaum* announced the arrival of a half dozen more of the faceless creatures. They materialized out of the wall, blades ready, and Kit found herself parrying desperately. Another pair attacked Jyo-raku and were immediately chopped down.

"Jyo-raku!" Kei pried futilely at the tendril holding her. Her hands passed right through it with no effect on its grip. "Help Kit!"

But the shadow spirit either wasn't listening or didn't think that merited a response. He chose the left branch and stalked around the corner, dragging Kei with him. She dried to drag her heels, but that merely forced the spirit to hold her a few inches off the ground.

"Kit!"

"Kei!" The younger draekere's wail faded into the distance as the shadow spirit rounded another corner.

"Jyo-raku! We have to go back! We . . ."

"It was apparent that you would become intractable without your friend," hissed Jyo-raku. "Now that we have arrived, however, your tractability is not required."

"You . . ." She was unable to think of an epithet vile enough. Another pair of guardians materialized in front of them and were summarily slashed to bits.

"Save your breath. Your beloved brother will be here shortly."

Kagerin Shuzan cast a long shadow as he approached Heaven's Gate, stained purple by the dancing sparks of light. He walked toward the curtain warily, with one hand on the hilt of the Blade. Its ever-present hum of screaming voices seemed to be getting louder, and it was only with an effort of will that he could ignore them and concentrate on the task at hand.

Jyo-raku took Shia in here. *Why* he'd done it was a question that was beginning to gnaw at Shuzan's mind. The spirit had to have some truly awful scheme in place in order to justify the effort it had spent to drag her halfway across the continent.

Enough. He stepped in front of the curtain, but the sparks of purple light seemed unresponsive. *Should I just step through?*

Almost unconsciously, Shuzan pulled the Blade from its sheath. The response was immediate. The purple curtain lifted, as though it were made of cloth, and cleared a space big enough for three men to walk abreast. Shuzan kept the sword out as he walked through. Once he'd passed into the dim hallway beyond, the curtain fell closed, blocking all light from the outside.

Whaum. Sparks flooded out from the walls when he reached the first junction. The Fifty-Fourth of Two Hundred spun in place, Blade raised, and found himself surrounded by a half dozen faceless women with milky-white skin and golden great swords . He smiled grimly and dropped into a combat stance, but the caryatids did not attack. Instead, after a moment, they bowed, pressing the tips of their swords into the ground before them.

The Bound Blade's hum seemed contented, somehow, as though recognizing this adulation as its due. Shuzan raised an eyebrow as the guardians dissolved back into purple sparks and flowed into the perfectly smooth flagstones, leaving the corridor empty once more. There was nothing to be seen in either direction except gently curving, perfectly featureless hallway, so Shuzan picked a direction at random and set off at a jog, Blade still unsheathed in his hand.

Whatever the secrets of this place are, it respects the Blade.

Someone wanted me to be here. Someone guided me to the Blade. Jyo-raku? Shuzan's brow furrowed as he tried to think. It was difficult to recall the exact circumstance in which he'd acquired the weapon; even the thought of a time without it was fuzzy in his memory. *That's ridiculous. I picked the thing up only yesterday. It just feels like forever.*

His footsteps echoed down the corridors, and the hum of the Blade grew louder still.

VEIL STARED UP at the massive arch of Heaven's Gate, and sighed.

"Why is it," she said, "that I'm the only one who's allowed to act impressed?"

Isobel and Corvus looked at each other, then back at Veil.

"Seriously. Would it violate some macho code for one of you to show a little surprise from time to time?"

Corvus shrugged, but Isobel actually chuckled. "I'll admit. I'm impressed."

"Thank you." *Now if I could get one of them to admit to being scared out of her mind.* "So now what? Do we just walk through the curtain?"

"No," said Sybian's chiming voice. "That would be a very bad idea."

"So what do I do?" Veil thought back at her.

"Just wait a moment."

"Veil?" said Isobel, curiously.

"What?"

"You got all distant there for a second."

"Figuring out what to do next?" asked Corvus sourly. He was clearly not pleased to have to rely on someone else for instructions. "Hurry up. Shuzan is just ahead of us, and I don't want to lose him."

"This is the only entrance, though," said Isobel reasonably.

"This thing is huge," the swordsman retorted. "It could be a maze inside. He could hide practically forever. And who knows what sorcery could do."

"Or he could get killed," commented Veil.

"Right. I'd like to catch up with him before that."

The conversation was cut off by a rising whine. The wind whipped back and forth, blowing Veil's hair first one way, then the other. It carried winter's chill with it, and the tang of ice. This was followed by a feeling of pressure, a great soundless *whomph* that rippled past the three and their two doglike protectors and continued out into the valley. When Veil next looked around, they'd been joined by another figure. It was a young woman, unclothed, and made completely of crystal-clear ice. Her hair was jointed and spiky, made of crystals that tinkled when she turned, and when she opened her mouth it was filled with needle-like icicle teeth. Her voice was the soft chiming that Veil had been hearing all along.

"Greetings," said Sybian. "We've never met, but I've been watching you for some time."

Corvus rounded on her, his hand on his sword, and Isobel dropped into a fighting stance. Veil waved her hands frantically.

"Wait, you don't understand . . ."

"Who in the name of the gods are you?" growled the swordsman.

"My name is Sybian," said Sybian, who had made no move to respond. "As I said, I've been watching you for some time."

"And providing timely assistance where necessary?" Corvus straightened up.

"Indeed."

"The ice-dragon in Corsa." Corvus ticked off points on his fingers. "These two hounds in the battle against Shuzan." He tilted his head. "What about the dragon at the Diem camp? That one was attacking Veil."

"That was conjured by one of the Diem shamans," Sybian lied smoothly. Veil opened her mouth to object, then thought better of it and stayed silent.

"So you're Veil's bottled genie." Corvus snorted. "I don't get it. Why should we trust you?"

"You just said I've been helping you all along." Sybian gave him her best smile, which was pretty horrible. "Why shouldn't you?"

"You're a demon," said Corvus shortly. "Demons don't do anything unless it's in their own interest or because some sorcerer ordered them to. Why did you sic your dogs on Saya?"

Saya? Veil was puzzled. *How does he know that name?*

"She was decimating our side of the battle, if you recall. I had to do something."

"I could have handled her."

"You seemed unwilling to do so."

"Please," said Veil. "Can we avoid a swordfight, here?"

"So what do you want?" growled Corvus.

Sybian affected a sigh. "Fine. I will admit to an ulterior motive. I need you to do me a little favor."

"A favor?"

"In exchange for which, I'll help you capture Kagerin Shuzan and get every answer you need."

"Why should I listen to you?"

"You can't get through that door without my help."

Corvus glanced sideways at Isobel, who nodded. The girl stooped, picked up a branch from the forest floor, and tossed it into the curtain. There was a crackle and a spit of light, and the branch vanished into a wisp of smoke. Corvus nodded, as though he'd expected it to do that, and turned back to Sybian.

"And you can get us in?"

"Of course. I'd hardly have dragged you all this way if I couldn't."

Corvus' lip twisted. He obviously objected to the thought of being dragged anywhere. "How?"

"I have one of the six keys. The one that belonged to the Frost King, before I killed him."

"I have no idea what you're talking about."

"Watch." Sybian walked around Corvus and stepped directly in to the curtain. The purple sparks flowed around her, as though they had a natural repulsion to her body. When she raised her arms, the bottom half of the archway was clear. "See? There's nothing to it."

Corvus stared a moment, then turned to Veil. "What do you think?"

"What do *I* think?" Veil raised an eyebrow. "What do you mean?"

"You've been talking with this crazy demon the whole time, right?"

"Right." It was admitting she'd lied, which made Veil feel oddly chagrined. "I . . . I have."

"So can we trust her?"

No! was Veil's first thought. *But without Sybian, Corvus won't find what he's looking for. And she's helped us so far. Maybe all she honestly wants from him is a favor . . .*

What ultimately decided her was a very different thought. *If it comes down to Sybian versus Corvus, I know where my bets will be.*

"I think we can. A little. She obviously wants something here, but she needs our help to get it."

"Okay." He turned to Isobel. "You agree?"

"Sure." She raised an eyebrow. "When did you get so democratic?"

"When this whole situation turned weird."

"That was a *long* while back," sighed Veil. "You're a bit late."

"For the moment," Corvus said to Sybian, "we'll help you. But I want to know what's going on *before* it happens."

"As you wish." The ice spirit smiled. "Kaal. Kuul."

The two huge ice-hounds passed through the Gate, one by one. They had to crouch almost to the ground to fit underneath. The three humans followed, Veil bringing up the rear. She caught a glimpse of a hallway, and then darkness closed in as Sybian let the curtain fall behind them.

"Give it a moment," came the chiming voice. "Let your eyes adapt."

"I can see fine," growled Corvus, stalking past the two dogs. "Come on . . ."

"Wait . . ."

Whaum. Purple mist rolled from the walls, solidifying quickly into a half dozen armed figures with blank, alabaster faces. Corvus' sword flashed from its sheath, faster than thought, and a moment later a half dozen golden great swords clattered to the floor, quickly dissolving back into purple mist.

"Damn it." The swordsman turned back toward Sybian. "Any other surprises?"

"There are more of them." The spirit pointed. "A lot more."

Purple mist was indeed flowing out of the walls again, crystallizing into rank after rank of caryatids. This time the two ice hounds surged forward to meet them, brushing past Corvus. The spirits shredded their way through the ranks of the guardians, whose golden great swords bounced ineffectually from the dog's flanks or chipped little bits of ice from their shoulders, which only seemed to make them angrier. They bounded forward, eventually vanishing around the curve of the passageway, but the sounds of combat continued.

Sybian gestured, calmly. "Shall we proceed?"

Kɪᴛ ᴅᴏᴠᴇ, ᴛʜᴇɴ ducked. A golden great sword whistled through the space where her head had been and bounced off the inde-structible rock wall. The draekere ran the caryatid through and let it slide off her blade, already dissolving into purple mist. No more seemed to be following, so Kit let herself slump back against the wall, gasping for breath. She worried the bandage on her neck—apparently the exertion had broken open the scabs from where the demon had clawed her.

You know, Wing Kitsu, if I didn't know any better I'd say you had no idea where we were going. She'd been forced in the opposite di-rection Jyo-raku had taken, as though the guardians had been purposely trying to separate them. *Maybe they are. Divide and con-quer. Split off the weak ones and kill them.* She let out a long breath in relative silence. *They're not doing such a great job now, though. Maybe Jyo-raku's got them distracted.*

So where am I? Kit took a moment to look around. They'd ducked into a small, square chamber with an arched doorway at either end. The flat sides held a pair of statues—one depict-ed a stern-looking father figure, holding a gnarled staff in one hand, while the other showed a kindly grandmother, down on one knee.

El and Zetz. Gods of the Imperial pantheon. This is supposed to be their tomb. Fair enough.

So what's the game plan? Find Kei, and get the hell out of here. She silenced the thought that asked, 'to where?' *Away. The key is away.*

The clatter of footsteps on stone made her reach for her sword. Seconds later, three caryatids burst into the room, driv-en backward by something that resembled nothing so much as a horse-sized dog composed entirely of ice. It had a mane, a long strip of pointed ice crystals, and as she watched it crushed the torso of one of the guardians between its jaws.

Kit backpedaled. With one of their number disintegrating into purple mist, the other two guardians attacked. One golden blade glanced off the dog's muzzle, but the other bit deep into the ice of its shoulder. The spirit howled and smashed the guardian against the wall with one paw, where it splattered. The other managed a last swing, shaving off a little bit more ice, before it was similarly disposed of.

Then the spirit turned to Kit, who'd backed up as far as she could go. She held her sword in front of her, in what she hoped was a non-threatening way.

So where did this guy come from? She hadn't seen any ice-spirits in the tomb as of yet. *And he's fighting the guardians. I suppose it's too much to think that he might actually be on our side?* She lowered her blade, carefully, then raised it hastily as the ice hound took a heavy step forward. It looked as though it couldn't decide what to do about her.

"Nice doggy?" said Kit, hopefully.

The hound raised its paw. Kit's blade licked out, instinctively, but did little more than chip a bit from the thing's foreleg. It caught her in the side, flinging her across the entire room to crash heavily into the opposite wall and slump to the floor.

Oddly enough, she felt no pain, just a gentle numbness. Kit lay in a heap, unable to do anything except strain for air, and felt the blood soaking her shirt with a clinical detachment.

So this is the end. Not what I'd expected, I'll admit. The thought of Kei wormed its way in, but Kit dismissed it. *She'll be fine. She has Jyo-raku to protect her. Just relax, Kitsu Meru, and enjoy dying.* She opened her eyes to find the hound standing over her, its freezing breath raising goose bumps on her face. *Goodbye, Zaneh.*

There was a sudden cacophony, as though a thousand voices

had screamed all at once, and the chamber resonated to the impossible drone of a million bees. The hound paused, leaned drunkenly to one side, and collapsed, its body already starting to melt into a puddle. Kit took a deep breath, feeling the pain in her chest for the first time, and let it out as a sigh.

Not yet?

Then another figure entered her field of view, extending a hand.

"Are you all right?"

Kit found enough voice for a croak. "I don't think so."

"Think you can stand up?"

"I can try."

She willed exhausted muscles into action. Any attempt to move her left arm produced shots of overwhelming pain, so she took the man's hand with her right. Her eyes were gradually focusing. She found herself holding the hand of a Khaev lord, and one she recognized, at that.

"Lord Kagerin!" *He came for Kei, after all.* And in his other hand—*the Bound Blade! Jyo-raku was leaving it for* him.

He pulled her to her feet, and to her surprise she managed to remain upright with a little help from the wall. It took her mind a little while to get over the idea that she wasn't about to die, but once it had, it presented her with a rather urgent list of injuries, all clamoring for attention. A deep cut on her stomach was responsible for most of the bleeding, and her arm hung useless at her side.

Lord Kagerin was looking at her and thinking.

"You're Kitsu Meru."

"Yes, my lord."

"Where's Wing Leader Keimani?"

"I wish I knew. Last I saw Jyo-raku was dragging her off."

"She's here in the tomb? Is she all right?"

"As far as I know."

"We have to find her." He cleared his throat, suddenly aware that his concern might not be easily explicable. "I . . ."

"Relax." Kit shrugged, with only one shoulder. "She told me."

"Ah." He let out a long breath. "Do you think you can walk? If you stay near me, I don't think the guardians will bother you. They seem to respect the Blade."

And no wonder, thought Kit, glancing at the decomposing remains of the ice-spirit. "I'll have to walk, won't I? But help me bind my arm."

"Is it broken?"

"It certainly feels like it."

Shuzan shrugged off his cloak and sliced it into strips with the Blade. A few moments of horrible agony later, Kit's arm was bound to her side and mostly immobilized. Another strap was wrapped around her stomach, to absorb the blood. Her legs, thankfully, had sustained only bruises, and she was able to walk without much trouble once the world had stopped spinning around her.

"I don't suppose you have any idea where to go?" Shuzan peeked around the corner. A pair of caryatids saw him, bowed, and flashed back into purple mist. Kit followed, cautiously.

"Not really. I was running for my life."

"The layout of this place doesn't make any sense."

"Jyo-raku said that all paths lead to the Trap."

"What's the Trap?"

"I have no idea, but it's where he was going."

"So we just pick a direction and start walking?"

"I guess."

Shuzan shrugged and started down the corridor, with Kit close behind him. Her mind still felt numb. *Kei. I'm glad I didn't die. I'd like the chance to kiss her a little more thoroughly.*

525

KEI AND JYO-RAKU turned another corner to find a hallway that dead-ended in a door, the first one they'd seen in the tomb. It was guarded by another half dozen of the caryatids. Kei winced, involuntarily, as the shadow spirit tore into the them, razor-sharp tendrils of darkness flaying about him too fast to follow. Once they were gone, she stepped up behind him.

The thought of escaping had crossed her mind, of course. But she'd been unable to keep track of the twists and turns Jyo-raku had taken, which meant that she didn't stand much of a chance of finding the way out. *Not to mention the guardians would get me. So it appears I'm stuck with him for the duration.*

I hope Kit's okay. She tried to imagine the younger draekere lying skewered in some corridor, gasping out her last breath, but the picture wouldn't come; that was some small comfort. *I'm sure she's fine. She's too stubborn to just up and die. And Shuzan . . .*

The portal was wooden, a set of arch-shaped double doors without handles or ornamentation. Jyo-raku touched them, and they swung inwards, revealing a room beyond. The shadow spirit strode in, without hesitation, and Kei hurried after him.

The room was shaped like a half-circle, with a high, vaulted ceiling that gave off more of the twilight radiance that illuminated the whole tomb. On the curved side, doors alternated with little alcoves, with each alcove bearing an exquisitely detailed statue of one of the Imperial gods. There were six statues, of course, and seven doors; she and Jyo-raku had entered from the left-most.

The other side of the room, the flat side, had but a single door in the center. It was larger than any of the others, and, while they were plain, it was inscribed with the same complicated sigils that adorned Heaven's Gate. Kei was starting to recognize what that signified—*another ward. What's* in *here, that needs so much protection?*

Jyo-raku's expression was invisible as always, but she definitely got the impression that he was smiling.

"This is it?" Kei looked around the empty room.

"This is the antechamber. The Trap itself, as you can probably guess, is behind that door."

"So are we're going in?"

"I cannot." Jyo-raku shrugged. "The ward excludes all sorcery and spirits, and is exceedingly powerful. I doubt anyone alive today could break it."

"So you're going to send a human in?" Jyo-raku had pulled that trick before, after all, at the caves that held the Bound Blade.

"Yes."

"Me?"

He gave a hissing chuckle. "No. Godsdoom was designed to protect the Trap forever. Bound behind that door is the Guardian, who makes the minor spirits we've been fighting up until now look like campfires beside the sun. The gods assumed that no human could defeat him, and no spirit could pass the warding, so their precious construction would be safe for all time." Jyo-raku spread his arms, as though he were stretching, and his dark aura extended to fill the room. "I'm afraid they underestimated you."

There's someone I need him to kill. Kei's mouth went dry. "You want Shuzan to go in there for you."

"Bearing the Bound Blade, created by the gods themselves. The Guardian will fall, and the road to the Trap will open."

"And then what?"

"Then, silly human." Jyo-raku leaned close to her, until she could smell his odor of old, wet stone. "Then the accumulated power of sixty centuries will be mine. This time there will be only one god, and no mistakes."

Two of the doors on the curved side of the room slammed inward simultaneously. Kei and Jyo-raku both whipped around. *Shuzan!*

Kagerin Shuzan was indeed emerging from one of the doors, the Bound Blade held in front of him. Its bizarre buzz filled the room, resonating at odd intervals that made Kei's teeth rattle. Behind him, battered but very much alive, was Kit; Kei felt a knot in her stomach relax. *Thank you, Shuzan. Thank you.*

It was on the other door, though, that Jyo-raku focused his attention. There were three people, none of whom Kei recognized—two girls and a swordsman in black—followed by an ice-spirit. The spirit was in the form of a young woman, made entirely of clear crystal; her hair chimed gently as she moved.

Jyo-raku ignored the three humans, focusing immediately on the other spirit. His normal hiss deepened to a kind of growl.

"Sybian."

"None other." The ice-spirit pushed past the surprised-looking swordsman and bowed. "You don't look happy to see me, Jyo-raku."

Kei felt his dark aura around her again, dragging her to the shadow spirit's side. Her arms were bound by ropes of shadow, and she could only watch helplessly as Jyo-raku turned to Shuzan.

"Kagerin Shuzan. Listen very carefully if you want your sister to live."

Shuzan! There was a gag across her mouth, as well. Kei couldn't even speak.

"What do you want?" Shuzan didn't lower the Bound Blade or take his eyes off the shadow spirit. He'd spared the other party of newcomers only a glance.

"Kill them." Jyo-raku gestured at the ice spirit. "Kill them all."

Saya materialized from pure light, standing outside Heaven's Gate. It was as close as she could get to the Trap without taking physical form. The purple sparks of the Gate swirled madly, as though disturbed by so many recent passages. They swirled aside as Saya stalked through.

I am Lady Light. The guardians of the tomb barely had a chance to form before they were blasted aside by focused brilliance. Saya ran through the corridors of Godsdoom, hurrying desperately toward the Trap. *The oldest spirit in the world.*

Corvus must be stopped.

chapter 20

> "This is the end of things, my friends. We have come
> to the end of days."
>
> —Van Seiger, Imperial general, after the
> report of the Imperial defeat at Tsankuun

KILL THEM ALL." Those words seemed to freeze the scene.
Veil leaned closer to Isobel and whispered. "Do you
have any idea what's going on?"

"The guy with the sword is Kagerin Shuzan."

"You mentioned him before . . ."

"He's a Khaev lord. And Fifty-Fourth of Two Hundred."

"Which means?"

"There are only fifty-three sword masters in the world who
can beat him. If you believe the Khaevs. But Corvus stopped
him cold last time."

"During the battle?"

"Right."

Corvus pushed forward and stepped in front of Sybian, who
showed no eagerness to confront the Khaev and his strange,
buzzing sword. Jyo-raku laughed: a horrible, choking sound.

"Still getting everyone else to do your fighting for you, Sybian? What purpose does it serve to have this mortal die first?"

"Unlike you, Jyo-raku," the ice spirit chimed, "I have been
paying attention."

This seemed to anger the shadow further. "Shuzan! Kill him!"

The two men locked eyes, and something passed between them. Corvus' hand dropped to his own blade.

"I find it irritating to be ordered into battle." Shuzan dropped smoothly into a guard position, his strange blade humming as it moved. "But I'm glad to have the opportunity to continue our little challenge."

Corvus smiled. "Likewise."

"Will you answer a question for me?"

The swordsman in black shrugged. "If I can."

"Are you the real Corvus?"

There was a long pause.

"Funny," said Corvus finally. "I was going to ask the same thing of you."

Both forms blurred, and the two met in the center of the room, mortal blade scraping against god-forged steel. The hum of Shuzan's otherworldly sword rose to an anguished scream, and a shower of sparks flickered and died against the flagstones underfoot. The air was suddenly filled with the tang of hot ozone.

As though operating on some unseen signal, the two men sprang apart, then came back together, the space between them filled with a complex pattern of flashing steel too fast to follow. Veil stared, her heart in her throat, as the fatal dance went on and on.

Corvus will be fine. Her breath caught as Shuzan's blade broke past Corvus' parry and licked out at head height; the black swordsman dropped underneath it, then lunged upward in a powerful thrust that came close to skewering his opponent. *He'll be fine. He's the greatest sword master there is, no matter what the Khaevs say.*

531

KEI STARED AT the battle, helplessly. At first she'd felt nearly as confident as Jyo-raku—*as if some Imperial swordsman could stand against one of the Two Hundred!* A few moments of watching Corvus had knocked the ground from under her.

Who is *he?* Shuzan was strong, fast, and incredibly well-trained, but it was as though Corvus was on another scale entirely. Every time Shuzan came close to matching him, the swordsman simply got faster, until his sword was nothing but a flashing blur and Shuzan was parrying madly for his life.

She wanted to scream. *Shuzan!* Kei's eyes misted over with tears of frustration. She did, however, notice what everyone else had missed. The girl in black—tall, gangly, with no figure to speak of—was creeping, step by cautious step, toward the door that led to the Trap.

ISOBEL HAD BLINKED, a moment after Veil had turned away from her, and when she opened her eyes she was in another place.

It wasn't a place, precisely—more of a *non-place*, the details barely sketched in. All that mattered was the occupant—a silvery metal giant, topping her by two heads or more, its jointed armor spurting little gouts of flame as it moved. Instead of a visor, there was a blank metal faceplate, but she could feel its gaze nevertheless. It was a figure she recognized, from the worst of her nightmares.

"Who *are* you?" Isobel tried to suppress a shiver, despite the heat that wrapped the creature like a cloak. When it spoke, its voice was the bass roar of a bonfire, the cracks and pops of burning wood.

"Vaalkir."

"What are you doing to me?" Isobel put on as brave an expression as she could. The cool, emotionless certainty that had served her all her life seemed to be draining away, replaced with the unfamiliar taste of fear. She could feel bile rising in the back of her throat. "Get out of my mind!"

"Are you certain you want to be rid of me?" The thing—a spirit, she had to assume—leaned forward. "I've been with you, Isobel. Always. I took a little girl a few weeks from death's door and turned her into you. Something to respect."

"You.." Isobel's voice dropped away, to a whisper. "You gave me . . ."

"I gave you a purpose. I gave you a reason for living. I gave you the armor you needed."

"What happened?" "I have been inconvenienced. Your mind proved an adequate hiding place." The spirit waved a gauntleted hand. "But that means nothing. You've have been working all your life, Isobel, to reach this point."

"All my life?"

"The one you must face is behind that door."

The one. The one man who can beat me. She saw her endless search for the best of the best in flashes—blood spraying from a slit throat, a woman's shocked expression as she clutched the dagger buried in her womb, the last shiver of an old man's hands pressed against hers as he died. *The end. This is the end?*

"You used me." Isobel crossed her arms, and shivered.

"I helped you. Without me you'd be dead a dozen times over by now."

"And how many people would still be alive?" Without the comforting insulation of the spirit's artificial detachment, a thousand staring faces rolled over Isobel all at once. She felt tears welling in her eyes. *Another unfamiliar sensation. I haven't cried since . . . since . . .*

"Since you came!" She turned from Vaalkir, felt his presence start to recede.

"Ah well," said the bass rumble. "Luckily, your cooperation

is not required."

Isobel screamed in agony as a white-hot metal gauntlet ripped through her mind.

VEIL ONLY NOTICED once the big doors opened. She caught a glimpse of Isobel disappearing behind them before they swung closed again, clicking shut with a crackle of arcane power. Both Sybian and Jyo-raku seemed to notice at nearly the same instant. Sybian put on an expression of calculation, as though thinking furiously, but the shadow spirit screamed in frustration.

"Her! Shuzan, kill her!"

Shuzan could not have obeyed, even if he were so inclined. Corvus had backed him against one wall, and now he had nowhere left to retreat to. A final surge had bought him a moment to breathe, but his strength was flagging, while the black swordsman's stamina seemed limitless. It was only a matter of time. Shuzan finally extended himself a bit too far, trying desperately to get a blow in between parries. Corvus' blade flashed against his hand, and the humming sword skittered across the room. The Khaev lord looked up, his expression unreadable. Veil couldn't have said whether he expected Corvus to cut him dead on the spot or not. His eyes were on the Khaev girl in leather that the shadow spirit held. Shuzan started to say something, but before he could finish Corvus slammed the hilt of his blade against the Khaev's head. Shuzan's knees buckled, and he slipped to the floor.

"That's impossible." Jyo-raku stared at Corvus. "Impossible. Who are you?"

"Corvus." The swordsman leveled his blade at the spirit's head. "I want some answers."

Jyo-raku responded with a snarl and a wave of his hand. A hundred darts of pure shadow flashed toward Corvus, but

before they could arrive a wave of light washed over the swordsman, obliterating the projectiles in mid-flight. Another door on
the curved wall had slammed open, revealing a young woman
with golden skin and long, silver hair.

"Saya!" Jyo-raku's voice was a shriek.

"I think we have all had just about enough of you." The
newcomer raised her hand. Jyo-raku countered with another
hail of shadow-darts, but none of them got close. The beam of
light Saya produced burned them away and caught the shadow
spirit square in the chest. His dark aura bubbled and frothed to
nothing under the brilliant radiance, and after one last despairing scream, Jyo-raku boiled away into a mist of shadows.

KEI FELT THE bonds holding her relax, and she almost managed to keep her feet when she dropped to the floor. Instead she
ended up staggering back against one wall, breathing hard. Kit
was there before Kei thought to look for her, propping her up
with her good arm.

"Wing Leader?" The girl's voice was anxious. "Are you
all right?"

"Shuzan," Kei breathed. "Shuzan."

"I think he's okay. That Corvus guy just knocked him out,
looks like."

Kei blinked, tears welling again. Kit was still surveying the
scene with interest.

"So who's the new one? Saya?"

"Do you have any idea what's going on?"

"I'm starting to get an inkling."

ISOBEL BLINKED, AND the massive double doors slammed closed
behind her.

What happened? The last thing she remembered was Vaalkir's

535

hand reaching into the core of her soul and *tearing* . . .

Gods! She sank to her knees, eyes closed. *What did he do to me?*

A soundless moment passed. Eventually Isobel got back up and wiped her eyes.

Okay. I feel like the same person. Though if I wasn't, how would I know? Vaalkir seems to be gone for the moment. So where am I?

The double doors, featureless on this side, were closed. She reached out to touch them, as an experiment, but they didn't budge. *No handles, nothing to get a grip on, and they probably weigh about a ton each. So I can't get back that way.*

She took a deep breath and turned around; most of the breath escaped in a gasp.

What in the Aether . . .

The surface she was standing on—the same perfectly-smooth stone that made up the rest of the tomb—was part of a bridge, hovering without support over a gaping void. It was perhaps ten feet wide and a hundred long, and ended at a cylindrical platform that also simply hung in the air. Floating over the center of the platform at about head height was a small sphere of almost perfectly transparent crystal, only visible because of the slight distortion of light passing through it. Past that, she could see the other wall of the chamber. Given the design of the tomb as a whole, Isobel guessed she was inside a sphere, with the glowing marble occupying the exact center. She edged closer to the side of the bridge—there was no railing, nothing to prevent one from toppling over the side—and confirmed this theory; the bottom of the chamber was another hundred feet below. She swallowed, and thanked the gods that she'd never had any problems with heights.

At the end of the bridge, sitting cross-legged on the platform, was a human figure draped in a heavy cloak. Isobel watched it for a moment, then shrugged. *There doesn't seem to be anywhere else to go.* Her footsteps echoed oddly in the giant sphere, and as she got closer the figure shrugged off its cloak and got slowly to his feet.

He was an old man, of the type usually described as 'spry.' His hair was pure white, as was his magnificent brush of a mustache, and his limbs held a kind of wiry strength rather than fragility. His expression was kindly, and a lively intelligence twinkled in his wrinkled blue eyes. Something about his smile, though, carried an odd undertone of regret. He was dressed simply, in loose-fitting grays, and had an unornamented sword sheathed on his left hip.

Isobel kept her hands away from her own weapons, for the moment, since the man didn't seem at all aggressive. Her mouth had gone dry. *The one. Vaalkir said he'd be waiting. This old guy, then?*

It could be. No assumptions. This is the most magical place on the continent. He could be anything.

"A girl." The old man had a surprisingly deep voice; it sounded like he was used to barking commands and having them obeyed. For all that, his tone was friendly. "That's a bit of a surprise."

Isobel raised one hand and waved, feeling idiotic. "H . . . Hello."

"What's your name, girl?"

"Isobel." There didn't seem to be any harm in telling him.

"Isobel. Odd name. I probably should have expected that, though." He stretched, and she could hear the muscles in his shoulders pop. "I'm Dominarius Zetz."

"Dominarius?"

"Does it sound odd to you?" He tilted his head, then chuckled. "I imagine it would. How long has it been?"

"How long since what?"

"Since the end of the war."

Which war? The Khaev invasion? Or . . . Her brain finally caught up with the conversation. *The Godswar. Has he been in here since the end of the Godswar?*

She cleared her throat. "A little more than six thousand years."

"That long?" He kicked his cloak back onto the platform and stretched again, bending over to touch his toes. "I'm surprised. I figured one, two thousand years at the outside."

"Have you really been in here for six thousand years?"

"Something like that." He cracked his knuckles. "Spent a lot of time sleeping, of course."

"And I'm the first person you've seen?"

"The second," he corrected. "One man got in here—I guess it must be almost three thousand years ago, now—funny little foreign fellow. I had a nice long chat with him. Apparently things have really fallen apart out there."

She shook her head. "What are you doing here?"

"He didn't even tell you that?"

"Who didn't?"

"Whoever brought you here. One of the big ones, I imagine—Samukyne, Kuron, Saya, Ghael, one of that lot."

"Vaalkir," said Isobel, feeling a sudden chill. "His name is Vaalkir."

"Vaalkir?" Dominarius grunted. "Never heard of him. I guess things change even for spirits, in six thousand years. But he didn't tell you how things are?"

"No." *He just told me—* "I think he wants me to kill you."

"Of course he does." Dominarius hooked a thumb over his shoulder. "That's the Trap. I'm the Guardian. I guard it, as you might have guessed. More precisely, I guard the ward that keeps spirits out of this place."

"Why?"

"Why?" He shrugged. "When a god asks you to do something, girl, it's not like you have a choice."

"A god?"

"The gods built this place, and they put me here to guard it. Anybody wants to get in, they have to go through me. The ward keeps spirits out, so they have to get humans to try it for them."

"Vaalkir wants me to . . ."

"Kill me, yes." He rolled his neck, which emitted an audible crack. "Ah. That feels so good."

"But . . ."

"You about ready, girl? 'Cause I was having a nice dream I'm about ready to get back to."

"You mean . . . now?"

"Yup." He drew his sword, and the twilight glow of the tomb glittered on the razor edge. It was a straight-bladed, Imperial design, longer than a modern short sword and a good deal heavier. Dominarius dropped into an unfamiliar position, one foot forward and his body turned sideways, and smiled at her. "It's nothing personal, you understand?"

"Right." Isobel's blades leapt into her hands almost of their own accord. "I understand."

"Excellent! I don't have any intention of being unsporting about this."

"You," said Corvus, "need to start explaining things."

Saya turned to him, her attitude imperious. "I don't like being threatened . . ."

"I wasn't threatening you."

"Oh?"

Corvus opened his hand, letting the sword of the First of Two Hundred clatter to the floor. His foot lashed out, and the

Bound Blade leapt into the air with a buzz and dropped into his waiting palm.

"*Now* I'm threatening you. Answers, Saya. Now. For starters, why do I know your name?"

"I left it to you." If Veil didn't know better, she would have thought the spirit was showing genuine emotion, as though fighting to keep tears from her eyes. "I couldn't bear to take it."

"Take it?" Corvus' voice was a hiss, nearly matching Jyoraku's. "So you're responsible for what happened to me?"

"In a sense, I am responsible for everything that has ever happened to you." Saya sighed. "I created you, after all."

"Wait, wait." Veil stepped up beside Corvus; the swordsman glanced at her, his eyes unreadable, but stayed silent. "You *created* him? Corvus isn't a spirit. He may be a bit weird, but he's still flesh and blood."

"He is, and he isn't." Saya shook her head. "It's a long story . . ."

"Talk. Nobody's going anywhere."

"Perhaps in private . . ."

"Talk."

"Very well." Saya took a long breath—for appearances, Veil suspected—and began. "I am Saya, the Lady Light, one of the founding members of the alliance of spirits that destroyed the gods. I am more than six thousand years old, and I have seen . . ."

"Get to the point." He waved the Blade.

" . . . I have *seen* the games that my kind play with yours repeated, over and over. We set ourselves up as deities, fight wars through human proxies, encourage you to worship, adore, and protect us. After six thousand years, I started to ask myself, *why?*"

"It took six thousand years?" asked Veil.

"Introspection does not come naturally to my kind. But eventually, I realized that we had lapsed into stasis. The oldest of us never changed, never grew, and never died, unless they chose to or were pulled down by younger spirits who only went on to take their place. So I began to experiment. There wasn't enough power in the world to support a spirit much greater than myself, so I reasoned that some other element must be needed.

"I found a human woman, in the act of conception, and I added something—extra. A portion of my essence. She died, of course. It took me nearly a hundred years to get everything right, but eventually I managed to produce something absolutely, impossibly new."

"Me, you mean?" growled Corvus.

Saya nodded. "Mostly human, but not quite. I hoped you would have a human's ability to adapt, combined with the power and immortality of a spirit. You were raised by humans, but I kept track of you, adjusted things so you would follow the proper path . . ."

There was a hoarse laugh from the corner of the room, and everyone's heads turned. Kagerin Shuzan got slowly to his feet, massaging his head with one hand.

"You had no idea what you were doing, did you?" He laughed again, through a dry throat. "Just experimenting. What do the lives of humans matter, anyway? And you created a monster."

"Corvus is not a monster!" insisted Veil, grabbing at the swordsman's sleeve.

"Unfortunately, Lord Kagerin is correct. Corvus was, in many aspects, everything I'd hoped for. But as his power grew . . ." She shook her head.

"Ebon Death." Shuzan whispered the words.

DOMINARIUS ADVANCED SLOWLY, shuffling his feet so as never to be off balance. Isobel remained where she was, blades crossed in front of her, feeling a touch of the old excitement. While Vaalkir himself was gone, something remained. It had been burned into her, over a decade and through hundreds of deaths. Watching the old man's stance, she felt a thrill—the uncertainty of something new. *That this, finally, might be the one.*

But this is the one. The one I'm supposed to kill, the one Vaalkir ordered me to kill. After all these years . . .

Dominarius attacked, a simple thrust—lazy, slow, easy to parry. Isobel knocked it aside and twisted inside his grip, sliding one blade along his to keep it outside her and bringing one toward his throat. It was a move that was close to reflex for her, but it took many opponents by surprise.

The old man wasn't even fazed. He let her blade slide until it caught on his hilt, ducked under her other knife, and grabbed her wrist with his free hand. With the leverage this gave him he turned around completely, sending her spinning away from him like a ballroom dancer. Isobel took a moment to regain her footing, stopping dangerously close to the edge of the bridge. The old man raised his sword in a salute, smiled, and dropped back into a guard position.

Why bother? His style seemed too . . .showy, perhaps. *Why not just drive me to the ground and disarm me?*

This time she launched the attack, a two-handed feint to his mid-section. Dominarius wasn't fooled. He stepped aside and aimed a cut at her head, which she checked with one blade while she poked at him with the other. Her stroke *barely* missed his side, and once again he spun past her, tapping her shoulder lightly with his free hand and dancing back into a guard position.

"You're not bad at all," the old man mused. "Not at all."

Isobel felt herself getting angry. "I could hardly have gotten here otherwise."

"True enough." He smiled. "Capable *and* spunky. Why, if I were ten years younger . . ."

He trailed off.

"If you were ten years younger?"

"I'd be six thousand, one hundred and sixty eight. So I suppose it wouldn't make much of a difference after all."

Isobel gritted her teeth. "I can see why they were so eager to lock you up in a tomb."

"Aw." He mimed regret. "You have to permit me my fun, girl! It might be another three thousand years until my next visitor. I've got to take my entertainment while I can."

She rushed him with a flurry of blows, which he checked one after another, dancing backward and grinning like a fool. They'd exchanged positions, so she was forcing him toward the double doors. Long before he got there, though, he stopped as though he'd put his back to a stone wall, blocking her every move. Eventually, Isobel was forced to retreat a few steps, if only to give some respite to her aching arms. Through all of this, Dominarius hadn't attacked once.

"*Very* good. I'm impressed."

Isobel was panting. "I . . . don't appreciate . . . being toyed with."

"Are you *that* eager to die, girl?"

Not anymore. But I hate games. She resumed her guard position, and he did likewise. Dominarius shrugged. "I'd never keep someone here against their will. So when you get tired of this, let me know."

"I'm tired of it already."

"As you wish."

Isobel raised her knives against the attack that had to be coming, but Dominarius' form blurred in between one breath and the next. She moved to parry, frantically, but the old man was so fast that a dozen swords seemed to be coming at her at once. Turning awkwardly in mid-step, Isobel lost her footing and stumbled backwards. She could *feel* the abyss behind her, pulling almost viscerally. Dominarius' free hand shot out and grabbed her wrist, yanking her back on to the bridge; at the same time, his other hand thrust.

There was a moment of shocked silence, and then Isobel let her blades clatter to the floor. Her hands moved, almost involuntarily, to her stomach, tapping the cool metal that protruded there as though she couldn't believe that it was real. She took a deep breath, and felt the warm wetness spreading. A moment later her legs gave out, and Dominarius lowered her gently to the floor.

"Sorry about that, girl." The old man put one foot on her shoulder and pulled his sword out with a wet shlick. "You did say, though."

Isobel closed her eyes, her hands clenched over the wound, and tried to relax.

This is it. This *is how it's supposed to be.*

Somewhere in the deep recesses of her mind, Vaalkir gave a last bass scream and faded away forever.

"Ebon Death?" This came from Kei, who had gotten to her feet. "What do you mean, Ebon Death?"

"Ebon Death is a kid's story," said Veil. "An evil man who lives in shadows and take bad children away in the night." She looked at the draekere, curiously. "I didn't know the Khaevs believed in him."

"We don't, really." Kei shrugged. "The same kind of stories. He's supposed to be the incarnation of vengeance, who brings death to those who don't obey their masters."

"The Diem believe," Saya put in, "that Ebon Death is a servant of the true masters of the universe, and comes to destroy those who have brushed too close to the truth."

"And you're telling me he's real?" Kei turned to Shuzan. "This fairy tale?"

"The fairy tale is standing in front of you." Shuzan gestured. "But . . ."

"There is a secret history, dating back more than two hundred years." He rubbed his head again. "Locked inside the vault of the Two Hundred in our fortress at Saido. It tells the story of peasant boy who rose from nothing to become the First of Two Hundred. He always dressed in black, and called himself Ebon Death. Nothing and no one could stand against him, and he ruled our order with an iron fist. Even the great families were subject to his whims. He fought his way into the Noboru household and killed their leader, single-handedly, despite being assailed by half a hundred men. In the end, he left because he claimed to be bored with Khaevar. Took a ship and vanished."

Veil tugged on Corvus' sleeve. "You don't remember any of this, do you?"

"No." Corvus kept the Blade pointed at Saya. "I'm afraid not."

"Once we took over the Empire," Shuzan continued, "the scholars among us wondered what had happened to him. Much to our surprise, there was a trail to follow: a trail of legends and stories, about a whirlwind demon named Ebon Death who raged across the land with the force of a summer gale. The riverlanders had heard of him, and the Diem, and even the people of the Red Hills. But there the trail ended. What do the Red Hills people say about him?"

"That he lived among the people," said Veil slowly. "And that one day, he walked into the high desert, and now he lives only in the dark places between what is and what isn't . . ."

"Two hundred years distorts matters." Shuzan shrugged. "But the man himself walked into the desert and never came back."

"And this was me." Corvus shook his head dismissively. "You're saying this was me, this terror of a continent? That's ridiculous."

"Right!" said Veil, embarrassingly loudly. She felt herself blushing, and tried to remind herself how ridiculous it was. *I mean, now is* not *the time.*

"How else could he have beaten me?" asked Shuzan. "Ebon Death was the First of Two Hundred."

"Just because Corvus is better than you doesn't make him a monster out of some storybook!" Veil retorted. "You just can't accept that there might be someone outside your precious Two Hundred who's worth a damn . . ."

"Unfortunately, Lord Kagerin is right," interjected Saya. "Corvus acquired the nickname Ebon Death. In addition to the power of a spirit, he had also apparently inherited our cruelty. Since I had unleashed him, I felt that it fell to me to remedy the situation."

"But you couldn't take the easy way out," chimed Sybian softly. Veil look back at her, startled. She'd almost forgotten the ice spirit was there. "You could have destroyed him then."

"I admit to a certain . . . reticence." Saya shifted uncomfortably. "He was my creation! It's only natural."

"Natural for a human, perhaps." Sybian sneered. "You've spent so much time around them you've picked things up . . ."

"Enough." Corvus flicked the Blade briefly in Sybian's direction, then back to Saya. "What happened?"

"I met you in the desert and placed you under a warding, a very special one of my own design."

"To erase my memories?"

"Yes. I planned to start the experiment over, as it were."

"So you are responsible."

"But only because I couldn't stand by and let you be a scourge upon the land . . ."

"I don't believe it." Veil shook her head. "I *know* Corvus. He's not anything like that."

"*This* Corvus isn't." Saya shook her head. "You've never met Ebon Death."

"Tell him the rest, Saya," said Sybian.

"The rest?" Corvus looked at Saya. "What does she mean?"

"You have to understand . . ." Saya began, but Sybian cut her off.

"The warding on the door to the Trap was created by the gods themselves. It's more powerful than anything any spirit could build, and it's specifically designed to keep out spirits and their creations. Walk through that door, Corvus, and Saya's ward will be blown away."

Corvus turned his head. "What's the catch?"

"The catch," said Saya, "is that you'll turn back into Ebon Death! He . . . you . . . a monster!"

Sybian rolled her eyes. "Finally. What, did you go via Saido?"

At first Veil wasn't sure who this comment was directed at; then the room burst into a flurry of motion. Another door opened up to admit a gigantic ice-hound—Kaal or Kuul, Veil couldn't tell the difference—which bore down on Saya with terrifying speed. Corvus spun, the Bound Blade at the ready, but he wasn't sure quite where to point it. In his moment of hesitation the hound closed the gap with the light-spirit and leapt. At the same time, Veil felt something cold and hard grip her from behind and drag her toward the wall.

A beam of light burst from Saya's hand, hitting the hound in the right foreleg. Ice vaporized, but the scintillating shaft took a moment to punch all the way through. Saya shifted her aim, and the beam slid across the dog's chest, but by that time it was on top of her. The light spirit shrieked as the ice hound closed its massive jaws over her head and wrenched, hard; her entire head tore away, and her body flopped to the floor. The dog followed her a moment later, whimpering, its right foreleg gone entirely. Another second and both had started to decompose—the dog melting and Saya's body breaking up into sparkling motes of pure radiance.

"And so ends the reign of Lady Light," chimed Sybian, right by Veil's ear. "Pathetic. This is what comes of getting involved with humans."

"What are you doing, Sybian?" Corvus' voice was low and dangerous. Veil tried to struggle against what gripped her and felt her back sliding across ice; more importantly, she felt cool sharpness pressed up against her throat. She stopped struggling immediately, and tried not to swallow.

"Leverage. In case she convinced you."

Don't panic. Corvus will figure something out. He always does . . .

"Don't come any closer." Sybian pressed her sharpened forearm tighter against Veil's neck, enough to draw blood. "I know exactly how fast you are, Corvus, and you're not fast enough."

"You assume I care what happens to the girl."

Veil's breath caught in her throat.

He's bluffing. He has to be bluffing.

"Not an assumption. I've been watching you for some time, remember?"

"That doesn't mean you know me."

"What Saya neglected to mention," Sybian mused, "is that her meddling created the perfect solution to the problem of the Trap. The gods built it to be impenetrable—a ward against spirits on the outside, and the greatest of human warriors within.

So in order to get to the Trap, a spirit had to have someone good enough to defeat the Guardian."

"You want me to go in?"

"Of course. I needed to get you here first, though, which Her late Radiance was not at all happy about. And how do you get a man who doesn't need anything to do what you want?" She sounded immensely pleased with herself. "You attach a lever. So I cast a net, and waited. You happened to run into Veil here, and she did quite nicely. Didn't you?"

Veil squirmed. "You . . ." She was unable to think of anything nasty enough to say.

"So it's not so bad, is it? You get your memory back. It's what you wanted, isn't it?"

"If you're convinced of that, put the girl down."

Part of Veil melted to hear that, even though Sybian only held her more tightly. "Oh, no. She's my insurance. One must be careful when dealing with a warrior of your caliber."

There was a long pause. The voice that finally spoke was unfamiliar. Veil turned her head and found that it belonged to the younger of the two draekeres.

"What do you get out of it?"

"Kit!" the other draekere hissed.

"It's a fair question, right? You said Corvus gets what he wanted. What's in the Trap that you need so badly?"

"A fair question, indeed." Sybian turned back to Corvus. "What's inside the Trap? Power. The spirits launched a war against the gods because they were jealous of their power. While the gods existed, they collected much of the natural energy that flows from the earth. Once they were destroyed, all that power would be free for the spirits to use. Undoubtedly some of them would have become gods themselves and destroyed the rest.

"But the gods had the last laugh. They built the Trap, which soaks up excess power like a sea sponge. Then they hid it in this tomb, layered over with wards and guardians. After they lost the war, the grand alliance of spirits disintegrated fast. They built the outer wards, to ensure that only the six most powerful spirits had access to the Trap, and none of them ever managed to get inside.

"Power leaks out, of course. Enough to grow the Doomwood, and feed the spirits that live there. But most of it just stays in the Trap. And once Corvus kills the Guardian for me, all I have to do is walk in there and take it. Sixty centuries of accumulated energy." She laughed, high and chiming. "I'll make the *gods* look like children."

There was another pause.

"That answers my question," said the draekere girl. Her companion shushed her violently.

"So, Corvus. What's it going to be? Does poor Veil have to lose her head?"

Corvus locked eyes with the ice spirit, silently. Then, without a word, he turned and stalked up to the warded double doors. They opened before him, and Corvus hefted the Bound Blade and walked into the Trap.

DOMINARIUS, SITTING ON his platform and carefully cleaning his sword, looked up. The little girl was a long time in dying—her periodic moans had disturbed his reverie several times now. But this sound was definitely the opening of the big doors.

"Another visitor? So soon?" He got carefully to his feet. "Well, well. Much more of this and I'll be all worn out."

He paused. It was probably a trick of the chamber's light, but the newcomer's eyes seemed to be glowing from within; the dark, sullen red of a dying fire. He had a sword in one hand, and as he moved it through the air it gave off a skull-splitting buzz. The sound increased as he got closer, as though the blade itself anticipated a fight.

"Interesting," said the Guardian. "Very interesting. My name is Dominarius Zetz. Might I have the pleasure of knowing yours?"

The stranger raised his head. His eyes were definitely glowing, now, and when he smiled his teeth looked like fangs.

"I am Ebon Death, the First of Two Hundred."

The buzz of the sword rose to a shriek.

"I am here to defend the Trap . . ."

"And I'm here for your head."

The blade flicked out, faster than thought.

OUTSIDE THE DOORS, things were quiet. Shuzan and the two draekeres were huddled in one corner, deep in conversation; that left Veil alone with her captor.

"Sybian."

"What?"

The ice spirit set Veil down, and the girl gasped a deep breath. Her throat was numb from prolonged contact with the ice.

"You really . . . helped me, with Corvus, just for this?"

"Of course. I told you as much from the start, didn't I?"

I'm using you as a pawn. Sybian had said that, at the outset. *I thought, after a while, things were different.*

"Don't ever say," the spirit chimed, "that I've been less than honest with you."

Veil jumped on that. "Then you'll let us go. After Corvus kills the Guardian or whatever. You said you'd let me go, that I'd be better off."

"As I said, I've been nothing less than honest. Once I have the power stored in the Trap, you can have whatever you wish."

Sybian smiled, revealing a mouth full of needle teeth. "I will look back on our time together fondly."

"What about Corvus and Isobel?"

"Isobel is most likely dead by now. I can't imagine she was able to defeat the Guardian, whatever that idiot Vaalkir thought she was capable of."

No. Veil held fast to that thought. *She's not dead, not yet. Somehow.*

"And what about Corvus?"

"I never made you any promises regarding Corvus."

"Why?" Veil felt her voice rise. "What do you need him for?"

"I don't need him for anything. I just neglected to mention that, as a side effect, the Trap destroys anyone who makes it past the Guardian. Just another safety measure—I think the gods believed that finding a mortal who could defeat their champion *and* was willing to sacrifice his own life would be very difficult. I seem to have managed it, however." She giggled, a series of high-pitched tinkles.

Veil stared. "You can't—"

The sound from behind the double doors was a single bass *whump*, more felt in the bones than heard through the ears. The glittering script that adorned the door flared blue-green, all at once, and a brilliant light of the same color outlined the double doors themselves. It got brighter and brighter, until Veil could see it with her eyes closed, the actinic brilliance burning right through her eyelids. Sybian laughed and laughed, until just as it reached the point of pain the brilliant light was gone. Veil opened her eyes and found her vision spotted with red after-images.

"You know," said Kei quietly, "it's good to see you again."

"Likewise." Shuzan sighed. "I just wish it were under better circumstances."

"What, you're not happy to reunite at the end of the world?"

Kit leaned forward, on Kei's other side. "This isn't *exactly* the end of the world, is it?"

"It might as well be. You heard what Sybian said. Once she goes through those doors, she turns into something that makes gods obsolete. How long do you think we humans will last?"

"I didn't think of that." Kit sighed. "I suppose we have to stop her."

"*We* have to stop her?" Kei stared at her, incredulously.

Shuzan cleared his throat. "I'm not sure we've been introduced."

"Right. Shuzan, this is my partner Kitsu Meru, a complete lunatic. We call her Kit." Kit nodded her head politely, and Kei continued. "Kit, this is my brother Kagerin Shuzan, the Fifty-Fourth of Two Hundred. Now, may I continue?"

Kit nodded again.

"You're an idiot."

There was a pause.

"Was that all?" asked Kit.

"Pretty much, yeah."

"I was just thinking that if you're right, and the whole human race is in trouble, then we might as well try to stop Sybian here and now."

"She'll just kill us all."

"If it's a choice between dying now, and maybe accomplishing something, and having to walk back with one arm broken through a demon-infested forest and then the world gets destroyed *anyway*, I'm pretty sure what I'd pick."

"She has a point," said Shuzan, grimly. "I don't think we can take Sybian, but we have to try."

"We *have* to try? Don't you start going all noble idiot on me, Shuzan."

"If I hadn't been a noble idiot, you wouldn't be here."

Those words hung heavily in the air between them. There

557

was another, longer, pause.

"I'm sorry," said Shuzan quietly.

"No." Kei shook her head and rubbed one palm against her eyes. "You're right."

"He is?" asked Kit.

"I," Kei took a deep breath, "am just a coward. But he's right."

"If you were a coward," Kit said, "I don't think you'd still be alive. I certainly wouldn't be."

"She's right," said Shuzan.

"But . . ."

"Are we going to sit here arguing, Wing Leader, or are we going to kill that ice bitch?"

Kei nodded and turned to Shuzan. "What's the plan?"

"You two get her attention. I'll see if I can get to the sword that Corvus dropped—I might be able to take her out. Get ready."

"What are we waiting for?" asked Kit.

"Some signal that the doors are open. She'll be distracted."

"How do we know what the signal is?"

"I suspect," said Shuzan dryly, "that it will be rather obvious."

Whump. The bass note was loud enough that it seemed to press them against the walls. The door and its ward started to glow with a nasty blue-green light, brighter and brighter until Kei was forced to throw a hand in front of her eyes. Then it faded, all at once, and she scrambled to her feet and heard Kit and Shuzan do the same.

This is completely and utterly insane. Kei sprinted forward, her notched blade sliding noisily from its sheath. She blinked desperately, trying to get rid of the flowing red afterimages—she could just make out Sybian, standing in front of the doors, her arms raised as though in prayer. Her back was unprotected—*if she's distracted, we might just have a chance . . .*

EVEN IF SHE wasn't paying attention, a spirit of Sybian's power couldn't be taken that easily. Kei's attack, a simple downward stroke, caught the spirit in the right shoulder but did little more than crack the steel-hard ice. Kei's blade rebounded and sprang from her hands, ringing like a bell, and Sybian spun around. Kei backpedaled, staring ice-cold death in the face. Before the spirit could strike, though, Kit arrived from her left.

The young draekere held her blade one-handed, catching the spirit just under the armpit and flicking off a chip of ice. Sybian caught another strike on her forearm, and then Kit was forced to backpedal as the spirit's arms elongated, forming a pair of needle-like blades. In her weakened state, the draekere couldn't quite keep up. She kept backing away until she lost her footing, going flat on her back and letting her knife skitter across the floor.

In the meantime, though, Shuzan had scooped up the blade of the First. He charged Sybian, sword pointed like a lance, and the spirit had to throw up both arms to deflect the blade over her head. The two began a furious exchange of blows, and the sound of ice on steel rang while Kei frantically searched for her weapon. Kit dragged herself across the floor until she was right in front of the doors, where her knife had fallen; she slid it across the stone to Kei, who picked it up with one hand and charged Sybian's unprotected side.

The ice-spirit saw her coming, and she ducked low under one of Shuzan's strokes and scythed his legs out from under with a vicious kick. The Khaev noble fell to one side, and Kei was forced to give ground or be skewered, backing up toward the fallen Kit. She had a hard time holding on to her long knife against the power of Sybian's strokes, and a misplaced parry let the spirit beat the blade out of her hands. Kei dropped underneath a thrust but caught Sybian's knee on the way down, leaving her sprawling on the floor.

The ice spirit wasted no time, moving to finish off her enemies as soon as all three of them were down. She stood over Kit, sword raised . . .

. . . *the girl's tongue, briefly—honey and smoke—*

"Kit! Are you okay?"

. . . *Kit found the catch and flew free, gripping Kei's wrist so hard it hurt—*

"I'm a coward."

. . . and Kei rolled toward Kit, shoving her through the doorway as Sybian's sword shivered down.

Shuzan, having gotten groggily to his feet, screamed.

"*Shia!*"

VEIL WATCHED THE Khaevs attack Sybian with a sense of detachment. Her vision cleared rapidly, until she blinked away the last of the red dots.

Corvus can't be dead. I don't believe it. She just couldn't wrap her mind around the idea. *He could be hurt, though. And Sybian will kill him if she gets the chance.*

Veil bent down, almost unconsciously, and retrieved the long knife that had skittered from the draekere's hand to bump neatly against her feet. She hefted it uncertainly, the weight unfamiliar in her hands, and slowly walked toward the spirit.

I can't let her kill him. I can't.

But, said the rational part of her mind, *you can't fight Sybian. You don't have a prayer.*

I trust Corvus.

He's not Corvus anymore. He's Ebon Death.

I trust him.

One of the draekeres pushed the other through the doorway

and took the needle of Sybian's arm right between her breasts, bone giving way with a nasty crunch.

"*Shia!*"

"Kei!"

The other draekere surged to her feet, as though she was ready to take on the ice spirit with no weapons at all. Sybian raised one arm, contemptuously, and Veil charged her from behind.

She swung the long knife, clumsily, drawing a scratch across Sybian's back. The spirit whipped around, clearly in a fury; in that moment, Veil locked eyes with the Khaev girl and mouthed a single word.

'Duck.'

The draekere threw herself flat, and Veil did likewise; Sybian's cut whistled over her head. Behind the spirit, the cloud of smoke that filled the Trap chamber billowed and spat out a singed figure, all in black, swinging a sword that buzzed like a swarm of angry hornets as it growled through the air. His eyes were glowing a deep, angry red, and his grin was like nothing human.

Sybian turned and raised an arm to parry, but the Bound Blade went through it like it wasn't there, chopping her from neck to waist in a single blow. The ice spirit gave one last, keening cry, then shattered into a thousand tiny crystals.

KIT RACED TO Kei's side and dropped to her knees.

"Wing Leader! Kei!"

"Kit." Kei's eyes stared sightlessly upwards, and her words were barely even a whisper. "Take . . .care of Shuzan."

Kit grabbed her hand, squeezing hard. "Wait. Wait just a minute. I know you think things are going badly, Wing Leader, but you always think that. We'll get you out of here, don't worry. Shuzan and I should be enough to get us back through the forest. Or maybe that Corvus guy will help, he seemed competent enough. Even if he really is Ebon Death, he seemed like a nice enough type. So we'll get out of this yet. We always do, right?" She squeezed Kei's hand again. "Right?"

Kei's chest had not moved in some time. Shuzan reached her side and crouched, tears already welling in his eyes.

"Shia . . ."

Kit felt warmth coming to her own eyes, which was of course impossible. *I haven't cried since Zaneh died. Haven't cared about anyone, really, since Zaneh died. This is just another day in my life-after-death. I don't care about any of this. I don't!*

She bowed her head, tears running down her cheeks.

CORVUS CLEANED HIS sword on a black cloth, then slid it smoothly into its sheath.

The glow had faded from his eyes, and he looked more like the man Veil remembered. The elemental force of destruction was still there, though, boiling just below the surface. She'd seen it, that night in the Diem highlands. *Is that who he really is?*

"C . . . Corvus?"

He snapped around and stared at her.

Oh. Dear gods. When the ward broke, did his old memories replace the new ones?

Does he even remember me at all? "Why are you staring at me like a landed fish?" asked Corvus irritably. He shook his head. "Gods. You kill the greatest sword master who ever lived, and you don't even get a round of applause. It's ridiculous."

"Corvus!"

She rushed to his side and wrapped her arms around him, which he tolerated for only a moment before pushing her away. Veil looked at him; there was something new in his eyes, a hard glint that was difficult to identify.

"Corvus. Are you okay?"

"Am I okay?" He shrugged. "I'm back."

"E . . . Ebon Death?"

He smiled. "Something like that. Spending a couple of hundred years in the desert gave me some time to think. And with everything that's happened since then . . ."

"What happened?"

He shrugged again. "They tried to kill me. Didn't manage it."

"I'm glad."

"Me too."

Veil's breath caught. "Isobel! Is she in there?"

"I think so. But . . ."

Veil rushed past him, coughing as the smoke of the explosion rolled over her. It took her a few moments to find a black-clad body, curled around its own private pain. Veil hovered over her, not sure what to do, and Corvus sauntered up behind her.

"Is she . . ."

The swordsman prodded Isobel gently with one black boot. "Hey. You alive?"

The response was little more than a whisper. "Somehow."

"Planning on dying anytime soon?"

"Not . . ." Isobel uncurled, one hand on her stomach, and gave Veil a shaky smile. "Not if I can help it."

Corvus glanced down at her, then over at Veil. "I suppose you expect me to carry her."

Veil couldn't say it, but the look on her face was apparently enough. Corvus sighed and reach down, hoisting Isobel to her feet and draping her over his back.

"You're just lucky there's no one here to see. It wouldn't do my reputation any good . . ."

He walked slowly, so as not to jostle the girl on his back. Veil kept a hand on his shoulder, but she looked down as they passed the three Khaevs and tugged on his sleeve.

"Corvus . . ."

He looked at them, expression unreadable, and then drew his sword. The buzzing filled the room. Shuzan looked up at him with dull, dead eyes. Veil's breath caught in her throat.

There was a long silence.

Corvus flipped the Blade around, handing Shuzan the hilt. "You'll probably need this to get out of the woods. Besides, if I used it people would accuse me of being unfair." He walked toward the double doors, with Veil trailing behind him. Half-way there he bent to pick up the sword of the First, which he slid back into his scabbard. "Me! Unfair! How could they even think . . ."

The swordsman's voice trailed off as the doors closed behind him. Shuzan looked down at the Bound Blade in his hands, then over at Kei's corpse.

She looks almost peaceful. The wound that had killed her was an angry red stain on her chest, but Kei's expression didn't show any pain.

No pain.

Shia. In the end, I couldn't protect you.

There was a long trek ahead—out of the tomb, out of the Doomwood. There were explanations that had to be made. The mistress of draekeres, four of her people, and six hundred riders were dead; Tashida Ikon would want answers.

And what can I tell him? Shuzan's mind rebelled.

Better to just stay here. Stay here, with Kei, until I rot.

He moved unconsciously, turning the Blade over until the point was level with his throat. Shuzan's hands trembled.

Better—

"Enough." Kit laid her hand on top of his.

"What?"

"Kei asked me to take care of you." She wiped her eyes with

the back of her hand, and gently pried the Bound Blade from his grip. "So I am."

He got to his feet as she walked away, carrying the Blade over her shoulder. She looked back at him.

"Come on, Shuzan. We're going home."

"Isn't the Trap just open now, for whoever wants to take it?"

"I expect the old guy will get himself put back together," said Corvus. "Give him a couple of centuries."

They walked in silence for a few minutes.

"Veil."

"Hmm?"

"You know what you promised, in the desert? You said you'd leave me alone, once we got back to civilization."

"I . . . I did."

"It's important to stand by your promises."

"I know." She swallowed.

Corvus chuckled. "Well, I wouldn't really consider the riverlands all *that* civilized."

Veil paused, then kicked him lightly on the shin. "You're a jerk, you know?"

"What, I'm not allowed to have fun with you?"

"I was really worried!"

"You worry too much."

This, she thought, *is going to take some getting used to.*

Don't miss Django Wexler's next exciting
novel from Medallion Press . . .

Shinigami

|djαngo wexleʀ|

ISBN#1932815716

Silver

$14.99

Epic Fantasy

August 2006

www.bloodgod.com

THE
DREAM
THIEF

HELEN A. ROSBURG

Someone is murdering young, beautiful women in mid-sixteenth century Venice. Even the most formidable walls of the grandest villas cannot keep him out, for he steals into his victims' dreams. Holding his chosen prey captive in the night, he seduces them . . . to death.

Now Pina's cousin, Valeria, is found dead, her lovely body ravished. It is the final straw for Pina's overbearing fiance', Antonio, and he orders her confined within the walls of her mother's opulent villa on Venice's Grand Canal. It is a blow not only to Pina, but to the poor and downtrodden in the city's ghettos, to whom Pina has been an angel of charity and mercy. But Pina does not chafe long in her lavish prison, for soon she too begins to show symptoms of the midnight visitations; a waxen pallor and overwhelming lethargy.

Fearing for her daughter's life, Pina's mother removes her from the city to their estate in the country. Still, Pina is not safe. For Antonio's wealth and his family's power enable him to hide a deadly secret. And the murderer manages to find his intended victim. Not to steal into her dreams and steal away her life, however, but to save her. And to find his own salvation in the arms of the only woman who has ever shown him love.

ISBN#1932815201
Gold
$6.99
Fiction
December 2005
www.helenrosburg.com

DARK PLANET

CHARLES W SASSER

Kadar San, a human-Zentadon crossbreed distrusted by both humans and Zentadon, is dispatched with a Deep Reconnaissance Team (DRT) to the Dark Planet of Aldenia. His mission: use his telepathic powers to sniff out a Blob assault base preparing to attack the Galaxia Republic. Dominated by both amazing insect and reptile life forms, and by an evil and mysterious Presence, Aldenia was once a base for the warlike Indowy who used their superior technology to enslave the Zentadon and turn them into super warriors to deploy against humans.

The DRT comes under attack not only from savage denizens of the Dark Planet, but also from the mysterious Presence, which turns team member against team member and all against Kadar San. The Presence promises untold wealth and power to any member of the team unscrupulous enough to unleash the contents of a Pandora's box-like remnant of Indowy technology. The box's possessor poses a greater threat than the entire Blob nation, for he is capable of releasing untold horrors upon the galaxy.

Kadar San finds himself pitted against a human killer, an expert sniper, in a desperate struggle to save both the Republic and the human female he has come to love. Like all Zentadon, however, Kadar San cannot kill without facing destruction himself in the process. and he has no choice but to kill. In order to save the galaxy, Kadar San must face the truth . . . No one will leave the Dark Planet.

ISBN#1932815139
Gold
$6.99
Science Fiction
www.charlessasser.com

L.G. BURBANK

PRESENTS

LORDS OF DARKNESS

VOL I:

THE SOULLESS

AN UNLIKELY HERO . . .

Mordred Soulis is the chosen one, the man ancient legends
claim will save the world from great evil. There's only one
problem. Before Mordred can become the hero of mankind,
he must first learn to embrace the vampyre within.

A FORGOTTEN RACE . . .

With the help of a mysterious order, a king of immortals and
a shape-shifting companion, Mordred is set on a dangerous
course that will either save the human race or destroy it.

A TIMELESS STRUGGLE . . .

Journeying across the sands of the Byzantine Empire; in the time
of the Second Crusade, to the great Pyramids of Egypt and then
on to the Highlands of Scotland, Mordred will face the Dark One.
This evil entity is both Mordred's creator and the Soul Stealer
he has become. As champion of mortals, Mordred must accept
his vampyre-self . . . something he has vowed never to do.

ISBN#0974363960
$6.99
Available Now
www.lgburbank.com

L.G. BURBANK

LORDS OF DARKNESS

VOL II:
THE RUTHLESS

Mordred Soulis, the Chosen One, has awakened from his
healing slumber and must now continue his mission to save
mankind. It is time to journey to the land of ice and snow, to
the place where earth and heaven meet. It is time to enlist the
aid of the second of the Vampyre kings, the mighty Lir.

It takes all the strength of Mordred's tortured soul to
convince Lir to aid him on his quest to save humanity. For
the blood of all Norse flows through Lir's steely veins,
including that of Odin's battle maidens, the Valkyries.

Together at last, the two sail across dangerous seas, discovering
a new continent where Mordred seeks what he needs to defeat
his nemesis, Vlad. The task is daunting. Plagued by the most
wicked of temptations, Mordred finally gives in to weakness
and finds himself a victim of the Spanish Inquisition. Once
again, he is forced to reconcile the evil men do with that of
his creator. Once again, he must question his own existence,
and the once clear vision of his quest blurs and wavers.

And always, as time ticks slowly by, the
destruction of mortals grows ever nearer.

Gold
$6.99
Fiction
October 2005
www.lgburbank.com

MORE THAN MAGICK

Rick Taubold

What if you were told you have a power you don't know about? What if you were told that you have to use it to save the universe from a major baddie? What if no one will tell you how you are supposed to do this?

A recent college graduate, Scott Madison is half-heartedly considering his future when he reads an ad on the dorm bulletin board. He ends up taking the job with Jake Kesten, Martial Arts expert and Ph.D. math whiz, and finds himself busting computer hackers for the government. It's an interesting job, if a little rough at times. Still, it's just a job.

Then Jake and Scott get a visit from what, apparently, is an old friend of Jake's — Arion. Scott thinks Arion dresses a little funny, what with the robes and all. But then Arion proclaims himself an Adept at Magick. Before Scott can even roll his eyes, he finds himself whisked away to another world where he joins his fellow adventurers, all plucked as unceremoniously from their own home worlds. Their mission? To save the Elfaeden and their friends, the Crystal Dragons. Their secret weapon? Scott Madison. Who is about to discover that there is something, indeed, **MORE THAN MAGICK.**

ISBN# 0974363987
$6.99
Available Now
www.ricktaubold.com

THE CARDINAL'S HEIR
JAKI DEMAREST

Cardinal Richelieu is dead, a victim of poison. The throne of France, which he has long protected, is once more unstable as rival factions vie for power. But the Cardinal has appointed two heirs: one to his religious position, and one to head the elite spy ring that has maintained France's fragile political balance.

Francoise Marguerite de Palis, the Cardinal's lovely but low born niece, is devastated by her uncle's murder and vows revenge, which she sets out after immediately. Though the task is daunting, she at least has some formidable tools at her command. Not only is she now the head of the Cardinal's Eyes, but is arguably the most powerful Sorciere in all France. Shapeshifting into her character Biscarrat, notorious swordsman, she sets out to find her uncle's murderer. But with an unexpected ally.

Handsome and dashing Jean de Treville, head of the King's Musketeers, is saddened to learn of the Cardinal's death, though both headed groups not generally fond of one another. Sadness turns to stunned amazement, however, when he learns who has been appointed to lead the Cardinal's spy ring . . . and who is also, in fact, the swordsman who has bested him on numerous occasions. Not to mention the beautiful, and untouchable, wife of Court favorite, Antoine de Palis.

But just as there is more, much more, to the enchanting Francoise, so is there more than simple murder afoot. Side by side, Francoise and Jean descend into a maelstrom of magic as they battle another powerful Sorcier, and enter a bloody race to obtain a fabulous jewel. And the throne of France hangs in the balance, supported only by the magic and mastery of . . .

The Cardinal's Heir

ISBN#1932815104
Gold
$6.99
Fantasy
www.jakidemarest.com

LINNEA SINCLAIR
WINTERTIDE

SORCERY. TREACHERY. LOVE.

For centuries the Infernal War has been waged by witches and sorcerers to control the Orb of Knowledge. The war must end. Then, at Wintertide, the Hill Raiders attack the village of Cirrus Cove.

The sea captain's daughter is raped, and a child conceived. "If the child is to be who the stones say she will, it's best I raise her. She will live with me." Bronya the Healer accepts the responsibility of caring for the unborn child.

Having read the truth in the Stones, Bronya tends the birth and, in the midst of a maelstrom, takes the babe to her cave. Warded now by the signs and symbols of magick, Bronya keeps the child, Khamsin, safe from the Sorcerer.

On the eve of Khamsin's eighteenth birthday, the Hill Raiders, those who wreaked havoc upon her mother, come again. They murder the inhabitants of her village, her husband and her family. Blaming Khamsin for witchery, for bringing the scourge down upon them, the survivors of Cirrus Cove nearly take her life. The enigmatic Tinker, selling pots and pans, heals Khamsin. And he accompanies her on a journey that magick omens have directed her to take.

One of them knows the truth. One of them is seeking, just as she is sought. The war for the Orb is about to end. But only love can win it.

ISBN#1932815074
Gold
$6.99
Fantasy
www.starfreighter.com